DREAMS of DARKNESS and LIGHT

Karen Stockwell

ISBN: 978-1-482-67829-1
DREAMS OF DARKNESS AND LIGHT
Copyright © 2013 by Karen Dilsaver Stockwell

All rights reserved. Except for use in any review, the reproduction or utilization of this work in whole or in part in any form by any electronic, mechanical or other means, now known or hereafter invented, including xerography, photocopying and recording, or in any information storage or retrieval system, is forbidden without the written permission of the author.

This is a work of fiction. Names, characters, places and incidents are either the product of the author's imagination or are used fictitiously, and any resemblance to actual persons, living or dead, business establishments, events or locales is entirely coincidental unless stated differently in the Author's Notes.

Cover and book design, author photo: Jill Zylke
Illustrations: Karen Stockwell

"Even so a faith, if it has no works, is dead, being
by itself."
James 2:17

to all those who long for a better world, especially the
people of Wellington Avenue United Church of Christ who work
hard to make it so

"The fierce power of imagination is a gift from God."
The Kabbalah

to artists, who see the world through the lens of their own
creativity, and who have the power to shape the vision and
understanding of others

DREAMS of DARKNESS and LIGHT

Part One

The darkest soil is the richest kind.
A seed placed in its womb may yield a flower
of pure light.

Darlene Howard
Teotenaca
Oaxaca, Mexico

1

"ARE YOU ALL RIGHT?"

The flight attendant's loud whisper woke me with a start as her breath brushed my eyelids.

"Yes, she is," a man answered from nearby. "It was a bad dream." He stated the words matter-of-factly. How did he know what was happening to me when I didn't know myself?

"Is that true?" she asked me as I opened one eye. I nodded without thinking. I just wanted her to go away. She turned to the man and said, "Let me know if she needs anything," before she disappeared up the aisle. But my fear lingered. My breathing was shallow, as if I'd been chased down a dark alley.

"You were very distressed," the man sitting next to me said. "*Are* you all right?" His voice was gentle.

"Yes! Yes. Thank you for asking," I said. "It was a *horrible* dream," I mumbled, rubbing my eyes. "I was trapped in a dark room and couldn't get out!" My heart beat rapidly. I was still reeling, but the stranger continued reassuring me. He had a slightly formal demeanor that provided distance, like a counselor talking to a patient.

"Is there something on your mind lately? Perhaps the dream is a message," he reasoned in a slight Spanish accent. We were sitting next to each other on the plane heading to Mexico City, but had barely spoken. He was a pleasant looking man with salt and pepper hair and a graying mustache that accentuated his smile.

"So much is on my mind lately." I admitted. I wanted to talk about it, but I wondered if he'd later regret giving me the chance. "Work is crazier than usual. Maybe I feel trapped. Or," I didn't want to get into the subject, but it slipped out, "maybe it's because my boyfriend broke up with me. We were almost engaged. It still hurts," I winced. Emotional pain has a physical aspect, of which I'd become keenly aware.

"Perhaps it is the boyfriend then. I can tell you are feeling much emotion," the man nodded. "Maybe you are lingering on what could have been and you can't let go, and so you feel trapped."

Was it work, or Neil? It could have been either. Or maybe it was my mother's concern about me traveling solo. She was convinced I was heading into drug cartel territory, or a rebel encampment, both of which seemed absurd to me at the time. But now that I was on my way to Mexico, maybe my own fears were surfacing. As I thought over the possibilities, I leaned toward Neil as the cause. I'd been thinking a lot about him.

"You can take away the dream's power if you talk about it," my companion offered. "I'm willing to listen, if you're comfortable with that," he smiled. I wondered if he really was a counselor. The dream hovered nearby, making me feel like I'd only taken a step from one room into another. I was happy to unburden myself to a stranger.

"I think it would help, if you don't mind," I said, trying to smile.

"It is no problem," he encouraged, with a shake of his head.

So I took a deep breath and began to describe my terrifying dream. I remembered it vividly. "It seemed so real," I told him. "I thought I was waking up from my nap on the plane. I opened my eyes, but I couldn't see anything! I was lying on a hard, cold surface, like damp concrete. It smelled like a musty old basement. I thought I was deep underground."

"That is *very* frightening," he agreed with a nod, his eyes wide.

I left out the next part, when I thought I'd been drugged on the plane, because he seemed the likely person who'd slip a pill in my drink. How ridiculous that seemed now! Instead, I told him how I'd stood up in the dark place, spreading my arms far apart to touch a wall or a door. But there was nothing. I tried to make sense of why I'd been kidnapped. Why would anyone want a person like me? Maybe I'd been mistaken for someone who was rich. The one question that mattered chanted loudly in my head during the dream. *How do I get out of this dark place?* But my senses were useless. The only sounds I heard were the thump of my heartbeat, the scraping of my feet on the floor, and the pathetic echoes of my own raspy voice as I called out. But no one answered. The still, damp air seemed to weigh me down. Then I noticed a pungent smell, reminding me of earth and rock and the slow, steady force that formed rivers and mountains. A shiver ran along my spine.

I shuffled forward until I saw a flicker of light. But I couldn't judge the distance. Ten feet? Twenty? Then it became a beam of light that grew bigger and brighter. At last my hand touched the bumpy, cool surface where the light leaked through a hole two inches across, just above my eye level. Dust particles danced there. I leaned against the craggy wall, standing on my toes, peeking through the opening. But now it was too bright to see. I reached through the opening and pulled the edge with my fingers. But it wouldn't give. By then, I was desperate. My fingers hurt from the effort. Finally a little of the wall crumbled, like dry clay. My heart raced with anticipation. I pulled again and more came loose, giving off a dense cloud of dust that got in my eyes.

As I brushed the dust away I heard a sound coming from the other side of the wall. Then there was a low rumble, a tremor that shook right through my feet! The wall began breaking open, as if an earthquake was pulling the place apart! I stepped backward, but fell to the ground. Light suddenly flooded the room, swallowing me in warmth and brilliance. I was engulfed in a wave of heat so intense that a fire-breathing dragon could have been about to storm the place. And then the most frightening thing happened. I saw a figure coming toward me, a misshapen form obscured by the cloud of dust so I couldn't tell if it was animal or human. In the nightmare, I began to scream, but it was at that point that the sound blurred and re-formed into the words of the agitated flight attendant. She'd freed me from that dark place. But that sudden shift back into the waking world had been disorienting.

"What a terrifying nightmare!" the man said, his smile gone. "Perhaps you are experiencing great pain in your life, or a great fear of the future," he interpreted. In my heart I felt it was the loss of Neil's love, the end of planning an anticipated future that included starting a family.

I still couldn't believe the love of my life had dropped me for a woman he'd just met at a sales conference. "I can't help it," Neil explained, looking past me. "It's like love at first sight, like meeting your soul mate when you weren't looking for her. I'm so sorry, Michelle," he told me with a feeble apology, "but this is out of my control." I wasn't sure what to make of that, but I knew it was completely out of *my* control. I asked what I'd done to make him stop loving me. He said, "Nothing." And nothing was what he left me. I felt stupid as I thought back on our two years together. Gone were my visions of our features blending in the faces of our children. I'd even imagined us walking arm in arm down the street, an elderly couple still in love. It was all wiped away now, just a cloud of dusty memories.

But I hadn't made up the vision of us sharing our lives into old age. He'd talked about getting married, as if it were the natural next step in our relationship. I was still in shock every time I realized the future I'd longed for had crumbled away, like the dried up wall in the nightmare. But there was no light for me, only the darkness that had entered my heart. I couldn't shake it. I told everyone this trip was a break from work, but I hoped it could be a distraction from thinking about my ex. I had to find a way of getting past my misery, and the trip would be a first step on that path. But if the nightmare was any indication, it would be a long journey.

"I think the nightmare was about my break-up," I concluded to the man on the plane. "But at least there was light in the dream, after the darkness. That's hopeful, isn't it?" I tried to convince him, along with myself.

"Yes, I would agree," he nodded and smiled. "And a person was approaching you, perhaps a new person in your life. You're an attractive young woman. You have blond highlights and blue eyes. It will happen."

I had to laugh with relief at the man's upbeat interpretation. "I could use a little hope right now," I said, though the "person" I'd seen in the dream didn't look like a guy I'd want to meet on a blind date.

"Is there more to worry about?" he asked with concern. "I don't mean to pry, but if you need to talk..."

His voice and eyes were steady and comforting. *Why is it that you can tell strangers things you can't tell your friends?* I wondered. But this part of the story was well known to my friends.

"Do you really want to hear the rest of my sad story?" I asked, secretly hoping he did.

"If it will help you feel safer, of course," he replied with no hesitation.

"Well then, besides breaking up with the man I thought was going to be my husband, I was supposed to be on this flight with three other people, but they won't be coming for two more days."

"And why is that?" he asked, concern in his kind voice once again.

"Because I messed up big time. It's my fault, but I'd prefer to blame it on the Internet, or the airlines," I frowned, looking around for the nervous flight attendant. "I wanted to go on this trip, but I was so busy at work, I hesitated. My friends had to book it to get a great deal on the airfare. When I got permission to take off the time from work, I went online with the flight numbers and was able to book on the same planes,

I thought. But I put in the wrong date, because I was in a hurry. I checked the confirmation a few days later and realized what I'd done. But I wasn't able to cancel and get on my friends' flights. Everything was booked up. Some kind of convention or something, I was told."

He smiled and said, "If you miss the window, you are out of luck. It has happened to me, too. But you decided to come, anyway? That is a brave thing to do, to travel alone."

"It may be a foolish thing to do, too," I laughed. "But I really needed to get away, so I didn't let that stop me. My friends weren't able to change their plans, either, so here I am."

The flight attendant walked by then, giving me a nod and an approving smile.

The man continued, "You said you were going to Oaxaca, which is an old and beautiful colonial city. You should be able to keep yourself busy with sightseeing and shopping until your friends come," he assured me. "You will be safe. And when you go home, you will find someone better, I think, someone who is more perfect for you," he smiled with assurance, as if he were predicting my future like a seasoned psychic.

"You're a very positive person," I laughed with relief. I had to admire his attitude. "I'm so glad you're sitting next to me instead of a mother with a crying child or a teenager as miserable as I am. My name's Michelle Hardtke, by the way. What's yours? And are you a counselor?"

"Roberto. Roberto Del Castillo. No, I am a marketing consultant. I was visiting my family in Chicago."

I was blessed to have him in the next seat, a man who in no way could be a kidnapper of solitary, miserable travelers like me.

2

The original idea for our trip to Oaxaca had come from my old college buddy Max, who had a knack for going off the beaten path. Our little group of Max, Angel, Maggie and I took turns picking the next vacation spot we'd hit, and this one was his choice. He'd had other places in mind, until he found an old travel book in a trunk he purchased at an estate sale. The book, titled *Inexpensive Adventures*, had intrigued him. Being a believer in omens, he opened to the page bookmarked with a raffle ticket for a red 1968 VW Karmann Ghia convertible. There was a huge, sloppy asterisk handwritten next to an entry that was only two paragraphs long. The description got his attention and he couldn't get it out of his head. It made the rest of us curious, too.

"Nestled deep in the mountains of the state of Oaxaca is a jewel of natural beauty. Accessible by dirt road, the town of Santa María Teotenaca lies on a wooded ridge in the shadow of a mountain the locals call El Anhelo. (NOTE: It is customary to drop the Spanish part of the town name and use the original native name of Teotenaca.) Hiking trails abound with outstanding overlooks throughout the area. Many descendants of the early inhabitants live in the town and in the surrounding countryside as farmers and artisans. Unlike many Oaxacan villages known for one particular craft, Teotenaca's artisans are a diverse group. The designs on their pottery, woodcarving, and textiles have roots in ancient forms. The old stories survive in the symbols appearing in these local crafts, some alluding to a mythical cave.

The town is also unique because it has welcomed the arrival of many artists from other parts of Mexico, and even beyond its borders, who live in the surrounding area. Accommodations in Teotenaca are inexpensive, but spartan. There is an inn with a restaurant called El Refugio and an area used for camping. Home visits can also be arranged if the inn is at capacity. The church of Santa María, sitting above the plaza, is stunning with its excellent painted carvings of the saints. You'll find that the people here are open to visiting outsiders. But be prepared for anything as you savor the stunning terrain in this ancient land."

If it's so beautiful, why haven't I heard of it? I wondered when Max showed us the book. There was a dark photo of El Anhelo on the next page. It was wide at the base and covered with trees and brush. Its top was jagged with one dominant peak that pointed straight up at the sky. I thumbed through the book and recognized many of the other locations in it, places that had become known and built up since 1968. Maybe it was the vision of author Dennis Lawley, who seemed to favor natural beauty over comfort, that made this book esoteric and exotic. We wondered what had happened to Teotenaca since then. Maggie volunteered to research the town and Mr. Lawley.

What she found only deepened the mystery and our curiosity. Lawley was an American naturalist and travel writer who frequented the Americas. He'd disappeared in a Brazilian rainforest in the mid-1970s while researching a book on rare flora and fauna in South America. He was in his late thirties then and had left a legacy of three books, including the one Max found in the trunk. Maggie said the logical way to get to Teotenaca was to fly into the city of Oaxaca, then arrange for a driver to get us the rest of the way through the mountains. The other option was to take a bus from the city, then walk for two miles after it dropped us off near the road leading into town, or arrange to be picked up at that spot. As for where to stay, she'd only found two places in the remote town. One was the inn Lawley had mentioned, El Refugio, which translates as "the refuge" in English. It made me wonder what it was a refuge *from*. The other was a bed and breakfast called Sweet Dreams. Maggie said she was leaning toward the B & B and included a link to their website in an email. "Sweet Dreams" was indeed a more comforting name than El Refugio. I checked out their website. The whole idea of a B & B in a remote mountainous area of Mexico had seemed absurd to me. But there it was, the Sweet Dreams Bed and Breakfast owned and operated by Darlene and Reggie Howard, an Australian couple. Their three guest rooms were pictured with unbelievably low rates, computed in several currencies. Each room had a colorful folk art theme. According to the site, the husband was an artist and the wife, a writer, and they'd lived in the area for over five years. Apparently they also ran a small, organic farm and had a cottage industry making goat's milk cheese and soap.

Their website attested to the area's natural beauty by using the mountain and the surrounding area as a backdrop. "Here's what you'll see from your window," the caption read below a turquoise and orange sunset casting its light on the mountain. Another image showed a sunlit meadow and a forest with the same peak as a backdrop. "Follow a path of wildflowers and pine trees to winding trails and foothills with spectacular views." I imagined myself walking through the meadow and looking up at El Anhelo.

So I decided to send the innkeepers an email just to check on availability, though I thought it highly likely there wouldn't be a problem. I shared all this in an email to my three friends. I hoped to hear back from the Howards before our group got together the following week to decide if we'd go through with our proposed trip.

Back in our late teens, Max, Angel and I met in a college philosophy class. We shared our opinions and confusion after class at a local coffee shop, where we discussed Plato and Nietzche over burgers and fries while drinking pop. In the process we became close friends. Now, years later, along with our new friend Maggie, we discussed our busy lives and careers over salmon and crème brulee, and washed the meals down with wine and espresso.

Travel had always been a frequent topic for our discussions, and it turned out we traveled well together. One trip led to another, it seemed, so we took turns picking the destinations. Of course, each of us had ulterior motives for our choices. Angel, a comparative religions teacher, had planned our trip to England, where he took time to study ancient stone circles and cairns in the countryside. Even though Max and I made occasional jokes about a professor named "Angel" teaching classes on religion, we'd come to respect his intellectual curiosity, as well as his capacity for research. When it was my turn, we went to northern Wisconsin, where I painted watercolors on location and hiked through the woods. Neil was on a business trip then and didn't go. I would have invited him to Mexico, but his new soul mate Samantha found him before I could ask.

And for this vacation, Max had chosen an obscure Mexican mountain village where he would photograph the highly recommended terrain. I imagined him towering over the locals and standing out with his short-cropped blond hair and blue eyes. He was ten inches taller than my 5' 3" frame, so I knew how it felt to look up at him. Then his shots of

Teotenaca would go into his stock photo collection, one of the ways he made money from his photography. It was more exciting than tabletop product shots, occasional weddings and portrait sittings, though he did those, too. He traveled whenever he could, sometimes freelancing as a photojournalist and putting himself in the middle of natural or political disasters. He sold those photos, too, and it always surprised me to see the name "Max DeBoer" next to images in national magazines.

Maggie always had the same answer when I asked where she'd go next. "Spain," she'd say, raising her hand as if in salute to that country. She was a physical therapist who studied flamenco dancing in her off hours. With her caramel skin, green and gold eyes, dark red curly hair and tall, slender body, she was amazing to watch as she danced. It was obvious she longed to see authentic flamenco in the country of its origin.

The night we met at a Mexican restaurant to talk about the next trip, I noted to Maggie that, "If we go to Mexico, at least you can practice your Spanish." She'd been listening to language CD's for the last year. But then I wondered if the language we'd hear in Santa María Teotenaca would be an obscure native dialect instead. Strangely, it seemed what English we'd hear would be spoken with an Australian accent. We all knew this vacation would be the biggest surprise package of all, either a dud or a gem. This was a trip we all had to agree on. So far, the only thing we'd done was block out time on our calendars, and mine was tentative. Sadly, we would miss the big *Guelaguetza* dance festival in Oaxaca city in the second half of July, but the only time we could get away was the end of June. Since this trip was Max's baby, he made himself facilitator at our discussion.

"Let's begin with the pros," he said. He grabbed a red crayon from a jar on the table and made a space so he could write on the white paper square that covered the red tablecloth at La Fiesta Restaurant. "Why should we go to Teotenaca? What's the attraction? What would we do there?"

"Max, sorry but your pronunciation is a little bit off. It's pronounced Tay-oh-ten-AK-a," Professor Fuentes pointed out. Max repeated it, as did Maggie. "That's right. You've got it now.

"OK, back to business. We know you'd be sitting on ledges capturing the view in your camera," Angel laughed and winked at Maggie and me, his longish dark hair framing his face with soft curls.

"Of course," Max replied, "and finding the best local Margarita." He swirled that exact drink in his fishbowl-shaped glass as he spoke.

"Beware of the ice in Mexico," I warned. "We should not drink the water unless it's bottled or boiled."

"Excuse me, señorita," he frowned. "We're doing pros now, not cons."

"But you do have to be aware of those things," I countered. Neil had broken up with me a couple weeks before then and I couldn't shake a negative attitude about almost everything. I made the effort to put a positive spin on what I knew so far. "OK, let me try again. I want to explore the hiking trails and take in that beautiful scenery. Have you seen the website for that Sweet Dreams place yet? The mountain and the trails will be worth the trip."

"Much better," he said writing "hiking" and "scenery" in the "pros" column. Before long our list included exploring the local culture and cuisine, looking for historical clues of Teotenaca's pre-Columbian past, spending time together, reading, practicing flamenco, and not hearing hair-raising news from the outside world. We even talked about leaving our cell phones at home, but knew we'd take them, just in case. Then Maggie asked Max if he had anything to add.

"I'd like to run," he said. "But I don't know if that thin mountain air will let me. I might just be hiking with the rest of you," he concluded, looking at us as if we were a bunch of out-of-shape wimps.

"I hope you're still wearing that elastic brace on your knee when you run," Maggie said, narrowing her eyes at him.

She couldn't help herself, because she knew the history of Max's knee. They'd become friends while he recuperated from a bad fall. Ironically, he'd slipped down his front steps, not off the side of a mountain, but had still managed to sustain a nasty fracture. She was his physical therapist in those painful days and made him laugh despite his agony. After the sessions ended, he'd bumped into her at a party and they'd kept in touch. There was chemistry between them, but they'd only settled into a close friendship. I knew it was Max's decision, and I had my theories as to why. But I sensed Maggie's frustration at times. She'd become my friend, too, and I hoped Max would one day come to his senses before another man snatched her away.

Then Maggie made a point about the reasonable cost of our rooms. But she questioned it. "Are you sure it's really that low, Michelle? Did you read the fine print on the website?"

"Actually I did. To get the low rate we have to help milk goats or do other chores around their little farm. But that could be fun, too. And they offer other meals besides breakfast, depending on how much work a guest is willing to do or pay, so that's an option, in case the restaurants aren't great or don't exist."

"Doing chores?" Max scrunched up his nose at the thought, but said, "Tourist labor. That sounds like an odd arrangement for a B & B, but let's put goat milking in the 'pro' column."

Maggie agreed. "We'd be learning a new skill," she smiled slyly. "In today's job market you never know what might come in handy."

"By the way," I said, "they only have three rooms, so we'll have to figure out how to divide ourselves up. Celia's not coming, is she, Angel?" She was his on-again, off-again girlfriend. Her plans were unpredictable and had the potential to throw ours out the window. She came from a wealthy family and lived a freer, more creative life than the rest of us. My envy of her freedom may have influenced my opinion of her, oh, just a bit.

"She'll be developing a new play with a director in New York at that time, so no, she won't be coming," Angel replied, looking disappointed. But I was relieved, as were Max and Maggie, judging by their quiet sighs.

"So it's the usual four of us. Any questions about the Sweet Dreams B and B?" I asked again.

"What if the rooms aren't available then?" Max asked.

"There's still the inn. I'm sure they would be cheaper than the city of Oaxaca, and that's not unreasonable," I said.

"So let's say the rooms are available at Sweet Dreams. Shall we go girls in one room, boys in the other? We're paying per room, after all," Angel suggested

"Definitely a pro," Max agreed. "What kind of breakfast do they serve?" he said, while savoring his crispy enchilada suiza.

"Maybe it's got an Australian/Mexican twist, like crumpets with chorizo on the side," Maggie suggested with a shrug of her shoulder.

"It was described only as 'bountiful' on the website," I said. "And I think they have an occasional afternoon tea on the veranda. You can see the mountain from there, it said."

"You could bring your sketchpad, Michelle, maybe get your mind off of what's his name for a little while," Max nudged me. I'd been bending his ear and crying on his shoulder about losing Neil maybe a little too often, I now realized.

"As a matter of fact, I do hope to get that asshole out of my mind while I'm away," I calmly stated.

There was silence for a moment. Then Max said, "Whoa!" while Maggie gasped and Angel's eyes widened. Ordinarily, I never used that kind of language. But things had shifted in my life. I shrugged and continued the conversation. "But you know there might be local crafts to buy, too. Lawley's entry mentioned crafts and village artisans. I love to shop for things like that."

"Shopping therapy?" Max smiled sheepishly.

"Why not?" I nodded, more defensively than I meant to. "I'm doing salon therapy at the moment." I said, aggressively fluffing my hair with its new cut and blonde highlights. It swung until it landed neatly in place just below my shoulders. I made sure he saw my freshly manicured fingernails. "Maybe I'll try shopping therapy *next*!" I almost shouted.

Angel just laughed and said, "Then, while I'm uncovering the history of the place, you can uncover the shops."

"And what's the weather like in the summer?" Max asked.

"It's in the mountains, but it'll still be sunny and warm most of the day. There'll be afternoon showers, but they're quick and they'll cool things off. Don't forget your sun block," Angel reminded us.

"I can't stop wondering, though," Maggie said with squinted eyes. "Don't you find it weird that there's this cute B & B run by an Australian couple in a remote Mexican village? What's everybody's take on that?"

"Maybe they're part of the drug trade," Max looked serious, then laughed. "Maybe that's what they mean by 'Sweet Dreams.'"

I wished he hadn't said that. My mother had come to that same conclusion and she kept harping on it. So I suggested it was because they were artists and they really loved the place for its scenery and simplicity. But what *was* the real story? "I'm anxious to hear how they came there from Australia," I said. "I wonder if they have visitors like us regularly or a totally different clientele."

"Only one way to find out," Max said. "We'll have to ask them ourselves."

"But we haven't talked about the cons yet," Angel reminded him. "Let's get that out of the way and then we can make our *real* plans."

"I open the discussion to the cons." Max held out his palm toward each of us.

Silence at first and then Maggie said, "Other than the scenery and the B & B, we don't really know what this vacation will be like. We have that little entry in the Lawley book to go by and what the Sweet Dreams website tells us. We could do more research online and see if anything interesting pops up. Otherwise, we might have surprises or disappointments awaiting us."

Max shook his head. "Maggie, I've had surprises and disappointments every time I've traveled. So I'm okay with that. How about the rest of you?"

Angel responded, "Don't forget that I'm fluent in Spanish, which could be helpful if we run into an unexpected circumstance." He'd grown up in a bilingual home where he was often left in the care of his Mexican grandmother.

"Absolutely. That's a big one for the 'pro' column," Max noted, adding it to the long list.

I wondered why I was apprehensive while everyone else was excited. "To be honest," I said, "I have mixed emotions. Part of me really wants to go. It would be like getting to Cancún before the tourists found it. So that unknown element is a pro, but it's also a con. Aren't any of you a little anxious about this?" I asked.

They looked at each other and then Maggie laughed. "Yes, but look who we're going with, a Spanish-speaking scholar and a strong, experienced traveler. We're in this as a team."

"Well, you're right there," I admitted. "And they do have two wise women to keep them in line," I laughed, brushing off my unfounded worry.

Then the waiter came by and asked, "Anything else today? More beer, or perhaps dessert and coffee?"

"What do you have for dessert?" Angel asked.

"Flan. But today's special dessert is a white cake covered in caramel sauce with almonds and whipped cream. It's a house specialty we call 'Una Sueña Dulce'."

Angel seemed surprised. "Una Sueña Dulce?" he repeated, incredulous.

"Yes, sir. It means 'a sweet dream,'" the waiter replied.

"That's it," Max said, slapping his hand on the table. "That's our omen. We're going!"

"Would you like the check, sir?" the waiter asked, caught off-guard.

"Not before we sample that sweet dream of yours. In fact, why don't you bring us a couple dreams we can share," Max insisted.

I missed that smart aleck Max as I sat on the plane heading for Mexico City. I felt the miles between us growing every minute. I missed them all as I glanced at the clouds below, but I was also looking forward to meeting my hosts at the Sweet Dreams B & B. My current plan was to stay in Oaxaca for two nights and then catch a ride into the mountains. My friends wanted me to wait for their arrival, but if I did I'd miss the weekly market on Tuesday in Teotenaca, part of my new "shopping therapy." So I made arrangements with the Howards to pick me up Monday morning. I looked forward to seeing the local merchandise, including crafts, flowers, fruits and vegetables, even chickens, from what Dar said in her last email. She and Reggie would be there, too, selling their own cottage industry products of goat cheese and goat's milk soap. No wonder they needed help with the milking. I envisioned my fingers around a goat's udders and started to laugh. I wasn't even sure how many udders they had.

"Ah, Michelle, it's good to hear you laugh," my companion Roberto said with a smile. "You must be feeling more like you're on vacation now." I was so glad he was sitting next to me, the right person at the right time.

"I'm definitely entering the realm of new experiences on this trip, Roberto. I'll probably learn to milk goats when I get to Teotenaca. But I can't see myself doing that. It's so strange, it made me laugh."

"But I thought you were going to the city of Oaxaca," he said, his head tilted.

"I am, but then I'm traveling into the mountains. Have you heard of Teotenaca?"

He thought to himself, then shook his head. "I don't believe so. It must be far from the city. Why would you go there?"

I lost count of how many people had asked me that question. My mother's words came back to me every time. "There could be terrorists or drug lords up there. The B & B could be a cover for drug traffickers. Be careful, Michelle. Send us an email or a text message as soon as you can so we'll know you're okay."

"It's a long story." I told him about the book in the trunk, the beautiful scenery it described there, the attraction of an unusual tourist destination.

"Oaxaca is a poor state, you know. But it has a rich culture," he explained. "Many villages are known for their crafts. Perhaps you'll see artisans at work."

"That's one of the things I'm hoping for," I affirmed.

"But why would you be milking goats?" he laughed with a quizzical expression.

"It's part of the arrangement where we'll be staying. They have a farm."

"Ah," he said with a nod, as if that made perfect sense. Even if it didn't, I welcomed his small gesture and the smile that followed.

3

Despite my fear, I must have fallen back to sleep. I awoke to the sound of the engines slowing down and the tug of gravity. The pilot was going into landing mode and we were right on time.

"When you land at the airport in Oaxaca, you can catch a shuttle bus that will take you from the airport to downtown where your hotel is," Roberto informed me. "It's very simple." When we landed in Mexico City, he advised me where to find the gate information for my next flight and where the gate would probably be located. I thanked him and we concluded our conversation. "Have a good time, Michelle. I hope your dreams are happy ones from now on. And I hope you have a safe and wonderful vacation." His eyes and smile were remarkably sincere.

"You take care, Roberto. And thank you for listening to all my troubles." I waved, and he was gone.

I was on my own again, but the time went quickly. Soon I was on the flight to the city of Oaxaca. The passengers on the small jet included Latinos, Americans and Europeans. I saw mountains, farms and roads far below us. A wave of relaxation washed over me, finally, as I contemplated the vacation ahead, which was my escape from routine and heartache.

My hotel was a couple blocks from the Zócalo, the main square in Oaxaca. I tipped the driver, who took my wobbly suitcase all the way to the hotel lobby. "Muchas gracias," I thanked him, being careful to slur the words together so the "s" in muchas practically disappeared, just like Angel had taught me during a practice session. Sadly, I'd had three years of Spanish in high school but had forgotten much of it.

"Enjoy your stay," the driver said in English and nodded to me as he got back in the van. I was grateful there were people who could speak my language. And the hotel clerk was no exception.

"Welcome to Oaxaca," he said. "Is this all of your baggage, miss?"

"Yes," I confirmed.

He informed me that breakfast began at 8:00 a.m. in their restaurant if I was interested, and then questioned my reservation. "I see you have one room tonight and tomorrow and a different room the next night with a friend. You will have to check out of one room before you go to the other room. Our checkout time is 11:00 in the morning."

"Actually," I told him with some reluctance in my voice, "I'll be leaving before my friends arrive. I'll only be here for two nights. I've had a change of plans. So I don't have much time to see the city. What can I see tonight?"

"You are very lucky," he smiled. "We have a show this evening as well as tomorrow night in our dining room. There is a stage there. We still have a few seats available for dinner and a *folklórico* performance of dancers with live music."

"What will you serve there?" I asked.

"Chicken with mole, a special dark Oaxaqueña mole, with vegetables, fruit, dessert and a drink."

"Can I buy a ticket at the event? What time does it start?" I wanted to weigh my other options before choosing the first thing I heard about.

"Yes, if seats are available. It will start at 7:00. Let me know if you wish to go, in case they are filled."

"I will," I said. "But right now I'd like to get settled."

"Of course, miss. Enrico can show you to your room."

Enrico was a young man who smiled a lot but didn't speak much English. It was a perfect opportunity for me to try out what little Spanish I could muster. I followed him to the second floor.

"Enrico, muchas gracias para ayudarme," I thanked him for his help as he left the bags near the bed.

"No problema." He said, "Bienvenidos a Oaxaca," welcoming me to the city. I tipped him and he smiled with a nod. "Have a good time," he said in faltering English.

My room echoed the lobby's Spanish colonial style with dark, carved wood. The floor's terracotta tiles and the ceramic bathroom sink were painted by hand. The view from the window was poolside with several greasy-skinned sun-worshippers stretched out on the lounge chairs below. It wasn't the stunning view I'd hoped for, one of mountains in the distance, but I was glad to have arrived. I traced the pattern of the design in the sink, as if my finger were the brush that painted it, then splashed cold water on my face and headed for the Zócalo.

But first I sent an email to Max and the gang from a computer in the hotel lobby. I'd sent him a text on arrival in Mexico City, but opted for free Internet access in Oaxaca. "This eagle has landed in beautiful Oaxaca. Off to explore. All is well," I wrote. I wanted to keep things upbeat so they wouldn't worry. I also sent an email to my mom to diffuse her fears. No one had kidnapped me so far. I got a reply back from Max before I signed off telling me to "behave" myself, which meant not to take risks he wouldn't approve of. We'd see about that!

On the way to the square, I decided to begin my shopping therapy when I saw how reasonable the prices were in the local shops. I bought a shawl, which the clerk called a *rebozo*, and a vest and wondered if I'd use up all the room in my luggage. The streets were crowded with cars and people walking, but I stood out from everyone else. Instead of the skirts of the city women, and the colorful ensembles and ribbon-braided hair of the *indígenas*, I wore a T-shirt and jeans with comfortable laced shoes. My thick, sandy hair was pulled back in a low-slung ponytail. It wasn't necessary to wear a badge that said *"turista,"* because that was obvious! And I planned on playing the tourist role to the max while I was in this beautiful colonial city.

I realized how far I'd come from home when I saw the cathedral's baroque façade, the ornate fountain and the wrought iron benches in the square. Along the periphery of hotels and restaurants were outdoor cafes crowded with diners, drinkers and local indigenous people hawking items to the customers. I'd decided to join the cafe society and not go to the special dance event back at the hotel. Maybe I'd make it there the next night. When I sat down at a table I got a few stares, probably because I was a woman dining alone. I'd forgotten my pocket Spanish dictionary in the hotel room, but the waiter spoke adequate English.

"You want dinner?"

"Yes, sí. What do you recommend?" I asked.

"You like fish, steak, chicken?" he inquired.

"Probably chicken. What is best?"

"Chicken with mole. Okay?"

"Okay," I nodded.

"And to drink?"

I deferred to the familiar. "Coca-cola, por favor. Pero no hielo." No ice for me.

"Gracias," he said and was off to put in my order.

It seemed fate was pushing me toward chicken with mole. He brought my drink, no ice as requested. While I waited for the food, I turned my chair to get a better view of the square. It was a great vantage point for watching the activity around me. I saw young tourists who'd gone native with bright colored blouses, and a group of nuns whose laughter turned to quiet smiles as they entered the cathedral. Tourists photographed each other in front of the fountain. A swarm of yellow and brown birds landed near my feet looking for crumbs, then flew to the next table.

There was a rhythm to life on the Zócalo. I could tell it was the heart of this city and wondered if its vitality echoed what life was like in the plaza of nearby Monte Albán centuries before the cathedral even existed. This was my second trip to Mexico and once again I was aware of the juxtaposition of the old, even ancient, ways with the modern world. Here the people still wore traditional clothing every day and observed customs like the Day of the Dead. I took a few pictures to document the Zócalo from my seated position.

Dinner surprised me. A chicken leg and breast lay in the middle of the plate completely covered by dark mole sauce with a few decorative sesame seeds scattered on top. But it was flavorful and I was grateful I'd done well in ordering my first meal in Mexico. As I finished, a couple of young indigenous women approached my table. They were selling small bouquets of flowers that I could smell as they drew closer.

"¿Señora, flores?" one of them asked me, extending a bouquet a foot from my nose. I had never smelled a fresh gardenia before, though I'd always liked the distinctive scent of it in candles and soaps. But the real thing surpassed them all. Then I think she said they had come a long way, just as I had.

"¿Cuanto?" I asked the price.

When I calculated her answer into American currency it was under five dollars. I nodded and dug for the pesos in my purse.

As we exchanged money for flowers she looked at me sadly.

"¿Dónde ésta su esposo?" She wondered why I was alone. Where was my husband?

"No tengo un esposo," I replied. "Pero mis amigos vienen." Yes, no husband, but my friends are on the way.

"Bueno. Usted está bonita. Su esposo viene en la futura, es verdád. Buenas noches, señorita," she whispered, smiled, and then moved to the next table as the birds had done.

"Buenas noches," I said. "Y gracias." I was relieved I'd understood what she'd said, but also that she'd predicted a husband in my future. It may have been part of her sales pitch, but I didn't care. As her partner negotiated with the next table, the young woman glanced back at me and smiled, as if she'd read my thoughts.

The bouquet was a blend of greens, tiny pink carnations and one large, white, seductively aromatic gardenia. It was simple, beautiful, and magical. An omen of good things to come, I told myself. After the meal, I wrapped my new shawl around my shoulders as the sun grew dim and walked back toward the hotel, taking an occasional whiff of my flowers along the way. It seemed as if everyone I passed was walking with someone. My upbeat mood went down a notch as a longing for Neil's company pulled at my heart. I took a deep breath over the gardenia and let its fragrance lull me back to being joyful.

As I walked past the fountain I noticed another woman who was by herself. She was dressed in a white dress and had long loose dark hair. She looked up as I passed, nodded her head and smiled directly at me. Had she mistaken me for someone else? It didn't matter. I was grateful for her kind gesture and returned her smile.

Right before I fell asleep, I read a poem Darlene Howard had e-mailed to me when I'd asked for a sample of her writing. We'd exchanged several messages by then, but I hadn't anticipated her poems would be inspirational. Her words had a straightforward, quiet power. There was one poem I found especially reassuring as I re-read it that first night in Mexico.

God Is in the Moonlight
by Darlene Howard

In the deepest furrow of a barren field,
in the darkest shadow beneath a fallen tree,
where no light is known,
no candle burns,
God is there and God will always be.

In the coldest winter upon the highest hill,
in the caves of sorrow and regret,
where no heat is known,

no fire burns,
God is there and God will always be.

For God is in the moonlight,
illuminating,
shining out upon the earth
in shafts of hope beaming down
through shattered clouds.

Divine love sleeps in all hearts,
in all places,
awaiting just a whisper
to ignite its flame.

When all is nothing but despair,
remember,
God is there and God will always be.

Despite my nightmare on the plane, I was comforted by the smell of gardenia filling my room as I fell asleep that first night in Mexico.

4

The next morning, when a slice of sunlight poured through an opening in the curtains and into my eyes, I couldn't remember waking during the night. I'd been dreaming again. At the center of the one image left behind in my sleepy memory was the gardenia bouquet I'd bought the night before. It was in my hand, but looked as if it had been through a windstorm. White and pink petals had fallen to the ground scattered in a rough line, the apparent route I'd just taken through a field. A short distance away was the edge of a thick woods where the petals stopped. *I must have been in there,* I thought, where the tall trees would have blotted out the stunning blue sky above them. The rest of the dream was gone. It seemed clear that I'd walked out of that forest, but what had happened there I'd forgotten. My only clue was the wilting flowers in my hand, a marker of time, perhaps days, spent behind those trees. Usually, when I woke from a dream I couldn't remember much of it, beyond the mood it left me in. But this time, my only clue was this image, with no emotions attached to it.

After breakfast I looked over a brochure outlining the sights of the city of Oaxaca and the surrounding area. I had a day to kill on my own and weighed my choices. They all looked interesting to me, but Monte Albán was the largest and most fascinating thing of all, hands down. With the concierge's help, I joined a tour that was just leaving to visit the site. The guide was bilingual and gave us the historical background of the ancient city as we drove up the road in a yellow school bus. I'd seen photos of the place, but its size amazed me. I wondered what ruins were still buried under the mounds of dirt and plants that had taken over the place. Everywhere our group walked, dutifully following our guide Joaquín, we were followed by a gaggle of local people carrying souvenirs for sale. When they got too close to us, Joaquín gestured with his arm for them to keep their distance, but I saw them pick off a few stragglers. One woman put the bracelets she'd just bought on her wrist, and another gingerly tucked a clay figure into a backpack. I stayed close to our guide so I wouldn't be bothered, or tempted.

But after he'd told us about the *danzante* carvings and the ball court (where the winning team's captain had the honor of being sacrificed to the gods) and pointed out the observatory and other interesting structures, he gave us another fifteen minutes to wander around on our own before boarding the bus to our next stop. In reality, this was a signal that we were now fair game. The souvenir hawkers approached each of us. I had to admit that the prices were cheaper than in town. Like the others, I succumbed. It was silver jewelry this time. It seemed that shopping was finding *me* on this trip.

Our next stop, Mitla, was some distance away. It was an ancient holy place designed with geometric stone shapes jutting from its thick pillars and walls. Joaquín explained that the ancients, as well as many of their descendants, believed that Mitla was the home of the dead. I imagined crowds of invisible souls watching yet another group of tourists traipsing through their turf. I wondered if these spirits included souvenir hawkers helplessly trying to get our attention. This time, no one came near us. But then I found out why. We got back on the bus and drove to a nearby village, also called Mitla, that specialized in weaving. Artisans demonstrated their work while Joaquín discussed the dyeing process and the looms they used. After that we were led to a store where we could buy their wares. It was shameless promotion and I had a feeling that our trusty tour guide was getting a kickback. But the shawls were beautiful. I couldn't help myself and bought two of them. One would appease my mother, I hoped.

Our next stop was lunch on our return trip to the city. We sat at long tables in a garden-like setting. All of us were served the same thing, a thin steak with a side of vegetables. Of course there was a nearby gift store, but I begged off this time. When we first boarded the bus after lunch everyone seemed animated, talking about their purchases and the wonderful sights we'd seen. But the rhythm of the bus wheels and our full stomachs made us drowsy. I stayed awake and watched the state of Oaxaca pass, mile by mile. I had clearly entered an unfamiliar world, one that was beautiful and ancient, but also poor.

By the time we got back, it was almost time for the official siesta from 2:00 until 4:00. I hurried to exchange money at the hotel's front desk and buy a few postcards at a nearby shop before it closed. While the rest of the locals took their naps or watched telenovelas, I wrote postcards, using words like "scenic," "exotic," "mysterious," and "friendly." I bought stamps for the postcards at the hotel desk and dropped them in the lobby's mailbox as I headed out again.

This time I went to a historical museum housed in a former convent. The cases were filled with pre-Columbian artifacts that echoed what I'd seen earlier in the day, objects found at both Monte Albán and Mitla. I was astounded by the craftsmanship of those artisans from long ago. Yet the convent itself was worth seeing with its gardens and walkways. I thought of the nuns who lived there centuries before and wondered what they would think of these "pagan" objects lining the rooms where they once worshiped the Savior. But then that was Mexico, a juxtaposition of the ancient ways and the Christian ones, like the pre-Columbian Day of the Dead celebration overlaying All Saints and All Souls Days. Back home we celebrated the same holy days with Halloween, no doubt a leftover from western pagan traditions. But in Mexico, the old ways seemed alive and meaningful while ours were forgotten, overwhelmed by Christianity and commercialization.

My time in Oaxaca was passing quicker than I thought it would. I was having second thoughts about leaving for Teotenaca ahead of my friends, but I'd already cast the die. My driver would be by in the morning to cart me off to the mountains. I walked to the Zócalo, sat on a wrought iron bench in the park and observed the people passing by. I wasn't sure what to expect in this old colonial city, but it seemed peaceful and comfortable, despite the political unrest it had experienced from time to time.

That night I decided to attend the 7:00 p.m. dinner and dance performance, one last blast before I left the city. I put on the only dress I'd brought, hoping there'd be room for one more tourist. There was. I watched Aztec dancers in full feather regalia, men suited in animal costumes representing jaguars, and women with wide woven skirts dancing flirtatiously with their suitors. The history, legends and culture of Mexico danced across the stage. It may have been a way of corralling more gringo money, but I found it totally enchanting.

5

After breakfast the next day, I calculated there was just enough time for one more stroll to the Zócalo. I talked myself out of a few shopping temptations along the way. I was all packed and that was that, I told myself. Time was spinning away from me so I walked quickly around the square, touching the cathedral of Santo Domingo and made a wish in the fountain with a dime. I sent one more email to Max assuring him that I was doing just fine and about to leave for Teotenaca. I wished him a safe trip and recommended the dinner show at the hotel, along with a couple shops and Monte Albán, of course. I signed off, "Hasta luego."

By 11:10 I was officially checked out of the hotel and awaiting my next leg of the journey. Dar Howard had told me to sit in the lobby until someone came in and called my name. That would be my ride to the Sweet Dreams Bed and Breakfast in Teotenaca. I had no idea what the driver's name would be, what he (or she?) would be driving, or if they even spoke English. I reasoned it would be a person local to the city whose usual job was transporting people to obscure places. But it turned out to be an English speaker like myself, though his accent was quite different than mine. There were a few other people sitting in the lobby, but I was the only single female, so he approached me.

"Would you be Michelle Hardtke? Did I get your name right?" the tall man inquired with a smile. He was dressed in jeans, hiking boots, and held a straw cowboy hat that matched the highlights in his brown hair. He had a wisp of gray at the temples and root beer colored eyes. The hat was trimmed with a colorful woven headband. His tan skin crinkled around his eyes when he smiled. I wasn't sure of his age, but I guessed forty-something.

"Yes, I am," I said, not hiding my surprise. "You got it right. 'Heart' plus 'key.'"

"G' day then. I'm Reggie Howard from the Sweet Dreams B & B

come to fetch you to Teotenaca. I hope your trip's been good thus far?" his voice swung upward.

I hadn't expected to meet my host so soon! We shook hands. His were dry and calloused, more like a farmer than a painter, I thought. He was solid as a tree with broad shoulders and sturdy legs. "I didn't think I'd meet you so soon, Reggie. It sounded like Darlene was going to arrange for a local driver."

He laughed. "Yeah, she did. Me. But it's no problem at all. I came in last night to drop off orders of our soap and cheese and stayed at a friend's house. We come into town most weeks on business. With you coming today, it seemed like the perfect opportunity to put the two together. And your friends will be leaving from here at the same time in two days, right?"

"Yes. They'll be arriving in Oaxaca later today and they'll spend all of tomorrow here. But I'm anxious to get to Teotenaca. I don't know what it is, but your website's photos put a spell on me. I want to see the mountain," I tried to explain with a shrug.

Nodding his understanding, he replied, "We have a fantastic webmaster, but when you see El Anhelo right outside your window you'll be even more mesmerized. Dar and I came to Mexico not intending to come back, let alone put down roots. But there's something about our little village. I can't explain, really." He stopped for a moment, then continued, "You may experience it, too, and then maybe you can explain it to us," he laughed. "Here, I can take that suitcase of yours. A bit wobbly on its wheels, eh? Maybe I'll just carry it then," and he lifted it like a small bag of groceries. "Can you manage the backpack or would you like me to get that as well?" he asked.

"I've got it, thanks. I have to keep my backpack-toting muscles in shape." I heaved it over my shoulder and we left. I followed him to a green jeep parked in a loading zone a half block away. The car was splashed with mud on both sides and looked as if it would disappear in a jungle landscape.

"Careful not to get any mud on yourself there, Michelle. It will be even worse by the time we reach home. This big, green fella will get his bath later today," he laughed.

He opened the back door and arranged my bags in between the boxes of supplies he'd picked up in town, then let me in on the passenger side. I closed the door and he sat there quietly for a moment.

"Gardenia?" he asked.

"Yes. I bought it from a young woman on the square. You have a good nose! Do you mind it up here with us?" I'd surrounded the flowers' stems with wet paper, then wrapped a small plastic bag around it and placed the bouquet in the cup holder.

"No, it's quite nice. It will make the journey that much more pleasant. Now be sure to strap yourself in good. The road will be rough in spots. Do you get car sick?"

"Not usually," I said. "Is it going to be that rough?"

"Could be, if you're not used to it. If you have any Dramamine, I'd recommend taking it now." Since I hadn't planned on being in a boat this trip I didn't have any Dramamine. So I braced myself like I'd just gotten on a roller coaster as we began the ride to Teotenaca.

6

The first part of the trip wasn't as bad as I'd expected. It was a hilly highway and had its share of curves. But the hills were really mountains and the roads got steeper. Reggie handled them with assurance, obviously knowing the way. But this was a new experience for a flatlander like me. I kept my eyes on the road more than the scenery and that manic, moving white line in the middle of the road was making me nauseous. But my driver didn't notice since he was doing most of the talking, about the history of the region and the scenery we were driving through. So I finally had to interrupt him. I had to get out of that car.

"Could we stop for just a few minutes? Please?" I interrupted.

"Of course," he said, looking concerned. At that point, we turned off the main road onto a gravel one and he shut off the engine. I slid out and gulped the fresh air, which wasn't easy at that altitude.

"It is a bit rough," he reminded me. "In the mountains you're dealing with less oxygen than you're used to back in Chicago. Just take a little time and walk around. Get your bearings. If you have to go in the bushes over there for any reason, I'll understand. We're very flexible in this part of the world."

I didn't need the bushes, but I did walk for a few minutes as I tried to acclimate to the high elevation. It also gave me a chance to look around from where we stood.

"Where are we?" I asked, not knowing what direction we were going.

"We're up on a ridge here. Quite a view, really. Take a good look behind you."

I did and what I saw below was part of the road we'd just come up, but also a forested valley with a stream. The sunlight reflected on the water turning it to sparkling silver.

"Why didn't I see that?" I asked him.

"Probably because you were doing what most people do when they come this way for the first time. You were watching the road. You wanted to be sure we were staying on it. But watching the road is my job and I'm good at it. You watch the scenery and enjoy the ride. It's a lovely one," he smiled.

After a few more semi-deep breaths I felt better, and I knew the scenery would be a helpful distraction. I tried to be brave and announced, "I'm okay now, more or less. Where do we go from here?"

"As a matter of fact we just stay on this gravel road. We're leaving that paved road for this one now. But it's only a half hour on this lot. Then we go to dirt and gravel. It's surprising how bumpy a dirt road can be. Oh sorry, I probably shouldn't have said that. Hop back in and I'll get you there as soon as I can." He was moving too quickly for my taste. I felt a little nauseous again at the thought of zooming along on a hilly, gravel road. No white line, but still.

"Actually, why don't you take your time, Reggie. Then I can relax instead of worrying about driving into a ditch, or over a cliff. I trust your driving, but I'm just not used to mountains." *So much for adventure*, I thought.

Once we were on our way again, he suggested I talk to keep my mind off the treacherous things that could befall us on the road. He asked how my friends and I had settled on Teotenaca for our vacation, so yet again I related the story of the Dennis Lawley book Max found in the trunk. Reggie smiled and nodded as if he'd already heard the story, though I hadn't told Dar. I explained that we were all looking for a different kind of vacation this time and that we thought we would find it in Teotenaca.

Again, he smiled and nodded knowingly.

I stopped talking and asked, "How often do you have guests?"

"It might surprise you, but we have guests every month of the year. Maybe not every week, but certainly every month."

"Are they tourists like us?" I asked, not knowing who else they could be.

"If you mean people looking for something different, that's often the case. Dennis Lawley's book may be obscure, but people have read it, found the entry on our town, and come. In fact, that's what we did. We went to the States to visit family and then we came along with them to Mexico. Before we left Texas, Dar and I found a copy of Lawley's book in a used bookstore and began reading it. It was pure chance all the way.

"The family took a side trip to Oaxaca and then Dar and I decided to find out more about Teotenaca, since it wouldn't be too far off. We meant it to be a brief trip, three days or so. But we stayed almost three weeks. We just fell in love with the town and the mountain. We couldn't stop talking and thinking about it when we got back to Melbourne. More than a few folks thought we'd gone off our heads by wanting to move here. But we're dug in now," he smiled. "So, you see, Lawley's book is a kind of underground, secret hit of a travel book. Many of the lot who come to our town have either read it or talked to others who have or to people who came here. And many of them are artists, interestingly enough. From what I hear, you fit that bill. What kind of art do you do, Michelle?"

"I'm a graphic designer. I design elementary textbooks. It can be stressful, but I like the challenge." That probably sounded sufficiently boring to a painter like Reggie.

He shook his head. "I'll bet you do more than that," he laughed. "Come on, you can tell me," he coaxed.

"Oh, I really have a degree in fine art, not graphic design," I admitted. "But I don't do much of my own work anymore. By the time I get home I don't have the energy. But I did bring a sketchbook along, just in case I get a chance to do a little drawing while I'm here."

"That's the spirit. You'll get inspired, no worries," he smiled.

"Dar told me you do a lot of sketching. Do you have any favorite places around Teotenaca?" I asked.

"Hmmm, favorite places. I move around quite a bit, but there are a couple of views I particularly fancy. I don't mind sharing them and you've got time to kill before the rest of the crew arrives," he offered.

"That would be great. I'm looking forward to seeing your paintings, too."

"I'm always happy to share them. I've got my own studio 'round back. We'll give you a tour."

Despite the bumpy road, I was feeling physically better as well as relaxed. After being on my own, Reggie's company was comforting. And the scenery was wildly beautiful. The trees were dense. As we drove upward, they dropped away. I saw other layers of forest in the distance. Instead of anxiety, I began coasting on an elevated level of excitement. Then I picked up my flowers from the cup holder and breathed in the aroma.

"Your bouquet is pretty, but that gardenia makes it special. What a wonderful work of nature that fragrance is," he marveled.

I sniffed and nodded in agreement.

"If you like flowers, we have quite a garden of our own," he said. "We have lots of herbs and vegetables as well. But what would life be without flowers," he laughed. "The native ones have inspired artists around these parts. Like I said, you won't have to go far for an opportunity to break open that sketchbook of yours. In fact, I hope it's got enough pages!"

Reggie made me laugh out loud. Dar had a friendly, but formal tone in her emails, much different than her husband's description of her. She was probably being professional. I grew more curious about her as we approached Teotenaca. Then Reggie slowed down to make a left turn onto a narrow road.

"About another fifteen minutes and we'll be home. Hold on to your bouquet," he said. He moved more slowly now as the car swayed between the potholes. They were impossible to avoid.

"We had a hard rain the other day and this road took a real beating from it. The village will have to fill these holes or it will be the death of our vehicles," he said on a serious note.

I wondered if he was referring to his and Darlene's cars or if the villagers owned cars as well. I pictured them driving oxen and riding burros. I was probably way off base, but I couldn't imagine them having cars, either, in such an out-of-the-way place.

"Are cars common around here?" I sheepishly asked.

"Somewhat," he said. "But there are more pickup trucks than cars. They're often used for hauling animals or crops. They have to work right because you're absolutely dependent on them out here. Thank God we have excellent mechanics in town."

As we hit a particularly bad stretch I wondered if this was how it felt to ride a camel. Reggie maneuvered around the potholes as best he could.

"Now you know why I'm wearing this cowboy hat. I feel like I'm riding a bucking bronco," he laughed.

"I had visions of riding a camel," I said.

"I've been on a camel," he replied. "They offer a much smoother ride."

Then he eased to a stop and pointed to the right.

"Almost there. The mountain is up ahead. You can see a bit of it through here. Can you see it?" He made sure I was looking where his finger was pointing. But I wasn't sure what he referred to. As we rounded a sharp bend to the right it became clearer. The view was becoming more familiar. I was looking at the base of the mountain but couldn't see the top through the trees. Another bend brought us to a clearing and I could see its form ahead of us. We were driving directly toward it.

Suddenly I felt a jolt in my body. It was something apart from the swaying Jeep, more like a muscle spasm in my stomach. Then my heart began to race and I wondered what was happening to me! Helplessly, I looked at Reggie who was staring back at me. He slowed down to a stop.

"Are you right? You look startled," he said with concern.

I couldn't speak at first. Then tears began running down my cheeks. Why, if I was past being anxious about the road, was I getting so emotional? I was stunned. But then I found my voice.

"What's going on? Is this altitude sickness?" I rasped. My head was reeling. "I have this awful pain in my stomach!"

He looked into my face. Then he reached over and put his hand on my shoulder. I could feel my body trembling through his grasp. He looked directly into my eyes without saying a word. And then the trembling lessened. Gradually, my breathing and heart rate calmed down to almost normal. All the while he kept his hand on my shoulder and looked me in the eye. But when he spoke, he startled me again.

"It may be a form of altitude sickness. But more likely it's the draw of the mountain," he said in all seriousness. "I can't explain why, but the mountain is like a big magnet for some people and you're experiencing a symptom of it. Is your heart racing, too? Not everyone is affected like this, but Dar and I were. It won't last long, so don't worry. Hang on. We're almost there." He turned back to the road and drove on. None of what he'd just said made sense to me then. "You'll see another road in a minute that splits off to the left. It leads to town. But I'm going home so I'll stay to the right, a little closer to our very tall neighbor, El Anhelo," he referred to the mountain looming before us.

And then I saw the split in the road and felt the subtle turn to the right, toward the mountain. There was a sign up ahead written in Spanish and English and I knew both said "Welcome to Sweet Dreams Bed and Breakfast." Above the words was the abstract image of a cloud with a half-moon shining a light beam across the rest of the sign. A smaller sign hanging below the first said, "Vacancy." As we pulled into the long driveway Reggie looked at me again. "How are you now?"

I was still jittery, but the involuntary crying had stopped, thank God! I took a deep, slow breath of mountain air and replied, "I'm okay. Really.

But that was frightening! Why would that happen? I didn't understand what you meant by the 'draw of the mountain.' Will it keep happening?"

"Sometimes it will, but it's usually an initial reaction as you get close to the mountain for the first time. There are ancient myths about this place." He looked away from me and upward toward the peak. "The descendants of the early folk hold the mountain in high regard. They say it can call people to it. You're not the first to have an emotional reaction to come from nowhere. Around here, that's considered a compliment," he said, tipping his hat toward me. On one hand I felt reassured, but on the other it didn't make sense. I wished Angel was there to sort out myth from fact.

"Hello," a female voice called from outside the car.

"Hello back, Dar," Reggie replied through the window. "This here's Michelle Hardtke. Michelle, this lady is your hostess, as well as my lovely wife, Darlene Howard."

"G' day, Michelle," she said, extending her hand as I stepped out of the Jeep. "Welcome to Sweet Dreams and Teotenaca. You've come a long way. How was your ride? Not too bumpy, I hope," she smiled warmly.

I tried to smile back, despite the wetness on my cheeks. I wiped it away with my hand and said, "It's a pleasure to meet you, Dar. Oh, it was bumpy all right, but I survived." She gave a quick look to Reggie and he nodded.

As we shook hands she asked, "Would you like a cup of *manzanilla* tea then? It will relax you. We'll help with your bags and get you in the room first, if you'd like."

"Yes and yes. Thanks," I said.

So what did I expect her to look like? I wasn't sure, but she surprised me. She was only a few years older than I was and several years younger than Reggie. She had coppery red hair tied back in a single braid that dipped to her shoulder blades, and pale blue eyes that reminded me of faded blue jeans. She wore a white blouse embroidered in bright floral patterns. Though I would have expected her to have a pale complexion, given her coloring, she was tan like Reggie.

A couple of dogs swirled around us, wagging their tails and sniffing my bags.

"Don't be afraid of those two. They're our friendly guard dogs," Reggie explained with a wink. "They should be out back watching the chickens and goats, but they're being greeters instead. The black one is

Jack and the brown and white one is Paco. Hi boys, did you miss me?" They both barked as Reggie put his hands out to pet them. They were medium-sized mixed breed dogs, full of energy.

The B & B stood out against the thick growth around it. It had adobe outer walls painted a deep yellow ochre, making it harmonious with the dark green color of the trees that surrounded it. The walkway was terracotta brick crisscrossed into a herringbone pattern with bright, low flowers lining the edges on both sides. Dar opened the screen door that led into the main part of the house while Reggie followed with my bags.

"We can start with a little tour," she said. "This is our lounge room, what Americans call the living room. You're free to come into this area whenever you like."

There were two large windows that faced the front where we had entered. A hand woven Mexican blanket rested on the back of the couch. The furniture reminded me of the Spanish colonial style back in the hotel, but these pieces were more simply done. The floors were yellow pine covered with several hand-woven rugs like the ones I'd seen in Oaxaca. The room was painted a pale cream, perfect as a backdrop for the paintings that hung there. Most were landscapes signed "Reg. Howard."

"These are your paintings, Reggie? They're wonderful." I was truly impressed. Though obviously done from the nearby landscape, they varied from long vistas to more intimate garden scenes of flowers and grasses. They had an impressionistic quality, yet the foregrounds were more defined, as if you could walk right into them.

"Thanks. I've got some extra canvas, if you're interested," he said, slyly tipping his head, apparently in the direction of his studio.

"I'm proud of him," Dar acknowledged. "He's really grown as an artist since we've moved here." She stepped forward and led me into another room.

"This is our dining room and kitchen area where we serve breakfast between 7:00 and 8:00 each morning." She must have seen the surprise on my face when she made that announcement. "Yes, I know that's early by most people's B & B standards. But it won't seem that early after you've been awakened by Rudolfo's crowing at daybreak. He's the big handsome rooster you'll see strutting about. Steer clear of him. He's a bit territorial. But we love him, anyway," she smiled, as if she were talking about a wayward child.

The dining room floor was lined with glazed terracotta tiles, some of them hand painted with various geometric designs. The walls were painted a more golden yellow here and a long, dark harvest table filled a good portion of the room. A hand-woven runner draped off each end. In the middle sat a black ceramic vase filled with white flowers. To the left and right of the vase were wrought iron candelabra, each holding three slender yellow-white candles.

"This is the part of our tour where Reggie wants me to mention that he built this table," Dar smiled with her hand on it. "He's developed impressive carpentry skills since we've been here."

"Very impressive," I smiled, affirming her statement.

There were several artworks in this room, too. A portrait of Reggie, Dar and a young girl hung parallel to the great table. It was painted in an entirely different style than the other paintings. Though contemporary, it borrowed from traditional portraits by adding symbolic elements like Reggie holding paintbrushes in his hand and Darlene's journal and pen on a desk beside her. The girl wore a garland of yellow roses on top of her brown hair. Her right hand rested over her heart while her left hand extended another rose toward the viewer. The mountain appeared in the background with a ring of clouds circling its peak, an echo of the girl's garland.

"What a lovely portrait," I said.

"Thank you. Geoffrey is one of our favorite artists," Dar explained. "He painted it as a thank you for our hospitality."

"He came all the way from London," Reggie added, "so he stayed a while."

"Is this your daughter? I didn't realize you had a child," I said.

"Oh, yes. I'm surprised Reg didn't talk your ears off about her on the way in. That's our own most precious work of art. Her name is Sondra, but we call her Sunny, because she truly is. She's visiting friends at the moment, but she'll be back in time for supper so you can meet her then. Oh, and by the way, since you're all by yourself, we'd like you to have supper with us tonight," Dar kindly offered. "Much of what we eat comes from our garden."

"Thank you." I had hoped she'd offer me a meal, because I didn't want to eat alone again.

"And no worries, Michelle. We won't charge you extra for it," Reggie smiled. "We don't want you going to town to eat alone in a strange place. That wouldn't be very considerate of us."

"I'm flabbergasted by your generosity," I laughed.

"Well, it happens to be the way we do things out here," Dar smiled.

"You know about helping with the chores?" Reggie reminded me.

"There was something about milking goats and helping out in general?" They nodded in unison without another word and then the tour proceeded to a door and a stairway.

"This door leads to our screened veranda, which you have access to. And up these stairs, right above it, your room awaits." She pointed upward with her palm and so I took the lead. As I reached the top of the stairs she announced, "You and Maggie can have the end room to the right. It has the most comfortable bed and the best views. I'll give the guys the other end room."

The doors of the three rooms faced toward a hallway off the stairs. Around to the right of the stairs was another door, which Dar explained led to their private rooms.

My room was painted in a rich blue, like the sky on the sunniest of days. There were two windows through which I could see much of the surrounding area, including the view I'd seen on their website. The reality of it almost set off my crying again. "I can't believe I'm really here," I said. "I'm so glad we decided to do this." So many times I'd been disappointed when I let my expectations get too high. But this house, this countryside, and these two people far exceeded what I had expected to find.

"And we're grateful you chose us," Darlene replied as she brought my backpack in and set it next to the bed. She pointed out a decorative ceramic vase I could use for my bouquet. "But as you'll notice, there's no private bath or sink in this room. There's only one bathroom on this floor that all three rooms share. That's one advantage the boys will have over your marvelous view. It's right across from their room. We have a water tank on the roof, which catches rain water used for the bath. You might find the water pressure is a bit slow at times. So keep that in mind."

"We try to make it comfortable for our guests, but we're a small operation. So the accommodations are cozy, but not luxurious. We don't have those terrycloth robes that some places offer," Reggie smiled with a wink. "I hope you brought your own."

"I did, more or less," I laughed, thinking of the oversized T-shirt I'd brought.

The room held a large bed with a patchwork quilt that didn't look the least bit Mexican. The dark, wooden bed frame was similar to the other furnishings but had a floral motif carved into the headboard. There was a large matching dresser with a mirror in a decorative tin frame hanging above it. One of Reggie's smaller paintings was on the opposite wall. A ceiling fan circulated the air above me.

"You'll be surprised at how bright it can be in here after dark. The moonlight often pours into this room." Dar gestured toward the window.

"But we did include shades on the windows if you need to block out sun or moon," Reggie pointed out.

"This is lovely, really," I smiled, helplessly gushing again. I felt right at home.

"Well, we aim to please. So I'm glad we are so far. Shall I put on a kettle for tea?" she offered.

"Absolutely," I nodded. "But first I think I'll try out that bathroom. It was a long ride."

"We'll see you downstairs, then. Reggie can show you around outside while the water heats."

"See you on the veranda," he waved as they descended the stairs.

I took the vase into the bathroom and poured tap water into it, then set my bouquet in it. While I sat next to the sink I looked at the pattern on the vase more closely. It was such an intricate design that its motif wasn't that obvious, but it looked like a ring of small snakes with their tails and heads intersecting. I thought that was odd, since I hadn't seen anything like it in Oaxaca. It must have been one of those "ancient art forms" Dennis Lawley wrote about.

I washed my hands with the creamy, rectangular bar of soap on the sink. Goat's milk soap, no doubt. As I rinsed off I noticed the soap dish. It was another handmade ceramic piece with a more visible snake-like form incised around it, as if the snake were embracing it. *Why snakes?* I wondered, echoing Indiana Jones's reaction to the creatures. I wasn't fond of them, either. It was out of sync with the pleasant atmosphere of the place.

As I set the vase down in the bedroom, I had the oddest sensation that someone was looking over my shoulder. Turning around I glanced out the window and saw nothing but the mountain. I pushed the odd sensation aside, but I wanted a closer look at El Anhelo. I headed down the stairs.

"Are you ready for the rest of the tour?" Reggie asked. I nodded and followed the tall man through the screened porch that was the veranda and out the door that led to the back yard. From that vantage point he motioned in several directions to orient me.

"The mountain is hard to miss. You see that formation to one side that looks like the profile of a large bird? If you stand in front of that and look this way you can see our roof and our Aussie flag. If you get lost, put yourself in that area of the mountain and you can find us. There are paths from here that join the one that goes around the mountain's base. The one leading here has a sign with our name and an arrow pointing this way. Am I clear?" he asked.

"Yes. Very." I studied the formation in the distance.

"Now I'll show you 'round the yard."

There was a windmill, and barrels for catching rain. We passed the gardens, which had chicken wire fencing around them. Paco and Jack followed us for a while, then ran off as if they'd heard movement in the bushes. Each dog had a small house with his name painted over the open door. Beyond that, there was a fenced-in area around a red chicken coop with a half dozen brown chickens scratching the ground. Nearby was a barn that connected to another fenced area with goats.

"Those chickens lay wondrous eggs, fresh every day, thanks to all the attention they get from my wife," he laughed. "She gives a little concert every time she feeds them and her singing agrees with them." He turned toward the other fenced area. "Our goats provide the milk. We make cheese and soap with it to sell locally and in Oaxaca city. Our dried herbs go into the cheeses, and our dried flowers go into the soaps. Our little cottage industry keeps us going, along with the occasional painting that sells, and guests like yourself. By the way, we have a friend who bakes a beautiful bread which works quite well with our cheeses. You'll get to sample a bit tomorrow morning for breakfast. We also have vegemite, if you're interested," he offered with a mischievous smile.

"A friend brought me some from Australia. I'll pass on the vegemite, thank you. Once was enough," I shook my head and probably made a face as I remembered the metallic taste of the stuff.

"Did your friend make it to Melbourne? That's where we're from."

"Yes, she did and she said it was beautiful. She loved the Victorian buildings. But she had an odd experience there," I suddenly remembered.

"And what was that?"

"Vicky was sightseeing on her own one day and almost got locked in the old Melbourne Gaol. On top of that, she thought she was hearing ghosts," I told him.

"You've got my attention now. What happened?"

"She spent a while looking at the death masks and reading the stories of each person and why they were hung right there in the jail. It was morbid, but fascinating, she said. Apparently she lost track of the time. And then she heard wailing or moaning sounds coming from inside the room. She thought it was the spirits of the people who belonged to the death masks. But the sound turned out to be pigeons or doves on the ledge just outside the window, she realized. But then she scared the guard, who thought she was already gone. He was about to lock the door."

"That place gives me the creepy crawlers," Reggie said, rubbing his forearms as if he were chilled. "I wouldn't be surprised if those souls still walk around the place at night. They probably even scare the pigeons away! I can't imagine being locked up in there all night."

For a moment I thought about being locked up in a dark place, like the one in the nightmare I'd had on the plane. I felt a chill, too, even though the sun was shining on us. "I can't imagine being locked up, either," I agreed. "I had this horrible dream on the plane to Mexico City where I woke up in a dark, damp room and then the wall broke open where a light was coming through it. Some horrible creature was coming toward me, but I couldn't tell what it was. It was a scary dream!"

"Sounds frightening," Reggie said with wide eyes. "I had a dream similar to that once. I took it to mean I was afraid of making a change in my life, that my own fear was stopping me from allowing it to happen."

"What did you do?" I asked.

"I decided my curiosity should play itself out. I really had nothing to lose, so I took the proverbial plunge, and I was glad I did. Fear can trap you if you let it. My advice is not to let it," he smiled.

"Will I have sweet dreams while I'm here?" I asked, trying to make it sound like a joke, even though I needed to be reassured that I would.

"It's part of our mission statement," he smiled. "I can guarantee you'll get a lot of sleep," he laughed. "But back to your friend and her trip down under. Did she enjoy the rest of her time there?"

"Oh yes. She raved about Australia. She especially liked climbing Uluru. I saw her pictures of it at dawn and they were amazing."

"It is indeed an amazing place. Now, unlike that huge red rock in the middle of the desert, our mountain's connected to a few other smaller ones. You can't quite walk all the way around unless you go over it at some point. It's not that hard to get partway up, but you need real gear to get to the top. Remember that and don't go it alone."

"I promise not to climb the mountain," I assured him. That wasn't on my agenda. As he walked on I followed until he stopped and pointed to a landmark.

"You see that large tree over there? That's where our path to the mountain begins. You can follow it to the main trail. It's a nice journey with lots of wildflowers and birds along the way. Just be sure to stay on, or at least close to, the trail, because there are places to twist your ankle if you get off of it. And you could be there a long while," he cautioned me. "We'd have to get a search party if you didn't make it back by supper. Or breakfast."

"Don't worry. I promise to stay on the trail," I insisted to Reggie, just as I had to Max that I wouldn't hike alone. We'd see about keeping *that* promise.

"To be honest, we haven't lost a visitor yet. They all come back, eventually," he laughed and looked away. "We'd best be getting back," he said, changing the subject. We walked past his studio, which was in a small building at the back of the house. It had a large window facing the mountain. I peeked in as we passed, but I couldn't see much. There were other outside doorways leading to workrooms for processing the cheese and soap.

"Where does Dar write?" I asked.

"She's got a quiet little room off the dining room. You might have thought it was a pantry or a closet. It's always closed and off limits to everyone, including me, although she lets Sunny visit and play in there. I think the girl's a bit of a muse for her. Precocious, she is. You'll see," he nodded.

We walked to the veranda where Dar had a pot of tea and three cups waiting. The cups looked European or Australian, but the tea cozy was embroidered with bright colors on a white background, like the embroidered clothes I'd seen in Oaxaca. I suddenly realized how hungry I was. She'd made a number of finger sandwiches and surrounded them with wedges of cut orange. On another plate she'd arranged a circle of thin cookies.

"I thought you would both be hungry," she said.

"We're a B & B with tea," Reggie joked.

And we were hungry. He and I managed to finish all the food to the last crumb while the sky grew grayer and a hard rain fell. The sweep of cool wet air whirled around us, dropping the temperature slightly. I saw something move from the corner of my eye. It was a long line of drying flowers and herbs hanging from pegs along the inside wall of the veranda. They bobbed in the breeze coming through the screen and sounded like rustling leaves.

"That hit the spot." I said, feeling happily full.

"Good! You seem more relaxed now, as if you're finally on vacation," Dar smiled. "We're here to make your stay as comfortable as possible, you know. You're a long way from home in more ways than miles," she reminded me. "By the way, the rain won't be long and it cools things off. Perhaps you'd like to get settled into your room in the meantime. Besides, it would be perfectly acceptable if you took a nap. It's siesta time after all. We'll be getting ready for the market tomorrow, but you're also welcome to sit here or walk around the yard."

"How close is the town from here?" I asked.

"It's a ways, more than a kilometer, not quite a mile. But the few shops and the cafe will be closed for a couple hours. Reg could give you a tour of that as well, if you'd like to see it," she offered, rolling her eyes toward her husband.

"That's fine," he said.

"Thank you both for your hospitality. But shouldn't I be paying you now?"

"No worries, dear. You can do that when you check out. We know you're not going anywhere without us," he grinned an enormous, toothy smile.

I opted for going upstairs to unpack and settle into my room. From there I saw that familiar vista from the website. The sun was coming back making colors richer after the rain. I tried to guess the distance from where I sat to the face of the mountain. It could have been one mile or five. It was hard to tell.

I left enough room for Maggie's things in the dresser and then pictured her, Max and Angel arriving in Oaxaca city in a couple hours. I texted Max, telling him I'd arrived and the place was better than he could imagine. And then the phone shut itself off unexpectedly and wouldn't start again. I wasn't sure if the message went through or not. I'd have to check with my hosts to see what the best way was to reach him. The plan was for my friends to spend the next day exploring the city before arriving in Teotenaca the following afternoon. I could have waited for them, but I was glad I'd opted for getting to the town first. There was something about that picture on the website, the view I now saw with my own eyes. "The draw of the mountain" Reggie called it. I sat on the bed and gazed at that mass of rock.

"Are you trying to get my attention? But why? Why me?" I asked out loud. But then I shook my head at the absurdity of my words and whispered, "Whatever," as I looked away. I remembered that Angel had translated "El Anhelo" as "longing or yearning," which would describe the tug in my chest at that moment. I faced the mountain again as a tear slipped involuntarily down my cheek.

7

A couple hours had passed by the time I went downstairs again. Dar was in the kitchen cleaning and preparing for supper. "Did you have a good siesta?" she asked. "That *is* a very comfortable bed."

"I did. But I can't even remember lying down. One minute I was looking out the window at the mountain and the next I was snoozing," I laughed. "It was so weird!"

"You must have needed to sleep. I suspected as much. We don't call this place 'Sweet Dreams' for nothing. It's quite peaceful here," she smiled warmly.

"I see that," I agreed.

"And did you dream?" she asked, widening her eyes.

"I don't remember, really. Well, then again, I have a vague memory of one of Reggie's landscapes as if I'd just walked out of it. It's not clear now, though. I guess his work made an impression on me."

"He would like that. If you want to see what he's up to, he could give you a quick run to town. He has to pick up Sunny and could take the long way there."

"Is he in the studio? I hate to bother him if he's working on a painting."

"Today there's another task at hand. He's in the back doing inventory on our soap for market tomorrow. He can break away from that easily enough." I was curious about these cottage industries of theirs so I headed over.

I knocked on the open door before entering. He asked for five more minutes and suggested I have a look at his studio, which was through another door around the corner in the same building. It was easy using up the time that way. As I poked around I grew nostalgic at the smell of turpentine. It took me back to my art student days. Reggie's studio was much more organized than I would have thought, given his casual manner. There were deep, narrow shelves where paintings were tucked away on their sides, paintbrushes arranged by size in paint-splattered cans, and tubes of oil paint piled neatly in boxes on a large worktable. When he came in he asked if I was ready for another bumpy ride.

"If that's the only kind I can get," I replied, while studying one of his half-finished canvases.

"It is these days," he laughed.

But before we left, I asked if I could somehow get a message to Max, who I pictured getting anxious because he might think I'd dropped off a cliff. I couldn't even get my phone to turn on, it seemed. "Not all phones work around here. But this one will." He handed me his cell and generously allowed me to send a text to Max.

"Arrived safe. Took a nap. Phone won't work. This is Reggie's. Beautiful here. Have fun there. MH" And then we got into the car for another ride.

The town couldn't be seen from the road because of the trees, though there was a sign and an arrow pointing toward it. We took a right turn and in a short time I caught sight of Santa María Teotenaca at last. The main square had a grouping of shops along the street that ran around it. The inn, El Refugio, seemed to anchor the middle of the street we were on. The church could be seen at the opposite end, set apart by a long row of steps that led to where it sat on top of a small hill. We passed a restaurant with an outdoor café where men were engaged in conversation, cigarettes in hand.

"Do they serve alcoholic drinks there?" I asked, with Max in mind.

"Yes, and the best coffee you'll ever taste," Reggie said.

"And how's the food in town?"

"Very good, but very local. They use exotic spices. The recipes have come down from pre-Columbian times in some cases. We think it's wonderful, but it may be an acquired taste." I pictured Angel feeling right at home there. "I'll drive around a bit so you can see just how charming and quaint our lovely town is."

We came closer to the church of Santa María, with its Spanish colonial façade. It had a small flower garden in front, but it was a far cry from the magnificent cathedral and the huge Zócalo in the city of Oaxaca. Beyond the main square, houses fanned out in various directions off the road. A few were spread far apart and I could see smaller buildings near the main houses. Reggie explained that some were kitchens, built outdoors so they could cook over a fire and the smoke could filter through the loosely fitted log walls. I saw chicken coops and garden plots. Other roads continued into wooded areas. All in all, the population seemed almost as small as I'd imagined.

"There isn't much to it, is there?" I said.

Reggie smiled. "There isn't and there is. It depends on your point of view. For us, there's a lot here. It's a friendly, cooperative community that allows, and even welcomes, outsiders living here, as long as they're cooperative, too. It's a more diverse community than most towns in Oaxaca."

He turned off the main road to a secondary one. "I have to get Sunny now. She's learning about pottery from my friend Fernán and his grandmother Flor. His daughter Carlita is a dear friend to her, too. We have our own little exchange program around here with the children. It gives them a cross-cultural appreciation for the arts and an understanding of other languages. I've been giving lessons to Carlita in drawing and English. Her mother suffered from a weak heart and died when the girl was only a year old, so I'm glad she and Sunny get along so well, since neither has a sibling."

"I'm sorry to hear about Carlita's mother. How sad." I was shocked, really.

"We're blessed in many ways here, but we still have our share of tragedy, like everyone else. On the positive side, you're in for at least another surprise or two today," he mysteriously added.

At that point, the road veered into the woods. In a clearing ahead of us was a light blue adobe house with two children laughing and chasing each other around a tree near the road. As we drove up, I recognized Sunny from the portrait in the dining room, though she'd grown since it was painted. Both girls wore woven blouses or *huipils*, but Carlita had a matching skirt while Sunny wore blue shorts. They both had dark hair, but Sunny's had auburn highlights while Carlita's was a rich black. When Sunny saw us she waved. "There's my sweet girl," Reggie smiled with love in his voice. Fernán greeted us in Spanish and Reggie responded with an authentic Spanish accent that surprised me. I tried to pick up on the conversation, but it moved too quickly. Reggie motioned to me, and his friend bowed slightly in greeting as my name was spoken.

"Michelle, this here's Fernán Morales and his daughter, Carlita, and my daughter, Sunny." Reggie introduced us and I nodded and said, "Hóla," to them all. Carlita and Sunny laughed and whispered in Spanish to one another. Then Sunny told me Carlita wanted to know if I had a boyfriend.

"Sunny, that's none of your business," her father responded in English.

"That's okay," I said. "The answer is simple. No." *Not anymore.*

Sunny whispered in Carlita's ear and she whispered back.

"Carlita says you should have one. You're pretty," Sunny translated, then hid her mouth and giggled.

It was awkward, but I hoped Carlita was right. "Gracias, Carlita," I said with a little wave.

"Okay, that's enough gossip," Reggie said. "I've come to fetch you for dinner. Are you ready?"

"Yes, Dad, but I have to get my pot," Sunny replied. She ran into the house and emerged with a small terracotta bowl decorated with green and white dabs of glaze. She held it out proudly for us to see.

"It's been fired and everything. I want to give it to Mum for her paper clips," she explained.

"Well, that's beautiful," her father beamed. "I'm sure your mum will be quite pleased that her daughter is such a clever girl."

I think he told Fernán he was an excellent teacher and talked about the market. Not wanting to keep me out of the conversation, Reggie explained in English that he'd asked his friend to make ceramic soap dishes. They'd set up stalls next to each other so customers could buy the dish from one and the soap from the other. I wondered if they'd be decorated like the one with snakes I'd seen at Sweet Dreams.

On the way home Reggie continued driving away from town, but after a few turns he ended up back on the main road. Along the way we passed more houses some distance from each other. People waved and Reggie tipped his hat. Sunny sat in front of me next to her dad and I could tell she was torn between examining her clay pot and examining me. Finally, she figured out a way to do both.

"Would you like to see my pot?" she asked me.

"Yes, I would," I said and carefully took it from her small hands while the car rocked.

"Do you like it?" she asked. "It's my first one."

"I do," I said in all honesty. She seemed to have a natural talent for one so young. The small bowl was made with a basic pinch pot technique. Yet the clay's thickness was relatively even and the base was almost perfectly round. The outside wasn't smooth, but that added to its beauty. "You *do* have an excellent teacher. And it looks like you're a very good student, Sunny."

"I love my Dad, but Fernán is my next favorite daddy, even though he's Carlita's. I love it when he shows me how to make pots," she explained, in an Aussie accent like her parents. She smiled warmly and I was stunned by how strikingly beautiful a child she was.

"What's your next project?" her father asked.

"A bigger pot. Just like this one, but bigger. Maybe I'll give it to you, Dad. You can put your pencils in it, or your keys," she suggested.

"Whatever you make for me will be wonderful, even if it just looks pretty on a shelf," he smiled.

"It will be pretty, but it will be more than that," Sunny stated with certainty. She had a radiant, dimple-cheeked expression.

As we crossed to the main road, Reggie turned and I saw a few more houses further down. One was nearly invisible because it blended right into the trees and wildflowers. "Does anyone live there?" I asked.

"They do," he said. "And they aren't as reclusive as you would think, given the way the place looks. It's just been there a long time. That's the way they fancy it, all overgrown like that."

"That's where my friend Zachary lives," Sunny added. "He's my dad's age and he likes to read to me. He writes stories for children and he asks me if I like them."

Reggie laughed. "That's true. You could say Sunny is Zachary's marketing consultant."

"He's very good," she insisted. "Some stories are funny and some are sad. My favorite one is about a goat who tells his master where to find a hidden treasure. The man is happy so he doesn't eat the goat for dinner. It has a lovely ending. I like that," she smiled.

"I remember that story," her father said. "It's traditional around here. But it doesn't end that way when other people tell it."

"I know," she sighed. "But I told Zachary he should change it. The way the story was before was the man eats the goat after it tells him where to find the treasure. He does find it, but when he takes it home, it sinks into a hole and it's gone. I told him the man shouldn't kill the goat and then he would have the goat *and* the treasure. That's better." She flung both hands in the air for emphasis.

"You're right. That's what's called a win-win ending, Sunny," Reggie nodded in agreement.

"What does Zachary do with his stories?" I asked.

"He has a publisher in New York," Reggie replied.

"Really?" I was amazed. "But that's so far away."

"I promised you surprises," he reminded me. "We have artists and writers who live in the area, and a few more who stay from time to time. Zachary and his wife Anna are permanent residents like we are. But they travel to promote his books and for her to lecture. Their last name is Kimball. They're from North Carolina, I believe."

"How did they come to live here?" I asked.

"Anna's done a lot of research on pre-Columbian cultures. She's written articles on the subject and taught at university. They were staying in Mexico City for a while, but they got tired of the congestion and pollution and moved to Oaxaca city. Then they found their way here and loved it, just the way we did," he related.

"They have lots of old masks," Sunny added.

"She collects them," her father explained.

"Can I have my pot back?" she asked me. Her bright blue eyes looked mildly concerned.

"Yes. Here you go," I said, being careful that it was firmly in her hands before I let go. "I'm sure your mother will like it."

"Me, too," Sunny smiled, exuding the bright enthusiasm that earned her that name.

8

We arrived back at Sweet Dreams where Sunny presented her mother with her first hand-built clay bowl, the perfect repository of paper clips, which Dar accepted with great fanfare. I hadn't meant to be such an active participant in the Howard family, but it all seemed so natural. The next thing I knew Sunny was introducing me to the goats. "This one is Miranda because she's so pretty and the one in the corner is Scout because she's always ahead of the lot. And that's Geoffrey. He's Scout's kid. We named him after a painter who stayed here. But soon he'll go live with someone else. I'll miss him," she frowned.

We were heading toward the hen house when Reggie called us.

"We need salad for dinner, girls." He handed me a kitchen knife and a bowl. "Sunny, take Michelle to the garden where she can cut us some lettuce for dinner," he directed.

The garden was in a bright spot where many healthy plants were growing. The girl unlatched the gate and we walked in. They kept it fenced so the dogs and other animals would be kept out. Paco the dog had been following us around and now he watched from outside the fencing. "Here, Michelle, these are ready," Sunny said while pointing to some small leafy growth. I'd never harvested lettuce before, so she told me where to cut it free. "Be careful. That knife is sharp," she warned me. I cut the leaves away from where they stood in the soil and tossed them into the bowl that Sunny held. Finally she said, "That should be enough. Save the rest for later," she advised.

Back at the house, I set the table while Reggie prepared the salad and drinks. Sunny's job was to put folded cloth napkins next to each plate. Dar and Reggie sat on one side of the long table while their daughter and I sat on the other. I was about to grab the tongs for salad when my small neighbor touched my hand and whispered in my ear, "Grace first."

"Oh, of course. Sorry," I said, my cheeks flushing. I'd gently been put in my place. I followed her lead and closed my eyes. Then I realized why she wanted my attention.

"Thank you, Lord, for blessing us with these gifts of food on our table," Sunny prayed. "We thank you for this day and for bringing Michelle to us to share it. And thank you for Fernán and Carlita and my new pot. Amen."

"Amen," the rest of us said in unison.

"Very nice, Sunny." Dar smiled at her and then at me.

"She never says it exactly the same way," her father explained.

I'd mentioned my concern about drinking the local water in an email so they'd provided me with a bottle of pop. "We were cautious when we came here, too," my hostess nodded. "We'd heard stories. But the water here agrees with all of us. There are lots of underground springs and it's remarkably pure. But Reg brought bottled water from the city if you're more comfortable with that."

"I will stick to that, I think. And bottled pop without the ice cubes," I insisted. "If I feel brave later maybe I'll try the water before I leave." But I had no intention of drinking it. I was even concerned about eating the lettuce, which had been rinsed off with tap water.

"By the way, your friends called while you were out. They said you don't have to call back, but they just wanted you to know they arrived safely. They got your text," she reported. "I believe the person I spoke with was Max. He sounded very serious."

"He's like that. Kind of a big brother."

"What are your friends like?" Sunny asked. I gave a brief rundown on each of them, explaining Angel's interest in religions and pre-Columbian culture, Max's photographic talents and Maggie's healing skills and mania for flamenco.

"I look forward to meeting them," Dar said. "What would you like to do in the meantime?"

"I'd like to go to the market with you tomorrow. And I'd like to get a head start on exploring the area around the mountain," I said, feeling that curious tug again. "Maybe I can get in a little sketching and hiking."

"I can show you around," Reggie offered. "We only got started earlier."

We all helped with the cleanup after supper and then Dar and Sunny went into the writing room and closed the door. Reggie and I walked outside to the tree where the path to the mountain's main hiking trail began.

"I'll show you a few of the best vantage points in this area," he said, stopping near a small creek and pointing beyond a grove of trees. "There's usually a nice play of light here, especially at sunset. The trees take on a glow, as does the mountain." As he spoke the words, the sun cast its magical light on El Anhelo. Again, my heart began to race and my eyes clouded with tears.

"It's happening again, Reggie!"

"Take a deep breath through your nose and hold it. That's right. Now release it slowly through your mouth. Good. Do it again. Yes. And again. Just one more deep breath. Are you feeling better?" He was acting like a yoga coach. But it worked. I was calmer, but confused.

"Better," I nodded, after another deep breath. "But I don't understand *why* that keeps happening to me." I wanted to find out more this time.

"It's not easy to explain," he said, looking me in the eye and then looking away toward the mountain. "It's El Anhelo, the mountain of longing. So who's longing for whom, eh? Or what?" He turned back toward me. "What do you long for, Michelle?" he asked in a hushed tone. It felt like a personal question that I wasn't sure how to answer. I took another deep breath first and replied cautiously, but truthfully.

"A place where I feel welcome and safe. Where I can get away from work and," I remembered Neil, "heartache, I suppose. To sit and sketch in a setting like this. It's been too long since I've done that."

"If that's why you came, then the draw of the mountain makes sense. It seems to open up one's creativity, and one's heart," he said, as if he could read my thoughts.

"But what can the mountain *do* for me, and *how*?" I wasn't getting it at all.

"If you open your mind to whatever may happen, you can learn a great deal here. But I can't predict what that might be." He was being mysterious again. I could tell he was holding something back.

"So what did you and Dar learn here? And why did you move here?" I asked, because I wanted to know the answers, but also to deflect his questions away from me.

He smiled and chose his words carefully. "In truth, we keep learning. It never ends. Our love for each other deepens all the time. Because of Sunny we're learning about parenting. We're taking our artistic lives more seriously than we had before coming here. Back in Australia I taught

French and Dar taught English at the same school. But on our first visit here," he laughed quietly, "we had to get right up to that mountain to have a good look at it." He stopped to glance at El Anhelo. In a more serious, even reverent, tone he said, "There's something at work here, Michelle. It's deep and sacred and very old. It stirs one's emotions, as it seems to have stirred in you. It broadens that creative part of ourselves and makes us more than we were before we came here." He looked hard into my eyes. "That's why people come back. Part of it is the natural beauty. Another part is the respectful, generous way people treat each other here. But it's greater than that. When you leave here, don't be surprised if you're not the same person who arrived today."

He must have seen skepticism and surprise in my eyes, because he became more animated. "It may not make sense now, but it will. The best advice I can give you is *not* to be afraid. Follow your instincts. They brought you here for a reason. And I *know* you'll sleep well here," he smiled.

I got a prickly feeling on the back of my neck. Sweet Dreams, huh. "I'm sure you mean well, Reggie, but what you're saying is confusing, maybe even a little scary for me."

There was an awkward silence between us.

"Perhaps I've said too much then. I wasn't trying to scare you, Michelle. Honestly." He looked away, not sure how to proceed. Then he repeated with more emphasis, "There's nothing for you to be afraid of here. Nothing at all, and least of all from me and my family."

He stared at the mountain, then at me, and surprised me by walking away toward the house. I hesitated. I was still facing El Anhelo, and in that instant I suddenly had a shred of understanding. In that brief moment I felt open to possibility and change. Maybe I could shake loose from my lingering sadness over losing Neil. Maybe the beauty surrounding the mountain would inspire me to return to my art. Silently I followed Reggie back, then helped him package the bars of goat's milk soap to be sold at market the next day.

9

At an ungodly hour the next morning, Rudolfo crowed. Loudly. That sound, so abrupt and unexpected, reverberated against my window. The next thing I noticed, a much more pleasant thing, was the aroma of my gardenia, still strong. My body was sleepy, but my senses were waking up.

I'd had trouble falling asleep the night before as I mulled over Reggie's explanation for the "draw of the mountain." I seemed to be missing a puzzle piece, not sure of what the whole picture should look like. But then the moonlight spilled through my window and onto the quilt. I tried to remember the words in Dar's poem and repeated the only line that came through intact: "God is there and God will always be." It was meditative and evolved into "God is here and God will always be." It was a comforting thought and then I fell into a solid sleep. Until Rudolfo's noisy interruption. It looked like night, but the sky began to brighten. What finally got me out of bed was my desire to see what the mountain looked like at dawn.

"Good morning, El Anhelo," I whispered with a half-smile.

The sun's early light began to spill over the top of the mountain from behind. I knew my curiosity and its physical beauty were drawing me to it, no matter how Reggie explained it. I wanted to touch it, just as my hosts had on their first trip. As I stood at the window I saw movement below me. It was Dar walking to the chicken coop. I imagined people across the area starting the same daily routine of feeding animals and making breakfast.

I felt privileged to have the bathroom to myself. The nights were cooler in the mountains, which made for great sleeping. But now that I was up and wearing my big T-shirt, I was missing that terrycloth robe Reggie had mentioned. I took a quick shower, since I'd been warned not to use up the hot water. I washed my essential parts, threw on my clothes and went down to breakfast.

"Good morning, Michelle," Dar greeted as she entered through the veranda door. "You're up early! I thought you'd be nestled under those covers until 8:30 and I'd have to knock on your door. Sleep well?" she asked.

"Yes. That's a great mattress!"

"Lovely. You know, I think mattresses always seem better when you're really tired," she laughed. Then she looked around, shaking her head, "That Reggie is always behind on market day. I don't suppose you know how to milk goats," she said.

"Is it like milking cows?" I asked.

"More or less. But you have two less teats."

"No," I laughed. "I don't know how to milk cows, either."

"Well, once we get the lord of the manor up and about he can show you how it's done. I think I hear him stirring." And then a sleepy-eyed Reggie appeared with a yawn.

"Did I hear someone calling me? What would you like me to do?" He looked at Dar who looked at him with her head tilted sideways.

"Oh, I know," he said. "My turn to milk the goats. I'm on it." And then he looked at me that way and I knew it was my turn, too. I carried a milking pail and a cup while Reggie carried two large milk cans. He blinked in the early light. "I'm surprised you're up so early," he said as we walked across the yard.

"So am I. Rudolfo is way more effective than my clock radio."

In the goat barn he pulled a chain that turned on a dim bulb hanging over a low table. The place smelled like a barn, but not as bad as I'd expected. "Sanitation is key in this business," he said as he poured water from a metal pitcher into a bowl and washed his hands, then wiped them on a towel hanging there. He described the process of milking a goat, then pointed to the low table. "That's the milking stand. I'll show you how to clean off the udder and teats before they get milked. You're an artist, so you're good with your hands. That'll help."

He began with Miranda. "Hey there, little girl, get on up here." He'd put grain in a bowl and held it in front of her nose, luring her to the milk stand. Once she jumped up on it he put the bowl on the other side of a narrow frame where she could reach it. When she stuck her head through the opening, he slid a couple of boards that gently held her in position while she ate. After pulling up a stool, he cleaned her udders with a disinfectant. Then he squeezed and the first squirt went into the cup. "Ah, I love a healthy goat," he said, inspecting the white fluid. He positioned the pail and got down to business with a hand on each teat.

"The idea is to squeeze the milk downward into the pail, then let the teat fill up again and squeeze it down again." He demonstrated the rhythmic technique, which included the grip and the fingers moving downward.

"You make it look easy," I said, "but I'm not so sure it is."

"It's like riding a bicycle. It seems hard at first, but once you figure it out, you never forget how it's done. When the flow slows down you hold the teat and push up. That's what the kids do to get the last of the milk out of Mum. Then squeeze downward, gently. After that it's time to go to the next goat."

When he finished with Miranda, he opened the frame and she hopped down. Then he poured the contents of the pail into a milk can. He washed the cup and repeated the process with the next goat, making sure I watched carefully. "Would you like to try it now?" he said after he'd finished. "These are the most patient animals on the continent, so don't be afraid."

He positioned the next one as I washed my hands. "This here's Trudy, the most agreeable one of the lot. Give her a go." I sat down and he positioned the cup for me. I did my best and got just enough out. "Fantastic! Looks good. Now switch to the pail." He coached from the sidelines until I got into the rhythm of it. When the milk thinned out he cupped his hand over mine to help get the last of it. It was awkward, but we were getting the job done. "You're doing great, Michelle! I knew you would." We took turns until both cans were full.

"Let's get these cans to the kitchen and I'll come back to finish up here." I walked slowly carrying one of the cans, but if there hadn't been a cover on it I'm sure I'd have splashed half of it on the ground. He had a good laugh. "It's quite the workout. You'll build those upper body muscles while you're here. Another benefit we offer."

We entered the building behind the house and placed the milk pails on the bottom shelf of a refrigerator. The room itself was cool. I noticed racks of cheeses curing along one wall. "Electricity is a wonderful thing, but we have a backup generator just in case. This milk is our life's blood. We do this twice a day so I may call on you again later. You're a natural, truly." He padded me on the back.

"It was fun, which surprises me. Maybe I'm not all city girl after all,"

I said, shaking my head.

"It appears you have talents you didn't know you possessed," he smiled. "I'm sure that's just the beginning. Who knows what you'll be up to in a few more days."

10

We ate breakfast in a hurry, but it was ample. The "beautiful bread" their friend had made complemented the soft goat cheese. On her slice, Dar spread a dark substance from a jar, the ubiquitous vegemite, a staple of the Aussie diet. We loaded up the car and on the way to market I asked her if she ever got homesick for the land down under.

"Oh, yes. We've gone back on occasion. But then we get homesick for Teotenaca," she replied. "It's tough to be from two places so far apart."

"I like Australia," Sunny added. "But I like it here better."

"Truth be told, so do we," Reggie agreed. "But there's no place on the planet like the land of Aus. I do miss it sometimes."

"By the way, thanks for your help this morning, Michelle," Dar said. "I hope you'll plan on having lunch with us," she smiled. "And what would you like to do with your day after the market?"

"Probably sketch a little and start inching my way toward the mountain. I really want to get a closer look at it. Max didn't want me to hike by myself, but it looks like an easy walk from what I can see. Are there any things to be wary of around there?" I asked, not expecting any. "Maybe snakes or highwaymen or places where the earth could swallow me whole?"

"Places where the earth could swallow you whole, maybe. But snakes and highwaymen aren't much of a threat these days," Reggie winked.

"Okay," I said slowly. "I'll watch where I step."

But before lunch and a hike, there was the market, the *tiangui* they called it. We drove to the main square in front of the church. A number of people were setting up their stalls when we arrived. Fernán waved for Reggie and family to join him. Dar and Sunny went to one side of the table with goat's milk, cheese and yogurt displayed on top of a tray filled with ice. Reggie sat on the other side near Fernán with stacks of goat's milk soap wrapped in plain brown paper. Their product label matched the logo on their sign – a cloud with a partial moon over the words

"Sweet Dreams" in English and Spanish, as if the label were a wish to all who bought their wares.

"Feel free to wander about, Michelle. There's a lot to see," Dar urged me. "We'll be here for a while."

After helping them set up, I took off on my own. The many merchants there had to have come from other villages, too, maybe from miles away. There were the traditional artisans with their handmade clay bowls, woven rugs, and embroidered clothes, as well as sellers of spun wool and natural dyes. But I also saw stalls manned by artists of other ancestries: an African-American jewelry designer with hammered silver bracelets, a Brazilian wood carver with intricate crucifixes, and an English potter with simple plates and bowls. I heard Spanish, English and indigenous dialects blending everywhere I walked. There were stacks of bread as well as open bags filled with dried beans, spices and herbs. There were brown eggs and live chickens, young pigs and goats. Like Sunny, children helped their parents in the booths.

But no one else had goat cheeses or goat's milk soap. When I went back to the Sweet Dreams booth it was surrounded by westerners and *indígenas* alike. I stood in front to get the perspective of their customers. And then I noticed a white-haired woman behind Fernán's booth. She seemed to know many of the customers, but she was also looking at me. She smiled and nodded when we made eye contact. Then she motioned for me to come closer. At first I thought this was just her way of getting new business for the masterful pots displayed there. I couldn't help but admire the craftsmanship. A few soap dishes as well as the bowls had flourishes scribed into them that looked like a sun with rays beaming out at an angle, as if the sun were spinning. But there was the snake motif again as well as other symbols: a repetitive bat-like shape and another resembling a fish with a visible skeleton, but no eyes. I wanted to interrupt Reggie or Dar and ask if anyone knew why *these* animals? What did they mean? But they were too busy. The white-haired woman nodded to me again and motioned to a small terracotta vase. I picked it up and held it. But when I realized a snake was carved in it just under my hand, I almost dropped it! What did she expect me to do next? I liked the way it felt in my hand, thin and light, but did I really want to buy it?

And then Reggie appeared at her side and introduced us. Her name was Flor Morales and she was Fernán's grandmother. "She wants you to have the vase," he told me, "as a gift."

"A gift? But why?" Weren't they trying to make money here?

"She says it was made for you."

"But what's with the snake motif? I'm not sure I really like it." Even though I was expressing doubt to Reggie, I smiled, not wanting to offend Flor. She turned to him and spoke. He translated for me.

"She senses that you're afraid of the snake and asked me to explain its meaning. It's a traditional symbol of renewal in Teotenaca. When the snake sheds its skin, it's because it's outgrown it. She feels you're about to outgrow your skin."

I kept smiling but said, "I don't get it."

"Flor says you'll outgrow it soon, so she wants you to have the vase, as a reminder of your progress."

"I still don't get it, but I'll accept her gift anyway, if it'll make her happy. Gracias, Señora Flor," I nodded with a forced smile. She nodded and smiled quite sincerely, took the vase back and wrapped it in a crumpled newspaper, then handed it to me and said, "Por nada, señorita. Estás una mujer del corazón."

I was a woman *of* the heart? A woman *from* the heart? I didn't understand that, either. "Reggie?"

"Trust me, it's a high compliment. It means your heart is connected with the heart of the mountain. It's another way of saying the mountain is calling you, but no worries. It's a good thing." They looked at each other and laughed a little, as if my ignorance was excusable since I was new. I smiled back, clutching the vase to my heart not knowing what else to do with it, then wandered down the aisle of stalls I'd missed.

After purchasing handmade souvenirs, I was about to return to the Sweet Dreams booth when I ran into Dar. "We're selling briskly today. We won't be here much longer at this rate. It's time for me to shop. Want to come along?" I nodded and followed. She carried a small cooler in one hand and a basket over her other arm.

"We barter quite a lot here. I've brought cheeses for people who I know will trade." She stopped at several of their booths and before long the basket began to fill as the cooler emptied. I was fascinated by this clever way of shopping. And then she asked what I'd bought. The first thing was a colorful woven bag to hold my purchases. I pulled out an embroidered blouse. It wasn't cheap, but then it had taken a lot of hours to make.

"Have you heard of *cochineal*?" she asked. "It's a deep red dye made from dried beetles. That sounds awful, I know, but it was sold in markets long before the Spanish came. I'm sure the thread in this *huipil* was dyed with it. It's a marvelous color and a staple of this culture. Unfortunately, commercial dyes have been taking over that market, but this color looks like the real thing. And what else have you there?"

I pulled out a few more items from the woven bag, including a pair of delicate silver earrings that had been wrapped in black paper. "They're quite lovely," she said, as I held them up. "You've a good eye, Michelle."

"Thanks, Dar. Oh, and then there's the vase that Flor gave me. Did Reggie tell you about it?" It was at the bottom of the bag.

"Ah, yes, he did. Most of the ceramics in that display belong to Fernán, but several pieces were made by Flor. Her pots are quite special and unique. They look so perfect, yet she and Fernán use a cone of clay and a corncob to hollow out and smooth the surface. They don't use a potter's wheel. To put things in perspective for you, that was a very generous gift for the time it took, but also because her work is highly praised."

"But, Dar, why would she give it to me, a stranger, a tourist for gosh sakes? I don't understand." I hoped she could explain more than Reggie had.

"Flor is highly intuitive. She sensed something about you and wanted to reassure you, I think," Dar interpreted, in a matter of fact way that surprised me.

"She said I'm about to outgrow my skin. I feel like I've been eating too much lately, but I don't think that's what she means," I said, trying to make light of it. "Do you?"

"Not at all," she assured me. "Hmmm, perhaps you're about to experience a kind of change, but she's saying it's one to look forward to. She's encouraging you to do whatever it is. Maybe you'll get past that break up with your boyfriend that's made you so sad lately. Flor may not know what it is herself, but it sounds like a new level of experience is coming your way, if she's right." Dar sounded encouraging, too, when she said, "Maybe it's time to start sketching again," and I knew she was right about that.

11

We may have looked tired as we packed up at the market, but I was energized. The Sweet Dreams crew had done well, selling or trading most of what they'd brought. There was no reason to stay, even though the market was still going on, so we went home.

"How'd you like your first Teotenacan market, Michelle? Was it what you expected?" Reggie asked.

"Yes, and a lot more. I was surprised by the non-Mexican artisans," I admitted.

"There weren't many this time, but there were also non-Mexican customers, you probably noticed," he reminded me.

"That's true, including myself, of course."

"And us as well," Dar added.

"It was fun," Sunny chimed in.

"And you did a marvelous job with the customers," her mother said, touching her daughter's cheek. "It's hard for people to say 'no' to that precious smile of yours." The girl smiled broadly, as if on cue. I had to admit, she was pretty irresistible.

"And Michelle was blessed by a gift from Flor, of all people. You're a lucky gal," Reggie emphasized.

"But her gift is still a mystery to me, and so are the symbols on Fernán's pots. I know about the snake shedding its skin, but what about the bats and the eyeless fish. Where do those come from? What do they mean?" I asked.

"They're all symbols that go back to ancient times," Reggie began. "There are bats around here, but perhaps not in the same abundance they once were. Bat guano is highly praised for its fertilizing effects and bats eat a lot of bugs, including mosquitoes. They're beneficial little critters, really. As for the fish, there are springs in the area with eyeless fish swimming around in underwater caves. No light, no eyes needed. But the pottery is quite beautiful, even if the motifs seem odd. You might even want to buy another one to take home with you."

"We'll see," I shrugged.

After lunch I decided to take a little walk. I'd been thinking about it since we'd gotten back. "And do a little sketching?" Dar asked. I nodded with a smile.

"Fantastic! Get on your way then, girl."

So I grabbed my sketchbook and a small box containing drawing and color pencils, then walked toward the big tree and the beginning of the trail. Along the way I heard small animals scurry away through the tall grass, but the birds kept singing. I noticed a weathered wooden chair that hadn't been there the day before. I sat down and decided my host had left it for me to discover, because the angle I was facing had an interesting perspective of the trees and the trail leading to the mountain.

Opening my sketchbook to the first page, I began to draw what I saw. The oak trees took on fluid shapes with branches pointing and bending at soft angles, richly covered with green leaves. Their shapes were contrasted against the backdrop of the mountain with its green foliage and dark pine trees. Portions of sky peeked between the branches. The sun warmed my shoulders and hands.

This was the first time I'd sat and sketched anything from nature since my last vacation the year before. My right hand seemed stiff and slow at first. But as I kept at it, the sketching took on a new energy and my hand moved easily as it transferred what I saw to the drawing paper. My vision seemed clearer, too. I wasn't adding color, but I was aware of the nuances of green and brown in the landscape. Then I found the appropriate color pencils in the box. Since I could only allude to the richness I was seeing, I laid the color down lightly, just hinting at it. I was surprised, and pleased, that this first sketch had come together so well. There was hope for this rusty artist after all.

As I moved along the trail toward the mountain I thought I heard chimes, a wispy music that came from the trees themselves. From that direction I saw a grove of trees with a clearing in its center. The remains of a campfire were surrounded by a circle of wooden plank benches. Before investigating, I made sure I could still see the trail and the house from where I stood. The Aussie flag waved distantly in the breeze. If I had plunged into the clearing and gone even further into the denser woods, I would have been disoriented. But then I remembered a hometown trick. In Chicago, as long as you know where the lake is, you know which direction is east. So it was with the mountain, which was east of Sweet Dreams. I decided to follow the music.

As I walked into the grove I heard a wind chime to my right. It was hanging from a tree bending toward the campfire pit. The chime looked like panpipes that had been separated. The breeze whistled through them creating a hollow, rustling sound as they bumped each other. Then an echoing chime came from my left with a deeper sound. It was actually three metal bells hanging from one tree, each with a slightly different pitch that formed a harmonious whole. Their sounds reminded me of the bronze bell hanging above my back porch at home. And then I detected a third sound coming from the trees. Walking toward it I caught its gleam in the sunlight. It was a wind chime of equal-sized metal tubes with a celestial sound, positioned equal distance from the other wind chime and the bells, with the campfire site in the middle. Together, the chimes and bells formed the points of an imaginary triangle.

I sat down on a bench and closed my eyes for a minute or two, just listening. The effect was musical as well as magical. The intersecting sounds of breeze, birds, insects, rustling leaves and manmade bells and chimes were comforting, filling me with a sense of peace. I'd discovered my own little sanctuary. Reluctantly, I opened my eyes. But I was startled to find I wasn't alone! Sunny sat directly across from me on another bench. She just smiled and dangled her legs back and forth. Her feet were off the ground.

"Sunny, where did you come from? I didn't hear you," I said, probably sounding a bit cross.

"I saw you sketching. Can I see?" she asked. I held out the sketchbook and turned to my drawing. "It's lovely," she beamed. "Dad was right. You are an artist. But you need to fill up the pages. I hope you do more. Would you mind if I drew a picture of you?" she smiled.

"If you want to, that's fine," I laughed with surprise. "And where do you want me to be?"

"Where you are," she replied with a confidence I hadn't noticed before. She chose a soft graphite drawing pencil and a medium blue color pencil from the box. I found a comfortable position on the plank bench and held it. She began to draw with the graphite. The music in the trees continued as her hand moved back and forth across the page.

"Do you like to dream?" she asked without looking up.

"Yes," I said, "but I usually don't remember what I dream."

"How sad," she said. "I remember mine. I make drawings of them sometimes."

"What do you dream about?" I asked, genuinely wondering.

"Mum and Dad or the goats or the chickens or the mountain. Or I dream about making pots with Fernán and how they will look when they're done. But sometimes I dream about people and places I don't know yet."

She left that thought drifting in the air between us until I had to ask, "What kinds of people and places?"

"People like you. I had a dream about you a few days ago. I do that when we have guests coming. They usually look the same as in my dreams." Her concentration remained steady as she relayed this unusual "fact."

"Is that so? Do *I* look the same as I did in the dream?"

"Yes, but you smiled more in the dream. Do you miss your friend Angel?"

"Yes, I miss all three of my friends," I said. "Were Maggie and Max in the dream, too?"

"Just Angel. He has thick dark hair and seems serious. He has a nice smile and he's clever." So far, she was right on, but how long could this imaginative conversation hold up, I wondered.

"Yes, he is like that," I confirmed. "What else did you see in your dream, Sunny?"

"Can you smile more? You look sad. I don't want to draw you looking sad," she insisted. So I smiled, but it didn't feel natural.

"That's better," she said and began moving the pencil across the page again as she spoke about her dream. "You were painting a picture on paper. It wasn't big like my dad's paintings. You had just started. You seemed happier than now," she smiled. "And that made Angel happy, too."

"Well," I said, "that sounds like a good dream."

"It's also true," she said seriously. "You'll see. My dreams are true."

I continued to smile as she drew my portrait, but I was confused again. It seemed that intuition was part of the local culture.

"How old are you, Sunny?" I asked. Her hair glowed with streaks of sunlight.

"Almost eight. How old are you?" she countered.

"Thirty-one," I replied, feeling the huge gap of time between us.

"Mum was younger than that when I was born," she said. "But Dad was older. Do you have children?"

"Not yet," I replied, thinking I wouldn't know what to do with one as precocious as she was.

"You will," she nodded affirmatively.

Then she took the blue pencil. Holding it on its side, she moved her hand across the surface of the paper, then declared she was done. "Do you like it?" she asked with a big smile, holding up the sketchbook.

I took it back to get a closer look. I couldn't remember anyone doing my portrait before, though I'd done my own in art school. It was definitely a child's drawing, but her perception and imagination were obvious. The blue pencil filled the background with sky around my head where a small winged creature hovered near my ear. She'd drawn a pattern resembling the texture of my top. And my hair wasn't rigid or straight, but moved slightly in one direction, just as it was doing in the breeze. My smile looked exaggerated so she picked up on that, too.

"It's very nice, Sunny. I like the way you drew my hair. But what's this in the sky? A bird?" I asked, pointing to the winged creature in the portrait.

"That's your guardian angel. She protects you all the time," she smiled. Such a sweet comment deserved a smile back and I obliged, willingly this time.

"May I keep this portrait in my book or do you want it?" I asked.

"It's for you, Michelle. I thought you should have a picture of yourself while you're visiting us. The sky is pretty today and I want you to remember."

"Thank you, Sunny. Will you sign it for me, since you're the artist?"

She beamed and wrote her name in the lower right corner, as her father usually did in his paintings. Her five letters stood straight up, as if they were at attention.

"You should sketch more," she said. "I'll go back now because Mum and Dad will be looking for me."

"I can walk back with you," I offered, afraid to let her go by herself with the woods so close.

"Can you walk me to the trail?" she asked. "Dad has his binoculars. He'll see me."

As Sunny headed toward the house, Reggie approached with Jack the dog, who ran ahead to meet her. Her father tipped his hat in a gesture of thanks and I waved back. Then I returned to the clearing and sat down, surrounded by the music of breeze, birds, bells, and chimes. I looked at Sunny's portrait again. My own laughter joined the musical sounds as I closed my eyes.

12

Time got away from me while I sketched. After nearly two hours, I decided to take a break. My hand was sore from the effort, but now there were five new drawings in my book, including Sunny's portrait of me.

Reggie was working in the yard when I got back. He nodded and said, "Filling in a few pages, eh?"

"I am," I smiled, feeling good about myself. "And I think I'm beginning to understand what you meant about this place. Are you inspired and motivated *all* the time?"

"Seems that way. It's exhausting and exhilarating, and I love it," he laughed. "Maybe it's just the air up here. I can't quite explain the why, just the what."

"I need to give my hand and my eyes a break, but I want to go out again in a little while. Next time, I'm walking all the way to the mountain," I declared.

"I'd allow at least three hours of light," he advised. "Siesta is the hottest time of the day, and you could get drenched in a quick, hard rain. We can outfit you with a few emergency supplies, in case something should happen. Who knows? You might get lost in a creative zone and forget to come back," he said, tipping his head to one side.

With Dar's help I prepared my backpack for the hike with bottled water, slices of aged goat cheese, bread and fruit. I added trail mix and power bars I'd brought from home. It seemed like a lot of food to take for a three hour walk, but my hosts insisted on it. Reggie gave me a flashlight with extra batteries, in case I stayed out too late and had to find my way back, though that seemed unlikely to me. Finally, I tucked in the sketchbook and pencil box. I wouldn't be traveling light this time. Since my cell phone refused to turn on, it got left behind.

"Wear long pants and socks and comfortable hiking shoes," Dar advised. "And bring another layer to slip on later so you'll have it if you need it. We told Max we'd take care of you."

Reggie gave me tips for how to be careful on my hike. "Stay close to the trail. Remember that bird's beak formation on the mountainside so you can orient yourself. If you don't see it, just stay on the trail. It will lead you to other trails and they all lead to town if you miss our sign. Anyone can get you back to us. Any questions?"

"No. I think you've covered it all. Thanks for your help. I can't see any problems, but you never know. I'm not planning on being gone for long, just a few sketches and a little exploration around the mountain. To tell you the truth, Max would be upset with me if he knew I was doing this. So be sure not to tell him." I nodded at both Reggie and Dar when I said, "I think El Anhelo is calling."

Reggie nodded back. "You'd better answer the call then."

I put my backpack on the veranda and went upstairs to make a few wardrobe adjustments. I knew about wearing layers from living in Chicago, where the temperature can drop or climb with little notice. I looked out the window one last time as I tied a sweatshirt around my waist. I was doing as I'd been told, even though I didn't think I'd need the extra layer. I took in the scent of gardenia and wondered if its fragrance would trigger a flood of memories in years to come, of this room, of my view of the mountain, of the Sweet Dreams Bed and Breakfast and the Howard family, of all I would experience in these magical days in Mexico.

As I strapped the backpack on, Reggie asked if I wanted him to walk part of the way with me. I said no, but asked him to keep an eye out for me and that I hoped to be back in time to milk the goats again.

"We'll watch for you. Take care out there."

He and Dar stood outside the screened veranda and waved as I began my trek. I put a ball cap on to block the sun from my eyes. Paco danced around my hosts, a brown and white flash of canine energy. I waved back. After about ten yards I turned to see them still standing there watching me go. We exchanged waves again. Another ten yards later and I saw them still standing there, talking, yet keeping watch as I slipped down the trail toward El Anhelo.

13

The trail around the mountain looked well-traveled, but it was siesta time and I was the only person on it. Occasionally I heard animals in the brush, as well as bird and insect songs. My plan was to sketch and hike the trail as far as I could in two hours, then turn around and go back to Sweet Dreams. Reggie had told me there were places where the trail went right up the side of the mountain, and that the view from these was highly recommended. One path seemed like an easy climb, so I left my backpack on the trail and went up about twenty feet with my drawing materials. I sat on a flattened rock near the edge and settled in. From my vantage point I could see much of the trail in both directions, but I couldn't see the Aussie flag through the trees. I did spy the tip of the church some distance away, though.

An hour must have passed while I drew the scenes around me. I checked my watch and knew I should start back. I was grateful Dar had supplied a heavy-duty sunscreen because the sun was brutal up there. I took a couple deep swallows from the water bottle before making my descent. I shook out my hair and then tied it back again.

Ironically, the climb down to the trail was trickier than the climb up. I scraped my left palm slightly when I slipped on a smooth rock and almost lost my grip. And when I put my backpack on it felt heavier than before. Maybe it was the heat or fatigue, but now I wanted to find a shady spot and rest for a while. I didn't walk far when I spied a log that had fallen near the mountain about ten feet off the trail. I headed straight for it. Dropping the backpack, I sat down facing the trail. Even though the log's surface was rough, it was a blessing to sit on anything with more give than those hard rocks back on the slope. After another drink of water, I let my muscles relax and let out a heavy sigh. Sitting there, I became aware of the natural sounds all around me. It was peaceful, like the grove with the campfire site and the chimes playing in the trees. I looked at the scratch on my hand. It stung. *A good time to take a breather,* I told myself.

I let my thoughts wander until I realized the sweat on my neck felt much cooler than the rest of me. At first I didn't think anything of it, but I began to wonder where the breeze was coming from, since my back was toward El Anhelo. Yet the source of the cooler air was definitely behind me, as if it was coming from the mountain itself. It didn't make sense. I got up and approached the rock face. I could feel the temperature drop slightly as I got closer to it. But where was it coming from? Like Reggie and Dar had done on their first trip, I got right up to the mountain trying to figure out this latest mystery for myself.

At first, I couldn't see anything. As I bent down, I felt the coolness against my face. Yet I still couldn't find the source of the airflow. Then a lizard darted past me from a ledge, I thought, but when I followed its trail backward I saw the gap where I could feel the air coming through. It was dark and when I felt along its edge my hand dropped off into emptiness. Was it a cave? Cautiously, I stuck my head inside the dark opening and saw a light emanating further down a tunnel that opened in front of me. It appeared to be radiating from inside the mountain. I could barely see, but as I stepped partially inside the narrow opening, I noticed that the floor of the tunnel was nearly flat, worn away by water, maybe. I wondered if people lived in it long ago. From the direction of the light came a sound like quiet singing. It wasn't like the chimes of birdsong I'd already heard in the area. It was mysterious and undefinable. It might have been echoing through the tunnel, but I had no idea what was causing that haunting melody.

Why hadn't Dar and Reggie mentioned this cave? How could they *not* know about it? Was it that well hidden? The entrance was unmarked after all. I vaguely remembered Dennis Lawley mentioning a "mythical" cave in his travel book. It might have inspired some of the local art motifs, he'd written. But this cave was no myth! "Be careful," my mother had said. "Look out for terrorists or drug smugglers hiding in the mountains." Could she be right after all? Maybe this was where drugs or weapons were stashed for safekeeping. I'd told Reggie I would watch where I stepped and meant it as a joke, but I wondered if the joke was on me, and he knew it. The mysterious sound in the cave began to merge with the internal rhythm of blood rushing to my brain.

This is so weird! Get out of here! I told myself.

I hastily pulled out of the opening and walked back into the sunlight trying to make sense of what I'd just seen and heard. I could find this place again. The fallen log past the trail up the mountain would be easy to remember. I could come back with my friends. I knew they'd want to check it out. But before we came back here I'd ask a million questions of Dar and Reggie, like why on earth didn't they know about this? And if they did, why hadn't they warned me about the cave?

Even though I was thinking in a logical way, my curiosity was in high gear. But there was more to it. I felt like I was being *summoned*. I know that sounds ludicrous, but I felt something pulling me, tugging me toward the cave. Reggie had insisted there was nothing to be afraid of, that I should follow my own impulses. But this was taking things to a whole different level! This horrible indecision kept me from sitting down again or walking back to Sweet Dreams. I was doing circles around the log, figuring out my next move, not willing to let go of this thing. I wanted to know where that light and the singing, or whatever it was, were coming from. I'd never experienced that in the three caves I'd been in, including Mammoth Cave.

I decided to walk away from the entrance and have a little heart-to-heart chat with myself. *Why is it so important to go in there this second?* I thought. I began a two-way discussion, partially in my head, but also out loud.

"Maybe it has something to do with 'the draw of the mountain.'"

And maybe it doesn't. Maybe it's just a crazy cult thing you don't want to go anywhere near!

"Only one way to find out."

There are other ways than going in there right this second. Go back and ask questions first!

"But I want to find out what's going on in there, *now*."

It is insane to even be thinking about going in there!

"Well, thank you very much, oh brain of mine! I *know* it's crazy, but I don't care. I'm going in!" I finally decided, against my own, logical better judgment.

I can't totally explain what I was feeling, but the urge to enter the cave wouldn't let up on me. The further I walked away, the more I wanted to go back. Even if this was an idiotic idea, I couldn't stop myself. My curiosity and will were more in control than my intellect at this point. Call it impulsive, but I had to go in. I even wondered if it was the mountain itself pulling me, because the urge was so strong. I could feel it in my gut, a kind of intense yearning. And yes, that was genuinely ridiculous and totally absurd, but I'd been told I had "the draw of the mountain" symptoms, and now I was turning into a believer as I felt that "longing" take over my ability to make a rationale decision.

Not knowing exactly how deep the cave was, but being unable to leave it behind, I went back to my gear. At first I thought it best to enter with only a few items, go as far as the light, leave and later return to this spot for a longer exploration with my friends. But then a voice spoke up inside my head. *No, take it all with you.* There was a sense of urgency in that thought. So I grabbed the backpack, but I felt even less sensible lugging that extra weight with me. "I must have left my mind at the border," I announced to the birds and the trees.

But before I went into the cave, I did do one intelligent and sane thing. I left a note written on a page from my sketchbook with an arrow drawn so it would point toward the cave's entrance. It said, "Michelle Hardtke entered El Anhelo's cave at this point." I looked at my watch, then wrote down the date and time. I wedged the paper under the log and put a large rock on top of it so it wasn't obvious, but could serve as a clue to my whereabouts, if anyone came looking for me. Knowing it was there was a tiny comfort I'd take with me. Of course I hoped things wouldn't come to that. I'd be careful. I'd still get back in time for supper, I told myself.

Max would kill you if he knew you were even thinking about going in there!

"But he's not here to stop me, so shut up already. I'm going in!" I declared to the logical side of my mind.

Be careful! I kept repeating those words in my head. I had no intention of harming myself. I just wanted to learn more about El Anhelo and then head back to Sweet Dreams to milk the goats and ask a few pointed questions.

I untied the sweatshirt from around the strap of my backpack and pulled it over my head, surprised that I was about to wear it after all. Fortunately, I'd been given a flashlight with extra batteries, and enough food and water to last a day if need be. Certainly this would be a short excursion, an hour at the most. When I put my hat and sketchbook in my pack, I saw the extra food my hosts had provided. They'd stuffed even more in than I thought. That was a relief! No wonder the bag was so heavy!

Then I had a brief flashback to the nightmare I'd had on the plane. But I wasn't going to let myself get trapped in this cave. After all, this was my idea. Plus there was some light in this cave and I could find my way out again. So I took the plunge.

The vines tugged at my ankles, almost tripping me as I stepped just inside the cave's entrance. I held the flashlight and moved slowly forward. The low roof angled smoothly away, reaching upward. The floor was flat and solid. I checked out the area with my flashlight because I wanted to recognize it when I came back. Sunlight leaked past the vines and wavered on the cave floor where I'd walked in. I'd see that and find the way out again. But I also put a half sheet of paper from my sketchbook right where the light fell on the cave floor, then anchored the paper down with a rock.

Having been in a cave before, I knew not to touch anything with my bare hands. The oil from my fingers could stop the flow of water that had dripped for eons. That's what made this a living cave as opposed to a dead one. I didn't want to harm anything, so I covered my scratched left hand with my sleeve and barely skimmed the surface of the wall as I moved forward toward the light. No telling what would be on the wall, maybe a wet crawling thing I didn't want to touch, anyway.

Then I noticed the light from down the tunnel pulsated slightly, like the rhythm of a heartbeat, almost as if it was connected to my own heartbeat. *Estás una mujer del corazón.* Is that what Flor meant? I remember wondering if my heart was matching that subtle beat or if I was creating it in my head. That blood pumping to the brain sensation was back.

I thought of Max's columns of pros and cons about this trip that we'd discussed at the Mexican restaurant in Chicago. Did I say I was a "wise woman" back then? I didn't feel all that wise now, since I was letting my curiosity take the lead in this unplanned situation. Yes, my logical, reasoning side insisted this was foolhardy. But I had the flashlight and there were no other passages intersecting this one. It was a straight tunnel, almost manmade.

The light was closer now. Waves, almost like smoke, wafted in the air in several directions. But distance and size were impossible to determine. So I moved slowly ahead, following the wall on my left while holding the flashlight in my right hand.

And then I felt a ledge, which the flashlight revealed to be a shelf dug out of the rocky wall. There was nothing on it, but carved in the space just above it was an etched drawing that looked like flames. The ledge and the carving looked too deliberate to be natural. Without thinking I looked to my right to check the opposite wall and found another shelf carved into the rock, but the symbol there reminded me of water. Perhaps these symbols were signifiers, remnants of an ancient language: fire and water, essential elements, opposites. Again, I moved toward the light, a little quicker now, continuing to feel the wall to my left.

But time was as fluid as the smoky light. How long had I been in the cave? I checked my watch with the flashlight and realized only ten minutes had passed. *Not bad*, I thought. *Lots of daylight left.*

The ground became bumpier all of a sudden. That would slow me down. And the tunnel was beginning to widen. I continued along the left wall as the right moved further away. Another few minutes passed and then the tunnel opened up into a larger space with other passages leading in various directions away from it. Then, for the first time, I saw the light reaching upward, floating near the top of a large dome-like room. It was as high as the ceiling of a cathedral and opened above the space I was approaching. There were slits in the rock above where the sunlight peeked through. The light illuminated the dust that wafted in the air there, apparently driven in a swirling, clockwise motion by the flow of air through what appeared to be three narrow slits in the ceiling. The "singing" was a series of whistling sounds that were loudest here and were also caused by the airflow through the three openings in the roof. I'd never seen or heard anything like it before. The effect was magical, like flimsy ghosts spinning and sirens singing through the dome, or thin clouds floating inside a cave. Before I walked into this larger space, I decided to leave some torn drawing paper on the floor like an arrow to mark the path I would take back to the entrance. I could easily slip down the wrong tunnel on my way out. It was easy to see the paper with the flashlight. Again, I found a loose rock to hold it in place. Opposite the rock was the corner of the paper that would serve as the pointer toward the tunnel I'd just come through.

As I stepped inside the dome, it was like being in a public space. The dusty light swirled above me in a mesmerizing pattern that was surreal and dreamlike. I walked to the center of the space and looked into the shapes above me. They were luminous and even golden at points from the sunlight. I wondered if moonlight would have a similar effect.

When I opened up my backpack on the trail, I'd found a small worn blanket Dar must have squeezed into it at the top. She was indeed taking care of me. Now I folded it into a small cushion and sat down on the dome floor near the tunnel that would lead me back out. The hard surface was relatively smooth and dry there. Looking up into the swirling dust had a calming effect on me. I watched the shapes float past like protective angels. It was hypnotic. My apprehension lifted. In that quiet state, I decided to try something I hadn't done in a while.

It had been a couple years since I'd sat in with a meditation group. It was only a short period in my life, but I missed it. I'd stopped because of longer workdays and spending time with Neil. Relaxing was one reason I'd come to Teotenaca and this was a fantastic setting to see if I could still meditate and visualize on my own. I turned off the flashlight and laid it in my lap. I didn't need it with the sunlight filtering through the slits in the cave's roof. I began with deep breathing, as I once did in the group and as Reggie had coached me the day before. I was surprised the air was so clear around me despite the dust cloud above me. I closed my eyes, slowly inhaling through my nose and exhaling through my mouth. As I inhaled, I thought, *I am...* On exhaling, *...relaxed*. I felt my muscles loosening from my toes up through my head and fingertips, as I mentally commanded each body part to let go of its tension. Our meditation group had listened to peaceful music softly playing in the background while candles and incense burned. But here, the cave made its own music. After a while, I heard more underlying sounds, like water trickling.

I was used to being told what to visualize during guided meditations by a lead person. I'd taken journeys to faraway places and met wise people, all filtered through my own occasionally wild imagination. *Just relax*, I told myself. *See what pops into your head*. More deep breathing, then I waited. The singing sound reminded me of the youth choir I'd been in years before. My favorite hymn was "Amazing Grace." Angel told me it was written by John Newton, the former captain of a slave trader ship who had become a cleric. Unconsciously, I began to hum that song and for an instant I thought of John Newton, that he himself was blind to the sin of slavery, then saw his horrible mistake and was changed by God's grace. His legacy was this inspiring song. I sang the words and the sound echoed around me like back-up vocals. An odd feeling came over me then. Not only was I extremely relaxed, but I felt comforted, as if the singing were a lullaby. I could have floated away on the lightness in my soul. I imagined rising and joining the slowly circling clouds of golden dust. In my mind's eye, I glided in a circle around the dome. I could see through the darkness as I explored the cave. I envisioned tunnels going out in many directions, as if the dome were the center of a wheel and the tunnels were the spokes.

I imagined floating to the top of the dome, examining it while the sunlight warmed me as I passed by it. Through the long, craggy slits in the rock I heard the wind outside sounding wild and raw, so different than the quiet inside. I floated to the edge of the dome and down a tunnel. The uneven ceiling occasionally opened into another channel of air above me. But I kept to the tunnel, floating and able to see through the darkness. There were both smooth and ragged surfaces with rocks jutting out in places, along with stalactites, stalagmites and perhaps more lights emanating from an adjoining tunnel. I kept riding the air through this freeform visualization until I got to the turn. When I moved into it I found myself back where I'd started, amid the lighted dust swirls of the dome.

I wasn't ready to halt these rich sensations, so I breathed deeply again and wondered what would come to my mind next. As if in a dream, I held a bamboo brush with horsehair strands shaped to a point. I dipped the brush into a bowl of water and ran it along a block of hardened black ink, then re-shaped it into a pointed tip. I drew on a piece of ivory paper, the thick and thin lines reminding me of an ocean shoreline. As the meditation continued, the lines resembled waves on a stormy sea and I saw the image of a boat on the water. And then, as if I'd closed my eyes and opened them to an entirely different scene, I was in a sailboat that mounted high waves and came back down until it was lifted up by the next wave. I was strapped down in a seat, feeling the sudden movements of the boat. But instead of being fearful, I was exhilarated. Everything seemed exaggerated: the sun was red as a ripe tomato and the clouds were a glowing white edged in gold.

And then the seas calmed a bit and I unfastened myself from the seat and stretched out on a beach blanket across the boat's deck. I looked up into the sky. Clouds passed and seemed to circle above me like the ones in the cave. But then the images became blurry and vague: a horse danced along the ocean shore like a streak of deep brown against the yellow sand; a bird hovered near me, white and curious, then flew away. There were hymns and children in red robes singing sweetly. I was sewing together a dress I was already wearing, red like the sun and the children's robes. And then I heard a sound like thunder and opened my eyes.

It was darker in the cave than I remembered when I'd closed my eyes. *How could that be?* I wondered. And then I realized what had happened and I felt fear for the first time inside the cave. My unguided meditation had apparently led me into a deep sleep. I was cold and stiff. My face was wet. Had it rained and dripped through the ceiling? I was wrapped tightly inside the blanket and lying on the ground. I couldn't believe my meditation had gone so out of control! The lighted shapes that circled inside the dome were dimmer now, lit by the pinkish haze of a sunset. It was almost dark!

I checked my watch and couldn't believe I'd lost hours! I'd been so foolish, betraying both my friends and myself by not being careful, by letting the moment swallow me up, leaving me in a risky situation. But I had been so compelled in those moments before I entered, that I couldn't resist the strong urge in my gut. In retrospect, I knew I would have done it all over again. No use beating myself up now. I just had to get out of there!

I gathered my belongings by touch. The flashlight had rolled a few feet away. My pack had been under my head like a pillow. I was hungry and thirsty and cold. I kept the blanket around me and stood, as wobbly as if I *were* on a boat. I dug in the backpack for the water bottle and drank, wishing it could be hot tea or soup instead. I found a power bar, too, then lost the wrapper in the darkness. The food and water woke me up, along with a shot of my own adrenaline. After locating the white paper that pointed me to the right tunnel, I moved quickly toward the entrance. I had to get back to Sweet Dreams before dark. Every minute was critical! My left hand steadied itself against the wall again and I searched the darkness with the flashlight in my right hand. Once again I ran across the ledges with the pictographs of fire and water, this time on opposite sides as I headed back. I kept moving, knowing I was walking in the right direction, continuing to follow the wall with my left hand, confident that I was approaching the opening. But after a long while, I wondered why I couldn't find the piece of sketchbook paper I'd left by the entrance. Even if the paper had blown away, my hand should have found the open space leading to the outside. I kept moving in the same direction. It had to be just up ahead. Maybe just another ten yards or so.

But it wasn't! I kept moving along the tunnel and couldn't find it or the paper on the cave floor. Did I miss the entrance? I must have, but how? I turned around and headed back towards the dome. I moved on and on until I came to the ledges again. But this time when I looked at them in the dim flashlight, they were not the same images. Instead of fire, there was a sun with beams radiating. And the water had been transformed into a crescent moon. I couldn't figure out how, but I'd managed to get into another tunnel. "This isn't happening," I said out loud. "This *can't* be happening!" I was shivering now and the hair on the back of my neck stood up. "Be calm. Be calm," I urged myself, in an effort not to scream. I kept talking to myself. "It doesn't look like you're getting out of here tonight. You have food and water. You'll be fine. Just get back to the dome!"

I pushed on, knowing the tunnels ran into it. Surely this one would, too. And it did. But it was darker when I returned to the dome. The swirls of dust were almost lost because of a cloud-covered moon. I was down to my only light source, the flashlight. I knew that even if I were able to find a way out of the cave, I couldn't find the path back to Sweet Dreams, let alone see it. There were no lights along the trail to guide me. I found a dry spot in the dome and sat on the blanket again, thinking of my options. Options? I only had one. To wait until morning and try again. I knew Reggie and Dar would come looking for me, which gave me comfort. If I couldn't get myself out, surely they'd find a way. Yet I couldn't get over the fact that they hadn't mentioned the cave. Maybe they didn't think I'd find it or that I wouldn't go in if I did. Or maybe, and I didn't like this thought, but maybe they were hiding something from me. Why had they been so concerned about giving me extra food, a blanket, a flashlight? Maybe they knew I'd be fool enough to enter the cave and get lost. I would have gone on like that all night, picking apart the details of how I'd gotten there and what would happen next. But as I sat under the dome a wave of fatigue washed over me and I closed my eyes. For a moment I remembered the line in Dar's poem I'd repeated the night before to help me sleep and whispered, "God is here, ... I hope." I turned off the flashlight, wrapping it in my arms, and fell into a deep sleep.

14

Darlene and Reggie had watched Michelle walk away from the safety of their home toward the trail that led around El Anhelo. As she looked back at them they smiled and waved. But as she turned around the second time, they were already discussing her fate on the trail.

"Reckon she'll find it?" Dar asked.

"I'd bet on it," Reggie replied. "Based on her first reaction, the mountain will find her. And if it does, she'll go in. She's full of curiosity, that one. I don't think I frightened her enough to keep her away. How well did you pack her bag, dear?"

"If she's careful she could go for three days or more. I gave her a small blanket, too. What will we tell her friends? It's so much easier when they go in there together," she sighed. "I wish she wasn't by herself."

"Ah yes, the friends. That's always a tough call. We'll have to be honest with them, if they'll listen to us. There's always the chance they'll think we've murdered her and hidden the body. That's just as believable as what we'll tell them," he chuckled.

"That's not funny, Reg. We came close to going to jail once before, remember? I have a feeling that Max will think the worst of us. We'll have to be cautious," she sighed again.

"We should be experts at this by now," Reggie sighed in return.

"We should, perhaps, but it's never easy. We tell a strange story, from their point of view." He put his arm around his wife as Michelle turned and waved one more time. They waved back.

"But Dar, haven't you heard it said that 'truth is stranger than fiction'?"

"Yes, love. But this is the strangest of truths."

They watched Michelle turn a corner and disappear beyond the trees.

Now, it was night and she hadn't returned. Reggie stood in the grove near the trail and listened to the chimes and bells mixing with the sounds of night creatures. He threw another log into the fire and saw the flames jump into the night air above him. He felt foolish for being there. But he had to go through the motions, just in case Michelle had merely gotten lost. Seeing the fire would be the last hope for finding her way back to Sweet Dreams that night.

Earlier, while it was still light, he'd walked around the trail and lingered in the yard doing his outdoor chores. Then he'd sat in the old chair by the big tree and read. He looked at the mountain, ancient and mysterious, and wished it could tell him what he already knew in his heart. It was too far to walk again so he'd brought his binoculars. There was a high point a bit further along where he could scan the trail near the mountain. Nothing moved. Then the sunlight began to fade and change. The sky turned a bright pink, but still no sign of her.

Now it was dark and he'd come to the clearing with Paco, who sniffed the brush around them. The fire might be partially hidden by the trees, but its flames would light the area enough to serve as a beacon. He stoked the burning wood and watched the trail of sparks lift into the air towards the moon. "Sweet dreams, Michelle," he whispered, praying they would be.

15

It seemed I had no other choice but to sleep. Ordinarily, I rarely remembered my dreams. But in that cold, stony cave I dreamt all night long and still can recall most of it. Ironically, I was left with a feeling of hope, not despair. What I experienced in that dream world was strange and wondrous. These dreams weren't blurry or hazy. Just the opposite. They were possessed of a kind of hyper reality. Everything about them appeared more real than the waking world. Maybe that was why they were so memorable, as if I were actually living through the situations and in the places I dreamt about.

As my unconscious mind took over, it brought me back to the sailboat from my earlier meditation, or should I say dream, in the cave. I was floating on the water again and looking up into the sky. The sun was warm, bright as a flame. I couldn't look into it, but I still saw its redness through my closed eyelids. I squinted around to see where I was. On the shore was a large promontory with buildings all along its edge. "That is the City of Light," I heard a voice say from inside me. "Your questions will be answered if you enter it."

"But how do I get there?" I asked. With sheer rock rising out of the water it was impossible to climb. There wasn't even a way of approaching it.

"There *is* a way," the voice said. "What looks impossible may only be a limitation of your own perception. Stay in the boat and let the current carry you to the other side of the rock."

"All right," I said. The boat bobbed along as I faced the craggy rock wall. Slowly it was pulled around to the other side by the current. There was a pier there, hidden by an overhang. As the boat pulled closer I noticed steps carved out of the rock face that led to the buildings above me. But it was narrow and steep there. I ducked under the overhang, maneuvering the boat with oars, and successfully docked. I didn't want to leave my backpack, but knew it would weigh me down too much to climb the steep path.

I can't do this, I thought.

"You *can* do it," the voice said. "Leave your bag and don't worry about it. If you don't shed it, you will not be able to climb to the top."

"What's up there? Who will meet me?" I asked. "Is it worth the effort?"

"You must answer those questions for yourself," the voice softly said. "But have faith."

And so I climbed, very slowly, trying not to look down or worry about my abandoned pack of supplies. I almost fell backwards when I took a quick glance toward the boat. After that, I concentrated on moving forward and up along the rock face. Occasionally there were handrails where I held tight and caught my breath. But it seemed as if hours had passed. I'd become thirsty and hungry.

"What is expected of me? Why is this so hard?" I protested out loud. It was drudgery. And despite the effort I'd already made, the buildings seemed further away, not closer.

"Your perception is tricking you," the voice said. "You think you are far away from your goal when you're much closer than it appears. Close your eyes. Take a moment to find strength from within."

Strength from within? I had a flashback of Sunny saying grace at meals and drawing me with my guardian angel. The line from Dar's poem repeated in my head. I prayed, asking for endurance and enough strength to get to the City of Light. When I opened my eyes, I saw the gate of the city for the first time. That alone was encouragement to keep going. As it turned out, the rest of the path was easy to climb. And then I was there, standing before a large, ornate carved door. I knocked on it and was asked the nature of my business by a man who looked through a small hole. I felt like Dorothy trying to get into The Emerald City.

"I'm trapped in a cave," I said. "I don't know how to find a way out of it. I'm tired and lost. May I rest here for a while? And can someone answer my questions?"

"What can you tell me about the cave?" the voice asked with a neutral tone.

"It's near the village of Teotenaca in the state of Oaxaca, Mexico. There's a dome inside where dusty sunlit shapes float in a circle, clockwise. There are tunnels off the dome, like spokes in a wheel. I'm sleeping near the tunnel with the wall carvings of water and fire. I wasn't able to find my way out along that same tunnel, even though that's where I came into the cave." Surely that was enough information, I hoped.

"You have described the cave well, though there is much you have yet to see of it."

With that, the door slowly swung open to a sunlit walkway. But I didn't see the man who'd opened the door. The path led to a park where the benches reminded me of those I'd seen in the Zócalo in Oaxaca city. They looked like stiff black iron, but when I sat on one it was comfortable, just what I needed after my long climb. The park was filled with roses, mostly pink and red, but also ivory. All were in full bloom. Their scent filled the air like an intoxicating potion. Sitting in that peaceful place brought a sense of relief. *Is this a sanctuary for travelers like me?* I wondered. Then I noticed a fountain that also reminded me of the one in the city.

"You've been to the Zócalo," I heard a female voice say from near the fountain, as if she'd read my thoughts. But I didn't see anyone standing nearby.

"Yes, on my way to Teotenaca," I said.

"What brings you to Mexico?" she asked, though I had a feeling she already knew.

"I'm on vacation. My friends will be arriving tomorrow afternoon," I answered. "We read about Teotenaca in an old travel book and were curious. It sounded beautiful and peaceful. We were looking forward to hiking the trail and being together," I spoke while I walked slowly around the fountain, but I still didn't see her.

"Was there any mention of the Cave of Dreams in your research on Teotenaca?" she asked.

"Is that where I am? No. I had no idea there was a cave in the mountain. I thought the cave was a myth."

"Does it surprise you that no one told you about it, that it *is* real?" she inquired.

"Well, yes. Is the cave a secret? But why would it be?"

"There are many who know of it, but they protect it. Not everyone is invited to enter here."

"I wasn't invited. This whole thing must be a mistake. When I found the opening, I couldn't resist the temptation to go in. Have I trespassed or violated anyone's rules? I'm really sorry. Can I leave now?" I asked with hope for my release, since I'd obviously made a terrible mistake. This was all so strange, I couldn't imagine what would happen next.

"It was the cave that chose *you*. Otherwise, you never would have found it. You're longing to enter was the cave's invitation to you, and you clearly accepted it," the voice said evenly, like it was not unusual at all.

I was shocked by her answer. "But why?" And how, after all?

"Surely you are an artist."

"I'm a graphic designer," I replied. "And I do love to paint."

"Then perhaps that is your answer. You have curiosity and an imagination that allows for vivid dreams, like this one. You will remember more than most people would. And that is essential here," she informed me.

"Excuse me, but who are you?" I asked. "And *where* are you?" It was disconcerting to have a conversation with a disembodied voice.

"I am a resident of this city. You may call me María." And then I saw her as she walked out from behind the fountain, though it looked more like she emerged from the spray itself. Her hair was dark, straight, and went half way down her back. Had I seen her before? She seemed familiar for some reason. She was neither young nor old, so it was impossible to know her age. Her skin was creamy with a healthy glow, but she was a Latina with dark eyes, and she had a slight Spanish accent. Her simple white dress seemed to be made of light, a stark contrast to her dark eyes and black hair. Then I had a flashback to the woman I'd seen by the fountain in Oaxaca city. She looked the same, I realized. She had smiled directly at me then, as if she knew me.

"And my name is Michelle," I said. "You look just like someone I saw by the fountain in the city. Were you there?"

She answered only with her warm smile. "I sense you have many questions, Michelle. You may ask me whatever you wish."

It must have been her. Why wouldn't she say so? In any case, I was glad she could answer my other questions! So I started asking them. "How long will I be in this cave? Will I be allowed to leave soon?"

She smiled. "I hear that question often. No one has died in the Cave of Dreams. You may emerge dazed and there is always the possibility of minor injury. But when the time is right, the cave will release you. You will be reunited with your friends." So, according to María, the cave had invited me in and it wouldn't let me out until it decided to release me. How can a "cave" do that? It made no sense, but I decided to follow along with her answers to see if there would be a shred of truth in them.

"And where am I now? I know this is a dream, but it doesn't feel like one. I don't usually smell roses in my dreams," I said, taking in a deep whiff of their fragrance.

"Physically, you are sleeping and dreaming in the Cave of Dreams. In your dream state, you are in the City of Light, a place that can only be reached through one's imagination. You can return here whenever you wish, even after you leave the cave. And I will be here to answer your questions when you do," she promised.

"María, are you a kind of spirit guide? I had a friend who believed in spirit guides. We were in a meditation group together. Or are you my guardian angel?" The words sounded juvenile to my ears. It must have been that drawing that Sunny had done because I hadn't thought about my guardian angel for years.

"Perhaps either description will work," she smiled. "I am part of your dream and I can be whatever you want me to be. Perhaps I am here because you need spiritual guidance. Is that true?"

"Spiritual guidance? I have to think about that. There are other areas where I know I could use help, besides the fact that I'm stuck in a cave!"

"Like what, Michelle?"

I told her about my breakup with Neil and how my job was whittling away at my free time. "Those two things have been wearing me down. Do they qualify for spiritual guidance?"

"Most situations do," she smiled again. Her voice had been gentle and calming. But it sounded slightly husky this time, maybe to emphasize her point.

"So what advice would you give me?" I wanted answers, but I was also highly skeptical.

"Listen to your intuition," she said. "You fight with it at times. You don't always think it's steering you right. But listen to it and don't argue. Divine wisdom speaks through your gut, which is where your intuition resides. Do what truly feels right. Otherwise you will never be happy with your life or yourself."

Her voice was soothing, flowing softly from her lips "As for your sadness over Neil, many people feel they must find another person who loves them to fulfill their happiness, that they cannot do this alone. Finding a person to love, who loves you in return, is a wonderful gift in life. But your life can still be complete without that love. Start by finding satisfaction in who you are. That will make you a happier person. That quality alone will make you more attractive. No one is drawn to a lonely, unhappy person. Is that helpful?" she asked, looking seriously into my eyes.

She was better than an advice columnist! "Yes, it *does* help." It made perfect sense to me (and my gut).

"I can advise you about your job in another dream. Perhaps it is time for you to end this one and go on to the next. You have much to learn while you are here. This dream is only an introduction. I am here when you need me." But I didn't want the dream to end. I wanted to see more of the City of Light.

"How can I come here again?" I asked.

"As I said before, you can reach this place through your imagination. I will see you soon. Learn much while you are here."

She was gone before I could ask another question. The City of Light melted away and then I was back in the boat, seated between two oars. I was glad to see my backpack was where I'd left it. A girl of about seventeen sat across from me holding another pair of oars. "Hi, Michelle," she smiled. I had no idea who she was. "Isn't it a pretty day? Of course, this is a dream and pretty days are always possible. But let's enjoy it." The more I looked at her, the more she seemed a younger version of me. She had the same sandy hair, blue eyes and dimpled chin I did. But her hair was like a waterfall that flowed down her back. She wore a long denim skirt and a light blue T-shirt that read "Peace is a state of being" with a peace symbol centered under the words. Bright blue flip flops peeked from under her skirt.

"What's your name?" I asked. She laughed and swung a clump of loose hair behind her shoulder. Her fingers were long and delicate, like mine.

"You know it. It begins with a 'T' and ends with an 'a.'"

"Is it Theresa?" I asked. That was my mother's name.

"Yes, but call me Terry like my friends do," she smiled. "Now which way do you want to go?"

I looked around and saw an island covered by palm trees to my right. There was only open water in every other direction. The City of Light had disappeared from the horizon. "The only place I can see is that island," I said.

"Off we go then," she laughed, turning around so we would both be facing the same way. She quickly pulled her oars into action. I began to row as well, but we couldn't synchronize our movements. The boat jerked from right to left and back again.

"This isn't working. Maybe we should take turns rowing," I suggested.

"We can do this. We just have to try harder," she insisted. "Why don't I start and then you can come in. When the oars come out of the water, that's the time to get ready to go in with yours. Try to follow the same rhythm and direction. I'll start slowly."

She sure acts like my mother, I thought. After studying the pattern of her rowing, I began to follow her lead until I was able to put the same effort into it. Team paddling worked well and we picked up speed as we neared the island. It was much larger than it seemed from a distance. There were no other people, just a flock of large flamboyantly colored birds that were singing like they were glad to see us. We rowed around the inlets until we found a sandy beach. As we landed she jumped out and pulled the boat further up so it wouldn't drift away on the next tide. Her skirt floated in the surf, but dragged on the sand.

"The water is warm," she said. I was the beneficiary of her efforts, stepping on the beach with dry feet.

"Where are we?" I asked.

"It's *your* dream. But I would guess it's probably the Caribbean. See how the water changes color in different places. See how blue it is over there and there. And over there it's more green. Yes, I'd say the Caribbean."

"If this is my dream, could I change it to the South Pacific?" I asked, since I'd never been there.

"I would imagine you could, if you knew what the South Pacific looked like. Apparently you're familiar with the Caribbean. Or it might take skill at dream manipulation. Are you good at that?" she asked.

"Probably not," I laughed. "I always thought my dreams were in control of me."

"It's different in the Cave of Dreams because you're not alone here. You'll learn more about that later. Under normal circumstances you would generate your own dreams. We all use them to deal with our fears and hopes, our concerns and relationships with others. It all gets filtered through our unconscious minds. But then we wake up with a deeper understanding of those things, even if the dream is gone. It's a magical process, but it's real. But enough of dream theory. Let's explore this place," she said with enthusiasm and beckoned me to follow with a wave of her arm.

I wondered what she meant by saying I wasn't alone in the cave.

Who else might be in there? I ignored her comment as we walked up a dune. Stopping part way, I took off my shoes and socks. I pushed my heels deep into the warm sand until it squished between my toes. At the top of the dune was a reddish brown rattan bench shaded by palm trees. We sat down and listened to the birds sing while they flit from tree to tree nearby. "So if you were stuck on this island, but you knew ahead of time, what one thing would you bring with you, Michelle? I don't mean a survival kind of thing, but what would give you comfort while you were here if you were here for a few months?"

"You know, I've thought about that from time to time, believe it or not," I realized. "I would bring my painting and sketching supplies. Do they qualify as one thing?"

"We could call them a set," she mused. "That's a good choice. You could be creative and document your surroundings, too."

"Or I might bring a photo album with a lot of family events in it, including my parents' twenty-fifth anniversary, which was a fun celebration. Wasn't it, Mom?" I wanted her to say she really was my mother.

"Michelle, I'm only seventeen in this dream. I'm not close to being married yet. So I really can't comment on that." But despite the disclaimer she whispered, "That's a great choice."

"Now how about you, Terry? What would you bring?" I asked with great curiosity.

She put her finger to her chin and squinted as if she were thinking deeply, a habit she still had. Then she smiled and announced, "I'd like my diary so I could keep an account of my experiences. It's beautiful here. And I love those chatty birds. They're noisy but it still sounds like music to me." She was so young, vibrant, and curious. I saw parts of myself in her, but I had trouble seeing my mother in this much younger version of herself.

"So Terry, why are you in this dream, and at this age?"

"While you're in the cave you'll gain an insight from every dream you have. For instance, this one is about how you view other people. Now you think you know who I am as your mother. From your point of view my identity is wrapped up in my relationship with you. But I was a person for years before you were born, and now I'm exploring the world as an older adult. That may be difficult for you to grasp at times. But if you're to truly understand a person, you have to think about who they were before you knew them and who they are to other people. It's helpful for you to understand who I am now by seeing how I was before I became your mother. That's possible by meeting me in this way."

"May I call you Mother, Terry?" I asked.

"If it helps you," she laughed.

"And why do you suppose I picked you, if I had anything to do with it, to be in this dream with me?"

She smiled. "Because you trust me to tell you what I think, even if you don't want to hear what I have to say. I'm here to tell you not to be afraid. It's not as bad as it seems right now. But I also wanted to tell you that you will have a great future, if you're willing to take up a challenge or two."

"How ironic, since you were so afraid for me to come to Mexico," I laughed.

"Oh, your older Mom is still worrying about you. But she'll have a reassuring dream tonight, too. She's sensing you're in danger, but you're not," she shook her head with insistence. "You can handle these challenges, Michelle. I'm confident of that."

"Are you just saying that because you're my mother?"

She shook her head. "I'm saying it because it's true. You're in this cave to discover things about the world and how you fit into it. The planet and its people are more interconnected than you realize, but you'll learn about that with each dream you have here. Just stop worrying. I know that sounds odd coming from me, since I put that thought in your head about drug traffickers hiding in the mountains. You almost didn't come in here, thanks to me. I have a lot to learn, too, but then I'm still a protective mother at heart."

She touched my shoulder and looked into my eyes, "I love you, Michelle, my daughter to be. Now listen to the birds. Their music will calm you even more."

She disappeared in the sound of the birds singing all around us. The whole scene faded then, along with the other dreams I had that night. When I finally woke up I was rested and refreshed, but boy was I stiff! I wasn't used to sleeping on rock. When I looked at my watch, it was almost 9:00 in the morning. My friends were due into town around 1:00 p.m. that afternoon. Dar and Reggie would have to tell them about my disappearance if I didn't get back, and I was sure they'd start a search for me, or so I hoped. Despite the curious and incredible dreams I'd had, I didn't want to be in the cave one more night. I wanted to get back to my vacation and see Max, Maggie and Angel again. If I was still missing by the time they arrived in Teotenaca, what on earth would my hosts tell them about where I was?

16

As Darlene got breakfast together after milking the goats, her thoughts were of Michelle waking up in the cave. It was a gray morning, but the sun looked strong between the clouds and would surely burn away the gloom. Reggie promised to check the trail before breakfast and scan the area around the mountain with binoculars. But she knew he would find nothing. She set the table for three this time and let Sunny place the napkins at each place.

"Didn't Michelle come home, Mum?"

"Not yet, dear. I checked upstairs and all around the house and yard. Your father thinks she's in the cave. What shall we do? We only have a few hours before her friends arrive," Dar sighed.

"Could you tell them she went to dinner and must have gotten lost," Sunny suggested.

Her mother smiled. "Well that's inventive, but I don't think they'll believe it, Sunny. The truth is better, anyway, even though it will be difficult."

"Do you think they'd be tired and just go up for a nap? Then you could tell them later." The girl was trying hard to find a solution, as she usually did when this happened. But she knew her mother was right about the truth.

"I have a feeling that if they don't find her here, they won't want to take a nap," her mother explained. "They'll want to look for her."

"Well, we could tell them what we think happened, that she's in the cave. But they won't know what that means," Sunny stated in a matter of fact way.

"We'll have to explain it to them, won't we?" Dar stated the obvious.

"I could tell them then. She's much safer there than on the trail where she could fall and be hurt in the dark. She's getting lots of sleep, too." Sunny tried hard to find a positive approach to their dilemma, as she often did.

"Sunny, you certainly know a lot about the cave for one who hasn't been in it yet," her mother pointed out.

"But Mum, I know so many people who have been in it that I can dream about it and what it's like. There are good things there, even if it is cold and dark and scary," she said, pinching her lips together in thought.

"Indeed. I keep telling myself that every time one of our guests disappears into it," Dar confided. "It's hard not to worry. And we don't make much money when they're in there because they're getting rocks for a mattress instead of the comfy beds upstairs."

"And they're not getting breakfast, either," Sunny observed.

They heard the door to the veranda open and looked up in anticipation. But instead of Michelle, Reggie walked in with binoculars in hand.

"Anything?" Dar asked.

"Not at all," he said. "No sign of her anywhere. She must have taken everything with her."

Dar smiled. "Well, that's a ray of sunshine. I hope she finds the extra tucker I put in her backpack. That will keep her going a bit longer."

"What did you put in her pack?" he asked.

"Slices of bread and cheese, cans of juice, oranges, and a sundry of other hearty things to keep her going, even a few biscuits. Too bad I couldn't include hot tea to go with them."

"Ah, hot tea. That sounds divine. Do we have a pot made?" He looked hopeful.

"Yes, of course. Have a seat and I'll bring it 'round."

"Start thinking about grace, Sunny," Reggie suggested as he sat down at the table. "Looks like another of your grand spreads, Dar."

They bowed their heads and Sunny began the prayer. "Thank you, dear God, for the yummy food Mum has made for our breakfast. And thank you for the sunlight that's coming soon. Please take care of our new friend, Michelle, who is in the cave. She will be afraid and hungry. Please help her find the bread and cheese Mum hid in her pack. And please help us when we have to tell her friends where she's gone. Thank you and amen," she prayed. With that they began eating breakfast and drinking the freshly brewed tea.

17

The light was filtering in through the cracks of the dome again and the illuminated shapes of dust continued their slow flight through the air in clockwise formation. It was so meditative and mesmerizing that every time I looked up at it my fascination overcame my fear. By itself, this light show put me at ease, and the musical accompaniment made by the breeze "playing" the slits in the dome added to the effect. But I wondered if there was more to it, if it was possible for a drug-laced vapor to be mixed in the air, quietly raining down on me, inducing a calmer state. Was that why I slept so soundly and had fantastic dreams? That was totally absurd, of course. But how else could this be happening?

While I watched the delicate dance above me, I drank more water and ate a piece of bread with cheese for breakfast. My stomach still growled after I finished as if to say, "Don't stop now." But I had to. I was saving the rest for later, hoping I could stretch it out, if I had to. Oh, to have hot food again! It was ironic that I was relaxed at all, of course, given my precarious situation. I theorized that I was in a massive state of denial. After all, what could the cave do to provide food and water after mine were gone?

Maybe dining in my dreams will help a little, I thought. Yeah, right! But oddly enough, the dreams *were* comforting. Yet I knew the key to survival was getting out of that cave. So I got up, brushed the dirt off my hair, and got my bearings.

The big question was how to find that opening again. I headed back down the tunnel where I first entered, but this time I held the flashlight in my left hand and followed the cave wall with my right. Gradually, I did see a point where a new tunnel began and stealthily led back to the dome. But I kept going straight down the tunnel I had entered when I first came into the cave. I had passed the ledges and the carvings of fire and water, so I knew I was heading in the right direction. I continued on, searching the wall to my left for an opening, a draft of warm air or a flash of sunlight, as well as the white paper I'd left on the ground. But there was nothing. *Maybe I walked much quicker when I first got in*, I reasoned, *and I'm going slower now. It will just take a little longer this time.* Then I thought I saw something white up ahead. Sure enough, it *was* the piece of drawing paper from my sketchbook. Thank God I was almost out of this strange place I'd been crazy enough to walk into! I was relieved at first. But then I didn't see any light coming through the opening. Maybe the sunlight didn't get in the opening at that time of day. Wrapping my sleeve around my left hand, I felt the surface of the cave's wall. But it was *solid*. That was impossible! I kept running my hand over the surface. But nothing! I tried a grid approach, touching the cold damp wall from left to right, from top to bottom, then up to down next to that. *Still* nothing! I forgot my cave etiquette and hit and scraped at the cave wall with my bare hands. I couldn't believe it! It was as if the entrance to the cave had closed behind me! Was I having another dream? I tried to make sense of it. Was it possible the paper was hit with a sudden draft of air and moved? I wasn't giving up yet. I couldn't! So I walked on and on touching the outside wall, and still found no opening.

I decided to go back to the piece of paper I'd left as a marker and tried again to find that narrow passage I'd walked through to enter the cave. I banged on the wall and had a flashback to my nightmare on the plane. Had the dream been a warning? My body started to shake with the memory. Then the tears came and I slid to the ground. "God! How can this be happening?" More tears flooded my eyes. In fact, it was an intense crying session, but probably overdue. I let the fear take over for a few minutes. But once I got it out, I was better. I got up and continued down the path through the tunnel.

And then I noticed that the tunnel started to shift slightly. I wondered if I'd end up where I started, back at the dome. The floor of the cave felt bumpier at one point and slowed me down even more. It was all so disorienting that I tripped over a huge lump that was rooted to the ground along the wall. I fell and hit my head on the way down. As I lay dazed on the damp ground, my head throbbed and I felt a warm trickle of blood running down my cheek. It came from a scrape next to my right eye. I knew head wounds bled easily and usually looked worse than they were. I hoped that was true in my case. I wiped the blood from my face and rubbed it off on my jeans. My right hand also stung from a scrape I got when I hit the floor. But I was grateful not to have broken any bones. My ankle stiffened up while I had that thought. Best to move it, so I grabbed the flashlight from a short distance where it had fallen and stood up. There was a soreness setting into my body. I began walking again, even slower this time. I could tell the path turned slightly at every step.

Maybe there's more than one way out of here, I thought. Rather than trying to find the way I had entered, which had mysteriously vanished, I kept hoping there would be another way out. The cave could go on for miles underground, but I tried not to think about that. If the messages in my dreams were true about this strange place, whoever was in charge of the sleep-inducing vapors would decide when and how I would leave. On one hand, it felt hopeless to look for a way out. And I should have been more worried about survival. But the dreams were so peaceful. Maybe they were a product of my unconscious speaking to my conscious mind as a self-defense mechanism. Was that why I kept remembering the dreams so vividly? But in the most rational part of my mind there was a constant thought insisting there *had* to be a way out.

I'd been exploring the tunnels off the dome for about a half hour when I decided it was time for a break. My joints felt better, having gotten a little exercise. I found a relatively smooth, rocky slab and sat down on it. But now that I stopped I could feel the cooler air wrap itself around me. There was a slight shift in the air coming from straight ahead and slightly to the left. Could it be another passage? Or a way out?

I thought about this for a while and turned off my flashlight. Everything went black. Absolutely black! But then, when I looked in the direction of the airflow, I thought I saw a small shaft of light. Yes, it definitely was a light source coming from up ahead, and this time it wasn't the dome. I studied it in the darkness. It appeared to drift slightly, as if, like the dust in the dome, it was affected by air currents. I stood up and walked toward it with my flashlight pointed at the ground and its hazards.

The beam of light grew as I approached. It came from another passage to my left. The slightly cooler air flowed from it. The subtle, rippling illumination reflected on the damp wall in front of me came from that direction, too. I turned off my flashlight once again and after my eyes adjusted I could see enough around me to move toward this new passage. But I attempted to remember the way back to the dome before I made the turn.

As I headed directly toward the passageway I heard a sound, like singing again, but very quiet, next to the familiar roar of the blood pulsing through my brain. *What will it be this time?* Slowly I turned the corner to face the source of this different light and sound. But for all the possibilities that had crossed my mind, I hadn't anticipated what I saw. A narrow waterfall stood right in the middle of the cave! Light filtered in from beyond the top of the tiny stream that trickled down the jagged rock. I couldn't see to the top because it disappeared into a chimney-like opening. The rippling water caught the light that leaked from above and projected it along the walls and into the passage I had just left. Perhaps the water came from a source near the top of the mountain, maybe rain that collected there. The other part of this surprise was a pool about twenty feet across at the base of the waterfall. The sound I'd heard was the gentle movement of water trickling down the rock and into the pool. Clearly the water was deeper than it looked and maybe not so calm below the surface as it flowed to another low point in the cave. But I also wondered if the cave ever flooded during a heavy rain. One more thing to worry about!

I used my flashlight to get a better look at this latest discovery. Ten feet from the pool I found a wide ledge that worked well as a bench. I turned off the flashlight again and within a few minutes my eyes became accustomed to the darkness and my ears appreciated the soothing sounds of the small waterfall as it echoed against the dark walls. The light floated on the moving water and the effect was similar to a crystal filtering the light of a subdued sun. Like the cloud in the dome, it was hypnotic and I thought I'd better be careful or I'd be off to dreamland again. As I looked from the waterfall to a darker part of the pool, thinking it wouldn't be very visible, I noticed what looked like small beams of light moving near its surface. I wondered if they could be fish. I remembered Fernán's pots and what Reggie had said about fish in underground streams, blind because eyes weren't necessary in a dark environment. I watched them move in circles, around each other, disappearing downward and reappearing as they came back up. They reflected what light bounced upon the pool and brightened it with their pale bodies.

I had the urge to investigate at a closer range, but decided to stay seated for a while and stretch my legs out in front of me, while pointing my toes and rotating my stiff ankle. As I worked on my upper body in the same manner, I stretched my right arm, then my left. When I did, my left hand touched a softer surface when it came back down on the rock where I sat. It felt like paper, maybe a food wrapper? I had left one back in the dome, but this was my first time by the waterfall. I picked it up and turned the flashlight back on to find a Lindt Chocolate candy wrapper. Definitely not mine. I couldn't tell how old it was, but it looked like it had been bought that day. My first thought was that I wasn't alone after all. Perhaps the person who left this piece of litter was still in here, too. But more likely they had moved on already, hopefully out of the cave and not to a forsaken corner to die! I so wanted to believe the dreams, that despite the dangers I'd get out of here and into daylight again, healthy and whole.

Still, it was reassuring to think that another person had sat where I now sat and viewed the waterfall as I did. But what to do next? Should I return to the passage I'd left or see if there was a passage behind the waterfall?

I decided to stick to familiar territory, such as it was, and go back to the passage where I'd been. The waterfall room would serve as a landmark if I came back this way. But I hesitated, because it was peaceful there with the sound of water bouncing against rock and into the quiet pool below. I thought of the person who had sat there and ate their candy bar. I wondered what they did next. I thought of the small beams of light darting around the pool. I wanted to get a closer look at them. After all, I might not come back this way.

I left my pack on the bench and stood up. Using my toes as a blind person would use a cane, I felt my way toward the water until I could bend down and sit at its edge. The light beams were indeed fish, moving like pale specters below the darker surface. I knew the water would be cold, but I touched it, anyway. Ignoring my own warnings about drinking the water in Mexico, I scooped a little up in my hand and tasted it with my tongue. It was slightly bitter, but drinkable. I hoped it was pure mountain water, flavored by minerals in its flow along ancient rock. I scooped and drank this time, and it was good, but cold as it traveled down inside me. My own water supply was getting low, but I thought it best to see how my body reacted before drinking more from the pool. I sat on the edge of the pool and tried to see my reflection in the water. But, of course, it only looked like a shadow on the surface. *I've disappeared*, I thought, *down into the belly of this cave. I should be screaming and clawing my way out of here, but I'm not. Why am I so calm about this?*

So far I felt fine, so I scooped up a bit more water and drank again. After that I washed the cut on my face with it. The wound stung a bit and my skin was stiff where blood had dried along my cheek. The water was soothing. I looked into it to see the fish again and tried to touch one that was near the surface. But then I thought better of it. What if they were hungry, too? What could they eat in here, anyway? Would the sudden movement in the water frighten them away or lure them closer for a bite? I didn't reach into the water again.

Instead, I looked around the room, which reminded me of a grotto. It was a smaller dome with walls that rose high around the pool and waterfall. The floor stretched behind my bench and to the left of where I'd sat. Then I saw there were more stone benches around the pool.

Something caught my eye near there. It, too, was white like the fish. I turned on the flashlight to find my way. Behind the bench was a higher ledge with a row of white objects running along its surface. What I found shocked me at first, but then I thought of the candy wrapper. There were white candles sitting in a row. Burned wax dripped over their sides like the veils of nuns at prayer. They had been larger, but had melted down to various heights, a couple no more than an inch tall. Each was uniform in diameter, probably about three inches across, but they'd melted into one other. I regretted not having any matches with me. Maybe Dar had included some, but I hadn't run across them.

But with this new discovery, the grotto assumed a sacred air to me. As a small girl sitting in a pew at church I'd felt at peace as I stared at the candles. I wondered if regular ceremonies or rituals took place here, and if so, who were the participants? And what did they do here? I turned quickly to glance behind me at the waterfall, and as I did I sensed movement in a space above it. But whatever it was disappeared by the time I trained my flashlight on it. I saw a kind of balcony above the pool, but no one was there. Whatever I thought I'd seen in my peripheral vision was pale and quick, like a speeding ghost, white like the candles. *Was* I alone? Or not?

I sat down on a bench closer to the candles and looked at the waterfall, this time from another perspective. If this were a church, what kind would it be? Christian? Pagan? Pre-Columbian? Who did the attendees worship? Would they lie on the stone benches and dream their way into the City of Light? Would their City of Light be different than the one in my dreams? Or were there ritual sacrifices here, like a scene out of a B movie? What if I'd fallen into the clutches of an evil cult and was never going to get out of here alive? A chill ran through me.

I thought all these things and wondered if the ghostly figure could hear me if I spoke. Would it respond? The mystery of this physical place and the wishful thinking of my dreams were fighting it out in my mind. I was confused and disoriented once again. I needed real, wide awake answers!

"Is this a church? Who do you worship?" I demanded of the ghostly spirit in a raspy voice. "And how can I leave? I don't want to be a part of this!"

I was answered by the echo of my own voice. I felt totally alone. This dark place I'd fallen into was frightening me again. Yet I had to admit to myself that amid the maze of changing passageways and disappearing portals, I kept finding signs of peace and worship. I wondered if this truly was named the Cave of Dreams. Obviously there were people who knew of it, though that didn't include Dennis Lawley, the travel writer who had so much to say about the beautiful, artistic village of Teotenaca. Why did he think the cave was only a myth? Or did he know better? I wondered what Reggie and Dar were doing to find me and when my friends would arrive. Wouldn't they all come looking for me? I watched the water trickle into the pool and prayed they would come soon.

18

Reggie and Darlene sat in the lounge room waiting for their guests to arrive. Juan, a friend from Oaxaca city, had agreed to pick up Max, Maggie, and Angel and bring them to Teotenaca, in exchange for lunch and a visit. Dar had prepared a pot of vegetable stew that quietly simmered on the stove. She was relieved Sunny was visiting Carlita and her family and would miss the drama she anticipated over lunch. "It's never easy when they don't enter El Anhelo together," she sighed.

"This lot is particularly scattered," Reggie nodded. "But we'll help them through it. That's why we're here." He reached over from his chair and touched the hand that held a book he knew she wasn't reading. She wrapped her other hand around his.

"I love you, Reginald Howard."

"I love you, too, my scarlet-haired woman of words." He leaned over, pulling on a lock of hair that had escaped her braid.

One of the things she loved about this man was his sense of humor, especially in trying situations like the one they were about to face. She laughed and said, "That's a new one. I like it. Now I'll have to write you a sonnet to prove you right."

"A sonnet, eh? When was the last time you wrote a sonnet?" he asked, squinting in thought.

"I don't remember," she laughed. "But maybe it's time I gave it a try." Their conversation was interrupted by the sound of Juan's horn in the drive. Her grip tightened on Reggie's hand.

"It's all right, Dar," he reassured in a soothing voice while kissing her hand, but his smile was met by her frightened eyes. "Be yourself. It's time to greet our guests." She blinked and nodded. She was glad he held her hand as they walked out the front door.

Juan helped Maggie down from the front seat of the Jeep as Max and Angel exited from the back. Reggie stepped forward to greet them in a calm and friendly manner. "G'day and welcome to Sweet Dreams Bed and Breakfast. I'm Reggie Howard and this is my wife, Darlene. I think I can guess who's who from Michelle's descriptions. You must be Maggie O'Rourke, of course." His smile was infectious enough to bring Dar's back to life. They took turns shaking Maggie's hand.

"Nice to meet you both," Maggie smiled as she took in her new surroundings.

"And you must be Max DeBoer," he continued, shaking the man's hand. Reggie noted that he was slightly taller than Max, a good thing given the conversation he was anticipating.

"Good to meet you, Reggie," Max nodded.

"Angel Fuentes," the shorter man introduced himself, extending his hand.

"Greetings, Angel," Reggie said, his broad smile unwavering.

"Good to see you, too, Juan," Dar said, regaining her composure. "Thank you for bringing our guests to Teotenaca. How was the ride?"

"Not bad, except for that last stretch. I don't remember it being that bumpy," Juan said in accented English as he and Reggie unloaded the luggage.

"A hard rain did it. We'll be working on that stretch soon and can always use another pair of hands, if you're in the neighborhood," Reggie invited.

"I believe I'll be busy that day," Juan laughed.

Maggie talked quietly with Angel, who leaned against the car as if unsteady on his feet. "Are you right?" Dar asked. "Did you get motion sickness?"

He straightened up and took a gulp of mountain air. "I had a bout of queasiness on that last part of the road. Maybe it was the car swaying so much. I got a terrible pain in my stomach just as we made the turn. But it's gone now."

Reggie looked at Juan, who nodded his head slightly in response. "Well, I hope you're up to lunch," he offered. "Dar's been slaving over the stove and you don't want to miss her cooking," he laughed.

"Lunch sounds good," Angel nodded, attempting a smile.

All agreed they were famished after the long ride through the mountains. Then Max dropped the first of the questions Dar had dreaded. But she was ready for it. "So where's Michelle? I thought she'd be here to greet us."

"She went on a walk to sketch," she replied.

"How far?" he asked. "I made her promise not to go hiking alone."

Dar sensed the concern in his voice and hesitated, so Reggie jumped in to say, "She went to the trail, which doesn't go very far up the mountain, less than ten meters. It's not far from here. She'll be fine." He replied with a confident manner that set them at ease. "But one can lose track of time out there and I'm sure that's what happened to her. Now let's get your gear upstairs." He and Juan grabbed the luggage as Dar led their guests through the front door. But before they entered, Juan whispered to Reggie in Spanish.

"Where's their friend?"

"Where do you think?" Reggie replied. "When anyone disappears around here, it's generally the same answer."

He sighed and rolled his eyes. "I was afraid of that. Her friends seem hurt that she didn't wait for them in the city. And now they'll feel worse thinking she's in danger. They seem like good people, but Max is the head honcho. He will not be happy about this," Juan warned, shaking his head.

"Now that you know, do you want to stay for lunch or go into town?" Reggie offered.

He opted to stay, as Reggie hoped he would. "I know them a little better than you from the drive. It might help," he shrugged.

"Thanks, Juan." Reggie gave him a grateful slap on the back. "You're a good friend."

They entered the house and brought the bags up to the rooms on the second floor, where the guests were viewing the mountain from their bedroom windows. "It's unbelievably beautiful here!" Maggie exclaimed.

"Which of these bags is yours, Miss Maggie?" Reggie asked. "You'll be bunking with Michelle in the room on the right." After depositing her bag at the foot of the bed, Maggie went to the far bedroom that Angel and Max would share. Her two friends stood looking at their bed in disbelief. It was smaller than the one in Maggie's room.

"What's the matter, you two? Haven't you ever slept in the same bed before in all your travels?" she asked.

"This will be the first time," Max said, still looking the bed up and down, trying to imagine how they would both fit in it.

"I'll *try* not to snore," Angel said, in a playful effort to placate Max.

"I don't care about that. Just be sure you stay on your side," his un-amused friend replied. Dar interrupted with another option, offering Max the middle room at no extra cost, since no one else would be staying while they were there. "Would you be offended if I left you?" Max asked his longtime friend.

"Are you kidding?" Angel laughed. "More room for me."

After Dar announced that lunch would be served in a few minutes, Angel asked her another unwelcome, yet predictable question. "So when do you expect Michelle might be back?"

She sighed and said, "It could be a while. She's been sketching a lot since she arrived. I packed food for her in case she got productive out there. If she's not back by the time we're done eating, you could look for her. We might even go for a hike with you," she smiled, even though she knew it would be no leisurely walk if they did.

"Well, we could," Reggie said, then tried to re-direct their focus. "But let's eat first." He rubbed his hands together in anticipation. Dar had included a place for Michelle, as if she might still join them for lunch. As they sat around the harvest table and ate their first meal in Teotenaca, the three newcomers studied the paintings on the walls and asked questions about the town. Reggie was hoping they would get through lunch before Michelle's whereabouts came back into the conversation. He encouraged them to eat by bragging about his wife's stew. It seemed to work. They settled into their chairs and began the meal.

"I tried to research Teotenaca, but there wasn't much information available," Maggie said. "Michelle told me you've been here for five years, so you must know a lot about the place. Besides enjoying the natural beauty, what do you think a tourist would be interested in doing here?"

"It's a fairly quiet place," Dar said.

"No casinos or discos," Reggie added. "We do have a friend who could rent horses to you for riding on the trails. There are three restaurants with open-air cafés in good weather, and a bar in El Refugio, the inn, and an Internet café. But you're welcome to eat with us, if you'd like. This stew is but one fine example of my lovely wife's wondrous cooking skills. There are also a number of artisans who sell their wares from their homes. If you're interested, I could drive you to a few studios. The Church of Santa María is worth a visit as well."

"And we have occasional gatherings here," Dar added. "The next one will be the night before you leave. Local artists come together and share their projects. There are a number of writers, artists, and musicians in the area who come from around the world."

"How did they come to live here? I keep wondering what their stories are," Max inquired, looking from Dar to Reggie.

Reggie and Juan laughed. "You mean why in the world would they come to this god-forsaken off-the-beaten-path place nobody knows about?" their host asked in a sarcastic tone.

"I didn't mean it to sound like that," Max apologized. "But I am curious."

"The answer is a long story," Juan replied. Dar braced herself. The great mystery of Teontenaca was about to be revealed to their unsuspecting guests. It was a story she and Reggie could relate, but she was glad Juan was there, because he told the tale well. "Perhaps we can explain it," he continued. "There is a reason why they come."

"Any more stew?" Reggie asked. Angel handed him his empty bowl.

"It's the reason why we're here," Dar added. "Where do we begin?"

"I'll start," her husband said, as he filled Angel's bowl full of vegetable stew. He set it before his guest and continued. "This village has an ancient history and a set of myths and stories that have been passed down for generations. It's helpful to know that our mountain, El Anhelo, which means 'longing,' has been considered sacred by the indigenous population since pre-Columbian times." He talked slowly, using wide gestures and taking time to stop and be thoughtful, as if he were carefully choosing his words. In truth, he had told this story many times before.

"One of the ancient tales is about a cave within the mountain," Dar continued. She also spoke slowly. "Its name translates into English as the Cave of Dreams. As the young men came of age, they went on a vision quest. In preparation they'd fast and pray for dreams to show them an entrance into the cave, since there was no visible way into the mountain." She stopped for a moment to be sure they grasped what she'd just said. "If a dream told them where to find the entrance, they'd gather a pack of provisions for the journey. Their family would follow and watch them walk toward the mountain, torch in hand. It was said that if the dream were true, the young man would be able to enter the cave."

"Can I take it from here?" Juan asked. "This is part of my family's history," he said, smiling at Max, who was listening with a skeptical look on his face. "It is said the young men stayed for a day or as long as a week, and then would be 'released' from the cave. They never came out the same way they went in. But still, there was no visible opening after they passed through the mountain's surface."

"That's fascinating," Angel said. "Are there local theories about how they were able to enter the cave? How long did the myth persist?"

"Let me answer that with this story," Juan said. "When the Spanish came to Oaxaca they were looking for riches, as they did everywhere they went in the New World. Somehow they had heard the story of the men here going into a mysterious cave. They must have assumed there was gold or gems in there, so they came to the village to investigate. But they *never* found a way into El Anhelo." He emphasized this point by slapping his hand on the table, making Maggie pull back with a start.

"One day, a couple of Spaniards walking along the trail happened on the scene of a young man entering the mountain, but they did not reveal themselves. Instead they watched and after the young man's family left, the Spaniards went to where they had seen him disappear into the mountain, but they could not find an opening. The next day they returned with the men in their company, who brought picks and chisels. They tried to dig their way in at the entry point. They chipped away a good portion of rock, but it never opened into a cave. They came back the next day to try again, only to discover that, despite the pile of rock that still lay where it had fallen, the gouges they had made in the mountain *were no longer there*." He stopped again, looking into each listener's eyes. Max looked bemused, while Angel seemed deeply engaged. Maggie rested her chin in her hand, eyes wide. "Yes," Juan nodded. "As impossible as it sounds, El Anhelo looked as it had before they laid their picks into it. It was as if the mountain had healed itself from the wounds they'd inflicted upon it."

Juan paused again to let them absorb the impossibility of what he'd said. Max stared at the painting of El Anhelo with the clouds ringing it like a crown. Reggie gave an encouraging wink as Juan continued to the next episode. "Since the locals believed the mountain to be sacred and the Spanish felt these people were pagans, the explorers reasoned that the mountain must be the work of the devil, not God. They became fearful and left Teotenaca with empty pockets. But back in the city of Oaxaca, they recommended that Dominican missionaries bring a Christian God to these presumed devil worshippers and their mysterious cave. And, indeed, the Dominicans came and built a church in town that is still in use. The indigenous population may have become Christian, but it still believes in the old ways, including the story of the cave," Juan concluded.

"So this story persists," Angel said. "Do the young men still fast and dream about the cave?"

"Some do," Juan answered. "Others are less spiritual and would prefer to live their lives without that experience. I think they may be fearful, also."

"I don't quite know what to think of this story," Maggie said. Juan could see her processing his words, trying to make sense of this bizarre thing he'd just told them. "Are there reports, eyewitness reports, of the young men walking into the mountain in recent times?"

"Oh, yes," Juan answered with confidence, surprising them all. "And, occasionally, there are those who have heard of the cave and have tried to enter the mountain by force like the Spanish did long ago. Now they come with power equipment, even with explosives. But all they ever find is more rock. They never get in. For them it is only a frustrating legend," he laughed, because he knew of those stories, too.

"So, Juan, forgive me if I'm having trouble swallowing this tale," Max said, " but if I were to believe it, my next question would be, what do the young men do when they're in the cave, presuming that they get in there somehow?" He gestured with open hands and shrugging shoulders.

"It's a sanctuary inside," Juan continued, opening his arms as if they were the way into the mountain. "It's a place for reflection and discovery of one's own purpose in life. Those who go inside the cave have vivid dreams that help them explore their own lives or problems they're dealing with, but they also discover contributions they can bring back to the world when they re-enter it."

"Are you sure this is still happening?" Maggie asked in disbelief.

"Yes," Juan nodded with a smile.

"Do you know anyone who has had this experience, Juan?" Angel asked. "I would love to talk with them."

A simple request. One that was easy to fulfill. But the irony of it made Juan laugh to himself. "Oh, yes. Artists and spiritual practitioners seem the most drawn to the mountain. It energizes them and broadens their creativity and faith in some mysterious way. But now they come from all over the world, even as far as Australia," he smiled. Maggie, Max, and Angel had a collective realization and stared at their hosts.

"It's true. Reggie and I entered the cave years ago," Darlene confessed. "It seemed a fluke that we even came to this place. But once we were here, we were drawn to the mountain." They didn't know about the cave, she explained. They only wanted to hike the trail. In preparation, their hosts at the inn told them to pack extra clothes. They gave them food, candles, and a blanket. "We thought they were crazy!" she emphasized.

"They told us that occasionally people got lost on the trail and they wanted to be sure we would have what we needed if that happened to us," Reggie continued. That had frightened them, but the mountain kept pulling them closer, he insisted. "While we were hiking, we found an entrance to the cave and wondered why there had been no mention of it. We only meant to go a little way in. We saw a light as we entered and we walked toward it. It wasn't far from where we entered El Anhelo. But when we tried to leave, the opening had disappeared."

"Maybe you just couldn't find it. Maybe you got lost," Maggie insisted.

"We felt very lost, indeed," Dar agreed. "I felt terribly foolish and certain we would perish. Reggie had more faith than I did."

"I would have been totally lost without you, dear heart," he kissed Dar's hand.

"So, if I choose to believe your story," Max said, "the next thing I have to ask is, how did you get out of the cave to tell the tale?"

Juan laughed. "You don't believe it, but you're still curious, Señor Max. That's good."

"Oh, we *know* how ridiculous this sounds," Dar insisted. It was easier for her to open up now that Juan had told the story. "And that is why people don't openly talk about it with those not from the area. That's why we weren't told and why we didn't tell you before now." They didn't want to scare their guests, she explained. "People who've been inside believe they were called to the cave, as if it wasn't their choice entirely. It's like a religious calling would be, very hard to ignore. The cave releases you in good time."

Maggie shifted in her chair and asked, "So why do you think you were 'called'?"

"Reggie is a painter and I'm a writer," Dar began. "That is the truth of who we are to the core. But we dedicated ourselves to other things. Reggie was a language teacher. I taught English at the same school in Melbourne. It was a good life. But here, everything is amplified. There's an energy coming from the cave that inspires artists and spiritual seekers. It's quite motivating. Just being near El Anhelo will influence you."

"People come here to live for various reasons," Reggie went on. "That special creative energy that comes from the cave is one. Even if a person never goes in, one can't help but be affected by it. It's very positive in Teotenaca. Lots of inspiration, yes. But cooperation, too. This is a community that supports one another, whether you were born here or arrived last week," he smiled.

Angel nodded. "An ideal, peaceful community. I've seen this tried before, but mostly it's theoretical, though the Amish have managed it for the most part. But they've had to commit to an old societal structure. This one sounds more flexible," he theorized. "But the sacred cave is something different."

"So if this is true, and I'm sorry, but I'm finding it hard to believe," Max asked, "why do people have to go *into* the cave? And why would they want to, since they don't know when or how they'll get out?" Reggie could tell that Juan had been right. Max was the biggest skeptic in the group. He wasn't buying their story.

"That's a question for the force that controls the cave, which we believe is a sacred one," Juan answered. "Artists have active imaginations, after all. They can infuse people with a deeper understanding of the world through their art."

Max laughed and shook his head in disagreement. "Excuse me, but how are they going to do that if they're here and not out in the world?"

"Dar's about to have a book published in Australia," Reggie replied. "My art is represented in galleries there and in Oaxaca city, Mexico City, Dallas, and Los Angeles. And you'd be surprised at some of the other artists whose influence goes far and wide. I'm sure you would know a few of their names. We also support those from the village who venture out into the world, most of whom are also artists."

"Dar, you said something that concerns me," Maggie interrupted. "You didn't tell us about the cave until now. Did you warn Michelle about the cave before she left? Do you," she hesitated, not sure if she wanted to know the answer, "do you think it's possible she's gone into the cave?"

"We didn't tell her. We aren't supposed to." Dar reacted by pulling her hands back from the table and into her lap.

Reggie sighed and quickly answered their guests. "We think she went in. We've looked for her along the mountain trail and there's no trace. That generally means a person's in the cave. But she has food and water to last several days. She should be fine."

Angel, Max, and Maggie were incredulous. "How could you let her go knowing that could happen and not even warn her?" Maggie asked, angry, but beginning to cry.

Max put his arm around her. "We'll go look for her. How can we trust you people?" he screamed at them.

"Look at my art," Reggie said, pointing to several of his works that hung on the wall. "I couldn't paint like this before I came here. Dar's writing is about God's presence in our daily lives. We are *not* evil people. If Michelle entered the cave, it's because she answered that unwritten invitation by listening to her own heart and going in of her own accord. She'll be out in a couple days or so. In the meantime, we should all go look for clues she may have left for us to find. That's a common practice. You'll need us to help you find the way."

The three friends looked at each other in disbelief. Maggie was in tears and Max tried to comfort her. Angel just shook his head as if he couldn't comprehend how this had happened. "If only I hadn't found that book in the trunk," Max said. "I should never have insisted we come here."

"*Inexpensive Adventures* by Dennis Lawley? We know it well," Reggie said in a triumphant tone. "We found a copy in a used bookstore in Dallas. That's why *we* came." Max stared at Reggie in silence, contemplating that odd coincidence. "We still have it," Reggie said, producing a dog-eared copy from a nearby bookshelf.

"You will have to trust us. We're *not* bad people." Dar spoke in a strong voice. "I said I'd look after her in your absence. I made sure she has plenty of water, food, and a blanket. She also took a flashlight and I packed extra batteries in her pack. She had her sketchbook along. Perhaps she left a note on the trail. We can look for that. Believe me, I worry, too."

The three guests looked at each other. "What choice do we have?" asked Angel. "Let's go look for her."

"Wear sturdy shoes and take a hat. If you need sunscreen we have plenty," Reggie offered.

"Even though this whole thing sounds ridiculous, I want to believe you," Maggie said. "Whatever happened, I want to find her safe and sound, as soon as possible!" This time *she* slapped the table.

Max nodded at her second statement. "You'd better help us find her or we'll go to the police."

"We can take you there first, if you like," Reggie said, calling his bluff.

"Just help us find her," Max said, more quietly. "Then we'll see." He turned to Juan. "Tell me one thing. Where did the story about the Spaniards come from? How would anyone know about that?"

Juan smiled and nodded. "That, Señor Max, is a story that has been passed down for generations in my family. My ancestor was among those Spaniards. But I'm Zapotec, too. Ironically, my father and his father entered the cave as young men. I have not yet been chosen. But then, I'm an accountant," he smiled.

19

I sat on the bench by the waterfall, doing a mental inventory of my remaining food. My water bottle was nearly empty, but deeper in my backpack I'd discovered juice and oranges Dar must have snuck into it, along with other food. I wondered how long I could make it last. Maybe a few days. But what would I do after that?

The water I'd drunk from the pool earlier had not made me ill, so I decided to fill my bottle with it. Besides, the pool was my only source of water in the cave. As I bent down and dipped the bottle into the pool, I heard metal scraping right next to my foot. It was a *milagro*, one of those silver Mexican charms that are pinned up on church walls to request miracles, or to thank God for performing one. This milagro seemed to be in the shape of an eye and had oxidized from silver into a tarnished black.

Catholic, I thought. The room *must* have been a place of worship. There were probably other clues hidden in the darkness. I picked up the milagro and wondered where it had fallen from, and how long ago. And now it was my turn to ask for a miracle. I placed it in front of the row of candles and silently prayed for the gift of vision. "Dear God, help me to see in this dark place. Show me a way out before I use up my food and batteries. Please keep me safe! Amen." I felt better then, relieved that I'd done one small thing. I slipped the milagro in my pocket. Its tiny presence gave me a sense of security, like a talisman. I drank some juice and ate a slice of cheese and felt stronger. I thought of my friends and what must be happening at Sweet Dreams. Surely they'd found out I was missing by now. What would they do to find me? Maybe this ordeal would be over in a matter of hours, not days, now that Max was on the case.

My mind wandered back to the last time I'd seen them all at Maggie's place right before I left for Mexico. She'd ordered a feast of authentic Mexican food from a local restaurant. Max contributed dark Mexican beer, and Angel arrived with homemade custard for dessert. I brought Mexican coffee. We'd joked about our off-the-beaten-path trip, that it was okay to be crazy for going because we'd be crazy together. That helped my nagging anxiety over what we'd find in Teotenaca. We practiced Spanish with our *maestro*, Señor Angel, who coached us through our bad accents and phrasing. "You can blend the vowels at the ends and beginnings of words more. Same goes for the consonants. Say 'BuenosDías,' not 'Bue-nos Dí-as.' Let's repeat that." And we did. We went over the most important phrases. Mine, as always, was "¿Dónde está el baño?" Where is the bathroom? I hoped I'd understand the answer when it came back in Spanish. I taught Max to say "No hielo," "No ice," so he wouldn't have to worry about bad water melting into his drink and giving him Montezuma's revenge.

I asked Maggie if she'd bring her flamenco gear on the trip. "The shoes, yes. The music, yes. But probably not the clothes. Well, maybe a shawl at least," she conceded. "I'm going to miss a class, so I have to get some practicing in." One thing led to another and after dinner she rolled up the rug, put on music and showed me a few moves. I tried to follow, but my sense of rhythm didn't match the music. I was pathetic. Then Angel and Max had a good laugh as I tried out the cold, steely femme fatale expressions Maggie did so naturally. The more I hammed, the more they folded over in laughter.

"Hey, this isn't easy. I'd like to see you try it," I dared them. Angel deferred, perhaps because he hadn't had as much beer as Max. But Max, always the adventurer, was willing to try. Our hostess gave him a demonstration, clapping her hands and moving her feet in syncopated rhythm. He followed surprisingly well. Then she showed him how to move his arms and wrists, undulating them like snakes. He seemed to understand that, somewhat. She tied her shawl around his hips, turned on the music, and let him go. He kept up the rhythm, flexing his hands and arms in a more supple way than I thought was possible. But when he tried out those haughty expressions, we couldn't hold back. His eyebrows moved up and down to the rhythm. When he crossed his eyes, I lost it! My throat hurt from laughing.

"Well, I guess you two have potential, but let me show you how flamenco *should* look," Maggie smiled, taking back her shawl. She moved the CD to another track. Poised and perfect, she began to dance, slowly at first, and then more boldly as the tempo picked up. She came right up to us, then spun away as if we disgusted her. I tried to hang on to the rhythm, but it kept eluding me. Yet she was right in time with her clapping and foot stomping.

Max was mesmerized and clapping with her. She reached down and grabbed his hand. He didn't hesitate to join her. They moved back to back with glances over their shoulders. When she twirled, he faced her. Then she turned away, but glanced over her shoulder at him. When the music stopped, she twirled toward him, but tripped on a corner of the rug. He reached out protectively and caught her in his arms. They stood together, catching their breath and looking into each other's eyes like there was no one else in the world, let alone Angel and me a few feet away on the couch.

We glanced at each other, not knowing what to do next. When Angel applauded and I joined in, Max looked up with a dazed expression. We all knew there was chemistry between him and Maggie. I wondered why they'd never done anything about it. But then Max had personal reasons for not getting close to women, and I doubted Maggie knew about them. Surely she would understand his reluctance, if only he'd confide his fears to her. But how could he not want to hold her? She was beautiful, a warm and wonderful person. The CD had moved to the next track, but the flamenco portion of our evening had officially ended.

"Custard and coffee, anyone?" Angel offered as our two friends stepped away from each other. We finished the meal like nothing unusual had happened.

"I didn't know you could cook this well, Angel," Maggie said between bites of the flan-like custard. "What other surprises do you have up your professor's sleeve?" she smiled.

He laughed. "I can't cook on a dance floor like you, but I *can* cook in my kitchen. I have traditional recipes to try on you another time, but they're a bit spicy. As for surprises, we'll see what I can dig up in Teotenaca." I was anxious to tag along with my professor friend as he played cultural detective in the mountains. He said he'd re-read notes from a trip to Oaxaca a few years before and that the place was absolutely fascinating. "It's a crossroads of different native cultures and Spanish colonialism, so there's a cross-pollination of languages, myths, and customs. I'm looking forward to going back there with my friends," he smiled. "This trip should be like tonight was, perhaps even more magical."

Maggie smiled. "I can't believe that this time next week we'll be there, looking at the mountains, hearing roosters crow, and even milking goats. Here's to Santa María Teotenaca!" she said, raising her coffee cup. The toasts kept coming.

"To magical mysteries of Mexico!"
"To Sweet Dreams to come!"
"To safe passage for Michelle!"
"To Michelle, who will not hike alone!"
"To the joy of hiking, alone!"
"Michelle!"
"Okay, to the joy of hiking with friends!"
"To a vacation like no other!"
"To surprises around every corner!"

We helped Maggie clean up and then Angel and I left. But Max lingered. "I wonder if they're practicing flamenco," Angel laughed in the car. He insisted on driving me home rather than watching me hop on a bus.

"What time is your flight?" he asked.

"At 9:30 in the morning. Maggie's taking me to the airport," I replied.

"I wish I could go with you. I do worry about you going alone," he confided.

"I appreciate your concern, but I'll be fine. I have another concerned person waiting for me on the other end and she'll take care of me."

Traffic was light so he got me home quickly. "I'll wait until you're inside the door," he insisted. I hugged him from the passenger's side and we exchanged kisses on the cheek. When I looked back at him, he seemed sad.

"Is something bothering you, Angel?"

"Maybe a little," he admitted. "I would hate to see anything happen to you." He touched my cheek. "I'm a serious guy, but you make me laugh," he smiled. "I need more of that."

"And I'd love to know more about what you're researching these days. I know you're up to more than hanging out with your rowdy friends," I joked. "I'm curious about other people's spiritual points of view, too, since I can't seem to settle on my own lately. What about you, Angel, you do believe in a deity, don't you?"

"Theoretically," he nodded. "And so I will say vaya con Díos, Michelle. May God go with you on your journey to Teotenaca. We can continue our conversation there. But now you'd better get some rest. Good night, sweet señorita."

"Good night, señor. I'll see you in the land of Sweet Dreams and mountains." I threw him a kiss as I slipped out of his car.

That was the last time I'd seen him. Of my three friends, I was missing him the most as I sat listening to water trickle into the cave pool. What would he think of this rabbit hole I'd foolishly fallen into?

The day after we'd parted, Maggie drove me to O'Hare for my flight to Mexico City. At the airport she pulled my suitcase with its unsteady wheels while I toted my backpack. There were long lines and I was surprised that Spanish was the predominant language. *I may as well get used to it*, I thought.

"How are you doing?" she inquired. "You look tired."

"Honestly, I never sleep well before a trip," I admitted. "I get so wound up with trying to pull everything together. And I'll admit I'm a bit more anxious about this one than I've let on. But don't you dare start feeling bad for me. It was my own fault for typing in the wrong date when I ordered the ticket. You'll catch up to me before you know it. And how are *you*, Maggie? You were quiet in the car. Is it Max?" I asked, already knowing it must be.

She smiled, then looked down, avoiding my eyes. "I suppose. He's the most frustrating man on the planet! I can never figure out what he's thinking or feeling. And you never know where he'll be from week to week! His impetuousness is attractive at times, but it's difficult, too."

"I know," I agreed.

"I keep thinking there's more to him than he wants anyone to know. I think he's really a sensitive soul, but he's so elusive! Am I nuts to have feelings for him, Michelle? You've known him a lot longer. Why is he like that?" She looked hard into my eyes then, as if she'd find the answer there. I didn't want to leave her in that state.

"I think Max cares a great deal for you, but he doesn't know what to do with his feelings, Maggie. He's developed a lifestyle that makes it impossible for anyone to get close to him. I know he's mushy underneath that tough exterior," I laughed, thinking about Max over the years. "He loved to discuss philosophy in college and I know he's read poetry." And then I remembered a poem that impacted his life shortly after he'd gotten out of school. I had hoped he'd share that part of his life story with Maggie, but he hadn't. She should know, I decided. She wasn't able to see the whole picture otherwise. "There was a time in Max's young life when, well, I really think he owes his life to a poem."

"His life?" she asked, puzzled. The line was beginning to move just then.

"He lost a girlfriend in a car accident," I told her. Even though years had passed, it still made me sad as I told the story. "She was the passenger and he was the driver. It absolutely wasn't his fault. A drunken driver in a pickup ran a light and hit them broadside. Anita was killed on the spot. There was nothing Max could have done." I must have told him that a dozen times, and still wondered if I ever got through to him. "He had broken bones and internal bleeding. It took him a long time to heal. But he survived and she didn't. He tortured himself wondering if he could have prevented it." He had really scared me back then as he fell into a depressive state. "Angel and I told him Anita would want him to get on with his life. But he wasn't responsive. I thought he was almost suicidal at one point, but he refused to see a therapist.

"Then one day I was at the library leafing through new books. Have you heard of Berta Corelli? She's a local poet who was getting a lot of press back then. I picked up her book and the first page I flipped to had a poem entitled 'Choosing to Live,' about someone who almost committed suicide, but decided they had too much to live for. It was an extraordinary poem, and so appropriate to what was happening to Max that I had to get it to him. I took out the book and told him to read that poem first and to *keep* reading it!"

"Poor Max," Maggie shook her head. "I had no idea. What happened next?" The line was moving quicker now.

"He read the book. In fact, he ended up buying it. I've seen it looking very worn on the bookshelves at his loft. He got better and gradually snapped out of the depression. But over time he evolved into the he-man he is today, strong and brave and hard to get close to, unless you're his friend. I can tell he really cares about you, Maggie. It's been years since Anita's death. It's time he moved on and showed his true feelings. I hope he can do that with you," I smiled with as much sincerity as I could muster. Then I turned and entered my information into a monitor, which spit out a boarding pass. I moved to the counter while Maggie, noticeably struggling with what I had told her, held back.

"Maggie," I said, "sorry, but I need that bag to go on the plane." She wheeled it up. Before long it was on its way to Mexico.

As we walked toward the security checkpoint, I wondered if I'd made a mistake by dumping that revelation on my friend right when I was leaving town. "Should I not have told you about Anita?" I asked.

But she smiled her warmest smile and said, "I'm glad you did. It all makes sense now. I won't tell him I know," she promised as she gave me a long good-bye hug.

And now, sitting and staring at the pool in the cave, I wondered when I would see them again, or *if* I would see them again. A wave of dread brushed across my heart. It was time to be more proactive about the mess I'd gotten myself into. I noted where this room was so I could come back for water. Then I resumed my walk through the passage in search of an opening out of the Cave of Dreams. I saw the undulating light again, reflecting off the pool and onto the wall outside that room. The wavy light seemed to be floating in the air. Hmmm, I thought, perhaps I should re-name this the Cave of Illusions since it also housed disappearing entrances.

Along that route, the floor was uneven and rough in places, but I found a fairly straight section and stayed on it. There was nothing of note along this tunnel until it began to twist and grow narrow. The roof lowered and I had to bend over. It was claustrophobic. I almost turned around when I saw a narrow opening ahead that was about three feet across and three feet high. I stuck my flashlight into the space to find another room, but I couldn't tell how far it went or if the path continued beyond it. As far as I could tell, the only other way to go was back where I'd come from, so I decided to check this room out.

The entrance was narrow for several feet before it opened to a larger space. The ceiling was around ten feet high at one point. At first I didn't see anything unusual. But then something in the wall sparkled when the beam of my flashlight crossed it. I moved the light back toward that spot and it quivered again, like a small sun. When I moved my flashlight further, it caught more of the glimmer in the dark rock. I took a closer look and found natural crystals embedded in the walls. It was like being inside a diamond showroom with only dim lights on. An electrical light would brighten the place tenfold. But there wasn't any way out of there and I'd reached a dead end. Discouraged, I left and went back to the room with the waterfall and sat near the pool again. What a waste of time that little exercise had been! I started crying, then stopped myself by taking a few purposeful deep breaths. I was almost overwhelmed by desperation at that point. "What now? I gasped. "Where do I go from here?" Without realizing it, my clenched fists began to relax. I slumped against the bench and lost consciousness without another thought.

20

Her guests had eaten most of the meal and Dar was grateful for that. Food was comforting and nourishing, much needed attributes for the unexpected situation they found themselves in. She scraped the plates clean, depositing the leftover bits into a bucket for the compost heap. Washing dishes was a kind of meditation for her. She looked out the window and daydreamed while the suds moved between her hands and the plates. From her kitchen vantage point, she could also see through the screened veranda and into the yard. She watched Reggie and Juan as they led Angel, Maggie, and Max toward the trail that skirted the mountain, and she was relieved to be staying behind.

The mood was silent and brooding as Reggie and Juan led the new arrivals toward El Anhelo. Reggie knew the brilliant sky, the music of birdsong, the meadow flowers and the mountain itself would be lost on them.

"How much further?" Max asked as they passed near the campfire area in the grove.

"Just a few more minutes before we connect with the mountain trail," Reggie replied.

"Oh!" It was Angel who called out. He'd fallen further behind the rest.

"What's wrong?" Juan came to his side as he bent over, apparently in pain.

"My stomach! This is like the ache in the car. What's making me sick?" he asked in a halting voice.

"Michelle had the same experience," Reggie said. "It's called the 'draw of the mountain,' which means you're a good candidate to go into the cave, Angel. If you're given the opportunity, you'll have to make that choice, though we haven't outfitted you like we did Michelle." Angel barely grasped what Reggie was saying.

"It could also be something he ate," Max insinuated.

"I suppose that's a possibility, but not at our house," Reggie smiled.

"Besides, the rest of you are fine."

"Is there a place where I can sit down?" Angel asked, leaning against a tree.

"Yes, there is, through those trees. Can you make it a little farther?" Reggie asked with a sympathetic tone. He'd experienced this same pain and knew it was probably peaking at this point.

"I can help," Max said.

"Me, too," Maggie agreed.

They stood on either side of Angel and supported him as they followed Reggie and Juan into the grove. The breeze was mild, which softened the musical sound of the bells and chimes that hung there. He was lowered onto the same bench where Michelle had sat the day before.

"Just relax," Maggie coaxed. "We won't budge until you're ready."

Max was uncharacteristically quiet. He moved to the other side of the campfire. "I have my camera," he said. "I want to document this as much as possible, starting now." He took out his camera and aimed it toward Maggie and Angel. She frowned while Angel grimaced with his face barely showing.

"Not now," she scowled. "Let him be. Do you need water?" she asked Angel.

"Maybe," he replied. "Just a little." She undid the water bottle hooked to her belt and put it to his mouth.

"Thanks, Maggie. It feels good to sit down. Do I hear bells?" Angel asked.

"You do," Reggie affirmed. "And wind chimes."

The breeze picked up for a moment as the sick man drank deeply of the water. The sound of bells increased, then subsided. The tall grass rustled and he realized what he was *not* hearing. He smiled despite his pain. "I don't hear cars or planes," he laughed. "No sirens, no train whistles, no car alarms. This is wonderful." They were all silent for a few moments, suddenly aware of their surroundings, and feeling very far from home.

"How are you now?" Max inquired.

"Better. The cramp, or whatever it is, is lifting. But I'd like to sit a few more minutes."

"You've had a rough day already, all of you," Reggie acknowledged, "from a tedious ride through the mountains to finding out the friend you hoped would greet you has disappeared. How are the rest of you doing?"

"How do you think?" Maggie flashed an angry look in his direction. "This trip was meant to be an adventure, but we weren't planning on becoming a search party. I'm sorry, but it's a preposterous story, and it doesn't add up. Why would she go into a cave alone? Why wouldn't she wait for us so we could explore it together, or find out more about it before she went in?"

"Some people *don't* go in for those reasons," Reggie explained. "They're afraid. But, speaking from experience, Dar and I felt very drawn to enter, despite our own misgivings. We marked the place where we went in and we didn't go that far inside. The tunnel opened into a dome where we saw the light that I'm sure Michelle has discovered. All tunnels lead to it. But what's tricky is finding the right tunnel back to where you entered. Even if you do, the opening will have disappeared by the time you get back to it. That happened to us. We couldn't believe it. We each blamed ourselves."

"So what did you do then? Didn't you panic?" Max asked.

"Oh, we did at first. We thought we were goners. But we took comfort in the fact we had each other and we walked back to the dome. It's peaceful there. So peaceful, in fact, that we fell asleep. And dreamed. And our dreams were similar," he explained.

Juan interjected, "My father and grandfather dreamed similar things, also, even though it was years apart. In their dreams they both went to a place called La Ciudad de la Luz."

"I still dream my way into The City of Light," Reggie said. "One can find answers there to the toughest questions."

"How about dreaming this – how do we find Michelle and get her out?" Max interrupted.

But Reggie spoke to Angel instead. "Are you certain you're up to going with us? Do you want to head back?"

"I can go," he said. "I'm feeling better now."

"All right then. Here's how we'll find her," Reggie said, "by looking where she would have gone, along the trail. We're bound to find something she's left behind."

"You sound pretty confident. How do we know you didn't plant it there for us to find?" Max accused him.

"If we find anything of Michelle's," Reggie sighed, "you'll know it's hers. I don't 'plant' things other than flowers, trees, and vegetables." He headed out of the grove not looking back to see if they followed, but they did. When they reached the trail along the mountain they spread out along the base and arranged to meet up again within the hour. Maggie tried to keep Angel in sight in case he had another attack, but he was walking upright. They looked everywhere for a sign of her, even off the trail in the meadows and down into ravines, ditches, and creeks. But no one found anything.

Max began photographing the area, switching his focus from looking for Michelle to savoring the views along the trail. Instead of documenting a perceived injustice, one that might have taken his friend's life, he began a visual diary of the scenes he encountered at every turn. He didn't realize it, but even he had fallen under the influence of the mountain.

They'd been searching for forty minutes, stretching out further from one another. Angel felt stronger, but his legs were tired from walking. He found a log to sit on that had fallen between the trail and the mountain. Facing toward the trail, he was aware of cooler air on his neck. It felt refreshing in the heat of the sunlit sky. Then he heard an odd sound from the other side of the log. He walked around the fallen tree and found a sheet of white paper pushed under the log and weighted down by a rock. The edges of the paper flapped in the breeze. There was writing on it, large letters written in dark pencil. Rather than remove it, he bent down to hold it in place and read what he realized was Michelle's note, dated the day before, which confirmed she had entered the cave. He followed the point of the hand-drawn arrow indicating where she'd entered. He knew the note to be genuine, a page out of the new sketchbook she'd bought before they left, and he knew she'd placed it there herself. The large, scrawled writing was definitely hers. He stood next to the mountain and pushed the vines to the side. Something glinted in the light. When he saw a hair tangled in the brush, lit by the sun, he knew that was hers, too. But where had she gone? He skimmed the rough rock with his hands, but there was no opening.

Then he discovered a place in the rocky surface that seemed colder to the touch. Did he feel air coming from within the mountain? He lifted the vines that hung from the slight overhang there. The sun was shining on the surface of the rock enough to take a good look. But still there was no opening. The rock was solid. Yet he was convinced that colder air was coming from inside. He looked closer for cracks or holes where it could be leaking through from the cave.

Then, as he scanned the surface with his eyes and fingers, his hand fell through and past the surface of the rock, where it remained suspended in the midst of what should have been solid and opaque! Yet it felt like a shaft of air and looked transparent to his eye. He stared at his hand. He moved it back and forth and it appeared to go through the rock again and again. He wondered if his whole body could pass through what appeared to be an illusion of solid rock.

But fear overcame his curiosity. He pulled his hand back so suddenly he almost fell. Was the rock mysteriously fluid? Could it become solid, then open? And who or what controlled it? Perhaps it wasn't solid at all and this was the opening Michelle had stepped through into the cave. But surely it would have looked more like an opening to her. But all this analytical thinking was hopeless. How could one reason with something so illogical? There was no obvious answer to such a mystery.

He walked back to the path and looked for Maggie, who was some distance away. He shouted and waved until he got her attention, then signaled that she should come quickly. She in turn looked further down the trail for Max and was able to signal him as well. She ran until she was nearly out of breath by the time she reached Angel.

"This isn't like jogging through Lincoln Park," she said. "The air is awfully thin here."

"You'd better catch your breath before I show you what I found," he said.

"Why? What did you find? Something of Michelle's?"

"Yes. She left a note for us. It's from yesterday. She did go in, like they said."

She just stared at him. "Are you sure it's her note? Could Reggie have put it there?"

"It's her writing. I also saw one of her hairs in the brush, so she was here. I'll show you the note." When he pointed, she bent down to get a better look. Like Angel, she recognized the writing as Michelle's and visually traced the direction indicated by the arrow.

"Did you see an opening?" she asked.

"Here, you try to find an opening. I want to see what happens when you look for it," he challenged her.

She cocked her head and squinted back. "What do you mean?"

"I can't tell you until you try to find it."

She walked to the same place where Angel had stood. "Are there snakes or lizards in these vines?" she asked tentatively.

"I didn't see any," he replied. "But that's where I saw one of her hairs."

"Let me see," she said. But after not finding any visible openings within ten feet of where the arrow pointed, she gave up. "There's nothing here. How can that be?"

"Try running your hands over the surface," he said. "Do you feel anything different?"

She reluctantly obliged, running her hands along the rock within the same span her eyes had surveyed. "Nothing," she said.

"How odd," he said. "That's not what I found." As he approached the area where his hand had entered the wall of the mountain, Max arrived on the scene. Both he and Maggie witnessed Angel's hand sliding effortlessly beyond what appeared to be a surface of solid rock. Maggie and Max took turns, but their hands couldn't penetrate the wall.

"Oh my God." Maggie could barely say the words.

"It's a kind of portal," Max said, trying to make sense of what they'd seen. "But it's only open to you, Angel. How far will your hand go in?"

"I don't know if I want to find out," he said, pulling his hand out again.

"They're telling the truth, Max!" Maggie couldn't believe what she'd just seen.

"Did you signal Reggie or Juan to come over?" Angel asked him.

"No, I didn't. They've probably noticed I'm gone by now. But it's almost time for us to meet up again," Max responded.

"Maybe they can shed more light on this," Angel said.

"How did you do that?" Max asked his friend.

"I have no idea!"

"What did it feel like?" Maggie asked.

"It's cold, as if I'm feeling cooler air coming from inside. Did you notice any difference in the temperature of the rock there?" he asked them.

"No," they replied at the same time.

"Do it again," she said. "I want to make sure I really saw what I saw."

"This makes me very uncomfortable, but curious, too," Angel said as he moved his hand once again past the surface of rock.

"How far can you reach through it?" Max asked.

"I don't know. I'll go slowly, inch by inch," he said, slowly moving in closer to the mountain. The shaft of cold air seemed endless. He was up to his elbow when he decided that was enough and pulled his arm out.

"What did you feel?" Max asked.

"Nothing. Just the cooler air. I could go further, but I don't want to.

What if I were able to walk right through it? How would I find my way back? What if it closed behind me like it did on Michelle?" Angel asked more emotionally than his professor side would have. This was too challenging for his intellect.

"If the mountain lets you in, it will shut the door behind you," a voice came from the path. It was Reggie with Juan.

"How would I know how to get out?" Angel asked. "How did you get out? And how will Michelle?"

"The force inside this mountain will show her the way out as it showed her the way in. But she won't know when or where until it's time for her to leave. Dar and I found out in a dream. It was as if the sun was shining in our eyes, but it was the cave beginning to open. It was so bright it woke us up. A strong wind pulled us toward the daylight that shone through the hole and we were able to walk out of there. When we went back a couple days later, both openings were gone," Reggie explained.

Suddenly, Angel reached into the opening again. He brought his head close to where his hand was suspended and pushed part way past the invisible entrance. He cupped his hand to his mouth.

"Michelle!" he shouted into the mountain. "It's Angel! MICHELLE!!! MICHELLE!!!" He waited, but no answer came back. "We will wait for you!" he shouted and then pulled himself away from the opening. He hadn't felt Max's strong arms around his waist until then.

"I was afraid we were going to lose you, too," Max said, letting go.

"Not now," Angel said. "But I have to say that the longer I stay here, uncomfortable or not, the more I want to go through the 'portal' and into the cave. I'm afraid, yet I want to go in, badly."

"Let us outfit you if you decide to go," Reggie offered. "But the time is limited, I'd say, since it looks like rock and not a way in."

"No. Let's go back," Maggie urged him. "I just wish we could know what's going on with Michelle and if she's all right in there."

Reggie smiled confidently at her. "She's all right," he said. "You'll see her again and she'll be alive and enlightened when you do. But there's a way of checking on her, if you'll trust me and what you'll hear."

"I trust you," Angel said. "After what just happened to me, I can believe anything about this place!"

"Do we have another choice? Better show us what you've got," Max said. "But I remain a skeptic. It had better be good."

"Oh, it will be," Reggie nodded. "You can bet on that."

21

    Maybe it was the sensory deprivation I was experiencing in the cave that forced my unconscious mind to compensate with incredibly vivid dreams. But I got an uneasy feeling when I began to long for the dream state more and more. Was I being lulled into not caring about leaving the cave? My sleeping state was comforting and reassuring, even though I had desperately wanted to find a way out of the mountain. But during one dream, things took a turn in another direction.

    It began in the City of Light where I met María once again. She'd been instructing me, as if she were preparing me for a mission. When I was with her, I felt safe and secure, but I also felt that I was in the presence of a spiritual being. She had an enlightened mind, a kind heart, and a smile that radiated warmth. We sat opposite each other on wrought iron benches. I couldn't help but notice the expanse of blue sky that filled the space behind her. She asked if I had a question for her. I asked the first thing that came into my mind.

    "Yes. This feels like a fantastic place, a place that only exists in my dreams. Yet it seems familiar. Is there anywhere like the City of Light on the physical earth?"

    "A good question," she replied. "There are aspects of this place on the planet, cities that have been built upon island fortresses like this. Some are off the coast of Greece. But there are places all over the physical world where you can find evidence of the spiritual plain."

    She rose and approached me. "But now, I have an important lesson for you. We have little time and I have much to teach you. Give me your hand," she said and I extended my right hand to her. She took it as if she would read my palm. But then she placed her right hand just above mine, as if it were hovering there. I could feel a heat generate between our palms until it became almost unbearable. Then she took her hand away, looked toward the sky behind her and held her arm straight ahead, palm out. She moved her arm from left to right in a wide arc and in the path her hand traced, the blue sky opened like a curtain on a window. But in place of the daytime sky there was absolute darkness, as deep as a starless night far from a city, or the bottom of the ocean, or, I suddenly realized, the inside of a cave.

"What do you see?" she asked.

"Nothing."

"What does 'nothing' look like?"

"Darkness. Shadows. An abyss. A cave," I answered.

"Very good," she smiled. "Do you see any light, any aspect of this city, in this 'nothing' space?"

"No, none at all," I replied.

"Or so it seems," she said mysteriously. "Look deeper into this space and I will ask you again." It seemed fruitless, but I did what she said. I stared into the darkness until I saw movement, but I couldn't tell what was moving. Then there were shapes, the silhouettes of people walking in opposite directions, but toward each other. I wondered how they could see where they were going.

"I see people now. They look as if they're on a crowded city sidewalk," I observed.

"Are they just walking past each other or is something else happening?" she asked. It took a while before I could distinguish two figures that were standing still. They were gesturing wildly toward one other and seemed to be yelling back and forth, but I couldn't hear any of it. Four-letter words, I speculated. No light in that discussion.

"Two people are arguing. They look like they're about to come to blows."

"If they lived in a more enlightened state, as we do in the City of Light, what do you think they would do next?" That was a difficult question, since these two seemed bent on hurting one other.

"If they lived here they wouldn't have gotten into this mess. I think they're going to beat each other up. If they lived here they would stop before that happened. One of them would have to back off or walk away or apologize. They would come to their senses before it got worse. The intention would have to shift," I realized.

"Excellent, Michelle. And what kind of intention would shift toward the light?"

I looked at the angry silhouettes. But now one was still while the other continued to gesture. The dynamic was changing. "If one of them would listen to what the other is saying, maybe compromise would be possible, or at least tolerance for the other person's point of view," I said. Then I saw the quiet figure begin to speak to the other who held a clenched fist, but had finally stopped to listen. I still couldn't hear them, but I understood their body language.

"What else?"

"Better communication. Real communication," I said. And the two figures began to speak to each other more calmly, occasionally nodding in agreement with each other for a change.

"And what else?"

"Respect for the other person," I said. And the two figures shook hands. Everything I said seemed to affect their actions. The tide had turned quickly.

"What else?" she asked.

"The possibility for forgiveness," I said. Why not? That would be a major stretch for most people.

"Anything else?" she continued.

I felt corny for saying it, but it seemed like a natural progression. "Love?" And the two figures embraced. As they did, the darkness fell away and their forms were filled with the missing blue sky. As they walked together, through the crowd of shadowy passersby, their sunlit silhouettes stood out from everyone else's.

"So how does one bring a spiritual light into the physical world?" María asked.

It all seemed so clear in my dream it surprised me. "It's available to people at any time. Perhaps it's really within us," I said. "Or we have to act like it is. If we don't, we'll never get there."

"Exactly! How do you think one must act to enter the light?"

A flood of words came to me then. "It's what I've already said and more. It's about being tolerant, merciful, patient, forgiving, understanding, communicative, respectful, even loving."

"Yes," she smiled. "For many people and situations that might seem impossible. But it *is* possible. It may take practice or time, but as long as the intention is from the light and not the darkness, there is hope. The darkness will eventually fall away if we undermine it with light. But if we build upon the opposite of your list of words, we build a wall around the City of Light, a wall with no door that will allow us to enter it. We shut ourselves out from those things that would sustain and nourish us, as well as those around us. Do you understand?" she asked.

"Yes." I got it easily enough. It seemed so obvious in my dream state. Why didn't it in the real world?

"Good. Then we will move from theory to practice. Remember the lesson. Remember to undermine the darkness with light. Your generosity of spirit can open a door to even greater possibility."

She seemed to be made of light as her white dress reflected sunlight. But then her figure faded into the sky and the sky faded into a background of skyscrapers. I didn't recognize the skyline. It wasn't Chicago or any other place I knew. Then I heard the sounds of a city all around me: buses, car horns, a siren far away. I was standing on the street of an expensive urban downtown with exclusive shops lining a boulevard. Looking down at my clothes, I realized they were the same ones I'd worn into the cave, and they looked dirty. My hair was snarled and I knew my makeup had worn off long ago. A heaviness on my back turned out to be my backpack. No one stopped to look at me. I felt completely out of place and very lost. Where was I and what should I do now? I hoped María was hovering nearby like the guardian angel in Sunny's drawing.

I stopped to look in a clothing store window and was shocked by my own reflection, so dirty and disheveled! Then another figure was reflected next to mine in the window, a man in his early fifties or so, with gray stubble coming out of his dark skin. His shirt pocket had come undone and hung like a gaping mouth. He seemed wobbly on his feet and smelled of liquor and sweat. I turned away from the glass and met his eyes.

"What *you* looking at?" he said belligerently. "You're no better than me." And he shuffled off down the street. It hit me then that I looked like him, like a homeless person. He stopped near the corner and put his hand out as the wealthy shoppers rushed by. They ignored him as if he were invisible. I could tell he was getting angry and I was afraid he might become desperate in an effort to get attention. I didn't want to confront him, but I was compelled to do something. I walked up to him, not knowing what to do. So I talked to him.

"What do you need?" I asked. "Are you hungry?"

He looked at me, half suspicious and half hopeful. "I'm always hungry," he said.

I felt in my pocket for a quarter or two, but I had no change. I had left all my money, U.S. and Mexican, back at the Sweet Dreams B & B. I had food in my backpack, but it had become precious to me. Still, I knew I had more than he did. "I don't have any money, but I have a little food."

"Oh really. I don't suppose you have a T-bone steak and hot mashed potatoes and gravy in there, do you?"

"I don't suppose I do," I said. I pulled out a power bar. Could I give it up, considering my own desperate situation? Before I could decide what to do, he grabbed it away from me and started eating it.

"I was going to give that to you." *Was I?* I wondered. "Why did you take it like that?" I said angrily.

"I'm not so sure you were going to give it up," he said. "You hesitated. A person in my situation has to seize opportunities as they present themselves," he laughed. "What else you got in there?"

"Not much now," I said. I had more than I let on, but I had to make it last for my own survival.

Before I had a chance to do anything else I felt another person sliding next to me. "Can you share with me, too?" a young woman asked. She had tattoos around her wrists and her stringy hair was streaked in electric blue stripes with light brown roots. She was another street person with a dirty shirt and skin that looked dried and wrinkled beyond her age.

"I don't have much," I said. But I pulled out an orange and handed it to her.

"Bless you," she said and ran down the street before the man next to me could grab it from her.

"Now why did you do that?" he said. "What else is in there? I love oranges."

"Nothing," I said and grabbed my backpack. He'd frightened me. I ran for two blocks. But the effort made me realize how hungry I was. I began to regret giving away what had been mine because it left me at risk.

In the distance, I saw a small park where I could sit down. I watched the crowds pass each other on the street. They reminded me of those dark figures I'd seen in the arc María had traced in the blue sky. Each was a separate being totally unaware of anyone else, except when they got in the way. Some waved the other on. But there were those who swore under their breath or out loud at those who had cut them off. They seemed almost mechanical. *This is a cruel place*, I thought. *Why are people fighting over such little things? Don't they realize how much they have?*

I was getting depressed and wondered what had happened to the City of Light. Why had I been transported from the cave into another dire situation? Could I dream my way back? While I was sorting all of this out someone sat next to me on the park bench. It was the man who had taken my power bar.

"I don't have anything else I can give you," I told him. "I don't have money like those people out there."

"Oh, I didn't come to take anything else," he said. "I actually came to thank you, and say I'm sorry. After you left I realized you didn't make me beg. You came to me on your own. I'm just wondering why you did that, especially since you're homeless, too."

I was relieved and less fearful of him after that because he sounded sincere. I looked into his face and saw a mix of emotions there: desperation, hurt, and gratitude. I felt like I was beginning to understand those emotions more with each hour in the cave. "I did that because I saw all those people ignoring you. It made me angry, because they have so much and they didn't even look at you. I was afraid you might grab a purse or hurt someone and that would get you into even more trouble," I explained.

"Even more trouble," he laughed. "Could jail be worse than this? At least they'd feed me there."

"How did this happen to you?" I whispered.

He was silent for a moment and looked across the park toward a row of hedges that formed a barrier between those who rushed along the sidewalk and us. "I'm not sure myself," he said. "I was educated, had a trade. But my job got taken from me and given to another person willing to work for a lot less over in Asia. My unemployment was over before anything else could bail me out and the debts started piling up. My kids were out of the house by then, but we didn't get along. They don't talk to me anymore. I was even getting abusive to my wife, so she left me and moved in with a man who had his own business fixing cars. I lost the house, too. It's all gone now, everything I ever had." A tear silently made a path down his right cheek. When he blinked another cascaded down his left. "You've shown me the first kindness I've known in a long time on these streets," he said. "Sorry if I got greedy. But I'm hungry and that makes a person more like an animal. I don't want to be like that."

I was moved by his story, which rang true to me. I'd been scammed out of money before on the streets of Chicago, but this was no scam.

"How long have you been out here?" I asked.

"Too long," he said. "Maybe a couple years. I go to the shelters and I get work sometimes. But none of it lasts. I keep coming back to the street."

"How does it make you feel when you see those people walking past you?"

"Angry. There but for the grace of God. They could be where I am. But they don't get that. They think they're above my misery. But nobody is. We all live fragile lives. But for a few it's more obvious, like me," he said with his hand on his chest. "But what's your story?" he asked. "You're still young. With a little clean-up you'd probably be a pretty girl. What happened to you?"

"Well, that's a strange story and I'm not sure I could even explain it," I said, "but I appreciate your asking. I'm hoping this is a temporary situation I've found myself in. If it's permanent, I'm in big trouble," I confided.

"Welcome to my world," he laughed dryly. "It's one strange story after another." He looked toward the people beyond the hedges.

Then I got to thinking about the City of Light and the idea of the spiritual plain intersecting with the earthly one. So I asked him a pointed question. "Are you a spiritual person? Do you believe in God? In redemption?"

"God? Well, I thought I did. But he forgot about me a long time ago."

"Not necessarily," I said. "A new friend of mine wrote a poem about how God is in the moonlight on the darkest nights one can imagine. Maybe God is nearer to you than you think."

"Is that right? So why has God been hiding from me? Haven't felt his presence in a mighty long time," the man said hanging his head. "Are you a Jehovah's Witness or something?" he asked me suspiciously.

"Oh no. I'm not recruiting. Just putting that thought into your consciousness. You look like a man who could use a good dose of hope right now."

"And a good dose of luck," he snorted.

I had a thought. "Let's see how lucky we both are," I said as I unzipped my backpack and looked inside. There wasn't any more food than there had been before. I dug deeper hoping to find a hidden treasure I'd missed. Then I felt a piece of paper. I pulled out a pink envelope with my name on it. I opened it and found Dar's poem about the moonlight. Perfect timing! I put it back in the envelope and handed it to the homeless man.

"I was hoping for more food," I said. "But this is food for thought. It's the poem I told you about. Please keep it. I know you don't have much faith right now, but keep reading this. It'll help." After a poem saved Max from his depression, I thought it was worth trying again.

The homeless man took the envelope and read the name on the front. "How did you know my name was Edgar?" he asked, incredulous. I looked at the envelope and the writing had changed from my name to his. *You never know what might happen in a dream*, I thought.

"What's inside?" I asked, thinking the contents might have changed, too. It was Dar's poem, as I'd said it was, but there was something else tucked in there. It fell out as he unfolded the paper. It looked like the want ads cut from a newspaper with circles around a few of the entries. He silently read the ads and began to smile.

"This has today's date on it," he said. "There are three ads here for jobs I can do. But I need change to make the calls. And if I get an interview I need money to buy clothes at the thrift store or the shelter. Wait a minute. I think there's something else in here."

I heard the rattle of change and saw the green flash of a twenty-dollar bill!

"Oh my God! It's the money and the change," he cried, and then hesitated. He was very intense and focused.

"This is a turning point," he said. "Normally I might go down to a bar and drown my sorrows. But this, well this is …" He was speechless and I saw more tears coming now. Then he looked at me as if I were from Mars.

"I don't know who you are," he said, "but I'm going to consider you my guardian angel." He leaned over and gave me a quick hug. "I've got to make these calls before I miss this chance," he smiled. "Thanks for the hope, and the food. Bless you!"

He ran back into the crowd clutching the envelope. And the constantly moving crowd turned dark until they became silhouettes once again, while Edgar stood out from the crowd filled with sunlight and blue sky.

"Michelle. Michelle, look over here," I heard María say in a whisper. Once again I was transported to the City of Light where she sat on the bench across from me.

"Welcome back," she smiled.
"It's mighty good to be back," I sighed with relief.

22

The group arrived at Fernán's house in two cars. Reggie was going to pick up Sunny, but his plans had changed completely once Michelle's presence in the cave was confirmed. He and Dar knew Flor, Fernán's intuitive grandmother, would be home and could use her skills to connect with Michelle in the cave. Dar carefully protected the fresh, brown eggs she'd just gathered as extra insurance to gain Flor's willingness. She knew Flor fancied them. The Australian had learned the trick of raising contented chickens from her grandmother. She sang to them, picked them up and petted them, called them by name, which resulted in happy hens and quality eggs. Lots of them.

"Buenas tardes, Fernán," Reggie began and continued the conversation in Spanish. "Has Sunny been behaving herself?"

"Oh yes. There are days she feels like my own," he smiled. "Have you brought your guests today? Are they interested in my pots?"

"I'm sure they will be. But first they have a lot on their minds. Their friend is in the cave and they're very concerned about her. I wondered if Flor could tell them about how she's doing. What do you think? Dar brought her a gift of our eggs," he smiled.

"She loves your eggs. I'm sure we can work something out with her. Let me go first and talk to her." Dar gently handed the egg carton to him.

"Sunny," Fernán called in Spanish, "your family and their guests are here." The girls were having a make-believe tea party in the shade with tiny clay cups Carlita had made for her doll. She'd learned about the custom from Sunny, who smiled and asked if the group wanted to join them. But when she saw Juan she ran over to give him a hug.

"Buenas tardes, Sunny. So you're becoming a potter, too," he laughed, speaking in English. "Will you make one for me?"

"Señor Juan! Buenas tardes. I'm still drawing, too, but if you want a pot I can make one for you. I have to finish Dad's pot first. Can you wait for it?" Sunny asked.

"Oh, that's fine. I'm not in a hurry. But I hear your workmanship is very good, so I want to encourage you to make more of them," he smiled, while lifting her in the air, which made her giggle.

While they waited for Fernán to return, Dar introduced her guests. They recognized Sunny from the portrait in the dining room. Maggie observed this little girl with the marvelous brown hair and blue eyes as she interacted with Juan. What was it like to grow up in Teotenaca? She wondered if this place was all the girl had ever known.

Once introduced to Maggie, Max, and Angel, Sunny freely talked to them about Michelle. "Your friend likes to draw," she said, exuding enthusiasm for the quality of Michelle's sketches. "She stayed out a long time the day she came. Dad said he thought she might fill her sketchbook while she was here. But then she went in the cave. It's too dark to draw in there. But she'll draw a *lot* when she gets out."

"Do you like to draw, Sunny?" Maggie asked.

"Yes. Do you?" she asked back.

"No. I don't have the talent for it. But I do like to dance," she smiled.

"Dance? What kind of dance?" Sunny asked with genuine curiosity.

"Flamenco. It's a Spanish dance. Have you ever seen it?"

"I don't think so. What's it like?" Sunny asked, her head leaning to the right.

"The women stomp their feet and clap their hands. They wear long skirts and move their arms and hands. The gypsies were the first to do it." Sunny looked either confused or intrigued. Maggie couldn't tell which.

"Can you show me?" she smiled.

"Sure. But first we have to find out more about Michelle and how she's doing in the cave."

Reggie and Dar were relieved when Fernán came back nodding and smiling. "She will see you all in a few minutes. She wanted to change her clothing," he said in Spanish. "I think the eggs helped," he nodded to Dar.

"Wonderful," Reggie laughed. "Flor will see us," he told Michelle's friends, changing to English.

They milled around the yard for a while and then Fernán led them to a small room. As they entered they were enveloped by the smell of *copal*, an ancient incense. The trail of smoke came from a family altar behind Flor where candles, photos, a doll, a man's hat and other mementos were displayed. Resting on the wall behind the altar were a heavily painted crucifix, portraits of Jesus and Our Lady of Guadalupe, and a carved and painted mask of a pre-Columbian god. A tall beeswax candle burned on a simple wooden table in front of her. Flor's white hair was bound with yellow ribbon into a neat braided bun. She wore an intricately embroidered blouse and sat in front of a rough, green wall. Though her skin was wrinkled, her eyes were alert, playful and friendly. She was welcoming and hospitable on one hand, yet maintained a formal demeanor. Despite her humble surroundings, she was the embodiment of dignity. Michelle's friends sensed this as they stood quietly awaiting the next step in this unfamiliar process. Fernán directed everyone to sit on the wooden benches and chairs that surrounded the table on three sides.

Flor spoke no English and her Spanish was peppered with words from her native dialect. Reggie translated her Spanish while Fernán quickly translated the indigenous words for Reggie. Even Angel needed Fernán's intervention to understand her at times. But before they began, Reggie gave the group a little background.

"Flor has lived in this area her entire life. She entered the cave in her youth often, and alone, which is unusual for women of her generation. That experience has affected her intuition. She can answer almost any question you throw at her, including what's happening to Michelle in the cave," he explained.

"So she's a psychic," Maggie said. "Does she need an article of clothing or anything? I've heard they work that way sometimes."

"Not really," Reggie said. "Prepare to be totally amazed." He smiled and winked at his wife who responded in kind. At the same time, Max rolled his eyes at Maggie who stared back, shook her head slightly, and smiled just enough to divert Max's negative influence. Angel looked around the room, attempting to preserve this experience in his scholar's memory, as Reggie began the questioning.

"We are seeking information on Michelle Hardtke who is in the cave. She is our guest, the woman you gave the vase to at the market. She went in yesterday afternoon. What can you tell us, Flor?"

The older woman nodded in recognition of who was in the cave, then bent her head, closed her eyes and chanted an ancient prayer. She stared into the candle's flame and breathed deeply of the incense. "She dreams often in the cave." She spoke slowly so her translators could follow. "Time is not relevant. Day and night have no meaning for her now. She thinks of her friends and of the world outside El Anhelo. She longs to be with them, but then the dreams pull her away into another world. Her imagination is very strong and grows even stronger with each dream. She is gaining understanding, even as her physical strength has weakened slightly."

"What's happened to her?" Maggie asked with concern. "Is she hungry?" Her words were quickly translated for Flor to answer.

"She has fallen and sustained minor injury," Flor reported. "But she is healing quickly."

"Where is she in the cave?" Reggie asked.

"She has been in several places. She first came to the dome. After that she could not find her way back to the place where she entered, but later she did find it. She could not leave, of course. She has found the waterfall and pool. And she has seen the room with the crystal walls," Flor answered.

"What is her emotional state?" Maggie asked. Reggie translated.

"It varies," Flor began. "She is frightened in her waking times, yet more at peace than she thinks she should be. She feels she could die in the cave if she cannot find a way out or if she has nothing more to eat. Yet the dreams give her hope. More and more she believes them to be true."

But Max wasn't convinced. "How can she dream if she only has hard rock for a bed and a pillow?" he asked.

Flor sensed his cynicism as his words were translated into Spanish. "When one is weary, one can sleep anywhere," she told him. Then she moved her attention from the candle to Max and smiled. "You do not believe me," she said. "That is your choice." She decided to give him a sign of her ability and sincerity. "Señor, you have traveled to many places, but have never known any like this one." She continued smiling as she spoke. "You travel to escape from a bad memory, from the pain of loss, and from the feeling that gnaws at your heart. You are not guilty of a loved one's death. You must let go of this guilt or you will not be able to go forward in your life. No matter how far you travel, you cannot move into a loving place until you realize this tragic loss could not be prevented. You must let this memory go. You cannot change what has passed." Her voice was tender and calming. But her words were as powerful as thunder to Max's ears. He was silent now and Maggie sensed a withdrawal into his own painful memories.

Then Flor turned to Maggie. "You are a healer, señorita. Your hands and your heart are powerful tools." She got up from the hard chair and walked over, reached out and folded Maggie's right hand into both of hers, held it for a moment, then let go. "Dancing is a way of channeling your passion for life and for your own need to express your emotions," she said. "You suppress your feelings because of others' needs. But your own must also be met, or you will suffer and grow weaker. And you do suffer in ways no one else sees. You have great love to give if a man will only open his eyes, his mind, and his heart to the riches you have to offer him."

As she said, "to offer him," Flor nodded in Max's direction to indicate she had someone specific in mind. Maggie could feel her face redden, though no one else noticed. Max's thoughts were fragmented between realizing the truth of Flor's words about his life and what she was saying to Maggie. His gaze connected with Flor's as she nodded to him, and then he looked toward Maggie. She wouldn't look at him at first, even as she felt his eyes on her. But when she did there was something different in his expression. He began to smile for the first time since they'd discovered Michelle was missing. Flor spoke words of encouragement to them. "Each of you can be a gift to the other," she said. "Together you can balance both pain and joy."

Maggie smiled back at Max who said, "I think we'd better have a little chat after this."

She just replied, "Uh huh," almost silently.

Angel thought of himself only as an observer to this proceeding, so he was caught off guard when Flor addressed him. Oddly, this time he understood the ancient words before Fernán translated them.

"You are looking for the divine, the Creator of all. You look in many places, many faiths. But you are not convinced. You think too much," she laughed. "It will be hard for you not to analyze things because it is a habit for you. But turn your attention to what you feel. Truth lies there. Listen more to your heart. You often deny what you feel because it has no place in your mind. You will find what you seek within yourself if you truly listen to your heart, to the inner voice that speaks this truth. And you will hear other words spoken by a friend who has been touched by the divine. Maybe then you will be convinced." She smiled enigmatically and left Angel wondering, and analyzing, her words.

Reggie and Darlene smiled to each other, feeling affirmed in their belief in Flor's intuitive abilities. Then she turned her attention to them. "You bring great faith with you," she said. "And your love for one another only grows stronger."

Sunny smiled as she sensed her parents' joy.

"And you, young one," Flor said to the girl. "You are already blessed with dreams almost as strong as mine. You will know, a dream will tell you, when the woman in the cave will be released. You may even be told where she will walk out of the mountain. When you wake up, share with your parents what the next dream tells you."

Sunny responded by talking directly to Flor in Spanish. "How is Michelle now?" she asked. "What is happening to her?"

Flor looked back into the flame and took several deep breaths. "She is asleep, but will soon awaken. When she does she will realize that she is not alone," Flor said. The response to her translated words was a collective gasp.

"Who else is in the cave?" Reggie asked.

She only smiled playfully and said, "Ask your daughter. She is wise and needs practice."

He looked at Sunny who seemed preoccupied with her own thoughts. She said one word as if it were a question. "Gardenia?" she said with a Spanish pronunciation.

Flor smiled and turned to her. "Sí, gardenia."

To Dar she said, "Thank you for the gracious gift of your eggs, Señora," then nodded to everyone. The session ended as Flor blew out the candle.

23

As I began waking up, I realized the night had been filled with dreams. Now I had a response to Sunny's question about remembering them and wanted to share them with her at breakfast. In fact, my imagination had cracked wide open with vivid colors and the most amazing cast of characters. I didn't see Angel in any of the dreams that night, but it was still comforting to hear his voice calling me from a great distance in one of them.

On the other hand, right before I opened my eyes, I had a repeat of the nightmare I had on the plane heading for Mexico City. This time the dream began at the point where I noticed light shining through the hole in a dark wall. Once again the wall crumbled and light flooded the bleak space where I was trapped. Again, I fell to the floor as the wall gave way and a mysterious figure approached. I saw more of "it" this time, but I still couldn't tell what it was. Its shape was distorted by dust mixing with the blinding light. In this latest version of the dream, the figure walked through the dust with a normal looking hand extended toward me, palm up. Instead of frightening me, the dream had a positive message. I was fixated on that hand. Someone was reaching out in a gesture of help, not in a threatening way at all.

I thought of my three friends and missed them terribly, and was glad I'd be seeing them soon. Then I smelled the gardenia's faint scent coming from a corner of the bedroom. *When will I hear Rudolfo crow?* I wondered. It seemed like the longest night I'd ever known, filled with emotions and extraordinary dreams, which I recalled in great detail. Slowly I opened my eyes. A faint light shimmered around me. But the next sense I had was pain in my back. I must have slept in the same place all night. The mattress had been comfortable when I first settled into it. I couldn't imagine why it felt so hard now. In fact, it had absolutely no give at all. Stiffly I raised myself and felt around. I was surprised because my hands weren't resting on a quilt, but on a thin blanket. And the mattress felt as solid as stone. My pillow wasn't filled with soft down, I realized with a start, because it was really my backpack, thinner now that much of the food in it had been eaten.

No. *No!* I didn't want to believe that the cave hadn't been a dream, too! I was disoriented when I realized where I was. But why did I smell gardenia? And why was there so much light around me, if I was still in the cave?

I turned my aching neck to survey my surroundings. The candles along the ledge near the bench where I'd slept were lit. *But by whom?* Standing up, I looked closer in disbelief. Sitting in front of the row of uneven candles was a white paper napkin with a large red apple placed upright in its center! My stomach growled in recognition. I touched the round fruit hoping it wasn't a delusion my hunger had conjured up. It felt like an apple, firm and cold in my hand. I brought it to my mouth and opened my stiff jaw. The apple's juice ran down my dry lips as I took the first bite and caught its sweet stream with my tongue. I'd never tasted an apple as wonderful as this one. With heightened awareness, I savored the texture of its skin, its pulp, its exquisite flavor, even the hard surface of its seeds. I was so hungry I devoured all of it but the stem, which I twirled between my fingers.

As I set the stem down on the napkin I saw there was another smaller candle burning in front of the larger white ones. Sniffing the air above it I realized it was releasing the scent of gardenia. I looked around, but saw no one. Then I remembered the place that could have been a balcony behind the waterfall and looked there. "Hello," I called in a raspy voice. I cleared my throat "Hello. Thank you for the apple. Would you have another one?"

At first there was no response. But then a shuffling sound came from nearby, not above me on the balcony, but to my right from the entrance to the room where I stood. I saw the beam of a flashlight come through first, but no one spoke. "Who are you?" I called, not knowing what kind of reply I would get. Maybe I should have asked in Spanish. But then the answer came.

"A friend," a male voice finally replied in English. I watched as the flashlight beam grew larger and then saw a figure in a white jacket enter the space. He looked like a ghost floating into the room to greet me. What do you say to a ghost?

"I didn't wish to startle you." His soft voice echoed against the cave walls. "My name is Father Moran. You must be Michelle." He was real, thank God! Was he from a search party? How else would he know my name?

"Yes," I replied. "I'm Michelle Hardtke. Are you here to lead me out of this cave? You must be. Please!"

"I haven't the ability to do that, I'm afraid. But I can help to prepare you before you leave."

"Is that why you're here? To help me?" This wasn't making sense. Despite my relief of being discovered, I felt a wave of panic shiver through me.

He laughed. "Well, if I can, I will. But I was told in a dream that you would be here to help *me*. It doesn't sound as if you had a dream about that, or did you?"

"No. What do *you* need help with?" I asked. My questions kept leading to more questions. Was this encounter just another dream?

"I'm here for a retreat," he said. "This year I was chosen to be the first to arrive, to put things in order before the others come," he said.

"Others?" I asked incredulously.

"Yes. There are twelve of us. It's highly unusual that you are here at the same time I am. Normally two of the participants enter together. At the inn I heard that more pilgrims were being summoned here in these difficult times. It must be true since you were chosen for the task."

"Pardon me, Father, but would you have another apple to spare?" I asked again. "I'm sorry, but I'm really hungry and I don't have much food with me."

"We could break bread together," he offered. "Do you like Irish soda bread?"

"Does it matter?" I laughed at the absurdity of his question.

"Perhaps not. But you will, I think. I'm warming up water for tea right now. Follow me," he said after blowing out all but one candle on the ledge. I couldn't believe my good fortune! I grabbed my backpack and blanket and followed close behind him with my flashlight.

"But how can you be making tea?"

"As I said, I'm here to prepare the way for the others. That includes setting up the kitchen."

"A kitchen? In a cave?"

"We have a loo, too," he said. I'd heard that term before.

"A bathroom? No!" I said in disbelief.

"Well, the latrine is a very deep hole with a seat on top of it," he explained. "That's why I brought the scented candle, for that little room. We throw lye down the hole. Still, it's not pleasant in there. But then I thought you might like to wake up to the smell of gardenia. Was it comforting for you?"

"I left a gardenia in a bouquet back at the Sweet Dreams Bed & Breakfast and I thought I was back there for a moment. I woke up thinking this cave had been just another dream." Oh, how I wished it had been!

"Not to worry. You'll be back there in due time," he consoled me. "No one has met their end in the Cave of Dreams, from what I've been told." And I didn't want to be the first!

"Cave of Dreams. That's what I heard it called in one of my dreams. So that's what it really is called?"

"Indeed. And the name certainly fits, as I'm sure you know by now," he said. Maybe it was the reference to dreams and sleep that made me take a deep yawn at that point. Or maybe it was the calming quality of his voice.

We walked into the adjoining tunnel and through another opening. I followed him into an area I hadn't explored yet. It wasn't far from the waterfall room, as it turned out. "This is the kitchen," he announced as we approached a hanging cloth. "It's quite rustic, of course." He pulled the curtain aside and I heard a whistling sound as we entered a long, almost rectangular room. The water was boiling in a metal teakettle, which sat on top of a camp stove against a far wall. The smells of burning propane and kerosene weren't pleasant, either. Besides the camp stove, there was a battery-operated light, a kerosene lamp and a few candles on shelves lining two walls. This was the most light and heat I'd known since I'd been in the cave. A long table and a couple of old wooden chairs filled the space to the right.

With a potholder, Father Moran lifted the kettle and poured the boiling water into a white teapot on a makeshift counter. The light that flickered in the kitchen illuminated his white jacket making it easy to follow his steps as he cut the Irish soda bread and brought it to the table. The plates were paper, and the cups were thicker paper with handles that came off from the side of each cup. He brought the teapot to the table and set it next to a lamp, then gestured for me to sit.

"Despite the fact that the openings to this cave keep disappearing, it's well ventilated in here. That's a blessing when you need to light a fire," he explained. "Otherwise, the flames might suck away the oxygen. Oh, one more thing," he said and returned with an apple. He placed one half on my plate, bowed his head for a moment of prayer, then poured the tea. When I saw his hand it reminded me of the hand in my recurring dream. He was here to help me, no matter what he said.

"No milk or sugar, I'm afraid."

"That's no problem. Plain tea is just fine," I said as I gratefully sipped the hot liquid. "I can't tell you how glad I am to see another flesh and blood person in here!"

"Well, company lifts my spirits, too, I must admit," he said. He spoke with an accent.

"Are you Irish, Father Moran?"

"That I am, from Dublin. And you're American? Midwestern, perhaps?" he asked.

"Yes. I'm from Chicago. We've both come a long way to meet in this odd place. How did you get in?" I asked. "And how will we get out?"

"I entered in my usual way," he said. "I had a dream and it told me where I would find the way in. This is my third time here, but I'm always directed to a different entrance."

The tea's warmth trickled down inside me as I devoured the slice of bread. And like the apple, it was the most exquisite bread I could remember. It had caraway seeds and raisins and a crispy exterior. "I guess that soda bread agrees with you then," he chuckled. I was embarrassed. I had only crumbs left on the plate while he had half a slice to finish.

"I've forgotten my manners," I apologized. "It was very good. Thank you, Father."

"Good. Now, if you drink more tea it will affect the bread like water to a sponge. Your stomach will feel satisfied, perhaps for the first time since you arrived," he advised.

"Have I taken too much of your food? Will you have enough for yourself while you're here?"

"It's quite all right," he said. "I wouldn't let you suffer knowing I can help you. Besides, during the retreat we don't eat much in the morning. It helps us to focus on prayer and meditation. I think it influences the dreams as well. At supper we share our food and reflect on our experiences here, as well as our different lives."

I had so many questions for the poor man that I was afraid he'd have second thoughts about enduring my company. But I had to ask them because the whole situation was so surreal. "Why do you come here?" I asked. "And how do you get out?"

"Perhaps I should start with your second question," he smiled. "You sound a bit anxious about getting out of the cave, which is understandable. Always, when it has been time for me to leave I've had a dream indicating where to find the way out. It's usually close to where I'm resting so I don't have far to go. I'm sure it will be the same for you, as well as for me and the others."

"How much longer will it be before 'the others' come?"

"A couple of days at the most. But there's a lot to be done before that. With your help it will take less time to accomplish my tasks. And we can keep each other company until they arrive."

"And once I'm no longer needed, perhaps I'll be let out. What do you think?" I asked, hoping I was right.

"That seems highly likely. And how is your friend Angel, by the way? I thought he might be here, too."

"You dreamt about Angel, too?"

"Yes. Perhaps he was meant as my back-up helper if you decided not to enter. Is he a good friend?"

"He is. But we traveled separately. He's probably in the area by now and is wondering what's become of me. I left a note just outside the cave. I hope they find it."

"Hmmm. They may find the note, but the entrance will be impossible to see."

"I couldn't see it when I got back to where I'd come in. I'd left a piece of paper inside the cave to mark the entrance. But the wall was solid. I couldn't believe it! That's why I'm still here," I explained.

"I can assure you that you wouldn't have found an opening once you came inside the cave. We all have to wait to be released." He said it so matter-of-factly I wanted to scream! I was truly the victim of an unseen force.

"But who's in charge here? Are there vision-inducing vapors coming from the ceiling? Mind-altering drugs in the water? Someone behind another curtain controlling openings in the wall? *What's going on in here, Father?*" I was experiencing a wave of disorientation again, followed by panic.

"None of the above," he said with great calm in his voice, trying to diffuse my emotional state. "As you continue to dream it will make more sense to you. Just remember not to be afraid. You're not here to be hurt, but to gain knowledge."

Before I could ask another question of him he asked one of me. "You are in the heart of El Anhelo, in the heart of the mountain that is called 'Longing.' So tell me, what is it you long for, Michelle?" His voice was gentle, reassuring. Hadn't Reggie asked me this same question? But in the meantime, everything had changed.

"I long for food, warmth, clean clothes, the necessities of living."

"Of course. This place brings one down to the level of basic survival. It has let you see how important those things are when you don't have them. But beyond the basics, what else do you long for?" he asked again.

The conversation seemed absurd, given the circumstances, but he was my one hope so I answered again. "I feel so removed from my life in here. I long for my friends, who don't know where I am. I want them to know I'm all right, for now. And being inside here, I long to get out. I miss the sunlight."

"And what else? Remember what you left behind," he prodded.

I couldn't hold back. He was stirring things up too much. "You want more?" I asked, hearing the anxiety in my own voice. "You're getting into personal territory, Father Moran. Truthfully," I sighed, "I long to be loved again. My boyfriend and I broke up recently. It's been tough. He was weighing heavily on my mind right before I came to Teotenaca. But now," I suddenly realized, "since I've been in here, I haven't even thought about him. How odd! But like I said, I feel very removed from my life back home right now."

He nodded in understanding. "The dreams take you to another realm, one that is familiar and yet strange and unknown. It's partially generated by your own imagination, as all dreams are, and what you long for. But there's much more at work. The dream plain has its own reality, its own direction of what you will experience there. You may have come here on vacation, but you will travel to many places beyond Teotenaca and this cave before you leave. It will change you as it does all who enter here." This was an echo of what Reggie had told me, too. I would leave a different person than when I arrived. Perhaps I was outgrowing my skin, as Flor, the woman in the market, had said I would. But how? And why *me*?

"Father Moran, I'm confused," I began. "You know why you're here, and I'm very curious about your retreat, but do you know why *I'm* here? I came to hike and sketch in the countryside and be on vacation with my friends. I had no idea I would be confined to a cave. That wasn't *my* idea. I'm kicking myself for walking in here, as a matter of fact. It's as if it was a trap set for me and I fell right into it." I remembered trying to walk away, but the cave had drawn me in with its mysterious force. "But at the same time, my dreams are so amazing. My host at the B & B said I was feeling the 'draw of the mountain,' but he never mentioned a cave. He must have known. Can you help me sort this out?"

He sipped his tea and smiled. He had short dark hair and a kindly face with a wide mouth. A shadow fell across a scar on his left cheek. His eyes were hard to see as the light's reflection danced on the lenses of his wire-rimmed glasses. He spoke in an animated way as he told me about his own encounter with the Cave of Dreams.

"Oh, I was quite confused myself the first time I came here. But I wasn't alone like you," he explained. "I was traveling with two other priests. We'd gone to the shrine of Our Lady of Guadalupe on a pilgrimage, but we wanted to see other grand churches in Mexico, too. We'd come a long way after all. So we went to the city of Oaxaca and attended mass in the cathedral of Santo Domingo. We were to stay only a few days there, but one morning we discovered that we all had the same marvelous dream. It was about an ancient, sacred place with a large natural dome to be found in a small village called Santa María Teotenaca. We asked the hotel clerk if such a village existed and he said it did. We made our way here and stayed at the inn. They said the dome was in the cave. But they didn't tell us we would be 'in the cave' for several days. They packed us a very large 'picnic' lunch, gave us each a blanket and told us to follow the trail along the edge of this mountain. They weren't clear about the cave's entrance, of course. 'Just keep walking and you will find it,' they said. We did and cautiously entered with flashlights, which they'd provided. We found candles, matches, and batteries, wrapped in a cloth napkin inside the basket. We went to the dome, prayed there for some time, and then decided to leave. But we couldn't find our way out again. We prayed very hard that night and finally fell asleep and had more dreams, all different this time, but we each learned we were in the Cave of Dreams. That time was extraordinary!" he said, becoming more animated. "My faith expanded here. My mind and heart became more aware of the good I could do, things I'd never thought of before."

He related all this with great passion, then continued his narrative. "After three days, we all dreamed we would leave. Upon waking we felt pulled to a different place to exit than the one where we had entered. The inn had been in touch with Father Hernandez from the local church and we talked with him upon our return. He was in this cave before he'd even thought to become a priest. You should talk to him, too, when you leave. He mentioned that a variety of religious come every year and it was possible we'd be back. Two years later, the dreams did call me again and I met the others as they arrived at the inn. We came into the cave as a large group. And here I am yet again, a third time. Circumstances aligned so I was able to come. It's a great blessing."

I thought of Angel. Would he call this a cult or a secret society? And I thought of all the secular people who lived in the area around the cave. Was there a connection between the spiritual urge of the cleric and the creative urge of the artist? The answer was becoming more obvious to me. I thought of Dar's poem about finding God in dark places and Reggie's paintings, which glorified the natural world.

"But why do you think *I'm* so blessed?" I asked him.

"You've been summoned and you'll leave with a purpose to follow, though it may not be apparent for a time. Are you a spiritual person, Michelle?"

I wasn't sure I knew the answer to that. "I was raised Catholic, but I haven't been to church in a while. But when I'm sketching or painting there are times I feel connected to something bigger than myself. I mean, how else am I capable of doing my best work with such little effort? It's like I'm channeling another, better artist. Kandinsky wrote about a spiritual connection in the creative process. Ever since I've been in this town, and now the cave, I've had an insatiable urge to either draw or dream."

"Artists are often called to the Cave of Dreams. You should have boundless creativity when you leave," he predicted. I hoped he was right!

"What about the purpose of why I may have been 'called'? Is the 'boundless creativity' part of that, do you think?" It all still seemed preposterous to me, but I was trying to follow the logic of it.

"That will become clearer in time. Just keep dreaming and drawing," he advised me with a gentle, yet enthusiastic, voice.

My next urge was a natural, rather than a supernatural, one. "Excuse me for changing the subject, but could you show me to the loo, Father Moran?"

"Follow me," he said. "We don't have soap and water in there, so this time I brought a marvelous antibacterial lotion along. I'll let you try it out." I followed close behind him on my way to the so-called "loo," grateful that such a place existed in the cave, but praying there might be toilet paper, too.

24

Angel sat on the veranda writing down his thoughts and impressions of the session with Flor. He had researched tribal seers, *curanderas*, and conjurers before, as well as Christian mystics and New Age psychics. But none compared to Flor. She connected with everything that was asked, thought, or even forgotten. There was no fanfare, no demands on their pocketbooks, no smoke and mirrors. Her only prop was a single candle in a rustic setting. Hers was a commanding, yet generous, presence as she sat before the icons of both Christian and pre-Columbian deities.

After their session, he'd viewed Flor's family pottery studio and work. It was an opportunity to show their appreciation for the reading, yet Angel found the black clay pots fascinating. He was drawn to two, in particular, and bought both, one by Flor and the other by Fernán. The traditional symbols of Teotenaca decorated them, but their exquisite craftsmanship took them to a higher level. Both were deep bowls with smooth surfaces. They had been incised with intricate patterns of repeating bat shapes on one and fish shapes on the other. They were meticulously done so the rows of intersecting shapes fit perfectly together without extra space between them. Fernán explained that this was a skill handed down through the family. Before the visitors left, Fernán discussed the symbols with Angel and explained how both the bat and the fish were connected to the cave in El Anhelo.

But Angel hadn't forgotten Michelle in all this. One reason to write down his memory of the session with Flor was to see if anything had been said about his missing friend that had slipped by them all. He wanted to talk with Maggie and Max, too, but he hadn't seen them since they'd gotten back to the B & B. He wasn't surprised. It was time they openly discovered their feelings for one another. Certainly Flor had revealed the truth that was hidden in both their hearts. Angel imagined them walking on the trail or sitting in the grove where the wind chimes played in the breeze.

It was quiet where he sat. Juan and Reggie were in the studio, Darlene was gardening, and Sunny swung from an old tire that hung from a handmade wooden swing set in the yard. He could hear the rope twist and looked up to see the slight bend of the top bar as the tire flew back and forth. With all the attention on Michelle's crisis, he had barely noticed the girl. Now he watched her swing as high as she could, a tiny human being who should have seemed out of place in Mexico, but who fit right into it. She sang, even as she propelled herself at top speed. He picked out a few words in Spanish, then recognized the melody. It reminded him of a song he knew as a young boy, a lullaby his grandmother had sung to him and his younger sister. The memory touched a nostalgic nerve.

He tried to go back to writing, but the girl distracted him. Or perhaps it was more of an attraction, because it drew him out of the veranda and into the yard. There were chairs behind the house on a small red brick patio and he sat in the one nearest the swing. His arrival there got Sunny's attention, too. It wasn't long before she slowed the swing to a stop and crawled out to see what he was doing.

"G' day. Isn't your name Angel?" she asked.

"Buenos días, Sunny. Yes, it is."

Her eyes got big. "I know someone else named Angel and he could be a real angel. He's very kind. You aren't an angel, are you?" she inquired.

"Not by a long shot," he laughed. "But that *is* my name. My grandparents were from Mexico, but further west and north of here. Tell me, Sunny, do you like it here in the mountains, and in Mexico?"

"What do you mean?" she asked.

"You're from Australia. Do you miss it?"

"I haven't been there in a while. I missed here when I was there," she answered. "This is where I belong."

He switched to Spanish to see how well she spoke it. "¿Cómo estás tu español?"

"Muy bien," she replied, with no hint of an Aussie accent. As she said, she spoke the language well.

"¿Qué te gusto mucho?" he asked. What did she like?

"Muchas cosas." As she became more thoughtful she switched to English. In answering his question, she had no end of favorite things. "I like to draw like Dad, and I like to make pots with Fernán and Carlita. I like the animals we have, so I like to feed them and pet them. Oh, but my most favorite thing is when I dream. My dreams are beautiful," she softly sighed as if remembering a particular one.

"What makes them beautiful?" he asked, bemused.

She looked at him silently, her head bent at a quizzical angle and asked, "Aren't your dreams beautiful?"

He hesitated, trying to recall if he'd had a "beautiful" dream. There was one. "They're usually blurry memories. But I do remember one I had when we were in Oaxaca city. Maybe it was a beautiful dream. I was walking through a forest and a large parrot landed on a tree near where I stood. He was talking instead of singing."

"What did he say? Was he talking to you?" she interrupted.

"Yes. He called my name and said, 'Angel, why are you walking through my forest? Did someone send you?' I was very surprised at first, but I *had* been sent there by a man who told me I'd find a beautiful waterfall on the other side of the forest. He said I must go there to see it. So I was on my way," he explained.

"What was the forest like?" she asked, intent on his answer.

"It was very green, but there were tropical flowers everywhere. It reminded me of a place I'd been to in Brazil. There were butterflies and birds flying around. But it was only the parrot that spoke to me."

"Then what happened?" she asked.

"The parrot told me to follow him and he would take me to the waterfall. So I did. I heard the waterfall before I saw it. It was long with a small lake at the bottom," he said, amazed that the memory was still vivid.

She smiled and looked mischievous, as if she knew a secret.

"What is it, Sunny? Do you have dreams like that?" he asked. She began to giggle.

"It's not that. Did you know there's a waterfall in the cave? Dad and Mum told me, but I think I dreamt about it once. Michelle has seen it by now. That's where Fernán saw the fish he puts on his pots. He said they don't have eyes because they don't need to see in the dark."

"That's very interesting. Do you remember what Flor said about your dreaming?" he gently reminded her.

"She wants me to dream about Michelle," she smiled and nodded.

"Yes. Can you do that tonight?" he asked, looking intently into her eyes.

"I will try. I'll think about her before I go to sleep. That always helps, you know, to think about what you want to dream before you fall asleep," she confided.

"Will you let me know what the dream tells you? I'm concerned about who is with her in the cave," he said. "You wouldn't know that, would you?"

"No. But I'll try to find out tonight. You should talk to Father Hernandez, too. He knows about people in the cave. Dad could give you a ride," she suggested.

"Thank you, Sunny. I'll talk to your dad about Father Hernandez. And I'll remind you about the dream later. Is that all right with you?" he asked.

"Yes, I'll remember, but you can still tell me, Mr. Angel," she laughed.

He talked with her a little longer and then decided to act on her suggestion about Father Hernandez. Angel had a feeling that the priest had been inside the cave, too. Visiting him seemed like a good alternative to spending time alone, even if he could get some reading done. How ironic that he was feeling left out on this vacation. With Maggie and Max off by themselves, he had only the Howard family to talk to. He was a stranger among strangers but, fortunately, they were friendly strangers. He walked to Reggie's studio and found him discussing his work with Juan. He noticed that one painting depicted a waterfall.

"Oh, hello, Angel. What can I do for you?" Reggie asked as he entered the room.

"Sorry to interrupt your conversation, Reggie, but Sunny suggested that I talk with Father Hernandez. I teach classes on comparative religions and I'd like to understand the cave and its significance from the perspective of the local spiritual leader. And I'm hoping he might know who is in the cave with Michelle. How can I talk with him?"

"Father Hernandez is quite accessible. In fact, he's probably in the confessional right now or the housekeeper can tell you where to find him. Would you like a ride to the church?" Reggie offered.

"If I could get a ride, I would be most appreciative," Angel nodded. "If you can get me there, maybe I can walk back on my own."

"We'll be eating in a couple hours. Sure you don't want to stay, Juan?" Reggie turned his attention to his Oaxaqueño friend.

"Thanks, but I should be going," he said. Then he looked around the studio and pointed to a partially completed painting on an easel and said, "Let me know when you're getting close to finishing that one. I know right where I want to hang it," Juan smiled.

"No worries. It's yours, my friend," Reggie nodded toward the painting.

The three men walked through the house and said their goodbyes to Darlene, who had an assignment for Reggie in town. "If you happen to see Raul tell him to stop by for that cheese he ordered."

"Will do."

She also handed a package of aged goat cheese to Juan to drop off at a restaurant in the city, which he was happy to take for them. Then Reggie and Juan got into their separate cars. "I wish you well, Señor Angel," Juan waved through his open window. "Your friend will be found alive and in good health. Do not worry so much." Then the car that had delivered Angel, Maggie and Max to Teotenaca drove down the mountains the way it had come.

25

Reggie drove past the inn and café, pointing out the same places of interest he had to Michelle. Angel could see the church ahead of them at the far end of the town square and wondered if it had been built over an existing pre-Columbian temple, as was often the case. It was a method used by the Spanish to transfer the sacred from the old belief system to their new one, from the ancient gods to the Christian one. The church's façade and garden were well kept up, with wooden benches near the entrance. Reggie opened the door and Angel instinctively made the sign of the cross and genuflected as they entered the last pew and sat down. Two people knelt in separate rows near the front. A young woman emerged from the confessional. As she knelt in the front row, another woman entered the confessional and closed the door.

Reggie whispered, "One more for confession and then he'll be free." They sat silently in the pew. Angel studied the church and was impressed by the richness of the carved and painted saints, the high ceiling with dark wooden arches, and the beauty of the stained glass windows. Rows of white votive candles burned along the wall near the entrance, each representing an appeal for divine intervention. The faint sparkle of a wall covered with *milagros* reflected the light of the candles.

In front of them, the altar sat on an elevated level several steps above the main floor. It was intricately carved in a darkly stained wood. Rows of saints looked down on the congregation from alcoves in the tall back wall. Angel knew they probably represented pre-Columbian gods as well, another example of overlaying two opposing faiths. High up, from a niche in the center of the wall, sat a large carving of Santa María, the Blessed Virgin, whose name had been added to the town's indigenous name by the Spanish conquerors. Like Our Lady of Guadalupe, she had dark skin. But the cross that hung below her on the wall behind the altar was larger than she was. The figure of Jesus was human-size and lifelike. His pale skin looked battered with purple bruises, scratches, and crimson ripples of blood that ran from the multiple wounds on his head, hands, feet, and chest. His head, encircled with a crown of sharp thorns, drooped to the left. But his gaze faced the congregation with eyes that were almost closed. It was clear the man represented was barely alive. Angel got a twinge of pain looking into that face. The reality of Christ's suffering was more apparent than he'd seen on any other cross, even in Mexico, where they were often brutal in appearance.

All the emotions that Angel had held back that day suddenly came forward as he looked at the huge crucifix. Surprising himself, he began to sob quietly. Reggie heard him and gently placed his arm around his shoulders, but said nothing. As he cried he realized he hadn't set foot in a Catholic church for over a year and hadn't been to confession even longer. Religions fascinated him as he tried to analyze their differences and commonalities. But he had been missing the emotional connection to his own faith for some time. When Flor told him he was searching for God, he interpreted her statement as a reference to his academic career. But now, as he sat in the worn wooden pew of this church in Teotenaca, he realized what she had meant. Would he find his faith here, in this glorious, yet humble, church?

His tears began to subside as the last penitent entered the confessional. Reggie patted his shoulder and whispered, "Are you right, Angel?"

"Yes. I'm worried about Michelle and I think looking into the face on that cross triggered my emotions," he whispered back.

"Not surprising. It's no ordinary cross, that one."

It was a couple minutes before the woman in the confessional exited and kneeled to say her penance. Shortly after, Father Hernandez realized the line had stopped and came out. Glancing around the church looking for more penitents, he noticed the two men in the back pew. Reggie nodded and smiled to him. The priest met them by the rows of burning votive candles and Reggie introduced him to Angel.

"Do you speak Spanish?" the priest whispered in slightly accented English.

"Sí, padre," Angel replied. From that point the conversation continued in Spanish.

"Perhaps we should step outside," the priest said, nodding toward the door. He was around forty years old, stocky and much shorter than Reggie. It was easy to see indigenous aspects in his facial features, yet his eyes were deep blue. Gray flecked his dark hair at the temples. He was dressed in black pants and a black shirt with a priest's collar. A colorful hand-woven stole draped around his neck. He gestured to the benches.

"So, Señor Angel, what can I do for you?" Father Hernandez asked. "You seem to be experiencing a strong emotion," he observed.

"Thank you for seeing me, Father," Angel nodded. "Yes, I have much on my mind. My friends and I only arrived in town a few hours ago. We hoped to find another friend here waiting for us, but she apparently is in the cave in El Anhelo. We have reason to believe that she isn't alone. I'm concerned about her and I'm wondering who is with her. Would you know of anyone else who has entered the cave recently?"

He smiled and nodded back. "Yes, I know who is with her. But I can't tell you who it is. It's an agreement I have. But what I can tell you is this person will take care of her and will make her feel safe. This is not anyone who would threaten or harm her. In fact, this person will probably act as a spiritual counselor to help her understand why she is there." And then he simply smiled at Angel, who was relieved, but still curious. Why couldn't the priest tell him who the other person in the cave was?

"Could it possibly be anyone else?" Angel asked.

"I suppose that's possible. But then there would be three people in the cave, not just two. I don't think that's the case," he replied. Reggie was smiling and suddenly gave a nod as if he understood who the second person in the cave was. But he said nothing.

"Is there anything else on your mind?" the priest asked Angel.

"Yes, so much, Father, but do you have time to talk?"

"I can give you more time, Angel, perhaps even an hour if you need that much. But if another penitent comes I will have to interrupt our conversation."

At that point, the church door opened. The last penitent left, smiling and nodding to them.

"Shall we go back inside?" the priest asked.

"Excuse me, but I have to get back to take care of a few chores," Reggie interrupted. "Are you all right with walking back, Angel? If not I can come back."

"I don't mind the walk," he replied, looking forward to having time to sort out his thoughts, as well as explore the town a bit on his own.

As Reggie drove back to Sweet Dreams, Angel and Father Hernandez re-entered the church. "This is a beautiful building," Angel commented.

"The craftsmanship is exquisite, especially these statues."

"Thank you. Yes, the community is active in maintaining it and that includes people who originally came from outside Teotenaca, like Reggie. The church has been here since the Spanish came, though it was seen as alien then, even a threat to the customs here," he explained. "Apparently the first priests who came told the people to stay away from the Cave of Dreams. I don't think they believed it really existed because they never found a way into it themselves. But that never stopped any of the townspeople from continuing their traditions," he smiled.

"Eventually, a priest came here who was genuinely interested in the people and in understanding their culture. His name was Father Vargas and they still talk about him. He was probably the first Catholic priest who had dreams that summoned him to the cave. And then he truly understood what a special place this is, that here we are connected to God's heart." He smiled and moved to the front of the church as Angel followed, taking a closer look at the windows and statues along the way.

"What do you think of our cross?" the priest asked, gesturing to the huge crucifix. Angel looked into the face of the Christ figure above him. The drooping lids revealed eyes that seemed to look directly into his soul.

"Reggie said this was no ordinary cross. I agree. I feel like he's looking right at me. It's unnerving!" he said of the Christ figure, but he couldn't look away.

"Our Jesús was carved by a local artisan named Bernardo Cansales. It is said he mixed his own blood with the red paint, but no one knows for sure. He was not asked to carve it. He was not commissioned to do it. But he was compelled to make this magnificent crucifix, probably through his dreams. It was the largest figure he ever carved and the only human one. Most of his carvings were the small animals you see richly decorated with bright paint. But this, ah, I have never seen anything like it. No one even knew it existed until he died. It was found behind a curtain in his workshop. He left a note there saying it was a gift to the church," the priest explained.

"I've never seen anything like it," Angel agreed. "And I've seen many churches."

"There have been paintings made of it and photographs taken. But none of them equate the experience of looking into this face. Occasionally people have said they've seen the eyes or the head move. One elderly woman claimed to be carrying on a conversation with Jesús when she came to mass. I've heard stories of men giving up their *pulque* and otherwise cleaning up their lives after they thought he looked at them. They may have been coming here for years. But one day, everything is different because of this cross."

"I believe it," Angel said. "I can't explain why, but I truly do." At that point, something shifted deep in his psyche, like a weight lifting, or a blocked artery flowing freely again. He felt warm and slightly lightheaded.

"I have to sit, Father."

"We can stay here or walk to the benches outside. Which would you prefer?"

"Outside, please."

Father Hernandez genuflected and signed the cross before turning from the altar. Angel followed his lead, dropping his head in respect, but also attempting not to see the statue's eyes again. Yet before he exited the church he glanced back at the crucifix. Had the head shifted slightly to the right? He must have imagined it.

They walked to a bench near blooming flowers and ferns where Father Hernandez motioned for him to sit. The garden was more manicured than the trail around the mountain and gave Angel a sense of order, which he badly needed after the disorienting experiences of the day.

"Father, I'm a scholar," he began. "My area of study is comparative religions. I've been interested in faiths that are not well known and I've researched tribal religions. I've heard of holy places before, sacred spaces infused with divine power that people can tap into. But they always seemed mythical to me. I've never been able to feel that power before. But in one day, without even looking for it, I seem to keep finding it over and over in Teotenaca. Yet this is a place I've never heard of. It was an accident that we came here at all. Nothing hinted at the energy permeating this place in what I read about the town. How is that possible?"

"Your question is a large one, Señor Angel," he acknowledged. "But I will attempt to answer it. The Cave of Dreams is a part of our community and has been for so long that no one knows when it was discovered. But we realize what a special place it is, that in our village the divine presence is felt in our lives every day. We accept it, but not lightly. We protect it. Occasionally people from the outside have heard of the cave and they want to see it for themselves, if it is real or not. We've even had people try to break into it with explosives and high-powered equipment. But they haven't been successful and they've gone away saying it was a lie, a myth. That's all right with us. We don't need that type of attention. We don't want to become a tourist attraction," he explained.

"But there are others who have been summoned here from many countries, who have dreamed about the cave or who didn't know of it at all, like you," he continued. "They are welcome here. You think you came as a tourist, but that was the means to get you here. Your purpose here is more than that. Perhaps it's a means of renewing your faith, or helping you understand the underlying meaning of why people need faith and the power one feels when one connects to divine energy. That combination can change a life or, perhaps, the world."

Angel looked into the priest's eyes. He was serious, but kindly, too, as if he were explaining a complicated lesson to a child. "Do you think that's why those entering the cave have become more international? Do you believe they can make a difference in the world because of this experience?" Angel asked.

"Anyone can change the world, my friend. It may seem impossible, but every person contributes to what happens all over the globe, to cause and effect, to the ebb and flow of history. It may be how a person gets along with his neighbors, or how he votes, whether he's apathetic, or if he keeps all his money or gives a little to someone in need. We make choices every day that change the world in some way, even in remote places like this," he said, gesturing to the town's buildings nearby.

"But those who have been in the cave have special contributions they can make," the priest explained with a nod in the direction of the mountain. "They dream and learn and then they teach by example. In these times, most who are summoned from outside this community are artists or spiritual practitioners like myself. They are people with strong imaginations and the potential for great faith, if they don't already have it. To consciously change the world, one must have vision in order to see it not as it is, but as it can be. Once you have a vision for a better world, you need courage and faith to make the vision real. A person who has been through an experience in the cave will always have dreams to guide and enlighten them. Does this answer your questions? Or only give you more?" the priest smiled.

"Mostly, you have answered them, Father, though there really is no end to the questions I have. The more you talk, the more I'm wondering about. For instance, why here? Why would the cave be so far from the closest city? It's not an easy drive to get here. And how can it exist at all? But I suppose those are questions that don't really have answers," Angel speculated.

The priest acknowledged the complexity of his thoughts with a nod. "Well, we do have theories around here, but only God knows the real answers. Have you ever gone on a retreat?"

"Yes. But mostly as part of my research," the scholar explained.

"And where were your retreats? Were they in cities?"

Angel smiled because he understood the theory Father Hernandez was about to explain. "They were in the country. One was even in the desert," he answered.

"And why were they in those places?"

"To get away from our daily patterns and distractions. By withdrawing into a small, private community we were more focused. It was quiet and naturally beautiful. I've meditated and prayed, and had thoughtful discussions. It's important to form a group dynamic. Yes, this town and the mountains would make an excellent place for a retreat. I understand your point, Father. But this is not a highly accessible town," Angel concluded, still wondering about the choice of this location.

"Exactly. The distractions of the outside world are minimal here. As for why the cave exists at all, I don't know," the priest admitted. "It's a divine gift and only the giver can answer that question."

26

"So where would you like me to begin?" I asked Father Moran. I'd agreed to help him "prepare the way" for the retreat in the Cave of Dreams. I hoped it would make the time pass quicker.

"I've made a list. There are several items you could do on your own and others you could help me do."

"Fine. What are they?" I asked.

"The candles need to be replaced in the chapel, where the waterfall is. The old candles from there can be used in the kitchen. This year I have smokeless candles in glass containers and that should be quite lovely as the glass reflects the light. But the candles from last year have melted onto the rock surface, with its high and low spots. They may be challenging to remove. I have a metal spatula that may work on them."

"What else?"

"The sleeping quarters. They're rustic. I have straw to lay on the floor and air mattresses on top of that. But the air pump is missing from the package so we'll have to use our own breath, I'm afraid. Thank God for sending you, Michelle. The pilgrims will put their sleeping bags on top of the mattresses, far superior to sleeping directly on rock, don't you think?" he chuckled.

"You have air mattresses? What about blankets?" I asked enthusiastically.

"I brought some. I can let you borrow one," he said.

"You said women come, too. What faiths do they usually represent?"

"It varies, as it does with the men. A Buddhist nun and a Protestant minister were among our community the last time I came."

I was curious about the languages they spoke to each other, too. "Father, how do you communicate? Do you speak the same language or say the same prayers? And it seems like differences between religions might be cause for conflict. It's been the cause of wars after all. How do you manage that?" I asked.

"Excellent questions. We do not all speak the same language, though we had several English and Spanish speakers at my last retreat here. Apparently it always works out that at least two people speak a common language and can communicate with others in the group. We take turns leading prayers and meditations, which come out of the various traditions we are from. And we are from very different backgrounds, but, ultimately, we know it is the same God we all believe in. It is safe to say we are more open to our commonalities than to our differences. In other words, we manage quite well," he concluded.

"Do you elect a leader, someone who directs it all?" I couldn't stop asking questions. This was a rare opportunity to find out about an event Angel would be fascinated with. And I was, too.

Father Moran hesitated and seemed thoughtful. "If we have a leader, it is the One who speaks to us through our dreams. We are united around a theme each time, which is revealed only in our dreams. As far as who goes when in the order of prayer, we do it by age so the eldest goes first. It works out.

"But I can't tell you what the theme is this year. I'm sworn to secrecy. Let it suffice to say that it is of great concern in the world. Some things are always a concern, of course, like poverty and war. We say general prayers for those. But we'll unite around a particular issue," he explained. "But I'll be thinking of you, Michelle, and thanking you for the help you are about to give me. Do you want to hear the other items on my list?" He brought us back around to our original purpose.

"Yes, though I'm leaning toward the candles in the chapel to start with. I can handle that," I said.

"I'll also need help setting up this kitchen. There are cabinets to organize, pots and pans to be cleaned, dusting and sweeping to be done. It's hard to see in the other places, but we try to keep this room as clean as possible. Apparently the candles and fires over time have essentially killed this part of the cave, so it's drier in here without the ceiling dripping on our heads. But I can't explain why the rest of the place is still so alive and beautiful," he said. "It's one of the cave's many mysteries."

We both hesitated for a moment and then he asked, "So where shall we start?"

"I'm still interested in the candles," I said.

"Then candles it is," he agreed. "While you're doing that, I'll place the new ones on the shelves along the aisles. They'll become beacons for finding our way around this place as well as stations for private prayer," he explained. "If you follow me, I have the boxes of candles stored near where I entered the cave. There's a little cart behind this curtain. This is our pantry and storage locker, by the way," he said while pulling a curtain aside. It hung from a jerry-rigged rod in a corner of the kitchen and seemed to connect to the wall. The cart was similar to the red wagon I had as a child, only bigger.

"You really know your way around here, Father. How did you get the air mattresses and candles and your sleeping bag and food in here?" I asked, dumbfounded by his organization. He described how the folks from El Refugio took care of the shipments and brought everything to the entrance, where he dragged and carried it into the cave. Even though they had also been directed there through their dreams, they were not to enter.

"The project manager from above," I said, looking upward, still wondering what I'd fallen into.

He pulled the empty cart to where it would be filled, avoiding rough spots along the way. The sound of the wheels on rock reverberated against the cave walls. I followed him to the place where he'd entered off the trail, which wasn't where I had come in. We loaded two boxes marked "CANDLES" onto the wagon and headed for the room with the waterfall. As we approached, I couldn't hear the trickle of water because of the noise made by the cart. Father Moran decided which group of candles in the room would be the last to be removed and then lit them, bringing the illumination I needed for my assignment. Whatever was left of them would be removed right before the retreat so the new candles would be unused until then. He used the spatula to cut through the tape that held the first box together and then began to line them up on the nearby benches. The white candles in their holders were packed like wine bottles, separated by cardboard dividers, but in two layers with bubble wrap between them.

"Michelle, I think it would work best if you remove the furthest candles to start, then work your way to this group you're using." He glanced at the candles I would replace, melted tightly into the pock-marked surface. "This could take longer than you think. If you get any clever ideas to make it easier, I would advise you to try them."

"Father, if I hurt the spatula, do you have another one?" I asked. I didn't want to ruin it, but knew I might.

"I believe there is a hard plastic one as well. In the meantime, I'll be putting the rest of the candles in place on the ledges. If you need me, you'll know where I am when that noisy cart is moving." He gave me matches and promised a break when our jobs were done, but gave me one warning. "Try not to sit down or relax or you know what will happen."

"I do, indeed," I said, trying not to think about it. "See you in a little while, Father."

Off he went with that wobbly cart. It reminded me of my unsteady suitcase. The sound echoed through the aisles that led to the dome. He planned to light the candles right before retreat participants arrived en masse. I imagined being in the center of the dome, the spokes of the wheel defined by the beacons of candlelight. I wondered what Father Moran had planned for the dome, which had its own natural light seeping through the cracks in its ceiling. My thoughts kept returning to that place. I longed to spend time there, but first I had work to do.

The candles I was trying to remove clung to their rocky foothold, almost as if they'd become part of where they stood, like the stalagmites that pointed up toward the stalactites a few feet above them. I couldn't seem to budge them with the spatula. But I knew there had to be a way to get them off, hopefully without damaging them or the spatula. So I appealed to the One I was told was in charge of the cave. I reached into my pocket and held the *milagro* of the eye while I prayed.

"Please help me find a way of doing this that doesn't destroy the candles or the spatula and that doesn't take hours to do. What is the best way to do this?" I asked out loud. Then I realized I was looking straight into the flames of the burning candles as I said the prayer. And I understood what I could do. I took the spatula and positioned it over the flames until I knew it was hot. Fortunately, its wooden handle kept my hand cool. Then I took the hot metal and placed it at the bottom of a candle and pushed. There was a bit of resistance, but it gave way. It seemed my prayer had been answered in short order.

I continued the process, scraping the excess wax until the ledge was as clean as possible. Then I positioned the new glass candleholders in a row. I stood back a few feet to admire my handiwork. I wanted to light the new candles to get the full effect, but Father Moran wanted them to be fresh for the retreat, so I let them be. But I could tell they'd make the space seem more like a church. What prayers would be said in this room,

I wondered, and in what languages?

As I lined up the last candle, I heard the cart creaking closer. When it stopped, Father Moran came into the room saying his work was almost done, but he needed to take his break.

"I'm just finishing," I said. "How does this look?"

He came closer and angled his flashlight on the first set of candles, and then the second. "Very nice," he exclaimed. "You did say you were an artist, didn't you? Well, it certainly shows. That's so much better than what I would have done," he laughed. "I hope you can do the last group, also, before your parting dream."

"I wish I could see everything lit before I leave."

"It should be quite impressive," he agreed, "thanks to you. I wish I had a more artistic project to give to you. But I can't think of any, sorry to say."

"Maybe I'll dream one up," I laughed.

We put the old candles in the empty slots in the box that had rumbled along on the cart, then walked to the kitchen. Father Moran put the teakettle on. I noticed a large plastic pitcher almost full of water on a counter near the hot plate.

"Where does the water come from?" I asked.

"From the pool in the chapel we just came from. It's actually quite good. Have you tried it?"

"Yes. I was leery of drinking anything but bottled water in Mexico, but I didn't have much of a choice, as you know. Fortunately, it seems to work just fine. I haven't gotten sick from it yet," I said, tapping my tummy.

"And neither have I," he affirmed.

We sat in silence for a few moments. But then the many questions floating around in my head began to surface. "Father, do you mind if I keep asking you questions?"

"It's quite all right, dear," he said. "It will help us pass the time."

"Where are you from and what's your parish like? Does your congregation have any idea where you are right now?" I asked in rapid succession. I was very curious about my companion's story.

"Well, Michelle, I didn't come to study the priesthood until I was an adult in the secular world. I'm most comfortable in an urban setting. Fortunately my parish is in Dublin where I'm the Associate Pastor. I'm quite certain that I've startled parishioners from time to time with my opinions and actions, so they are seldom surprised by anything I do, I dare say. I'm quite certain this situation would surprise them all, however." He gestured around to indicate the cave as well as me sitting next to him. "All they know is I'm on a retreat. Father McNamara, our pastor, has an idea of what I'm about, but he doesn't fully understand it. Still, he trusts me," the priest explained. "He knows I have both a mystical nature as well as one that's aware of the earthly demands on people. Perhaps I'm an enigma to him. But I've advised him on many occasions when he found himself in a quandary over one thing or another. He hasn't said 'no' to me yet as far as coming here."

"What did you do before you became a priest?" I asked.

"I worked in a large store in Dublin as an assistant buyer," he laughed. "Surprised?"

"Yes! And no, considering all the things you've brought with you. So why did you become a priest?" I asked. "That's quite a switch, to go from retail work to church work."

"Ah, yes. But it wasn't under ordinary circumstances," he continued. "One day as I was walking home from work I was struck by a car. I was severely injured, in a coma, and was given the sacrament of the dying. But on some mysterious level of consciousness, my mind was still at work. I had a dream about deciding whether I would live or die. I knew I wanted to live. I promised God that if I were spared, I would become a priest. Well, I came out of it and remembered the dream, so I was beholding to the Almighty. My mother couldn't believe it! She was grateful I'd survived. But her son becoming a priest, now that was clearly a miracle!" he laughed. "Looking back, I'm glad I followed that path. And God continues to lead me and bless me."

At that point, the teakettle began to whistle. Before long, that wonderful hot fluid was warming me up from the inside out. *How odd*, I thought, *to be drinking hot tea in a Mexican cave with an Irish priest.* And our source of water was equally unorthodox. I couldn't imagine where I'd be if I hadn't decided the water in the pool was drinkable. "Water is such a precious thing," I said.

"And like many things in life, water has its place and can be either a blessing or a curse," he began. "Too much can wash away crops or cause death and destruction. Yet we need it to survive."

That got me thinking about my fear of Mexican water. "Or if it's polluted, it can make you sick when you drink it. It might even poison everything that lives in it," I added.

"Clean water is indeed a blessing," he said slowly. "Those who are fortunate to have it all the time seldom appreciate it." I felt a twinge of guilt with that comment, since I was among the blessed who enjoyed daily showers and ready access to water through a faucet. I longingly looked forward to my next shower.

"When I decided to take a drink from the pool in the chapel, I wasn't sure how my body would react," I told him. "But that was the only choice I had, since my supply was so low. There must be people who know they're flirting with death every time they drink from the one water source they have. It must be so hard, especially when you're giving it to your children, knowing it could hurt them."

"Water is a powerful symbol of cleansing, too, which Christians use in Baptism," he reminded me. I wondered if other religions used water as a symbol. I'd have to ask Angel. And what would he make of all this? I hoped my friends knew about the cave by now, and that I was in it. At least with Father Moran for company, my journey had taken a turn for the better.

Then I noticed how the lights in the kitchen reflected in shimmering patterns on the liquid surface of the drink in my cup. "Thank you for sharing this most precious water with me," I smiled. He nodded his response and we raised our cups to each other before bringing them to our lips once again and sipping a most extraordinary tea.

27

Max and Maggie sat beside each other on a bench in the grove. He poked at the ash of the dead campfire with a stick in his right hand while his left hand grasped her by the waist. She watched the small dust clouds he made dissipate into the whispering breeze. "You've been carrying that pain around for a long time, Max. How strong a grip does it have on you?" she asked him.

He stopped moving the stick and sat quietly. "That's not easy to answer," he replied, "but I'm sure that who I've become since the accident has everything to do with it. To be honest, there's more to the story than what Michelle could have told you. I never shared all of it with anyone, but I want you to know about it."

"Please," she urged.

"Anita and I were talking about getting married. No date, we just talked about it. Then she found out she was pregnant. We decided to go ahead and get married. But there was a part of me that didn't want to be tied down yet. I was only twenty-two. I still had lots of things I wanted to do." He turned to face her, a desperate man trying to express the horror that still haunted his memories. "That's where the pain really kicks me in the gut. I know I probably couldn't have stopped that crash, but part of me wonders if I unconsciously let it happen, if I had seen the guy in my peripheral vision, but just let it happen. I remember driving in the car with her, but I have no memory of the accident, so there's no way I'll ever know. My friends thought I suffered from survival guilt, but it's deeper than that." He turned away for a moment, gazing back at the ashes. "I wonder what my life would have been like if we'd gotten married and she'd had the baby. Would I have stayed, or left them?"

He retreated into silence. She could see the pain etched in his expression and put her arms around him. "How horrible for you! I'm truly sorry, Max. But I can't believe you would let that happen to anyone. You have to get past it," she assured him, stroking his back.

"I haven't been able to let it go." He threw a fallen twig into the ashes. "There were times when I wished I'd died, too. But then I began thinking about it in a whole other way. After my recovery I felt almost like I *couldn't* die, because I should have died with her. Since then I've taken a lot of chances by traveling in dangerous places. But I'm still here," he said, throwing a hand in the air.

"And you're still afraid."

He didn't answer at first. The chimes and songs of birds filled the empty space that hung in their conversation. "A big, bad guy like me, afraid?" he laughed. "What am I afraid of, Maggie?"

She simply said, "Me," and he knew she was right.

"Let's see now, you're several inches shorter than I am and you probably weigh at least sixty pounds less than I do. And you don't have these muscles." He demonstrated his strength with a tight grip around her waist.

"Ouch!" she exclaimed, jumping with surprise. "I get your point. That's not what I mean."

"All right, all right. So *why* would I be afraid of a willowy, attractive woman such as yourself?" He let go of his grip and faced her. But when she looked into his eyes, he pulled away.

"So why can't you look at me?" she challenged him.

He tried again, first glancing, then connecting with her green and golden eyes. He found them to be warm and inviting, yet angry. He turned his gaze back to the ashes. "Whoa! You have very intense eyes," he said. "What are you thinking about?"

"What do you think I'm thinking about?" she asked back.

He took a deep breath, then looked into those eyes again. "I know you like me," he began. "But there's something else. I'm not sure, have I hurt you?"

"What do you think?" she asked with a bitter twinge in her voice.

"I must have. I can see it coming straight at me. I didn't mean to hurt you, Maggie. It's just that I'm …"

"… afraid?" she finished his sentence.

He sighed, turned away, and nodded. "Okay. I admit it. There's a fear factor at work here. I never meant to hurt you, Maggie. I am *so* sorry! I do care about you, a lot. We both know that, now that Flor blew my cover." *How had she read him like that?* he wondered. "You're an extraordinary person. I've never known anyone with the qualities you have all wrapped up in that Maggie package. Maybe I'm afraid I might lose you. Maybe I can't protect you, either. Or maybe you'd just reject me totally for being a kind of macho jerk. It wouldn't be the first time," he sighed and went back to poking into the ashes. She grabbed the stick and gently took it from his hand, then dropped it on the ground. She wrapped her hands around his.

"It doesn't matter how much you stir those ashes around. That fire's out and it's not coming back. Now, it doesn't matter to me that you're occasionally a macho jerk, Max. I can deal with that and I can see past it. I don't think that's who you are at all. Is it?" she asked, cocking her head.

"Well, I hope it isn't, to tell you the truth," he replied. "But if you act a certain way long enough, I suppose you can believe it *is* who you are. So, since we seem to be in a psychoanalytical mode here, why do you think I act like a 'jerk'? And you might want to define the term, while you're at it. I should be angry about that remark, by the way, but I'm not. It's weird, but it's a relief to admit it," he said, shaking his head.

"Well, if you're the one acting that way, surely you have a theory. I could tell you what I think, but it's better if you can see it for yourself," she said.

"You're not going to make this easy, are you?"

"Uh, uh," she replied, turning her head from side to side.

He took a deep breath and looked into her eyes again. "Perhaps it has to do with being very attracted to you, and when you seemed to be attracted to me, turning and running. But not too far. We did stay friends. How hard has that been for you?"

"What do you think?" she countered.

"I'm sorry, Maggie. Truly! I buried my feelings, but I couldn't let go of you. I was in an emotional limbo and I stuck you there, too. That wasn't fair. I knew that. But you *stayed*. You didn't give up on me. How hard was that for you? Really. Please, just tell me." He held her hands firmly in his and this time gazed deeply into her eyes to plumb the depths of what she was feeling in that moment. That's when she began to cry. It was like a tropical shower, a quick burst of tears and then it was over. Neither of them said anything until the storm passed. She took back her hands and wiped her eyes, but he could see more tears gathering there like a new set of storm clouds ready to flood their conversation.

"It hurt," she said. "You seemed not to care as much as I did, but I hung on to you as a friend, if that was all you'd allow me to be. I tried to be hopeful because it seemed like you cared, too, but something was getting in the way. Now I know it was about Anita. But, Max, it hurts to love a person one way and only be able to express it in another. Maybe I should have walked away. But I couldn't. I didn't want to." The storm clouds burst open again.

"I am so sorry, Maggie. I'm an even bigger jerk than I thought I was! Here, you can use my sleeve," he said, offering his T-shirt to wipe her tears.

"Damn you, Max! I wasn't planning on acting like this! I'm letting down my guard totally. Look what you've done to me!" she scolded.

"Perhaps you'd like to beat me over the head with this," he said with a little smirk on the edge of his sad smile. He offered her the branch he'd used to stir the ashes. "Will that make you feel better?"

She stopped, looked at the stick in his hand, and started to laugh. "It helps me metaphorically," she said. "It gives me an image to work with." She took the stick, raised it as if to strike him, then dropped it behind her.

"Did I scare you?" she asked with a half-smile.

"Only for a second," he admitted. "Let's be friends, Maggie. I mean, more than friends from now on, if you'll still have me. This isn't easy for me, either. I've shut away my emotions and gone into a 'numb state.' I've made a mess of things! Do you want to try again?"

She picked up the stick and began prodding the remnants of the old fire, as he had. She spoke, only looking his way a few times. She had secrets to reveal, too. "There are a couple things I have to say to you, before we go any further," she began. "When we first became friends I told you I'd been married and you said you wondered how anyone could let me go. Well, it seems my story picks up where yours and Anita's left off. When I was twenty-two I got pregnant. Like you, Martin and I had talked about getting married, so we did. But we were too young to settle down. About a month later I lost the baby. We decided to stay together, anyway, but he became abusive. First it was verbal, then physical. So I left. I had to. I've had my own set of fears about getting close to anyone since then."

She felt his arm around her as he brought her closer and said, "You've been hurting all this time, too." He kissed her cheek, but instead of lifting her gaze from the ashes, she pulled gently away.

"There's something else. Let me get it out," she insisted, as he tried to pull her toward him. He let her go. "It's about who I am. My ancestors came from all over the world: I took a DNA test to find out what I could. My roots go back to Africa, Spain probably, northern Europe, Ireland, of course, and even North America before Columbus. People expect a person named 'Maggie O'Rourke' to have red hair, green eyes, *and* fair skin. They can't hide their surprise when I show up. That's left me cautious, especially around men.

"And then I met you, this tall, very white guy named Max DeBoer," she said, pointing her finger at him with wide eyes, then glancing back toward the old campfire. "He's cute, he's funny, he's got the most amazing scars on his legs and all I can do is treat his poor battered knee. I'm a very professional therapist. I couldn't let my feelings show, but I had them even then. Are you listening?" When she checked, she saw a smirk on his face.

"What is funny here?" she asked incredulously.

"You are the most beautiful package of genetics I've ever encountered, and I've traveled a bit in this world. But even when you were treating my twisted knee and I was in agony, I was falling for you, too." He cleared his throat, surprised by his admission. "I didn't think it was proper to make a pass at my therapist and try my luck at an inappropriate moment. And when I bumped into you at that party I knew it was my chance to get to know you, Maggie. But it's ironic that you've got this rich blend of ancestry and I'm about as white as anyone can be. My ancestors were Dutch and English. Are you sure I'm not too white for you?" he asked in a sheepish tone.

She looked at him with a cross expression and then burst into laughter that she couldn't stop. "What if I said, 'Yes, Max, you're too white for me.' What would you do about it?"

"Hmmm," he said, thoughtfully stroking his chin as if he had a beard, while suppressing a laugh. "I could become a regular at the local tanning salon. But I'm still stuck with these genes. I can't change that. Are you going to say I'm too white?" he asked in mock terror. "Sorry, but I am who I am."

She just laughed. "And so am I. Don't worry about it. Just behave yourself," she said. "That means, show your true feelings. I'm not planning on dying on you. You know, you could give me a lot to live for."

He looked deep into her eyes and knew this was a moment that could change both their lives. "Maggie, I truly care for you. You've got an incredible heart, a generous personality, you make me laugh, and you're gorgeous! If you'll forgive me for hurting you, I hope we can be more than friends from now on. I do love you, you know," he whispered, then seemed surprised at his boldness. "There. It's said. It wasn't that hard," he laughed. "I love you, Maggie," he said with a deeper, confident voice.

She kissed him on the cheek and whispered in his ear, "I love you, too, Max."

He felt her tears run down his cheek as they mixed with his own.

28

While Father Hernandez drove Angel back to Sweet Dreams, Reggie helped Dar fix supper. "Smells great, dear heart. Where did you get the chicken? It isn't one of ours, is it?" her husband asked.

"No. I made a trade with Fischer; his chicken for our goat cheese," she explained.

He smiled his appreciation. "You have a way with our customers," he laughed. "Chicken for cheese, eh? I think you got the better part of that negotiation."

"Oh, do you now? Well, he got quite a lot of cheese. By the way, have you seen our guests?" she asked. "We're about ready to eat. Did you tell them about the bell?"

"In all the excitement today, I don't think so. But I'll use it. They'll get the idea, if they haven't run far away from here by now," he smiled.

"Give it a try, dear." As Reggie went to the back of the house to ring the bell that hung just beyond the veranda, Dar called Sunny to help set the table.

"How many, Mum?"

"Well, let's see. If we have everyone but Michelle, that's six people. If she or anyone else shows up, we'll set another place when they get here."

"Yes, Mum," Sunny said and went off to get the napkins.

As Reggie rang the bell it could be heard for a distance. Maggie and Max were walking back to the house hand in hand when the first clap sounded. "What's that?" she said, startled.

"Sounds like supper," he answered without concern.

"Or maybe something has happened."

"My stomach is chiming in time with the bell. I'll vote for supper," he asserted.

"There's only one way to find out for sure. Let's go."

Max found himself falling behind as she let go of his hand and speeded up almost into a run. "Wait for me, Maggie."

Angel was going to knock before entering Sweet Dreams, but when he heard the bell he tried the door, found it open, and stepped inside. "What's happening?" he asked as he entered the kitchen and dining area.

"Welcome back, Angel," Dar greeted him. "Supper is happening and you're just in time."

"Any word on Michelle?" he asked.

"Nothing has changed," she shook her head. "Not to worry. She'll be back in a day or two."

"Have you seen Max and Maggie?" he asked.

"Reggie's bell should get their attention, I reckon," she smiled. "They're probably hearing it in town, the way sound can echo around here."

As Max and Maggie approached, Reggie let the others know they were in sight. By the time they arrived, supper was on the table. Dar was relieved the conversation had turned more cordial. The earlier hostility toward her and her husband had subsided. But the subject of Michelle's condition weighed on everyone's minds. "There's nothing more we can do tonight but get some rest ourselves," Reggie recommended. "Father Hernandez hinted that she's in good hands, and that's a comfort."

"Who do you think it is?" Angel asked. "I got a sense that you knew even though he said he was sworn to secrecy."

Reggie looked at Dar who shrugged and nodded slowly. "All right then, but this is only a guess," he said. "Once a year, but not always at the same time of year, there's a religious retreat that takes place in the cave. I've heard about it, but I've never met the participants. Father Hernandez plays host to those who come, as do the folks at El Refugio. Apparently two or more people come before the others to get the cave spiffed up and ready for guests, and I think one of them is in the cave with Michelle. Perhaps she's helping clean up, too" he explained.

"Is it a Catholic retreat or something different?" Angel inquired.

"From what I've heard, it's an interfaith gathering with participants from many countries," he answered. "It's a very ecumenical place, the Cave of Dreams."

"Even so, wouldn't she be an outsider, even an intruder, to a retreat?" Maggie asked. "That could get a bit sticky, especially if it's such a private event."

Reggie smiled in answer. "I have another theory. I think she'll be out before it starts."

"Let's pray for that," Angel nodded.

"I hope I can sleep tonight," Maggie confided. "I'm still worried about her. I know I'm not alone here."

"I'm going to dream about her tonight," Sunny declared. "Flor and Angel asked me to. If I can, do you want me to say hello for you?"

Maggie was caught off-guard. She looked at the girl's parents, who only smiled back. "Yes, say hello and tell her we miss her and that we hope she's all right. We want to know when we'll see her again," Maggie responded, but only to humor Sunny. How could she think she'd be able to talk to Michelle in her dream?

"Will she know when we'll see her again, Dad?"

"Maybe. If not, you might still find out something. Be open, Sunny. Ask the question and see what happens. The answer may come through to you," he counseled the girl.

"Do you really believe that?" Max asked, not willing to humor anyone. He was still being the skeptic, despite the marvels he'd witnessed that day.

"Yes," Dar answered firmly for her husband. "Who knows what *you* might dream tonight, Max," she smiled warmly, diffusing his attitude a bit.

And then Sunny disarmed him further by giving the same advice she'd just received.

"Be open, Max. See what happens," she said in a serious tone.

After Maggie gave him a gentle kick under the table, he just smiled and said, "OK, Sunny. You're on."

29

Father Moran and I shared our accomplishments during our next meal. We hoped to finish eating before another dream session began. We both sensed it would be soon and could come any time, even in the middle of eating. He contributed tea and an apple, while I shared what food I had. But all I found in the backpack was bread, cheese and trail mix. There'd been more food in there the last time I'd checked. Where could it have gone? Had I been so hungry I'd eaten it in my sleep? As I savored the tastes that lingered in my mouth I wondered what the people on the retreat would be eating. "You'll have a lot of mouths to feed, Father. What will be on the menu?"

"Everyone brings their share plus a little more, which is often supplemented by the kind people at El Refugio. They'll give us fresh vegetables and fruit, canned goods, perhaps even beans and rice with tortillas or bread. As I told you before, we fast while we're here for most of the day. Then we share our supplies for the evening meal. It can be quite international."

I wasn't sure when I was overstepping the poor man's right to privacy or secrecy, but I trusted he'd tell me. So I kept asking questions. "Do you pray and dream for the entire day?"

"Yes, we do a bit of both," he yawned. "It's a very intensive process. In fact, when we pray in unison, whether it's the same or different words, there's a kind of murmur that echoes through the cave. It has an ancient quality, particularly when one doesn't understand the words the others are speaking. It's like whispered prayers in a very old cathedral. It drives me deeper into meditation. I do feel privileged to be a part of the history of this place," he said. I sensed a humility in his words.

"But you don't always pray together, correct?"

"Correct," he answered mechanically. I could sense that his thoughts were beginning to drift. "We spend part of our time praying privately for our own intentions. Pardon me, Michelle, but I'm getting sleepy. There's little time to reach the air mattress I set up. Could you help me? Take an air mattress for yourself, too," he suggested.

But I wasn't sure where to set mine up. "Where are we going?" I asked, taking one from the box and following close behind him. He looked wobbly when he stood.

"Follow me," he said. "If it looks like I need support, please help me. Not going far. Women's section is on the way."

I turned off the lights and blew out the candles, except for one, then followed him as closely as I could without stepping on the backs of his feet. "Around the corner here." He pointed his flashlight to the right. "Hurry!" he whispered with urgency as he shuffled slowly along. I took his arm to steady him. "That helps. Straight here, curve around ahead. Light's on there." He was slurring his words and getting harder to understand. I wondered if he'd fall asleep on the way and I'd have to make him comfortable against the rocks. Then he stopped.

"Here," he said. "Your place. Candle there, but not lit. I'm ahead."

We walked another twenty feet or so and then I saw a light. His bedding was on top of an air mattress, as he'd described. I got his shoes and jacket off and discovered his white jacket was a thin windbreaker, its pale surface now textured with grime from the cave. He said he wore white to reflect any available light, but I knew it would get darker from the moisture and dirt in the cave. His shirt and pants were dark. When he crawled into the open sleeping bag, I zipped it up and gently lifted his head so I could push a small pillow under it.

"Thank you, Michelle." His words became a snore. I was alone again.

"Sweet dreams, Father," I wished him, knowing the same thing was about to happen to me. I made my way back along the cave wall to the place he had pointed out. The candle was on a stool with matches next to it. Once lit, I got a better sense of the women's space. On top of a rickety wood chair sat a pile of folded blankets. Pillows were stacked on another. Straw was mounded in four places on the ground.

The quiet hum of Father Moran's snore in the near distance comforted me, reminding me of a train passing in the night. Sitting down on another chair, I began blowing through the air mattress's tiny funnel in time with his snoring. But the steady rhythm and sudden lack of my own oxygen left me lightheaded. I knew I wouldn't be able to finish filling the mattress when I felt that familiar wave of fatigue wash over me. I capped the funnel and pulled the mattress to one of the straw piles. Grabbing a pillow and blanket with the last of my consciousness, I laid down on the partially inflated air mattress. At least the firm pillow would protect my head. My eyes closed on that thought and my unconscious mind quickly transported me to the City of Light.

"Welcome back, Michelle," María greeted me. "I'm sorry you didn't get the air mattress filled all the way. You can finish it when you wake up and then you will have a comfortable bed the next time this happens. And now that you're here, do you have questions for me?"

There were many floating in my mind, like the fish in the pool by the waterfall. *Which one to catch first?* And then I knew. "I want to ask about my friends. But first I'm curious about what the requirements are for a person to enter El Anhelo. It seems that being an artist qualifies you, or being a cleric like Father Moran, or even someone knowledgeable of religions, like my friend Angel. But what about faith? Does one have to believe in God to get in here? I ask because I know several incredible people, who are talented and imaginative, as well as kind and caring individuals. But they don't believe in God. Would they walk around El Anhelo and never find the way in?"

She smiled and nodded slowly, as if she'd heard this question before. "The answer to your question may surprise you. Faith is important, but there are different kinds of faith. Besides faith in God, there is faith in truth and what is right. There is faith in knowing what can and must be changed, and faith in the future. For instance, if a person has great imagination and the potential to become a noted artist, and if he or she believes and acts on the basic principle that people should be treated as one would wish to be treated themselves, yet they do not believe in God, they are still welcome here.

"On the other hand, if a similarly talented person does not act on that basic principle of respect, even if they say they believe in God, they are *not* welcome here. Our hope is that those who enter El Anhelo become active in promoting change toward the good. That doesn't require belief in God, but belief in what is truly fair for all people. It isn't about one's individual relationship with God as much as it is about one's relationship with other people, even if they're on the opposite side of the world, or one's political beliefs. So I would say that your friends *would* be welcome here. They would find the door open. It's also possible they might discover a spiritual faith that explains what happens to them while they're here."

That did surprise me. "You've answered questions I hadn't even thought of. But I was hoping you'd say something like that. I haven't been consistent in my own religious faith, so I keep wondering why the cave opened to me."

"But I sense you have a spiritual faith, and that will grow stronger here. It will make you stronger, too. You will see that very soon," she encouraged me. "But back to your friends. What do you wish to know?"

"I'm concerned about how they're reacting to my predicament. I hope Max isn't threatening Reggie. I know Angel will be worried, too. I'd like to think they're concerned, but I don't want their vacation to be ruined. Can I find out what's happening with them?"

My dream guide didn't reply in a straightforward way, but I trusted she'd direct me to the answer. "You have a lot on your mind. Perhaps it's time you took a break and enjoyed the cinema instead," she said, turning to her right where a marquee lit up nearby. The featured movie was "Club of Dreams."

"Who's in the film?" I asked.

"You'll see," she smiled. "They may be unknowns to most people, but not to you."

Next, I was standing at the entrance to the theater with a ticket in hand. After I gave it to a young, *indígena* woman in an usher's uniform, she handed me a large bag of buttered popcorn and a super-sized carbonated drink with a lid and straw already in place. Inside the door of the dark theater, another usher escorted me down the aisle to a row of seats in the middle of the place. He directed me with his flashlight, which reminded me of being in the cave. When I looked around, I was the only patron.

"Enjoy the show, dear," he said as he walked away. Did I detect an Irish accent?

I slid the drink into a cup holder and began putting a dent into that delicious bag of popcorn. It was perfectly buttered and salted. I was hoping the fluffy kernels would expand in my stomach as I drank the pop. It turned out to be root beer, my favorite. Now if the movie was as good as the snacks, this would be a fantastic dream! Suddenly, the curtain parted and bright colors exploded onto the dark screen, accompanied by surround sound. It was startling after the quiet cave and the dark theater. I expected previews, but the graphics and music announced the featured presentation. The film began with a man whistling a tune I didn't know. Instrumentation filled in with the same tune until the melodic theme was established. Then the music switched to another, bouncier theme, followed by flamenco rhythms. The movie seemed to be a musical set in Europe around the early 1950s. Like film noir, it was shot in black and white with a smoky, nostalgic feel. The camera followed the whistling man as he approached a nightclub. Its marquee read "Club of Dreams," which became the title of the film. The credits rolled quickly by as he handed his trench coat and hat to a young woman at a coat check. (Did I see my friends' names listed as actors?) The titles continued as he made his way to a small table and ordered a drink. Everyone knew him it seemed, but I didn't recognize him at first, with his dapper suit and his hair slicked back. But when he moved his head and smiled I saw it was Reggie!

Then the lights on the club's stage came on and the crowd grew attentive. The black and white film morphed into dazzling Technicolor as the stage lights grew brighter. Music was playing and a slender woman in a satiny, green spaghetti strap dress stood with her back to the crowd, snapping the fingers on her right hand in time to the music. The microphone rested in her left hand. As she turned to face her audience, the crowd went wild, as if she was a favorite performer. The crystal beads of her necklace and earrings sparkled, along with her white teeth as she began to sing. She reminded me of Lena Horne and I thought it might be her biography. But then I realized it was my friend Maggie O'Rourke, looking quite sultry as she sang.

> *I loved you, but you didn't know.*
> *Thought I'd lose you if I let it show.*
> *I wanted to shout out loud,*
> *but would you have heard?*
> *What I wanted from you*
> *was that special word.*
>
> *But you didn't make it easy, oh, no.*
> *You didn't make it easy on me.*
> *But the tables are turned now.*
> *So how easy should I be?*
> *How easy should I be?*

Hmmm. Had Max finally figured things out and given in to his feelings for Maggie? Her frustration came through in the next verse.

Let's be friends? Well, I tried to be.
So we're friends now, but I'm still not free.
I've loved you all this time.
And you loved me, too.
Let's not get it wrong.
Let's let our love be true.

Then the music took over. Maggie moved to its rhythm, occasionally humming into the mike. She stood next to the pianist and sang to him during the chorus. After singing "How easy should I be?" she faked hitting him over the head with the mike! When he faced her in mock protest I saw it was Max, looking classy, yet edgy, with a black shirt and bright red tie. There was chemistry between them as he winked and she smiled back. This was good news!

The music played on as the camera panned the crowd. It stopped briefly on Reggie who was looking for someone. Then he gave up and watched the show as Maggie scat sang along with the sax player, who took the lead. His shiny hair was greased back. I hadn't noticed him until the camera came closer. He and Maggie improvised, echoing each other and getting further from the original tune. She won the contest with amazing vocal range. He acknowledged this with a laugh and a nod. That's when I realized the sax player was Angel with a different look, but I liked it! The quiet scholar had transformed into a lively jazz musician with a flashing smile and a handsome face. If he slicked back his bangs, would he really look like that? Then Maggie moved back to center stage and sung the concluding verse as the music came back around to the melody. The verse included the lines "Now I can shout out loud, we're in love and proud." Then she sang the final chorus and ended with "How easy should I be?"

There was a little musical interlude and then she answered herself, with accompaniment from the drummer after each number in the lyric.

As easy as one,
two,
threeeee.

She ended on a sustained high note. It was happy and triumphant and I sensed that she and Max truly were a couple now. I would have clapped along with the audience in the film, but I was holding that gigantic, partially eaten bag of popcorn. As Maggie's song ended, the camera moved away from the stage and back to the table where Reggie sat stirring his cocktail and looking around. Then a red-haired woman in a gold dress sat down at his table.

"So Mr. Howard," she said, "what brings you to the Club of Dreams tonight?" Her Aussie accent tipped me off. It was Dar all dolled up and gorgeous in makeup and pearls, her hair pulled back in a chignon right out of a Toulouse Lautrec painting.

"Hi, Ruby," he smiled back. "I'm looking for a missing person. My clients seem to think she's here. Maybe you could help me." *Is he looking for me?* I wondered.

"What's her name?" Dar asked.

"Michelle. Michelle Hardtke. She disappeared near here. Ever heard of her?"

"What's she look like?" He pulled out a picture and showed it to her. It was my passport photo. "I'm not sure," she replied. "I'll keep my eyes open for her. Is there a reward?"

He handed her a card. "Oh, yes. Her friends are worried about her. I'm sure they would pay a high price to get her back." That made me smile. As their conversation continued, I felt my bag of popcorn move. I looked down to see a tiny hand reach into it, grabbing a handful. As my eyes adjusted, I realized I was looking into the face of Sunny Howard!

"Sunny, what are you doing in my dream?" I whispered in surprise.

She laughed. "You're in *my* dream, Michelle."

"Oh, really," I said. That seemed odd.

"I'm supposed to dream about you and find out how you are and when you're getting out of the cave," she explained.

"How sweet," I said. "Who sent you?"

"Flor, Fernán's grandmum, and your friend Angel," she said.

"Angel! Please tell him I'm fine."

"I will. Max and Maggie say hello, too."

"You can tell them all that I miss them. But I have food and company from a kindly Irish priest who is also in the cave. I don't know exactly when I'm leaving, though. But Father Moran seemed to think it would be within a couple days. There's a religious retreat about to happen," I said. "I have to be out before the others come."

"Then Dad was right!" she said loudly.

There was a collective "Shhhh!" directed at us. When I looked around, the theater was still empty. And then I realized it was Dar and Reggie on the screen who were shushing us. They had stopped the action and were looking in our direction.

"Sorry," I responded and they went back to their dialogue.

Then I saw María sitting next to Sunny. She tapped the girl on the shoulder and gestured for her to follow. They left me there with my popcorn and drink, but I was content to be left alone watching the movie. The scene continued as Dar walked away from the table with Reggie's card in her hand. She discreetly cast her eyes toward a catwalk at the side of the club, but kept walking. The camera lingered on the catwalk as the curtain of a French door was pushed to the side slightly. The room behind the door was in darkness, but the camera brought the light of the stage into the room just enough to show who was behind the curtain. It was me again, of course, looking as disheveled as ever. Did Dar know I was there? Was she protecting me or keeping me a prisoner?

But before I learned any more, the film broke! My face was twisting around the spool, over and over. Now what? The lights came on. I walked to the lobby where I saw Sunny and María talking. "The film broke!" I shouted, throwing my left hand in the air. I'd forgotten my drink. My right arm still held the bag of popcorn. "What happens next? How does the story end?"

But María didn't look up. She was giving Sunny a hug and whispering to her. The young girl waved to both of us, then walked out the door and out of my dream.

30

The day began as it usually did, with Rudolfo's crow ushering in the morning. It was the first time Angel, Max, and Maggie had heard it, but each was slow to react. This was unfamiliar, even disorienting. All of them were exhausted from the travel and emotional drain of the previous day. In the meantime, Sunny and Darlene were busy in the kitchen.

"Well, you're quite excited this morning, Sunny," her mother noted. "You'll have to share it with us at breakfast. Can you hold on a little longer?"

"I have to talk to Angel, Mum, but I can wait a little longer," she said with disappointment in her voice.

"If you help me it'll take your mind off it," she said, handing her silverware and napkins to put at the place settings. Eventually everyone, despite their sleepy states, had come to the table. Sunny began the blessing.

"Dear God, thank you for bringing everyone here so I can tell them about my dream. Also thank you for the wonderful food Mum has made for breakfast." She concluded with a hint of her announcement. "Please watch over Michelle until she can have breakfast with us in two days. Amen."

Everyone looked at each other and then at Sunny. No one lifted a fork or a cup or began to eat.

"All right then, Sunny. What's the word from your dream? What did you learn last night?" her father asked with genuine curiosity.

"Dad, you were right about the retreat," she nodded enthusiastically. "She'll be out of the cave tomorrow afternoon, right before the retreat starts. She was in my dream last night, but she thought I was in hers. We were watching a film and all of you were in it. I talked to her, but I made too much noise. A woman named María told me more about Michelle leaving the cave. It will be late in the afternoon. She told me where we should look for her, too. You know where the path goes up the mountain?

She'll be coming out near there." Then she giggled. "Michelle was eating a big bag of popcorn that tasted salty."

"You ate popcorn?" Dar asked in surprise.

"A little. It was all right," she answered. "But Michelle liked it 'cause she kept eating it, even when I was talking to her."

"She was probably happy to be eating anything, even if it was only in a dream," her father smiled.

Maggie was fascinated by the concept of a crossover dream. "Sunny, how did she look?" Max couldn't hide a slight smirk.

"Well, it was dark in the theater," Sunny explained, "so it was hard to see. But I saw her in the lobby for a moment. She had a dirty sweatshirt on. Her jeans had a tear in the knee. Her hair was quite messy and her face looked dirty, too. She was upset because the film broke. An Irish priest is taking care of her in the cave, and she's helping him clean the cave. He's very kind. She misses all of you. That's probably why you were in her dream, too," she concluded. "Oh, and I told her that you asked me to dream about her, Angel," Sunny added.

Angel tilted his head and looked into her eyes. "Thank you very much, Sunny," he said with appreciation.

Maggie helped Dar clean up after the meal while Angel and Max did outside chores with Reggie. It was a bright day so Sunny went outside to play, which gave the two women a chance to talk. While Maggie dried the dishes she said, "Your daughter is an extraordinary child, Dar. Do you think her dream will be accurate?"

"Thank you. Yes, I do. She has intuitive skills that seem to grow as she does. Flor's been helpful in giving her little assignments so she can stretch and play with her abilities. For one who has never been in the cave, she has vivid dreams and remembers them well. But it's not a total surprise. She's always been connected to the cave."

"Is it because of your experience there?" Maggie asked, not sure what Dar meant.

"That's part of it. But there's more to the story."

Dar looked into the soapy water where the glasses bobbed. She was silent for a moment or two, then shared information she hadn't told many people. "I have to explain something first. Reggie and I had been unsuccessful in having a baby. I couldn't get pregnant to save my life. We went to a fertility doctor and learned there were problems on both sides. There wasn't much he could offer other than surgery for Reggie and drugs for me, but it was quite expensive with no guarantees. So we gave up at that point and decided it was our lot in life. We talked about adopting and were looking into it before we came here that first time. But it was just as well we didn't adopt," she laughed, "because I got pregnant after all."

"That's wonderful! Was it after you were in the cave?" Maggie asked.

"Oh, I know exactly when it was," she smiled. "When Reggie and I realized we were trapped in El Anhelo, we didn't think we'd get out. It's odd how one reacts in anticipation of an imminent, slow death. In our case, it drew us together. We made love in there. Even though we couldn't have babies, we performed that life-affirming act, that act of love. I don't think I ever felt closer to Reg, or more intimate. It was so dark and damp in the cave, yet those moments felt beautiful and light. It took away our fear for a short time. Afterward we fell asleep and we both had a similar dream, that we *would* survive and a beautiful child would come into our lives. I truly believe Sunny was conceived in that act of love in the cave. She's our daughter, but she's also linked to the Cave of Dreams. She herself is a dream that came to life, after all," Dar explained.

Maggie began to understand something for the first time. "Is she the reason you came back here?"

"Yes, to some extent. She's definitely one reason we've stayed. She's an extraordinary child and has unusual skills that other children outside of this community might not understand. To be honest, we were afraid she'd be made fun of in Australia. But here, she's appreciated as a special person. It also seems her gifts are expanding because of her proximity to the cave. I believe that when Sunny leaves here, perhaps for college, she'll take the world by storm." Dar smiled at that possibility. "Until then, we'll try to prepare her as best we can. Of course, another reason we came back to Teotenaca was because one's creative abilities grow here. We've matured as artists, as many others here have."

"I know you write poetry and Reggie paints wonderful landscapes. But what do the other artists do who live in the area?" Maggie inquired.

Her hostess laughed. "You name it. We've got quite the variety around these parts, everything from very fine traditional Oaxacan crafts to contemporary fine arts. Isn't there an art form you're interested in? Did I hear it was dance?" she asked, but already knew the answer.

"Flamenco," Maggie replied with conviction. "It's my passion. I've been studying it for six years now. I don't suppose there are any flamenco dancers around here."

The other woman smiled mysteriously. "Dancers, no," she said. "Flamenco guitarist, yes! And a great one."

"A flamenco guitarist?" Maggie gasped in disbelief.

"Oh, yes. He's a composer and singer, too, and blends the traditional music with jazz. But Salvador, who is from Seville, is an outstanding guitarist," Dar nodded with appreciation. "You should meet him."

"I would love to meet him. I know more flamenco dancers than musicians. I dance to live music for the occasional performance, but that's about it."

"I have an idea," Dar said, dropping the dishcloth in the water. "We're having a salon here Saturday night. It's an occasion when we invite everyone to come by, bring a dish, and share what they've been working on recently. We'll have performances, too. I can talk to Salvador. If he's coming, maybe you could dance while he plays and sings. It could be quite exciting!" she smiled with mischief in her eyes.

"That would be fantastic! Can we make this our little secret? Don't tell Max or anyone else. If I can work this out with Salvador, to dance to his music, that would be so amazing! If it doesn't work out, it doesn't. But I would love to surprise your guests with a dance performance. Think of me as your top secret act," Maggie laughed.

"I'll be your co-conspirator," Dar agreed. "You'll be wonderful!"

"And Michelle will be back by then. All the more reason to celebrate," she said, striking a pose, "with flamenco!"

31

When I woke up, my back and sides were sore despite the cushion of straw and the partially filled air mattress. I swore I'd finish blowing up that thing before I fell asleep again! I didn't hear Father Moran snoring, so he must have been up and about already. Checking my watch by flashlight, I saw it was nearly noon. The candle still burned, but was dim. I'd check the kitchen to see if he was there. If not, I'd surely find food at least, though I wasn't as hungry as I should be, which was odd. Had my stomach shrunk?

When I stood up, I felt something small and hard inside my right shoe. It hurt, pushing deep into my ankle. The shoelace's knot was so tangled and tight it was hard to undo. I pulled the shoe off and heard the object hit the ground, bouncing away. I trained the flashlight on the cave floor, but all I could see was the uneven surface. Whatever it was had been round like a small pebble. I remembered the bag of popcorn in my dream and realized that thing in my shoe felt like a kernel of unpopped corn. But that was impossible! I put my shoe back on, grateful that the "pebble" had rolled far away.

Once I got my bearings I blew out the candle to preserve it for later and slowly made my way toward the kitchen. I heard singing further down near the room with the waterfall. Since Father Moran wasn't in the kitchen, I followed the sound. It got louder, but I couldn't understand the words. They weren't English or Spanish. There was a light in the chapel and I recognized the mellow tenor voice as its sound bounced around the cavernous space. Was he singing an ancient hymn or prayer? I hadn't meant to disturb him or let him know I was there, but he probably saw my flashlight's beam as I stood outside the room.

"Michelle?"

"Yes, Father. I didn't mean to interrupt you," I said as I entered the sacred space. "I'm so sorry."

"Not to worry. I was just finishing my prayer."

"Prayer? Whatever you were singing was very moving. What was it? You weren't speaking in tongues were you?" I asked in obvious confusion.

"Oh, no," he laughed. "That was Gaelic, though some might think it sounds like tongues. It's an ancient language. That was a prayer written and set to music by my grandfather. I memorized it as a young lad. Even though I've learned the prayers of a priest, that simple hymn is still with me. It allows me to express a variety of emotions that the standardized prayers do not. This room is the perfect place for singing. Did I sound like a choir?" he asked with a smile in his voice.

I laughed. "I wasn't sure what I was hearing. Your voice reverberated so that, I guess it did sound like a choir. But what does the prayer mean?" I asked, sitting down next to him on a stone bench. "It was beautiful."

"Well, let's see if I can translate it into English," he said. "It won't be as poetic, of course. It means,
Oh, you who are my guide, lead me to the righteous paths.
You who know the truth, speak it through me.
You whose love is eternal, let it flow through me.
You who can heal, teach me the way of it.
For you are the maker of all that is good
and I am yours to that end."

"It's beautiful in English, too," I said, in awe of the power of his words, even in a rough translation.

"I'm glad you like it. It touches on what I believe and try to live in my own life."

I looked around at the trickling waterfall and the pool, at the burning candles and the shadows playing on the ancient stone walls. The cave's formations hung like soft, translucent draperies. This indeed was a sacred space, one in which prayers were meant to be spoken, or sung. "Father, it's been a long time since I've prayed on a regular basis. I've meditated every now and then, even in the cave before you found me. But I'm a fallen away Catholic who occasionally searches for her own way. Now and then I think I've found it, but it's not one religion. It's pieces from several. Father, can you advise me on the best way to pray?" I asked.

"The answer is simple, Michelle. Choose prayers you learned, like the 'Hail Mary' and 'The Lord's Prayer.' They may be comforting to you and you can convey your feelings and appeals through them. Or you can merely speak to God in a conversation that comes from your heart.

You can pray for guidance, or forgiveness, but don't forget to express thanks for God's grace. A response can come to you in many forms. For instance, you'll recognize the truth in your heart when you hear it said or you'll think of a solution to a problem that had once seemed impossible to solve. It may surprise you. But, of course, not all prayers are answered, especially the selfish ones that could hurt another person," he cautioned. "Don't pray for hurtful things, or you may pay a price. But talk to God, in whatever way works for you. I suspect you're already praying, but don't realize it." I heard that smile in his voice again.

"One of the things I liked about meditating, when I did it a while back, was listening to quiet, calming music or no sounds at all," I told him. "But now, when I'm alone, I usually fill the silence with music, TV, the Internet. I suppose that's a substitute for human companionship."

"Yes. People fill their lives with distractions," he said.

"There are so many technological toys out there. They suck your time away, if you're not careful. My ex-boyfriend Neil was into buying the latest everything," I sighed. Now how had he gotten into the conversation?

"Do you want to talk about him? He must be on your mind," he advised.

"He was briefly in a dream I just had." I thought I'd seen him in the audience at the Club of Dreams, I realized.

"Do you miss him, Michelle?" he asked in a soft voice.

"You know, Father, with everything that's been happening on this trip, I haven't thought much about him, which was one of my goals for coming here. But he's seeping back into my consciousness, or unconsciousness," I realized in frustration.

"Perhaps it's time to talk about your feelings for him. Tell me, what do you miss about Neil?" he asked in his soothing voice as I sat with him on a stone bench.

"Neil Jones. Huh! He has a great smile, with a little dimple in his right cheek, right here," I said, pointing to my own face. "He was funny, easy going when he wasn't working, ambitious when he was. He was generous and considerate to me. He had more great qualities than any other guy I ever dated. So I appreciated him for that. I thought we'd grown close enough to become more serious about our relationship. We'd talked about marriage. And then, out of nowhere, he announced that he found his soul mate, and it wasn't me after all." I had to stop talking and let the wave of sorrow and disappointment wash over me.

"I'm so sorry, Michelle. Truly," the priest said, putting his hand on my shoulder and squeezing gently. "Now tell me what you *didn't* like about him, even back when you were close to him. Surely there's something. No one is perfect."

I was so hung up on what I was missing about him that I hadn't thought about the break-up in that way. What would I *not* be missing about Neil? "Hmmm, that's a good question, Father. He had a habit of putting dishes in the sink and I was always the one who had to move them to the dishwasher, or they'd pile up. It wasn't a big deal, but I asked him not to do that, but he still did." Maybe he wasn't as considerate as I thought he was, in retrospect. "I did get tired of that. Oh, and there were times when he was rude to his assistant at work. I overheard their conversations a few times when he called into the office. He was always nice to me, but he occasionally talked down to others. That did make me uncomfortable, I must say. I won't miss that."

"What did he think of your art? I know that's important to you. Was he supportive?" the priest asked.

I froze, because Father Moran had hit a nerve. I could forgive Neil for the small things. But this was different.

"I thought he was," I replied. "He complimented my watercolors and told me they were beautiful, that I had talent." That was the good part. "But at one point I realized he didn't take my work seriously. He referred to it as my 'hobby.' I can see why he might think that, since I didn't do it on a regular basis. But that was because I was so busy with work and spending time with him." Maybe I hadn't been serious enough myself and he was picking up on that, I realized now. "Father, I could have used some encouragement, some moral support, even some space so I'd have the time to paint even when he was around. My art is a part of who I am, even if I don't do it as often as I'd like. But Neil never got that. You know, that did hurt me. I wonder how it would have played out if we'd stayed together. I might have given up my art entirely."

"Perhaps he needed some convincing of your sincerity," Father Moran concluded. "You are serious about your art now?"

I remembered the sketches from the days before, the satisfaction of being able to draw again. I was in that zone once more, becoming one with my creative energy. I wanted to keep that flow going, even when I got back to work after this crazy trip I was in the middle of. "I am, Father.

More serious than I even realized, before I came to Teotenaca."

"Well then, perhaps you've lost Neil, but you've gained something else you hold dear, something that is part of your own identity," he concluded. "Remember that the next time you miss him."

"Thank you, Father. I will." And I meant it.

Shortly after that, I followed him back to the kitchen where we drank water with lemon slices floating in it and ate a mixture of sliced apples and pears with grapes. The taste was wonderful, but, because of the dim lighting, I missed seeing the beauty of the colors next to each other. I longed for the return of color in my waking hours.

Our tasks that day would include blowing up the air mattresses and putting the kitchen in order. "We need to sleep, I mean sweep, the floor and clean the counters," he said. He had biodegradable plates, utensils and cups to put away and tasks to be completed in the chapel.

"Father, excuse me, but we haven't been in that large domed room for a while. Is there anything we should be doing in there? I kind of miss that space." That's where the mysterious singing had first lured me into the cave.

"Yes, we could set that up as well. But I have a tendency to fall asleep in that room. It must be that golden dust cloud floating overhead. Just thinking of it makes me want to yawn," he said, promptly doing just that.

"In other words, you'd like to get everything else in order before you tackle that room, right?"

"Correct. I've had my most interesting and fascinating dreams in there. But I have too much to do before I can indulge in that. I'm leaving it for last," he declared with certainty in his voice.

"What are *your* dreams like, Father? I've never had dreams like the ones I've had in here. And I've never remembered them so clearly before. When I think back on my dreams in the cave it's like replaying a movie in my mind, as if I'm watching it all over again. Is it like that for you, too?"

"Yes. It is," he replied.

"There's a person named María in my dreams here. She guides me and answers my questions, usually by putting me into a very lifelike experience. Some have been unsettling, but I don't wake up in the middle of them like I would at home. Instead, I'm a captive of the dream like I am of the cave."

"Have you had any dreams in the City of Darkness, Michelle?" He almost whispered the question.

"No," I said. "Do you think I will? It sounds scary, like a horror film."

"It is frightening, and very real, right out of the dark nature of human history. If you are taken there by María, remember that for you it's only a dream. You'll be safe. She won't let the dream get out of hand," he warned me. I hoped she wouldn't put me in such a dark place. I'd find out soon enough, though.

"You're making me anxious, Father. That could be my next dream! I'll have to trust María, I guess. By the way, do you have a dream guide?"

He smiled. "His name is Antonio. We meet in the City of Light."

"No!" I said incredulously. "I go there, too!"

"I'm surprised we haven't bumped into each other," he laughed. "Maybe we will someday. I would like that. In the future, think of me before you fall asleep and maybe we will meet again, on that dream plain."

"I would like that, too," I agreed. "You've been a wonderful spiritual guide in our waking moments, Father. I appreciate that. Do you write sermons or ponder the big spiritual questions in your Cave of Dreams' dreams?"

He grew silent for a moment and then answered, "I've traversed history, geography, and time in my dreams since I first entered this place. The most memorable dream was when I walked among the crowd lining Christ's route to Calvary. I could feel his sorrow and fatigue as he slowly passed. I wept to see his ordeal. He left a trail of his precious blood all the way to the top of that ghastly hill. When you are out of here, Michelle, visit Father Hernandez and the church in town. The cross in that church bears a Christ figure that may have influenced my dream. That figure came to life for me. Now, when we do the Stations of the Cross in my own church or talk about Christ's suffering, I remember that dream and how real it was. I try to convey that to my parishioners." Given my own dreams, I knew how hyper real it must have been for him. I could understand why his congregation would be awed by his descriptions.

"My dreams also give me advice on counseling, and that is immensely helpful. For instance, one young parishioner came close to committing suicide. He was considering hanging himself and I saw him preparing to do it in my dream. As soon as I could the next morning, I went to see him. I told him the Holy Spirit wanted me to check on him. He was caught off guard, but opened up to me. I was able to help him. His life and his soul were saved because of my dream," he said with emotion in his voice.

"And because you acted on the dream, Father." I wondered what my dreams would tell me to do. "Your dreams are truly a gift, not only for you, but for those you can help and influence. Do you think my dreams might move to a more profound level?" I asked. "Could I help others, too? I did in one dream so far."

He smiled and nodded. "I've talked to others who have been here, of course, and eventually the dreams moved from their own concerns and interests to that of others. It will depend on what your mission is, I think. Time will clarify it."

"Oh, Father, it's all so mysterious, this 'mission' thing," I said in frustration.

"Don't worry," he counseled. "Your calling will make itself known to you, when the time is right."

"And when it does come, what if I don't act on it, what if I decide it's something I don't want to do? Or what if I miss the boat entirely and don't get that *this is it*?" I asked, running my hand through the snarls in my hair.

"That will be your choice, my dear. But you'll surely get more than one opportunity to jump on board," he reassured me.

"OK then, I'll try to be patient. But it won't be easy," I replied.

"Well, here's a thought. I can give you a mission right now. How about helping me clean up this room?" he laughed.

"I guess it's time to get back to work," I sighed. "But I'm going to keep asking you questions, even with a broom in my hand!" I laughed.

While he continued to answer my questions, the very patient Father Moran and I worked hard for the rest of that day sweeping, wiping down the surface areas of the kitchen, putting things in order on the shelves in the pantry, and eventually going back to the sleeping areas where I helped blow up air mattresses. But that was the hardest thing of all. I kept feeling short of breath as a result.

"Father, what happened to the air pump? How did that get missed?" I gasped.

He breathlessly answered, "It was on my list and was supposed to be shipped with the air mattresses. But unfortunately it wasn't in the box. This is harder than putting hay down."

"I'm afraid I'll lose consciousness due to lack of oxygen," I complained, "especially since the altitude is higher than I'm used to."

"All the better to help you sleep well." I knew he was right about that.

"If you need a break there are other things to be done, or we could take a walk to stretch a bit," he offered. "We could try out the new head lamps at the same time." They were meant for the retreat, but he wanted to road test them before everyone arrived.

"A walk sounds great. Do you have anywhere in mind?"

"I do, if you're up for a bit of climbing. It's not far from here. It's an amazing place."

He was more familiar with the cave than I was, but I could only think of one amazing place I hadn't been with him. "I did see a small space with a crystal ceiling. Is that it?" I asked him.

"Oh, the crystal chamber is a wonderful space for private prayer. But this is different. It will require going up into another part of the cave, if you're game after being so out of breath. Interested?"

"Yes!" I didn't want to stay and keep blowing into those mattresses! "Lead the way."

We stopped to pick up two of the headlamps. Taking turns helping each other, we adjusted them to our heads. We still took the flashlights as a backup source of light. But the lamps were great. The beams went right to where we were looking and our hands were free. It was more instantaneous than relying on the flashlight. I followed him to a place where the passage became narrower and snaked its way in several directions. I almost voiced my concern about getting lost but decided to trust him. But then the path seemed to end.

"This is where we go up," he said. "It's not as bad as it looks, once you get past the first three steps." His flashlight outlined the new opening and passage we were to take. "I'll go first." We left the flashlights behind and relied on the headlamps. I followed the movement of his feet until I couldn't see them. "Are you coming?" he called down to me.

"Can you shine your light where I should be stepping, Father?"

"Start here," he said and shone the beam onto a foothold. "Then go here." He moved it to the next step.

I set my feet in those places and pushed into the sides of the narrow passage with my elbows for balance. His light's beam guided me to where he stood. I tried not to look directly into his light. The footholds evolved into steps that led to another open space with a fairly even floor. We walked through it for some distance.

"You'll be surprised when you see where this takes us," he said. I let him lead again and then I heard a sound like a quiet wind getting louder with each step I took. It was familiar and when we emerged into another opening my thought was confirmed. We stood on a ledge beside the formation where water trickled down from above and into the pool in the chapel. This is where I'd first seen the white shape of Father Moran, as I stood below wondering if I was hallucinating. He had seemed a ghost then as he disappeared behind the cave wall.

"You scared me the first time I saw you standing here," I said. "I can't believe *I'm* here now. It gives me a different perspective on the waterfall and the space below." A few candles lit the chamber and I could see the stone bench where I'd slept. The trickle of water had a more echoing sound where we stood. But when I looked around me, I realized this wasn't a dead end. "Where does this lead?" I asked.

"To where I am taking you," he answered mysteriously. The passage curved slightly. There were a few more steps leading us through a tight space that opened into another large room. I had the sensation that we weren't alone. There were stalactites and stalagmites on a grand scale there with a yellow color permeating many of them. They seemed to radiate as I trained my light on them.

"Aren't they a wonder?" he asked, with awe in his voice.

"Indeed," was all I could say.

He gingerly walked through them, like one would enter a crowded party. "Be careful not to touch these formations, especially on their tips. They're still dripping together and the oil from your fingers could do permanent damage," he warned.

"I know that," I said, but it was a good reminder, since I did have the urge to touch them.

He led the way through the chamber, with its walls that slanted to our right. I hoped our lights wouldn't go out. The formations were immense and a few had met each other to form lopsided columns. He stood waiting for me, ten feet beyond the largest of these.

"How did you ever find this place?" I asked.

"The last retreat," he said. "A Lutheran minister showed me. And he wasn't the first. You'll see that soon enough." I followed him through the narrow passage with a low ceiling that forced us to bend over for about ten more feet. Then it opened up into a room with a high ceiling. Long, thin spikes hung from above us.

"Do you know what those are called?" he asked. I'd seen them before but couldn't recall their name.

"I'm not sure."

"Soda straws. A perfect name, don't you think?"

"Yes," I agreed, and certainly the longest straws of any kind I'd ever seen.

"They've been dripping for eons and are hollow inside, I'm told." They were outrageously delicate. I was amazed that a thing so fragile could be so old. "But this is what I wanted to show you," he said, shining his light on a wall behind where the thin straws dripped. At first I couldn't make out anything but a fairly flat surface with odd coloration on it. But then I realized it was a mural that expanded from a central point. And it was huge, maybe fifteen feet across.

"Is it a mandala?" I asked.

"It's reminiscent of one, I agree. Have you seen mandalas before?"

"Only in books. But this is simpler than what I've seen before. It's crumbled away quite a bit. It must be very old."

"I would venture to say indigenous people did it hundreds of years ago. Or perhaps an artist more recently got in there with a ladder or with ropes to paint it on the wall. But they would have knocked down the soda straws. I think it was done a long time ago when the straws were younger and short. Yet it's perfectly symmetrical and round," he observed. The central point of the mural was the remnant of a dark horizontal line. From it emerged a long, black snake's body that wound in a clockwise spiral with the head stopping above the middle point.

"I've seen the snake motif before, on the local pottery," I said, thinking of the vase Flor had given me. "That middle section may be the skin it's just outgrown and shed. And I've seen that background image before but I don't understand what it means. Do you?" I asked. There was a circle of yellow, like a giant sun, that served as background for the snake. Around it there were rays of yellow, maybe sun rays, that whirled away from it. I had the impression that it was also going in a clockwise direction. The rays made the huge disc look as if it were in motion.

"Anyone who's been in this cave has seen that whirling sun when they've left. I daresay you'll see it, too, Michelle. I don't want to say more than that about it. You'll find out soon enough." So another mystery would be solved when I exited, or so I hoped.

"It's so huge, Father. Why do you think it's here?"

"Traditional mandalas are used as a form of meditation, usually, and this may have been, too," he replied. "I'd like to think it's the product of several artists from another age, perhaps a group project. Maybe our tradition of a retreat in the cave started in ancient times," he theorized.

Then something caught my eye. I stood back as far as I could to take in the whole form as we both shone lights around the mural. On either side were similar shapes, but both were quite deteriorated.

"I'll bet these are hands on either side of it, as if the whirling sun is being held in them," I observed.

Father Moran took my thought one step further. "I hadn't noticed them before. I think you're right, but I think the hands are doing more than holding the sun and the snake. I think they're giving them to the viewer. A divine gift, perhaps."

"You mean the hands would be . . . God's?"

"It's a metaphor for divine guidance, I think. It seems this has been a sacred place for a very, *very* long time," he concluded.

32

Max and Angel were left behind after lunch at the Sweet Dreams B & B while Dar, Maggie, and Sunny ran an errand and Reggie met with a group of local people in town about the road repair project.

"Did you see Maggie's expression as she was leaving?" Max asked his friend.

"She seemed happy. I heard them laughing as they were getting into the car," Angel replied.

"Doesn't that strike you as odd?"

"Well, I know we're still concerned about Michelle and what may have happened to her. But the Howards truly are a wonderful family. I think Maggie really likes Dar. She's the only adult female here, so I think that's comforting for her. Are you still being the skeptic?" Angel asked.

"It's my nature, I guess," Max admitted. "Trust doesn't come easy for me. Besides, I'd rather Maggie put herself in my hands," he smiled.

"Maybe she needs a little break. After all, she carried a torch for you for a while, and now you're hovering around her like a moth to the flame," he laughed at the irony.

"Yeah, I finally acknowledged the light from her torch. We could've been together all this time," Max said with regret in his voice.

"But now she understands why you couldn't be."

"And I'm relieved she knows. Well, this leaves our little group down to two," Max observed. "What shall we do with ourselves? Do you feel like hiking a bit? I'd like to take some shots around the trail and the mountain."

"Sure. I need to change my shoes and grab a water bottle. Any chance you might also be looking for openings to the cave?" Angel asked, theorizing that could be the real motive behind Max's desire to hike and photograph while everyone else was away.

"If we happen to find one, I just might take a peek inside," he confessed. "How would you feel about that?"

"I just might go in, too," Angel nodded. And then he added, "But we won't find any openings. You saw how the one I found closed up while we were standing there. It seems unlikely that the cave would open to us again. In fact, any openings might be camouflaged to us, the way that one was."

"Really? Well, let's say the cave does open up to us, or we find a camouflaged place that can be entered," Max theorized. "If we go in, we should have flashlights, batteries, water and food with us. That would take a while to pull together right now. Why don't we just go for a hike, and if we find any openings we'll mark them so we can find them later."

Angel just smiled, understanding that Max thought of himself as their leader. It was natural that he'd want to rescue Michelle himself. But Angel also knew in his heart that there would be no opening in the cave that day. He'd missed his one opportunity to enter and now he no longer felt that urge, that "draw of the mountain," in his gut.

But walking along the trail would put him closer to Michelle. He kept thinking of her, wondering what was happening to her and how she might be changed when they saw her again. His thoughts kept slipping into the prayers he learned as a child, into entreaties to a higher power, to keep her safe, to bring her back to her friends. And he prayed Sunny's dream did become true and that they'd see her the next day. He needed an activity to occupy this time while they waited. Perhaps that was why Maggie seemed glad to leave. It was her opportunity to not think about Michelle for a while.

"I'm with you, Max. I'm happy to hike and play the tourist while you look for the mysterious opening to the cave," Angel said.

Looking into his friend's eyes for a moment, Max observed, "So who's the skeptic now? Let's see what we can find. You grab your shoes and I'll grab my camera and a couple of water bottles."

It was the hottest part of the day, not the best time to go for a hike on a mountain trail, but the two men set out, anyway, rather than walking to town or staying at Sweet Dreams. When they reached the grove of trees, they stepped off the trail, sat down in the shade on the old plank benches that surrounded the campfire ashes and took a break. A slight breeze swayed the branches around them, making music of the wind chimes and bells that hung there. Angel breathed deeply of the calm he felt in that setting. He wanted to stay there listening to the sounds, basking in this sense of peacefulness. But he noticed the tightness in Max's face and the nervous energy in his legs as they swayed back and forth.

"Max, could I have a swig from that water bottle?" he asked. His friend had an elaborate camera case that included a place for food and water. They agreed to take turns carrying it.

"Oh, sure. I may as well join you," he said, extending a bottle. They toasted each other and took deep swallows.

"Can you feel how peaceful it is here?" Angel asked, while speaking slowly.

"I suppose," his friend nodded quickly.

"Why don't you close your eyes and take a deep breath and you'll see what I mean. Let's do it together. Come on, Max, on the count of three. One. Two. Three. Breathe..."

"I am breathing!" he protested.

"Max, listen. We're on vacation. There's nothing we can do to find Michelle. We've already looked. We *will* see her tomorrow. I don't know why, but I really feel it'll happen, just as we've been told. I don't think Father Hernandez and the Howard family are part of a conspiracy to keep her or her fate hidden from us. You need to get a grip," he reasoned with his friend in a sincere voice.

"What are you talking about?" Max protested again.

"Look at yourself," he said. "Your muscles are taut. You can't sit still. Your worry is showing. You're miserable because Michelle is missing and you can't do anything about it. Are you worried about Maggie now?"

"Yes, I'm worried about both of them. Aren't you? Who knows if Maggie will disappear next? I'd feel better if she'd stayed behind with us," he revealed, letting his concern spill out in a voice that broke the calm mood of the clearing. Almost in answer, the breeze blew harder and the music of the chimes and bells increased their volume with a dissonant sound. "How can you be so at peace, Angel? Did they slip Valium in your juice?" he asked in irritation. But then he relented a bit, not wanting to hurt his friend, the only ally he had left, it seemed. "I'm sorry. But I still can't accept everything we've been told. Despite what we've seen, I can't help thinking this is all so farfetched!"

"I can't explain everything I feel," his friend replied in earnest, "but I had a long talk with Father Hernandez that gave me several insights into the history and people of this place. There's a kind of inherent harmony and balance here. The peaceful mood where we are now is a good example. You've brought your distrust and honest concern with you, Max. You can't change who you are, but you're seeing everything through that lens. Somehow you have to open your eyes and your mind beyond that. Or just stay calm and see what happens, if that's possible. If we don't have Michelle back by tomorrow, it'll be time to talk to the authorities. And watch our backs."

"What makes you so sure about these people?" Max asked indignantly.

Angel knew he wouldn't like his answer. Despite Max's early interest in philosophy, he believed only in what he could see and touch. Angel tried to explain. "I'm basing my feelings on my own intuition, I will admit. But it's usually right. I've been in field situations when I knew not to trust the locals, that I couldn't believe what they told me. I've had close calls on occasion, in fact, but my intuition always warned me before it was too late. You can see it in people's eyes, their true intent. And I have to say that I feel very comfortable here. These are generous people. They don't mean us harm. What would they have to gain by hurting us?" he asked his worried friend.

"I don't know. I'm trying to maintain a clear head to see all the angles here. It's possible they could be identity thieves." That sounded desperate to Angel. Max was grasping for any excuse not to trust their hosts.

"All the way out here?"

"Why not?"

"We're not rich, Max," Angel reasoned.

"But we do have good credit."

"That's probably true," Angel smiled.

"Can we talk about this while we walk? I'm getting antsy."

"Maybe we should just walk," his friend replied. He took another drink of water and handed the bottle back to Max. They returned to the trail and headed toward El Anhelo in silence. As they walked toward the mountain's face, Angel was struck by the beauty all around them. There were stands of colorful wild flowers, birds with voices he'd never heard before, and the intense blue of the sky reminded him of an ocean. But Max was oblivious to all of it.

Angel wondered why he didn't feel a little of his friend's mistrust. But he knew the cave's opening up to him was genuine. After all, he could feel the cooler air from within the mountain when he reached through what seemed to be solid rock. Max must have rationalized this as a trick. But how could it have been since it was Angel himself who'd found the note and the apparent opening in the mountain? He'd recognized Michelle's writing and found her hair on the vines. But Max could argue she was forced to write the note and Reggie placed it there for them to find. Yet Max couldn't enter the cave. It had rejected him, so he couldn't understand what Angel had experienced, that impossible reaching into the mountain.

And then there was Flor, who had access to the secrets of the universe, or so it seemed. She had read their hearts. Without her help, Max wouldn't have had the courage to acknowledge his love for Maggie. What could be more real than that?

Father Hernandez had confirmed everything previously said by the Howards. And there was that crucifix in the small church of Santa María, those penetrating eyes of the Christ figure. This town and the rugged mountain they now faced were uncanny, like nothing he'd ever encountered. He realized it would be impossible to share his experiences with anyone back home, especially through his academic writing or in his classes. Max was typical. No one would believe him.

As he walked beside his friend on the mountain trail, Angel was astounded at how their perspective on things differed. Where Max wondered what the Howards or the people of Teotenaca might want to take from them, Angel attempted to understand what this remote place was trying to give them through its people, its mountain and its cave. As he looked over at his worried friend, he remembered the Biblical passage from Matthew 10 when Jesus advised the disciples who were going to "proclaim the good news" to the masses that they should be both "wise as serpents and innocent as doves." He and Max were both trying to uncover the truth, but approaching it from two very different angles.

33

After seeing the mural, I knew I was hungry when the golden stalagmite formations started looking like giant Cheetos coming out of the floor. We stopped by the kitchen for a snack, which helped to mildly invigorate us again. Father Moran told me there were other mysteries in the cave, but he'd only heard or dreamt of them.

"What about bats, Father? I know they're a motif on the crafts in Teotenaca. But I haven't seen any in here. Have you ever seen them in the cave?" I asked with some trepidation.

"Oh, they're here," he assured me. "They keep their distance from us. But there's a large nest deep in the mountain. You'll know when you're getting close to it because it has a strong ammonia smell." I made a mental note to head the other way if I smelled ammonia. "Their droppings, or *guano*, are supposed to make a wonderful fertilizer. It has quite a reputation in these parts. Father Hernandez claims that when the local people access the cave, some go to there to collect it. It helps the crops grow, so the bat is seen as a positive creature, not demonic at all."

"Is that it?"

"As far as I know. Why do you ask?"

I was disappointed with his answer. I'd heard of harvesting bat guano before. "It just sounds so normal, that's all. Normal seems unusual in the Cave of Dreams."

"Point taken," he laughed.

We went back to work inflating the air mattresses. But in the back of my mind I kept wondering how much time I had before I'd be falling asleep again. Maybe I dwelt on it too much. Call it the power of suggestion, but before long the fatigue set in again as I finished filling a mattress and capped its air tube. "Father, I'm sorry but I have to take another break," I said with a yawn. "Seems like I just got back to work."

"Use this mattress, Michelle. It's nice and full of air. I'll get a blanket for you."

I was conscious enough to remove my sweatshirt this time. It had become soiled with blood from the cut on my head, as well as the moisture, mud and dirt of the cave. I didn't want to rub that mess into the blanket. Instead of untying my shoes, I pulled them off and dropped them on the ground next to me. It was great to wiggle my toes again. But before I could take off my dirty jeans, I fell asleep wrapped in the fresh blanket. It felt soft on my arms and the full air mattress created the most comfortable surface I'd surrendered my back to in days. I heard Father Moran's voice in the distance as I drifted off into unconsciousness. "Sleep well, dear."

If I'd known what was coming, I'd have been more wary of falling asleep that time. My dreams had been a mix of emotions as María guided me through lessons that ranged from inspiring to frightening. The Cave of Dreams' learning process had revealed many aspects of my own personality and life as well as that of other people, like Edgar, the homeless man. But what came next altered my understanding of the world forever. It was this dream that turned the tide of my life.

It began quietly. My body was floating on the air in the mattress and my mind seemed to be floating as well. Then I became aware of a breeze blowing my hair into my face, obscuring my vision. As I pushed the tangled mess on my head aside, I realized I was standing on a high bluff overlooking a blue sea. The water's surface rippled under the heavy wind until white caps topped the choppy waves. Behind me, in the City of Light, I heard shutters banging against houses. The wind rose in intensity as if a huge storm was approaching. But where was María?

"I'm here with you, Michelle. I have not seen you for a while. Father Moran is keeping you busy, huh?"

"María!" She stood behind me. "I'm glad to see you. Yes, we've been preparing for the retreat," I replied.

"And now I need you back. Your time in the cave will soon end and you still have much to observe and learn while you are here. In fact, this dream will be the most important you'll encounter." She spoke quickly.

"Does it have anything to do with this weather? It feels like a hurricane is coming." I could hear my voice competing with the howl of the wind. She motioned for me to step inside a small courtyard with high walls. It was easier to talk in its quiet space.

"Yes. Soon the sky will darken and we'll be engulfed in a storm. It's the natural course of things. There is sun and light and warmth, but then there is rain and darkness and cold. Opposites pervade the Creation. In the physical world where you live this is common: day and night, land and sea, birth and death, male and female. Opposites create order. They even help to define each other. For instance, one cannot truly understand day until one experiences night. And so one cannot truly understand the City of Light until one experiences the City of Darkness. We are opposite entities, yet we are linked. Michelle, from your experiences in the cave, how would you describe what light means to you?" she asked.

So the City of Darkness was up next. Father Moran had warned me about that place. But I tried to focus on what my guide was asking, as she prepared me for the next sequence of events that would take me there. I thought about her question for a moment. "Light has so many meanings. It's illumination, certainly. No one can see in total darkness without a form of light. If there were only the dark, there would be no hope of being able to see to move around in the cave, for instance. I can't imagine being alone in the cave with no light." The thought made me shiver. But I was talking about light, so I switched to a metaphorical approach. "Light represents enlightenment and understanding. Hope. And even life. Where would we be without the sun?" I concluded.

"By contrast, how would you define darkness as a metaphor?" she asked.

I thought over what I had just said and answered, "Darkness is the absence of light. If it's the opposite then it could also represent ignorance and misunderstanding, despair, and death." I could hear the wind getting louder just beyond the walls.

"Exactly," she nodded, coming closer to me. Her expression had become more intense. "The earth is extremely out of balance because there is far more darkness than light in it. For many, life is like sailing in a relentless storm on a dark sea or entering a cave without a light source. The world is desperate for more light, Michelle. Many people, even nations, need to believe in hope and possibility. But they need light to find their way. And now, you will learn more about the darkness so you can bring more light into the world. You have the capacity to become a beacon of light and enlightenment, even a messenger of hope, through the lessons of this dream."

I was dumbfounded by her words. "How can *I* do all that?"

She smiled saying, "Don't underestimate yourself. Too many people do. They have that ability, as well, but their doubts keep them in shadow. But now it is time. Follow me, please." She quickly led me toward a door as the rain fell heavily in the courtyard. The sky above us had become darker with a strange greenish hue behind the clouds. We stepped through the door and slowly descended a long staircase that was lit with torches.

"What am I supposed to do?" I asked. "Father Moran warned me that this would be a rough dream."

She ignored my comment and explained the "simple" rule. "You must walk through the City of Darkness alone. There is a single street, a path that will lead you through it, but you must stay on it. Even when it seems it has disappeared, follow your intuition so that you are moving forward. If at any time you can no longer bear it, stop along the way and a door will open to you. But before you walk through the door, see who is on the other side of it. Look into their eyes to determine if you can trust them. If you feel you cannot, walk on. Another door will open," she instructed me.

"But what will I be doing there? Just walking through?" I pictured a crime-ridden street in a rough neighborhood, but my expectations were often wrong in these dreams. It didn't sound easy, whatever it would be.

"Yes, observing and experiencing everything around you as you travel through it. You may stop, but be careful if you do. Don't lose direction," she warned in an urgent tone. "Keep your senses alert at all times. Learn all you can about the darkness so that you can remember it when you're back in your own world. In this dream you will be able to see and hear the darkness as well as feel it, even smell and taste it. Father Moran is right. This is a difficult dream, but the most necessary one. When you return to the cave, you can talk to him about it. He will help you understand it."

"You're frightening me, María. What if I'm not up to this?" We had reached the bottom of the stairs where there was a large door, the only one I had seen in that long, deep passageway.

"This is the entrance to the City of Darkness, Michelle. I cannot go with you, but I will be near. You can stop this dream at any time. Call my name and I will answer when you need me." She paused to see my reaction to her words. I was leery of the whole thing, even with her reassurances, but I wasn't being given another choice.

"Are you ready?" she asked in a serious tone.

I didn't really feel I was, but my dream self said, "Yes," and the door creaked open. I stepped through it and surveyed what lay ahead of me. What I saw seemed normal enough, a tree-lined street on a sunny day, in fact. Surprisingly, there was no storm here. I turned around to ask my guide how this place could be called the City of Darkness, but she and the door were gone. Then I heard her voice reply to my unspoken question.

"Appearances can be deceptive. That is one of the lessons you will learn here. Pay attention to what is truly happening because it may be hidden at first glance."

I stepped into this new place with fear, but curiosity, too. The first thing I smelled was a sweet scent of roses, but then I detected an underlying chemical odor. It was subtle, but I felt my throat react with a sudden scratchiness. Perhaps there was a chemical plant nearby or a toxic dump. Yet I saw large pink roses climbing a trellis beside a beautiful white house. Two rocking chairs stood on the wide front porch. I heard voices coming from the backyard. They were quiet at first, but then I heard shouting and the sound seemed to get closer. A young girl around ten years old ran through the bushes and toward the front where I stood. But her body lurched backward suddenly. A male adult had run after her and he pulled her arm to stop her.

"When are you going to do as I say?" he shouted and pulled her arm again. I could tell she was in pain.

"Okay, okay. But stop hurting me, Dad. Please," she begged.

"I'll show you what to expect if you ever do this again," he shouted.

"No!" she screamed, pulling her arm away from his grasp. She ran toward me and as she passed I saw the look in her eyes, as if she were a wounded animal running as fast as she could from a hunter. I saw blood and tears on her cheek and a rip in her blouse. Her arm was already turning a darker color where she had been held. When I looked back at the man he just stared at me with as cold an expression as I'd ever known. *Poor girl*, I thought. But she'd disappeared down a side street and I knew there was nothing I could do. So I walked on.

It wasn't long before the well-kept houses changed to apartment buildings that needed painting and repairs. People sat on the steps on both sides of the street chatting and laughing. Several cars passed by with loud music blaring from their speakers. I could feel the rumble of the bass reverberate through my body and it set me on edge. One of the loud cars pulled up in front of a building further up the block. There was shouting and swearing between the people on the steps and those in the car. And then I heard a sound like firecrackers and the people on the steps screamed as the car sped off past me. I made eye contact with a young man in the car who was holding a gun. Looking wary, he scowled back and lowered it out of sight.

On the stoop where the bullets had been fired, three people lay wounded, including a child. Their blood trickled down the stairs like a slow moving red waterfall. A woman screamed, "My baby! Why did he shoot my baby?" The young girl was limp in her arms, with blood staining her tiny chest. Soon afterward there were sirens. An ambulance and a police car drove up, followed by a News van with an antenna on top. I walked through the crowd standing and staring from the sidewalk. Only a few came forward to offer help to the wounded and their family. I hoped the child was still alive, but I had a feeling she wasn't. I started crying at that, at the waste of an innocent life, at the coldness of the triggerman.

This dream will only get worse, I thought. These two incidents were the type of thing I had heard in the news but had never witnessed myself. I wondered what would be next as I passed several abandoned lots filled with weeds and garbage. As I looked toward them I saw things going on in the block behind them. The houses there were really shacks next to a few scattered trees. I saw a burning cross in front of a building and something large hung from one of the trees. Was it human? Where was the fire department now?

"María, what am I seeing?"

Her voice came back in my head. "It is what you think it is, a manifestation of racism, and it was common once. In this dream, you will see historical connections to the current darkness." And then I understood the horror in the distance. I thought of Billie Holliday's song "Strange Fruit." It caught my breath. I walked faster.

Further down, on a corner on the other side of the street stood a young, black woman, maybe a teenager, in a clingy red short skirt and revealing blouse. She stood provocatively while holding a lit cigarette. Every time a car drove by she smiled at the driver through bright red lipstick. As I waited for the light to change, she talked with the driver of a late model silver car through the passenger's window. The older well-dressed white man opened the car door to let her in and they drove off, leaving only her smoking cigarette on the curb.

When I crossed the street, the scene shifted. I wasn't in urban America anymore. It felt as if I'd crossed an ocean and stood in a foreign city. A store sign written in both Hebrew characters and English clued me that it was probably Israel, but the cars on the street were from an earlier decade. As I approached a group waiting for a bus, a man grabbed a large purse right out of the hand of a young woman standing there. She screamed. He'd timed his theft so that he was able to run across the street and hop on a bus going in the opposite direction. No one ran after him and the victim seemed to be in a daze. Everyone standing there was caught off guard.

"Are you all right?" the people around the victim asked.

She was silent at first, then laughed with a kind of relief. I thought I heard her say under her breath, "One bus is as good as another," and then she ran away toward a side street. As she turned the corner, we felt the tremor of a huge explosion only a block away. The bus the thief had boarded had blown up! I heard metal fragments whiz past my head. The people that stood at the bus stop began to wail.

"That could have been us!" someone screamed. "It was the stolen purse!" Sirens soon droned louder as ambulances came from all directions. I walked quickly away from the destruction behind me. I couldn't bear to watch the smoke and listen to the screams.

María's voice whispered in my head, "How are you doing, Michelle?"

"Shaky," I said. "But I'm sure there's much more to see."

"It never ends," she replied in a flat tone.

I crossed the street again and saw signs with Arab characters this time. People were coming back from the market, baskets in hand. Suddenly I heard a helicopter that sounded very close. The people ran in all directions, screaming and cowering toward the ground. A man motioned for me to get down. I braced myself against a wall as the low-flying helicopter passed right above me. The rotating blades whipped up a dust cloud full of the heat from its engine. The smell of diesel filled the air. Then the copter hovered above a building in the next block. There was a loud noise and a huge explosion. Fragments of brick and glass flew past us. I covered my head even tighter with my arms. The copter had fired a missile and obliterated whatever it hit. Whoever it hit. I ran, crossing the street again, but still moving in a forward direction.

When I did, the scene changed again. It was quieter now, but a few moments later I walked past a gigantic crater in the street. It was larger than the helicopter's missile could have made and I wondered what had caused such a huge hole. As I stared into it, I viewed what seemed to be a silent black and white documentary movie. First I saw a vintage plane flying. Then it dropped a large bomb. The camera followed the bomb down for part of the way, then panned back to the plane. In the plane's window I saw a familiar reflection, and then saw the thing itself, a mushroom cloud. The familiar and frightening image was followed by horrendous scenes of destruction and human suffering. I knew it was Hiroshima or Nagasaki, Japan, 1945. I saw dazed women with kimono patterns burned into their bare flesh. People were missing limbs and bleeding helplessly. One mother carried a baby, but the blanket was covered in blood, like the young shooting victim I'd just seen. Many people were burned and cut from falling debris. The buildings were piles of rubble. Other people, who seemed unharmed, were walking aimlessly in shock. Smoke and ash filled the air where homes had once stood. I witnessed scene after scene of devastation until I had to look away. I felt my stomach churn and I began to gag.

"It was an American bomb," I heard an older man say. He was looking into the hole, too. "They wouldn't admit it. They said it had been Iraqi, that it had gone off course. But a British journalist traced the serial number on a fragment to a weapons plant in Texas. Many people died here, including my daughter and grandchildren. But why?"

"Are you talking to me?" I rasped, since we were the only people present.

"I'll talk to anyone who will listen," he said, shaking his head. "How can anyone say these people died in the interest of freedom or democracy? This war, this occupation and violence, all have brought a plague on our people. So many have died because of it! What did we do to deserve such a horror?"

All I could think to say was, "I'm very sorry for your loss, sir. *Very* sorry." And then I stepped around the crater and kept walking. I heard bombs exploding in the distance. María answered my unspoken question. "That's the city of Aleppo in Syria being shelled. Their ruler is murdering multitudes of his own people."

"Horrible!" I mumbled and shuddered, knowing women and children were dying along with the rebels. Still, I managed to stay on the path moving forward.

But suddenly I found myself at the end of a long line of ragged people. Many had cloth wrapped around their feet instead of shoes. The street had become white with snow and the temperature dropped. We were in a rural setting this time. The buildings were gone. As I got closer to the people I asked where they were going.

One man replied, "Does it matter? They want to kill as many of us as they can. They say we're going to a new home, but the truth is they stole our homes and our land. They don't care if they kill women, children, and our elders. They just want the land. Why else would they move us in winter?" he cried. I looked into his eyes and realized he was an American Indian.

"Are you Cherokee?" I asked.

"Yes," he replied. I realized I was now on the Trail of Tears.

"Keep moving!" I heard a voice yell behind us. I expected a soldier on horseback, but I turned to see a Japanese soldier. When I looked back to the group I was following, it was only white women and children now, dressed in dirty 1940's clothes. The temperature had jumped to a tropical heat. They smelled of sweat.

"Where are we?" I asked.

"I don't know exactly," a young woman replied. "But I know Manila is far, far away by now."

"No talking!" a voice commanded from behind us. This time when I turned around I saw a German soldier from World War II. "Stop here," he yelled.

When I turned around again, we were being herded through a gate. There was a train standing nearby and people were coming off of it behind me. I was motioned to go to the left. I looked around for another clue and saw the name of the place. As I'd feared, it was "Auschwitz." Now what was going to happen? There were mothers separated from their children and husbands from their wives. The crying and wailing reminded me of the people at the bus stop.

"Keep moving!" a voice screamed behind me.

It was hot now. When I turned around it was a Latin American soldier this time. The people ahead of me were indigenous women wearing colorful woven clothes, some carrying their children. And they were terrified. I had read about the genocide of the Maya in Guatemala by government troops, and now I was witnessing it as one of them! We were herded over a hilly area, then stopped at a deep ditch. The soldiers told us to stand in front of it. The women held onto each other and wailed. One of them grabbed my arm as the soldiers began to fire at us. I didn't feel the pain of being shot, but I was yanked backwards into the hole with the other woman. Then someone landed on top of me and an elbow stabbed deeply into my left side. Blood splashed my cheek. I heard a moan a few feet away and a gun fired, then silence. I closed my eyes and tried to look like I wasn't breathing. But I wanted to scream! This time I felt pain from the elbow wedged into my left side. I could barely breathe because a body was lying across my chest. I felt the weight of death all around me and kept my eyes shut tightly.

Then it grew quiet and I feared I was passing out, until I heard a creaking sound as if a heavy door was being opened. Another deep male voice rang out. "Wake up! Wake up! We're in port and you'll be leaving this stinking ship for your new lives. Now, get up and move!"

When I opened my eyes I was in the hold of an old ship. I was chained at the ankles. The bodies next to me had been transformed into living, but gaunt Africans. The smell of sweat, urine, and feces filled the air. I wondered how long they had been in these cramped conditions. I knew that for them, this was the terrible beginning of a lifetime of enslavement. Stiffly, we moved in sync as we left the ship. Then we stood in bright, hot sunlight on the dock. The humidity was tropical. The Africans could barely see after spending weeks in the hold of the ship. They stumbled and tried to shield their eyes. We moved in unison as we were told. I closed my eyes from the sun for a moment.

But when I opened them, I was no longer with the same group. I heard singing and realized I was now part of a chain gang. Still shackled, we were walking along a road toward a field where other men were working. They were the ones singing, accentuating their beat with hammers as they broke stone into pieces. As we approached the group, I saw how exhausted they were. A guard monitored their movements at gunpoint. They were given a break to eat while we were told to take over the work. *What had I gotten myself into this time?* I thought. My shackles were removed. I stretched before doing anything and that's when I noticed there was a church in this field. Men with machetes were standing in front of it. One of them gave a signal and the armed men ran in screaming, machetes raised. I heard screams and wails, metal slashing flesh and cutting bone, people crying for mercy and getting none. Rwanda! Despite the pain in my side, I ran as fast as I could, not knowing or caring if I was on the path going forward anymore.

I tried to get my bearings, which was virtually impossible. I looked over my shoulder to see rice paddies this time. People in large straw hats bent in the mud, moving swiftly and mechanically in line. In the distance there were groves of trees. It was steamy here, but beautiful and peaceful, until I heard the sound of planes approaching. The people scrambled out of the rice paddies and ran toward the trees. But as the planes came near, I saw a fiery substance descend on the trees. They burst into flames! From the strong chemical smell in the air I figured it was napalm and this was Vietnam. I fled as the planes passed over again and their shadows outran me in the rice paddy. I couldn't have been more obvious in that setting. There was nowhere to hide. Then something else flew over. It was a drone heading for a target, and I was glad it wasn't me!

As I reached the road I saw that time and place had shifted again. I'd gotten back to the street where I'd started my walk and now the planes were commercial jets high above. Their white exhaust trails crisscrossed in the sky creating a fluffy, white "X."

Like María had told me to do, I kept moving. But I was exhausted! I felt like I'd been on a real death march. The constant shifts in history, location and weather were disorienting. Was I still on that forward moving path or not? My muscles were tired, I was out of breath, and I still felt pain in my left side where the elbow had lodged against me in the ditch filled with the dead and dying.

"What next?" I cried out loud.

"You're back to your own time, Michelle. But that is not necessarily a comforting thing. Let me know when it is enough."

I was approaching a viaduct with cars driving at top speeds above me. They were traveling so close to each other I was afraid they might crash. As I crossed under the bridge, I heard it happen, a chain reaction of crashes. The sound reverberated in the tunnel, then traveled further away like an echo. The people above me had to have been seriously injured or killed. Pieces of broken metal lay in the street ahead of me.

"Crazy people! You'd be surprised how often that happens around here. I can't sleep sometimes, it's so loud!" a slurring man yelled. I hadn't seen him under the bridge. He'd blended into the background on the other side of the street where he lay on a piece of cardboard. He smelled as if he hadn't bathed in weeks. His leathery skin had weathered to a reddish color. "You'd think if they owned fancy cars like that, people would be more careful. All they care about is getting ahead of everyone else. Crazy!"

He scurried out of the tunnel to see what had fallen from above. He found two cell phones and a wallet with cash in it. Then he gathered pieces of the twisted metal.

"Do you live here?" I asked.

"It's as good a place as any in this town," he said. "Except for the noise. They honk a lot, too," he laughed. "The sirens are something else! They'll be starting up next." He focused on me and said, "You got a buck, lady?"

"No, sorry," I said. "I left my wallet behind and I don't have any money with me."

He laughed. "I should have known. You look a mess, like you've been to hell and back."

"Yeah," I replied. "Something like that. Only I'm not back yet."

"Watch yourself when you walk out of this tunnel. It's dangerous out there," he warned, as if I didn't know already.

"Thanks," I said and looked above me as I walked back into the daylight. I gingerly stepped over pieces of burning car parts, then looked up at the smoking, twisted wrecks on the bridge. I heard moans and sirens, but kept walking.

In the next block there was a row of storefronts. The windows had been painted black but I could see light through a few openings in the paint. There were no signs to identify what was happening in these buildings. When I passed them I heard screams coming from inside.

"What's going on in there, María?"

"People are being tortured."

"What! Why? Who are they? Who's doing this to them?"

"Are you brave enough to look closer? There's a window where the paint has peeled off next door."

Cautiously, I looked through that clear place in the window and saw a man in his underwear with a hood over his head. He was being led to a place not far from the window by a couple of men in military uniforms. They tied his hands behind him, then attached a lever to the rope. They turned a crank and I saw a rope move up toward the ceiling. Then the man was hoisted upward until his feet were off the ground. He screamed as his shoulders seemed to pop out of their sockets. He was suspended from the ceiling. As he cried out from the pain, two men below laughed and talked to each other, but I couldn't hear them. I stepped away from the window, then noticed another opening in the dark paint at the next storefront. I looked in and this time I saw a woman being led past me. Her head was hooded, too, and all she wore was a torn, dirty slip. Her hands were tied in front of her and she walked awkwardly with her feet wide apart. Blood dripped down between both her legs. Someone inside approached the window, so I quickly walked away.

"María, that doesn't answer my questions. Where is this happening? And why?"

"It happens all over the world, Michelle. It happens to innocent people, to those who resist authority and policies they don't agree with. It happens when one group de-humanizes another and wants to exercise their power over them. It happens for the amusement of soldiers, mercenaries, revolutionaries, and terrorists. It happens in police stations, even where you live in Chicago. But there is no just reason *why* it happens." I knew she was right, and it made me feel sick again.

"It's enough, María. I've had enough of this dream," I screamed out loud. "How do I stop it?"

"Keep walking, Michelle. Try to be calm. You'll see shops up ahead. One of them is a gallery. You'll be safe if you enter there," she informed me. "But be careful on the way."

"Thank God," I whispered, hoping I would get there before anything else happened. But as I crossed the street I heard a siren approaching. I was halfway across when a huge black vehicle swerved into my path, narrowly missing me. Its side was badly scratched and it squealed as it made the turn. I ran to the other side safely, before a police car screeched around the corner in hot pursuit, sirens screaming and lights flashing.

I picked up my pace, too, as I looked for the gallery. It was in the middle of the block. In the window, under the sign that read "Crossroads Gallery," was a large abstract painting that reminded me of the white "X" I'd seen in the sky made by two jet trails. When I opened the door a chime sounded somewhere in the building. As I turned to close the door behind me, I saw a boy a short distance away. What should have been the other side of the street was now a dry, dusty field. He was about 12 years old, with a gun almost as big as he was strapped across his shoulders. His right arm rested on the barrel as he turned toward me. His clothes were ragged and dirty, and his expression was cold for one so young. I'd always remember him, a nameless African boy forced into fighting as a child soldier. For all the things I'd seen in the City of Darkness, this corruption of innocence was one of the saddest. I quickly pulled the door closed and stepped inside the building.

But instead of the open gallery space I'd expected, there was a long hallway with no signage. The walls were painted a soft blue with a hint of white that resembled clouds. I followed it cautiously until it opened into another larger hall to my right. A radio was playing, so I walked in the direction of its sound. The news was being given and I heard a familiar voice lamenting, "Why did he shoot my baby?" Details of the shooting followed in graphic detail. And after that there was more news and, of course, it was all bad.

At the end of that hall was the gallery's sign with a large arrow pointing toward an open doorway. I walked in the direction of the arrow and finally found the place. The radio stood on the reception desk of a young Asian woman dressed in black with hair as dark as coal. Thick black-framed glasses offset her pale skin. A small, red heart-shaped pin seemed to float as it projected out from her glossy, black blouse.

"Hello," she said cheerfully. Her eyes seemed friendly, too. "Welcome to Crossroads Gallery. Have you been here before?"

"No," I said, wondering if I was really safe here. I looked from left to right to see what was coming next.

"Well, we feature outstanding artists, many of whom are international. You can learn a lot about the world by looking at their work," she smiled. The news continued almost as a background sound. Its gloomy pronouncements didn't seem to faze her.

"What station are you listening to?" I asked.

"The all-news one. I forget the call numbers. But I don't really listen to it. It's too depressing. I just keep it on for the customers, when they come, so they can find the gallery." At least she had customers. That was hopeful. "We have a wonderful show on right now. It's a Mexican photojournalist named Rodrigo Guzmán who documents refugees all over the world. They're beautiful black and white photographs, despite the occasional gruesome subject matter. Please, come in and take a look. He deserves as much attention as he can get from the public. And we're donating a portion of his sales to a local charity," she revealed.

That was the only bright thing I'd heard in this entire dream. But his photographs were difficult to view, especially after what I'd just experienced. I could see the despair in the eyes of Guzmán's subjects. Each print had a large label below it that bore an explanation of the documented scene. Hope was dimming for these people. They owned only the clothes they'd worn as they fled for their lives. Many of the children were orphaned or had been separated from their families. They were from Africa, South America, and Central America. Guzmán had obviously been doing this for years, based on the quality of his work and the number of refugees he'd recorded.

I was moved, as well as fascinated, by the intricate contrasts of light and shadow in the images. The artist's depth of field was remarkable, too, with amazing detail in the backgrounds. But there was one photograph I found impossible to walk away from. The scene was a group of Afro-Colombians walking down a road carrying belongings on their heads, their backs and in small carts. They'd fled their town because the paramilitary wanted their land and had terrorized them to get it. The label for the photo said those who resisted had been killed. The survivors were on their way to another town, hoping to be taken in and given a place to stay. Even so, I suspected it would be overcrowded and they'd be dependent on others for food, water and shelter. There was also the strong possibility they might never get their land back. From my own experiences in the City of Darkness, I could imagine what it was like for this group of people. It looked sunny and hot. There were probably flies everywhere. People were squinting and I saw sweat dripping from their faces. Their feet were probably calloused and tired, their muscles weakened by the effort of carrying so much.

The face of one young mother in the foreground of the photo was particularly heart wrenching. I tried to decipher her expression and determine if the young man walking beside her was her husband or a relative. In an effort to see the detail in the photo, I closed my eyes for a second to refresh them, then opened and closed them quickly a couple more times. But when I looked ahead to where the woman should be in the photograph, I found myself on the side of the road pictured in the photo as the mass of fleeing people passed by me. I had entered the actual scene myself! In the distance, I saw the young woman with the baby approaching. It was as I'd imagined it. Flies buzzed around my head in the humidity and heat. It looked like a rainforest in the distance. The sky was intensely blue and the sun almost blinding. There was the sound of moving feet and wheels, but no one was talking. As the woman came closer, I heard her baby whimpering. She whispered soft words to calm it, not slowing her pace, and not looking down into its face. There were bundles strapped to her back.

Without warning, there was a flash of light and everything froze! The entire scene, both people and landscape, had changed to black and white with that flash. It had transformed into the image that hung in the gallery, but it was life-sized and three-dimensional. Startled, I realized that I stood only a few feet from the young woman who'd captured my attention, so I walked over to face her. She was still as a statue and without any flesh tones. Both her clothes and skin were exactly the same black and white shades as they were in the photograph. The whole scene was like that. I could have walked down the road to get a better look at those who were only shadows in the photo. I could have followed the journey to where it began. But I was the only flesh and blood, living person in this tableau now, and it was eerie. How did I get there? And how would I get out?

I walked among the people frozen in place on the road. But from one area I heard movement and saw color. I was hoping to discover who else was there when I saw a man with a camera moving among the people as I was.

"Good day," he said matter-of-factly.

"Good day," I said. "You must be the photographer, Rodrigo Guzmán?"

He stopped and pointed at the camera. "Good guess," he smiled.

"Where am I?" I asked.

"You're in my photograph," he replied with no hesitation.

"Why?"

"I don't know why. I suppose you were drawn into it, metaphorically at first, and then physically," he said. "This is a dream, after all. Anything is possible."

"This dream has been so real, I keep forgetting it's just a dream. So I can dream my way out, right?"

"Theoretically, yes," he replied.

"But I'm not ready yet," I said. After all, I had a chance to talk to the artist now.

"Something on your mind?" he asked.

"What can you tell me about these people, especially this woman with the baby?"

"They were all moving past me," he explained. "I captured them as a group, after all. But let me look at her more closely."

He walked over and looked into her face. "She's definitely younger than she appears. Her face is very drawn. She's quite tired, probably worried about her child. He doesn't look well, either."

I took a closer look at them both and came to the same conclusion. The baby was thin. "What about this young man?" I asked. "How do you think they're related?"

"He may be her husband, but he has the same nose she has and similar eyes. He's probably her brother, or a cousin. She may have lost her husband. Hopefully they'll help in each other's survival. They may have been separated from the rest of their family, or the only survivors of it. They seem to be together, but set apart from the others," he surmised.

"Your label for this piece says the group is fleeing from a town invaded by paramilitary forces. What do you think happened to them after you took this photograph?" I asked.

"I don't know. They walked to another town. Perhaps they were eventually relocated. Perhaps they went to the city to look for work. The obstacles would be high. Many refugees must contend with disease, poverty and a deep depression. I've seen it in many of the people I've photographed. But there is hope for them, too. The best thing these three people could do is stay alive until things improve. Hopefully, they did," he said with concern, looking into the eyes of the woman, who seemed more like a girl at this range. She was a couple inches shorter than I was. "But since I took the photo multi-nationals have come in to plant African palm oil trees on land like theirs. It's a fuel substitute, among other things. They won't get their land back, I'm afraid."

I was appalled but before I could say anything, he took a deep breath because he had a lot to say. "A photograph preserves one moment in the continuum of time," he explained. He became more passionate as he spoke. "I try to pick a representative split second in the story of these unfortunates. I flash a light into their lives, by illuminating the truth of their desperate situations. I want people to see the images and I want them to understand that the news they see on TV or the Internet is *real*. It is someone's *reality*. I want them to see the faces of the millions in the world who suffer because of power struggles and wars. I want people to be moved by these images, to be empathetic and try to understand this pain." He shook his head. "Perhaps that is a lot to ask, but then I want them to help these people, to take away their suffering. I want to see empathy replace selfishness. I work for understanding to replace ignorance in this world," he emphasized and then shifted his argument.

"And what if those who live comfortably in safe places had a change in their circumstances, perhaps a fire, or a hurricane like your Katrina or Sandy, or a terrorist attack? What would they want the people who hear news of such a disaster to do? How would they want those who see pictures of them in crisis to react? I want to motivate people to make a difference, because they can.

"Just think," he said, coming close to my face, "what if *you* traded places with her? What if it was *you* in my picture instead of this young woman?" he asked, pointing his hand toward me and then toward her. "What would you want people to think when they saw you? What would *you* want them to do?"

I didn't know how to answer his question. I meant to, but I didn't know what to say. I had to look away from the intensity of his eyes and when I did, everything shifted again. I found myself outside of the photograph, looking at the small, distraught faces of the young woman and man. But I found that her face had been transformed. It bore the same expression, but now it was like looking into a mirror, because, despite the difference in our skin color, her features had become my own.

34

"This food is surprisingly good," Max nodded. "What do you think, Angel, does it pass your taste test?" The three friends sat at an outside table at Café Puebla on the main street in Teotenaca.

"It reminds me of my grandmother's cooking. Very tasty," he exclaimed as he washed down a morsel of tortilla with a dark beer.

While they ate, Maggie sat silently, mentally rehearsing her surprise performance at the upcoming salon. Salvador's composition was rich and exotic with elements of jazz and African rhythms. It would be difficult for her to remember all of the music, since her rehearsal time with him was limited. But he promised to cue her each time the musical energy was about to shift. She'd fake her way well enough.

Michelle, her missing friend, also came to mind. The three of them had one more day to carry on without her, or so they'd been told. But what would they do if she failed to appear? Were there authorities in town who would help them? She wanted to be upbeat and hopeful, yet Max's cynicism kept invading her thoughts. But now, late in the day, even he seemed resigned to wait and see. For Maggie, the idea of a conspiracy in this friendly place seemed even more ludicrous than the cave's mysterious portal had been. She'd looked for signs of conflicting information, for exchanges of knowing winks and nods. But what she saw over and over was generosity, warmth, and an openness offered to them, despite their being outsiders. Finally, she decided to put her concerns on hold and trust appearances until tomorrow. Within twenty-four hours everything would either be resolved or completely unraveled. She dipped her fork into her plate of roasted pork with tomatillo sauce and attempted to rejoin the conversation, which had shifted to the subject of the next day's community road repair project.

"Are you going to take your camera?" Angel asked Max, who had volunteered to help on the road.

"That's the real reason I'm going. I should be able to get great shots of the local people at work. Repairing a road is hard labor. I've done similar work during my summers in college. And I helped out once before on a mountain road when I was photographing in South America," Max explained.

"How's your knee?" Maggie, his former physical therapist, asked.

"It's fine. Really," he nodded emphatically. "We did some major hiking today, even a little climbing. And it's not sore. You underestimate your healing powers, Maggie," he smiled.

"Are you going, too, Angel?" she asked.

"I'm not much for road repair," he laughed. "But I intend to use my time well. When this guy gets up bright and early, I'll get up, too. I promised to help Dar with chores to fill in for Reggie."

"How early are you and Reggie going to start fixing that old road?" she asked.

"Let's just say we may be waking up Rudolfo this time," he laughed grimly.

"Will you be able to see what you're doing?" she asked, tilting her head with a smile.

Reggie had assured them they would. "The trucks are supposed to arrive just before dawn. We'll be working in the earliest light. It'll be cooler then, but we'll get warm soon enough. I'm looking forward to it," he said.

"So you get a good workout, take photographs and fix a beat up old road, all in the space of one morning," she smiled. "I'm sure they'll be glad to have your help. But I have to confess I'm a little surprised."

"I need to keep myself occupied until tomorrow afternoon," he explained. "Otherwise, I'm worrying about Michelle. I want to see her come walking out of that cave right on time. But then I think, *What if she doesn't?* I don't have a real handle on what to do next. What do you two think will happen?"

"She'll be there," Angel said. Maggie was stunned by his confidence.

"How can you be so sure Sunny was right?" she asked. "I wish I could feel the same way. I want to trust these people because I've grown to really like them. But why are you so sure, Angel? What's your secret?" she asked, truly wanting to be as certain as he was.

"It's an odd mix of things," he began. "Part of it is intuitive, which is a weird thing for a researcher to say. But I like these people, too. They seem authentic. I'm also feeling that Michelle will be with us again, alive and well. And part of that comes from talking to Father Hernandez about the cave. There's nothing shifty or dark about him," he assured them, shaking his head. "But I'm not giving up there. Reggie told me about a couple of local historians who collect data on outsiders who've been in the cave. I intend to talk with them tomorrow morning. Father Hernandez said he'd arrange it for me. They live just down the road from Sweet Dreams."

Maggie picked at her food with a fork. "How will she look when we see her again, Angel? What do your research and intuition tell you about that?" she asked with obvious concern.

"She'll be tired and dirty, and hungry. I'll find out more tomorrow. But there was one thing Father Hernandez mentioned that surprised me. We've seen and heard a lot of unusual things on this trip, but this was really strange. He said he just wanted to caution me that it could happen."

"And what's that?" Max asked with worry in his voice.

"He told me that she might have blood on her clothes as if she's been badly wounded. Yet she won't have any wounds," he said.

"How is that possible? Whose blood will she be wearing?" Max asked in a skeptical voice.

Angel looked at them as if he weren't sure how to reply. His certainty had this one flaw. He knew his answer would sound surreal to them, as it had to him.

"According to Father Hernandez, the dreams in the cave are incredibly realistic. When a person has a particularly strong imagination, elements of a dream may manifest in the conscious world as well. For instance, when Father Hernandez was in the cave, he dreamt about his great grandmother who had died long before. In the dream, she gave him a small lock of her white hair. She asked him to keep it close to his heart to remember her love and remember the power of his dreams. During the dream, he put the lock in his shirt pocket. But it wasn't until he came out of the cave that he thought to look for it there. Surprisingly, he found it."

"The lock of his dead great grandmother's hair was in his pocket?" Maggie asked in disbelief.

"I know how it sounds," Angel nodded. "Over time the hair dissolved into dust and then disappeared. It looked like real hair, but it wasn't. That's one reason I want to talk to the local researchers, to see if they have hard evidence of such incidents."

Max just shook his head. "I wish you hadn't told me that," he said.

"I almost didn't," Angel said.

"Even if we did buy it, why would Michelle have blood on her clothes?" Maggie asked.

"Apparently it's not unusual for these cave dreamers to encounter tragedy or violence in their dreams. These are cautionary tales, lessons they're learning through the dreams. The result may be what looks like blood on their clothing, but it's not real. Father Hernandez felt we should be warned. It's so dark in the cave that Michelle may not even be aware of it. But when we see her, it will be the first thing we'll notice."

"This just gets weirder and weirder," Max reacted, shaking his head.

Maggie seemed more purposeful. "I intend to check her out," she said. "I'm going to check her bones and her responses. She could be extremely dehydrated and delusional. Even if there is another person in the cave with her, how much of his food and water would he be able to share? Their resources may be running low by now."

Silence fell among the three friends. Once again, uncertainty penetrated their hope, making the remaining wait increasingly difficult as the hours collapsed into the appointed time of Michelle's deliverance. Angel said a silent prayer for her safety. Afterward, he looked toward the street just as a mini-van passed by. From inside the vehicle, a passenger smiled as he surveyed the town through the window. He wore the traditional turban of a Sikh. There were at least two other passengers in the van, including the man at the other passenger window, who was Asian with a shaved head. Angel watched as they continued down the street and stopped at the inn. He felt his heart lift and knew with more certainty than before that they would see Michelle soon.

35

Dar watched passively as Reggie and Sunny cleared the table of dishes. She was usually the first to get up after a meal, but her attention had slipped away. As Reggie ran the water to rinse the dishes, the sound brought her back. "Oh, sorry. Let me help you," she offered as she rose from the table.

"No worries, dear heart. We can handle this. Can't we, Sunny?"

"Yes, Dad," the girl replied with a quick nod.

Dar gathered leftovers from the table and put them in the refrigerator. "Thanks," she told her crew of two. "I've just been so preoccupied today. I should be planning the salon. It's so close."

"Will Michelle be here for the salon?" Sunny asked.

"I will insist upon it," Dar confirmed. "She'll need to rest tomorrow night. But, if she's willing, I want her to be our guest of honor. And it would be helpful for her to meet others who've been in the cave."

"I heartily agree," Reggie nodded in affirmation.

"Will you read a poem, Mum?" Sunny asked with a hopeful smile.

"Oh, indeed, dear. I'm almost done with one. It's uplifting, but it starts in a dark place," she explained.

"Is that what you were thinking about at the table?" Reggie asked.

"In part," she admitted, "but I always worry about our guests before they come back from El Anhelo. I'll prepare a basket of food for Michelle, but I wish I could take off a bit of her burden. There's always a period of adjustment, as you know. I wish I could soften that for her."

Reggie wiped his hands dry and rubbed her back and shoulders. "You take off more of other people's burdens than you realize," he said. "The rest is part of the process. And that's why we're here. To make it easier for them, not for us." She felt her muscles relax. His hands were capable of hard work, of painting intricate landscapes, and of applying his calming touch.

"Thanks, Reg," she smiled back, grateful for his gentle hands and emotional support. "I'll try to tidy up the place while you're out fixing the road tomorrow," she told him. "You don't need to worry about anything else."

"I'll be the one needing a massage after that," he laughed. "Oh, and did I tell you Max is joining us?"

"Astounding news!" Dar replied in genuine surprise. "Perhaps he's having a change of heart."

"Whatever it is, we're grateful. He's a strong man. But he's asked to document the repair work and us workers with his camera. I agreed to it."

"Do you suppose he'll document Michelle's release as well?" Dar wondered out loud.

"I'm certain he'll attempt it, but it's all so unpredictable. He's a determined fellow, that one."

"Can I be there when the cave lets her out?" Sunny asked.

"Of course. Want to carry a hat and sunglasses for her?" Dar asked and Sunny nodded.

"She'll have a large greeting committee, then," Reggie laughed. "We'll fan out with her friends so we spot her before she wanders down the path somewhere."

"I'll make sure she comes home with us, Dad. I promise!" Sunny insisted.

Reggie couldn't help but laugh at her enthusiasm. "Sunny, you are a marvel," he commented. Then he turned to Dar and whispered, "And so are you."

36

"Are you all right, Michelle?" Father Moran asked with obvious concern in his voice. He was standing by my side when I woke up from that horrible nightmare in the City of Darkness. "You were flailing around so much I thought you might fall off the mattress or hit your hand or head on rock. Do you hurt anywhere?"

It took a moment to realize where I was. "Is that you, Father Moran?" Who else could it be? But I wanted to hear his confirmation. No way did I want to be alone or stuck in that dream any longer!

"Yes, it is. Do you feel any pain?" he asked again, softer this time.

I tried to stretch a bit, but I was shaking all over. I felt wet and chilled. I must have been sweating for the first time since I'd entered the cave. My eyes were opening, but the cave was so dark I could barely see. And then I felt the pain in my ribs.

"Ow! Yes, I do hurt. In my ribcage on the left side."

"I can give you a painkiller, if you'd like. Did anything happen to you in the dream where you might have been injured there?" he asked calmly.

There were so many possibilities that it was hard to remember one. But when I rubbed my side I had a flashback of falling backward into a mass grave as the woman holding my arm had been shot. With painful clarity I recalled the dense weight of an elbow wedged into my ribs and not being able to move for fear of being killed. "Yes, Father. But it was so gruesome, I don't want to think about it now." I started crying then as that scene replayed in my mind.

"I'm sorry, Michelle. Now close your eyes enough that I can shine the flashlight on your face. Let me know when you're ready." He spoke slowly, but insistently. I was too dazed to question his motive.

"Go ahead." I kept crying, but closed my eyes. And then I heard him gasp. "Father, what's wrong?" I asked, but he didn't answer.

"Michelle, move the blanket so I can see the rest of you." I heard concern in his voice again.

"All right," I said as I slowly moved it, afraid of his reaction, as well as more exposure to the cool air of the cave. I was flat on my back and kept my eyes closed. I heard him gasp again, which frightened me even more. "What are you seeing?" I whispered, afraid of the answer, but wanting to know. "How bad do I look?"

"I understand now what you've experienced," he said with sadness. "It's what some of us call the 'Hell on Earth' dream, because it is relentlessly dark and chaotic. Did you walk through the City of Darkness?"

"Yes, Father, and I thought I'd come out in the City of Light. But here I am, straight from that horrible place!" I wiped my eyes and felt a sticky spot as my hand brushed my cheek. "What are you seeing, Father? *What's on my cheek?*" I screamed.

He took a deep breath before he spoke. "It's blood. It's probably not yours, but belongs to a person you dreamt about," was his bizarre answer.

"What?" I gasped, sitting up in surprise.

"In your dream you touched suffering and death and it left its mark on your psyche, but it also manifested on your clothes and body. You must have a powerful imagination, and that is a gift," he said with conviction.

"Then why does it feel like a curse?" I asked through a downpour of sudden tears. "Why is this happening to me, Father? Is this some sort of punishment?"

I bent over with my head on my knees and pulled myself into a fetal position. No one could comfort me now as I began to rock back and forth on the air mattress. I felt like I was finally losing my mind and the cave was just another corner in the City of Darkness. Father Moran put his hand on my neck and softly massaged my damp skin. I felt a shiver go through my bones. What an emotional and physical mess I'd become! Maybe I'd bottled up all my apprehension of being cooped up in that dark place and now, because of that horrible dream, it was spilling out of me, spinning my emotions in all directions at once!

"Michelle," he said softly, trying to get my attention, "the first thing you have to do is stay warm or you'll get ill. Here, let's put the blanket back on you," he said as he wrapped it around me. He sat down behind me and straddled the mattress, putting his arms around my neck to hold the blanket in place around me. I was surprised the mattress didn't burst from our combined weight. But slowly the shivering lessened as his body heat came through the blanket to my back. The warmth seemed to radiate all around and through me then.

"Better now?" he asked, still holding me.

"Yes," I replied. "Thank you for being here, Father." I was more grateful to him than I knew how to express, yet I still felt a tremor deep inside me.

"I can heat water for you," he said. "Tea would be good to warm you. And you might want to wash yourself a bit, too. You would feel better if you did. I have an old shirt you can have, if you like. The one you're wearing is probably soaked through."

"Oh, Father, I can't take your clothes, too! I've already eaten half your food," I protested. "I can wear my sweatshirt. That'll be fine. But please, *please* explain your comment about the blood! And while you're at it, why are my ribs so sore if this was just a dream? Do you know?" I could hear the shaking in my own voice and knew I was losing it again, despite his efforts. I took a couple of deep breaths.

"Firstly, I *know* what I'm about to say will sound incredible, even impossible. But now that you've been in the Cave of Dreams there will be times when your dreams will wander onto a plain of existence that bridges the unconscious mind and the physical world. One's first reaction is to deny this, of course, because it's so illogical. But there are times when it is blatantly obvious, as it was in the intense dream you just had. And then it cannot be rationalized away. Secondly, as I said before, it means you have a strong imagination, which will serve you well after you leave here. And lastly, it indicates you are an empathetic person. You've taken on some of the suffering you witnessed around you. That's a good quality, but you must be careful not to take on too much or you won't be able to function. There is pain everywhere you turn in our world. You'll have much to do when you get back home," he said, alluding to my "mission" again.

I was still confused, still shaking. "But how can this be real blood, Father, if it was only a dream?" I asked, not grasping his explanation.

"I don't believe it's real," he said. "It certainly appears to be in its obvious properties. But if one attempted DNA testing on it, it would not be actual blood. However, the effect of seeing a person splattered with it is quite startling, as you know from the dream."

"Can I see it, Father?" I asked, apprehensive but wanting to know what he'd seen.

"Are you certain you're up to it, Michelle?" he asked. "You're already quite upset by this."

"Maybe just a little then. Is it on my pants?"

"Yes."

"If I stretch out my legs, can you shine the flashlight on them?"

"Yes, of course." When he did, I was shocked! I had dark red splatters on my jeans and so I assumed that was how I looked from head to foot. It was appalling!

"Is it hard to wash out?" I asked.

"You said you're staying at the B & B. I'm sure they must know how to get this out of your clothes. It will need more attention than I am able to provide with the rustic conditions here. But we can clean your face and arms. Yes, there's a bit on them, too. But you should get those pants off. Let me give you a pair of mine while we try to dry what you're wearing now. I'll be right back."

"I don't want to be alone, Father. I'll come with you," I insisted.

"Very well." He helped get my shoes back on. "Let me help you stand," he said and shone the flashlight on the floor so I could see where my feet should land. Then he took my arm to steady me as I stood. We found where the sweatshirt had fallen and he picked it up.

"Thank you, Father. Let me wrap this blanket around a bit tighter. Okay. I'm ready," I said.

I held on tight to his arm with one hand while my other hand held tight to the blanket. We made our way slowly to the kitchen. He put a kettle on and briefly left me sitting alone in the lamplight while he went off to fill a bucket with water from the chapel's pool. I took the opportunity to shed my top and replace it with my sweatshirt. Maybe I was foolish, but I left my bra on, even though it was also damp. I was just being modest, since I was in the company of a priest after all. When he returned, he took a box from a pantry shelf that contained towels.

"Once this water is heated, I'm going to start with your face and hair," he said. "Surely that will wash out with no problem."

After the kettle whistled and the teapot was filled, he poured a little hot water on a towel. It was comfortably warm by the time he walked over to wipe my face with it.

"Is it working?" I asked.

"Yes," he said. "You look much better. Touch your cheek now."

The stickiness was gone. "Much better," I agreed.

While I drank tea, he went off to get another blanket. The tremor had subsided and I felt my muscles relaxing. The dream had been overwhelming in its scope as it moved me through time and across continents. And yet I knew I'd seen the tip of the proverbial iceberg. There was darkness across the globe, across centuries of human existence. I knew there were pockets of hope as well, but the dream had offered little of that. Where was the light to come from that could chase away such deep wells of despair? María told me to discuss the dream with Father Moran and I was hoping we had time left to do that.

"How are you doing now?" he asked as he re-entered the kitchen.

"Better, Father. I think the anxiety attack has passed, at least for now. But that's not to say the anxiety has."

"I understand," he replied. "The horrors you witnessed in one dream are more than most people will experience in a lifetime. You've just taken on the suffering of the world."

Then he offered me a pair of his pants. "You'll feel better in these. You're quite a bit shorter and smaller than I, but we'll just sit here instead of doing more cave explorations or chores."

He left the room while I removed my pants, wiped my legs with the damp towel and then dried off. His pants hung past my feet, so I rolled up the cuffs. Then I pulled my sweatshirt off and cleaned the rest of me as best I could. It was a humble sponge bath, but it did wonders for the way I felt. I had to get by with the same underwear for a little longer but, oh, how I longed for clean replacements! As I wrapped the fresh blanket around me I called him back.

"Much better?" he asked as he entered the room.

"Much!" I assured him.

He laid the clothes near the camp stove and hoped what little heat was there might dry my sweat from them in the next few hours. Then he set about slicing bread and setting out some cheese. "Maybe we'll have a proper laundry in here one of these days," he laughed. "But I think in the meantime we'll be operating on a primitive scale."

"As soon as I'm out of here I intend to take a long bath and just soak," I mused. "But I might start off with a large meal before that. Maybe even a beer."

"It's so easy to take those things for granted, but not in here," he said. "I look forward to sleeping on a real bed again, I will admit."

"That's what I'll do after the bath," I nodded. And then I shuddered as I realized something. "But I'm afraid to go back to sleep. I'm afraid of being stuck in the City of Darkness again. In the dream, I never left it."

"Don't be afraid," he whispered. "It's made its impression on you. You'll see the world in a whole new way from now on. I can assure you that it's highly unlikely you'll have such a dream again, unless you need to be reminded of it," he surmised.

"The world is such an evil place, Father. I've led a sheltered life. Being from a large city like Chicago I've witnessed a few things, including having my purse stolen right out from under my chair in a restaurant. But that's nothing," I realized. "Where does all that violence come from? It was so out of control in my dream!" Before he could answer, another possibility occurred to me. "Do you believe in satanic forces, Father?"

"Evil is indeed a force that is alive and, unfortunately, doing well in our world," he agreed. "But where does it come from? The hearts of human beings, I would argue. For Satan can do nothing without human will and assistance. Perhaps it isn't Satan at all. Perhaps he is merely our excuse for the evil we perform on each other."

"Really!" I said, surprised at his response. "Then why are we so incredibly mean to one another? Pardon my language, but after that last dream I think this world is just plain fucked!"

My language didn't faze him. "Think about it, Michelle. For instance, why would anyone steal your purse? You didn't do anything to them. Should you take it personally?"

"I did at the time. I must have been an easy target and they needed money. Maybe they had a drug habit to support. It hurt and made me angry. It felt personal because I felt violated," I said, remembering the shock when I realized my purse had disappeared.

"Maybe the poor of the world are easy targets, too. Who'll defend them from corporations who mine or drill for oil on their land or cut down their forests for cattle grazing and coffee growing? Surely they feel violated, too," he argued.

"But where does that level of greed come from, Father? It's so inhuman."

"There are many insecure people in the world. I have a theory about greed. I think it comes from fear of not having enough or not having more than your neighbor, even on a corporate level. Money, power, and possessions are compensation for something missing in one's life. There's a certain satisfaction in having all you want, I suppose. But there's a greater satisfaction in sharing it with others. And, to paraphrase the Bible, one may win the world, but lose one's soul. That's an eternal error in judgment. And, yes, it happens all the time," he said with regret.

"Father, whenever anything terrible happens, some people say, 'Where's God? How can God let this happen?' What would you say to that?" I asked.

He threw his hands up and shook his head. "Well, if not Satan, who else to blame?" he answered with a bitter question. "Yes, I hear it. There are many mysteries in the universe and God is the greatest of all. When I was struck by a car and almost died, I asked those same questions. But then I never would have been a priest if it hadn't happened. Why do people have cancer or die in their youth? Why do they have illnesses and accidents that leave them in pain or crippled? Why do innocents die in the crossfire of a war zone or a gang fight? No one knows the answers to those questions.

"But God gets blamed for things that have a human cause. People forget that our world is blessed with abundance in so many ways. In the twenty-first century, with modern technology, we should be able to feed the world and see that everyone has a decent place to live, enough clothing, food, education and medical care. Clearly your dream showed that we're not even close." He paused to sigh and take a deep breath. My questions had hit a nerve. He continued in a quieter, concerned tone. "Humankind's selfish ways have put things terribly out of balance. Even our planet is at risk. There may always be poverty, disease, ignorance, and violence. But our hope is to trust in tolerance and sharing, to put our personal fears to the side and work for the greater good of all. And that is why we come to this cave, to learn and pray so we can bring the light of hope back with us. We appeal for divine intervention and guidance through our prayers. In this dark place, ironically, we are often heard. Perhaps you will hear some good news reported soon, if we are successful here."

"What kinds of things can you change?" I asked, wondering how much their prayers could affect.

"The things that God allows in nature, but occasionally the hearts of human beings, too," he revealed. It seemed like he didn't want to say more than that. He poured the tea and we continued our discussion. His passion was invigorating and I wanted to see how he'd react to other hot-button issues.

"There are times I think there's entirely too much testosterone loose in the world," I said. "No offense to your gender, Father, but I find young men with guns a frightening proposition. I saw them in my dream, too."

"Guns," he shook his head in disgust. "There was a time when men would face each other with their fists and they'd hurt each other, but they'd survive. But a gun does irreparable damage in an instant of anger, or error. It may make a weak person feel powerful and in control. But once it's used, it shows how weak the person, or the government, really is. Patience and diplomacy require more control than violence, and they offer the potential for a peaceful resolution. Non-violence offers hope, but it's a rare practice these days," he sighed again.

"So how do we fix the world when we're dealing with such overwhelming forces, if we're up against fear, greed, the power of corporations and the military? " I asked. "I saw patterns of violence repeating in my dream. How do we stop that? Revenge is part of many cultures, it seems."

"Decent people have a responsibility to try to make things better," he said. "There are more ordinary people in the world than there are multi-national corporations or leaders with their armies. If we can keep at it, like Davids against many Goliaths, we can make a difference. Look at South Africa and apartheid, for instance. There are humanitarian and human rights workers all over the world already risking their lives, but they need money and volunteers to keep up their work. Small amounts of money can change lives in many parts of the world," he insisted, then continued. "And there are easy things like signing petitions, phone calls and letters to governing officials, voting for responsible candidates and against unfair practices, supporting unions and fair trade, and being informed from a variety of news sources about what's happening in the world. These are things an average person can do. And numbers of average people add up," he concluded with a confident tone.

"It all seems so logical when you say it, Father. Why don't people see that and act on it?" I wondered.

"Distractions, I suppose," he answered. "People focusing on their own lives, not understanding how connected we all are, no matter where we are on the planet. After a hard day on the job, it's easy to sit in front of the tube, watch nonsense and forget the problems of the world. It's an escape. And then there's the adverts. We're constantly being told to buy things that we could easily live without. And people buy them, even if they go into debt to get them. Lives are so complicated with the endless need for possessions in this modern world of ours. I find it beyond understanding," he said in disgust.

"What about those who think we're getting closer to the end times, Father? There are people who think it's okay to use up the world's resources because it won't matter anyway, that the Apocalypse is near and the Bible predicts it's coming." I was hoping they were wrong, of course, but how do you change people's minds?

"I would call that a self-fulfilling prophecy, Michelle. If you think the world will end and you push it closer to that point, that's not a *real* prophecy. God meant us to be stewards of this wonderful creation. The world has so much promise that has gone by the wayside. We need to honor that creation by taking care of it, and each other."

As I sat there, cozy and comfortable in my blanket, I understood what he meant. His kindness had taken the edge off my trauma and the simple pleasure of another person's concern and care for me was deeply satisfying. In that moment, I was as content as I could ever be.

"You know, Father Moran," I said, "I have to agree with you. There is something to be said for living a simpler life with fewer distractions. But no TV after work? That will take real discipline!"

"I'm sure you can handle it," he laughed. "In fact, I'm sure you are capable of greater things than you can begin to imagine in this moment."

37

"You'd better go to sleep soon, Max. You've got a big day tomorrow," Maggie said, shaking her finger at him. A slight breeze came through the screen of the veranda where they stood.

"Yeah, I know, Mom, but I'm just not ready to call it a night," he defiantly teased back.

"You'll thank me in the morning, you bad boy. Go to sleep!" she commanded, pointing her finger toward the room above them.

"Make me!" he challenged back.

"Hmmm. No goodnight kiss if you're not on your way soon, young man."

"Ouch! Okay, okay. That's too harsh. I'll go, but not until I collect my kiss," he said, leaning forward.

"Very well," she said, pursing her lips and closing her eyes. It was a cartoon pose.

"Sorry, but that's not exactly what I had in mind," he laughed.

She unpuckered her lips, opened her eyes and shrugged, then reached up to take his head in her hands. She kissed his cheek. He was about to protest when she kissed his other cheek, much closer to his lips this time. Smiling, he waited expectantly for the third kiss, which brushed his top lip. The fourth kiss was warmly delivered on his slightly open mouth. The fifth kiss was mutually given and received and lasted a long time. His arms were around her as the fifth kiss ended and the sixth began, until Maggie broke away to take a breath.

"Ah, I wish this night would never end. You're quite a kisser," she sighed.

"Sweet Maggie," he whispered, "from your sweet lips to your flamenco toes."

She shifted in his arms and declared, "You know, Max, you're a much sweeter person than I thought at first. I'm sure you've managed to fool lots of other people, too."

"Really? So how can you tell I'm so sweet?" he teased.

She looked him in the eye. "Because you're helping with the road tomorrow. Because you'll be with us waiting for Michelle to come out of the cave instead of taking a siesta after your hard work. Because beneath your tough exterior there's an artist and a philosopher. Because you're patient and not asking me to jump into bed with you. And by the end of tomorrow, I have a feeling my list will be even longer," she concluded.

"Is that so?" he laughed. "Guess my secret is out. Where do I go from here?"

"To bed, young man," she reminded him, pointing above them. "You got your kiss-es." She stroked his cheek. "You have to get up mighty early and it's getting late. We can kiss, uh, talk more tomorrow. Lord knows we'll have a lot to say then."

"Are you going up?" he asked.

"In a few minutes. I want to talk to Dar first."

"Good night then, Maggie." Max kissed her one last time on the cheek. He was tender as he caressed her shoulder, smiled, and walked toward the stairs. She blew him one more kiss when he looked back before his ascent.

And then she stood alone on the veranda looking up into a clear night sky. She felt herself grow smaller with the immensity of the starry ceiling that rose above her. The moonlight trickled through the fingers of trees and drizzled itself on the ground. She heard the music of the night, the exotic mixture of creaking and croaking animal voices. It had sounded like noise the first night there. It had kept her up, along with her worry. But now it was familiar and soothing, as if it appealed to an unknown part of her being, calling down through the genetic lines of her ancestry. It was odd, but she felt more connected to this place every day. And then she thought of the day to come and wondered what it would bring.

She looked into the depth of the night sky, curious if a small whispered prayer would be heard. She thought of Sunny's approach to saying grace and decided to express gratitude. "Please bring Michelle back to us safe and sound, dear God. Thank you for all you've given us while we've been here. All we want now is our friend. Please release her tomorrow. We love her dearly. We miss her very much."

As she lost herself in the music of the wild things, and in the immensity of the night sky overflowing in stars, she heard the wind whistling through the trees, suddenly adding another layer of sound. Was it her own thoughts or did she hear a voice? Did it say, "She is well"? Or was it just the word "Michelle"? Or was it both at the same time?

When the wind picked up she listened carefully, and thought she heard it again.

"Michelle."

"She is well."

With that, the wind subsided and the other night sounds dominated the dark landscape again. "Thank you," she whispered back, feeling that the answer had been given. It didn't matter if she only imagined it. Then she felt the day grow heavy on her and went inside to talk to Dar.

Angel sat in his room writing in a journal he'd begun in Oaxaca city on the first night of this unpredictable journey. He had noted the sights in Monte Albán and the Spanish colonial architecture in the Zócalo. And then it had all taken a more personal turn when they reached Teotenaca. But after talking with Father Hernandez, he was back to being the researcher. This was a town he could not write a paper or lecture about, or divulge to the world in any way. Yet he had to make sense of it for himself. As he wrote the questions he would ask the local researchers the next morning, Max knocked on his half-opened door.

"Hey, Angel, can I come in for a minute?"

"Sure. But shouldn't you be asleep by now?"

"Yeah, yeah, I'm on my way. But I wanted to ask you something first."

"And what's that?" Angel asked with concern.

"You'll be seeing those local historians while I'm working on the road, right?"

"Yes. Dar's taking me there."

"Could you ask them how people are when they get out of the cave? I'm just thinking about Michelle and what our roles should be when she's back with us. What will we need to do for her?" The concern was obvious in his voice. This development surprised Angel, that Max had reached a point of acceptance and anticipation of their friend's return.

"I'll ask them. I've been thinking about that myself and talked to Reggie and Father Hernandez about what happens next. But these researchers will have more recorded data. I have a *lot* to ask them," he smiled. "We may be in for more surprises."

Max was quiet before he responded with a question. "You really think she'll be there, don't you, Angel?" he asked in a quiet, yet urgent, tone.

"I do," he replied. "I overheard someone in town saying there are several religious people from different faiths already here for the retreat. You may see more arriving while you're working on the road. Michelle has to be out before they all go in, so it should be soon."

A huge smile rose on Max's face like a sudden burst of sunlight. "Thank you. That'll help me sleep better. Good night, my friend," he said, squeezing Angel's shoulder.

"Good night, Max. Sleep well," Angel smiled, patting his friend's back as he turned and headed for the room next door.

As Dar slipped into bed beside Reggie, he woke from a light sleep. "What time is it?" he asked.

"Past my bedtime, dear. Go back to sleep."

"I've been tossing around a bit."

"You've a big schedule tomorrow. I'm not surprised," she said.

"Right. Maybe I need a little lullaby," he suggested. "Why were you up so late?"

"It was Maggie. We're making arrangements for a special performance at the salon. And she needed a little reassurance about her friend. I have no worries so I said all would be fine. She'll help me prepare the food basket for Michelle. Maggie is a wonderful person. I'd like to know her better, but Max is quite protective," Dar noted.

"She'll be free from his protection in the morning so take advantage of it," her husband whispered.

"Too true," she nodded. "I shall."

"Now how about that little lullaby for the old man, eh?" he asked again.

"Close your eyes. And keep them shut," she said softly.

"They are already."

She began with a hum. She hadn't sung to her daughter in a while, but tried to remember the song she wrote when Sunny was a baby. The words came in phrases, so she filled in the rest with humming.

Close your eyes, my darling, you precious gift of joy.
Tomorrow is another day, hmmm, hmmm, a toy.
I'll take you to the market. I'll take you far away.

We'll make it home by supper. And then you'll get to play.
Close your eyes, my darling, you precious gift of joy.
Close your eyes.
Close your eyes.
Tomorrow is another day.

She sang until she heard Reggie's snore, then kept humming until she fell asleep beside him, her dreams filled with anticipation of the day to come.

38

After a long and reassuring discussion with Father Moran, I was less apprehensive about dreaming again. According to my watch it was after midnight and I desperately wanted to go back to sleep. You would think with all the sleeping I'd already done in the cave I'd be rested. But the "Hell on Earth" dream had exhausted me, leaving me more tired than if I hadn't slept at all.

Did I look like I'd been through hell? Feeling my hair, I knew running a brush through it would be no easy task. *What will my friends think when they see me again?* I wondered. No doubt Max would find me a shocking image in his viewfinder. I kept wondering what my friends were doing, what they knew of my situation. I hoped Max hadn't called in the troops. According to Father Moran, being in the cave was a common experience in Teotenaca. My hope was that Reggie and Dar had explained it all in a way that made everything seem normal and predictable. That would have been a Herculean task, especially convincing Max, but I had a feeling this wasn't the first time they'd explained things to a missing person's friends or family members. I didn't envy them that task. And what would Angel make of all this from his scholarly perspective? I missed him especially. And I pictured Maggie's warm smile and longed to see her again. Yet I was grateful for my kindly Irish companion.

"Michelle, you should rest, get some real sleep," he advised me. "I had a dream about you earlier today. Your time in the cave is about to end. You have been marvelous company for me and a great help."

"Thank you, but I don't know how I would have survived in here without you, Father. Helping you was the least I could do. I'll miss you, but I have to say that I'm getting cave fever."

"Cave fever?" he asked with a quizzical expression.

"It's like cabin fever, when you've been cooped up for too long, like having to stay home during a rough winter season. But, of course, we're in a cave, not a cabin. I long for sunlight and my friends. I haven't seen that much of Teotenaca, either, and I still want to do that."

"I'm feeling a bit of cave fever myself, I must confess," he laughed. "But it will get better when everyone else arrives. We'll be focused and the retreat will go by quickly. It's a very enlightening, very rich experience and I'm looking forward to it."

"How soon will it start?" I asked.

"The retreat participants will enter the cave late tomorrow. I'll have the candles lit so they can find their way to the dome more easily. That's the last place I have to prepare. We can work in there tomorrow."

"That's the room that first drew me in here."

"And you'll be there when it's time for you to exit," he said. "So you should sleep as much as you can tonight. Let me see how your clothes are doing." They were surprisingly dry. I asked him to leave for a few moments while I put my dirty, but now dry, clothes back on. I thanked him profusely.

"You're very welcome, dear. Now, again, I would advise you to get more rest. Tomorrow you can get your things together before we work in the dome so you're prepared for your exit. I need to rest, too. By the way, how are your ribs feeling? I haven't heard you complaining." He'd given me a couple aspirin and I took an extra one for a boost of pain reliever. I told him I felt much better, but I still had a dull ache on my left side.

We walked to the separate sleeping rooms. I had a buoyant air mattress again and a clean blanket wrapped around me. It didn't take long before I was comfortable. I heard Father Moran's distant snore while my eyes began to close. I said a quick prayer, a hasty appeal for a peaceful dream this time. As I drifted off, his snore grew more distant until its rhythm was replaced by the sound of waves hitting a sandy shoreline. I found myself back on the island where I'd been with my teenaged mother. The sky was blue and filled with birdsong.

"It's so peaceful here, don't you think?" a familiar voice said. As I turned around, I realized it was my grandmother this time.

"Grandma?" I said with surprise and joy.

"How are you, Mishi? I haven't seen you in so long. I've missed you."

"I've missed you, too," I said as we hugged. She kissed me on the cheek.

Mishi was the nickname she'd given me when I was a girl. She'd died of cancer ten years before and I still missed her. My last memory was of a withered woman who looked much older than she was. The fire in her spirit had been replaced by a sad quietness. She knew she was dying. Pain and medication had become as much a part of her life as breathing. Finally, she was put in hospice care. I visited often, as the end of her life approached.

But in my dream she was restored to a person full of good cheer and healthy color. And I remembered what she'd said one of the last times I saw her. It was hard for her to talk, but it was important to her to speak to me. The morphine made her drowsy and she struggled to stay alert.

"Mishi, come closer," she'd said. I put my ear close to her mouth as I spoke quietly into her ear.

"Yes, Grandma. I'm here," I said.

"I won't live much longer. I don't want to. It hurts. I'll miss you. I love you," she whispered.

"I love you, too, Grandma. I love you, too," I replied, beginning to cry.

"Be happy, Mishi. Art makes you happy. Do great things. I know you can. Find love. We all need it," she whispered. It was slow, halting, painful to listen to. I told her I'd miss her very much, that I'd follow her advice. I wanted to say more. I had so much I wanted to tell her. But the tears kept coming and I couldn't talk. Then her eyes slowly rolled back and she lost consciousness again. I saw her two or three times after that, but by then she could barely speak at all. Her advice about pursuing joy, art, and love was the last meaningful exchange we had, but it stayed with me. There were times I felt an unexplainable sadness. I knew it was a lingering grief for her, but it was also an underlying memory of her last words to me. Was I living up to her advice? I knew I wasn't. I was working for a decent wage and living a cushy life. The things she'd talked about required risk. My excuse was always that the time wasn't right yet. Now I wondered if the time had come as our conversation began in my dream.

"You look wonderful, Grandma. It's so good to see you again!"

"It's very good to see you, too, my sweet granddaughter. But you don't look well at all. They've put you through a lot in the Cave of Dreams. But I can help by taking your mind off the pain from your last dream," she smiled.

"You know about my last dream? It was horrible! And the scariest thing is I know it's all true. I know the world is really that bad with no end in sight." I trembled just to think how overwhelming the troubles in the world had become for me now.

"Do you feel paralyzed?" she asked. "Do you feel like there's nothing you can do that can stop those terrible things from happening?"

"Yes. That's part of it," I said.

"And what else?"

"Even if I'm active in trying to improve things in this world, I'm wondering how much I can really do. I'm one little person who might make a microscopic difference. And if I do more, you know, really get involved, when is there too much risk? How much am I willing to sacrifice?" At that point, I had no idea.

"I understand," she reassured me. "Those are important questions." She pointed to a couple of rattan chairs on a grassy patch close by and we sat down in them as we continued our conversation.

"I think of the advice you gave me before you... passed." Even now it was hard to say. "I haven't acted on it as much as I could have. There's risk in that, too."

"And what troubles you the most, Mishi? What are you afraid of?" she asked with concern.

"You told me to do great things in my life, but I don't feel like I've even started. I don't know where to start," I said, sounding frustrated.

"Maybe you should start small," she said. "Opportunities to do great things are always there. Keep your eyes and ears open. A person could walk right into your life at any time with an opportunity you should pursue, and you'll feel you should. Do it from a place that feels like it's the right thing to do. You'll know what I mean when it happens. And you can be a great artist, my dear. I've watched you develop over the years, even since my passing. You do your job very well. But there is a hunger within you. I saw the sketches you did since you've been in Mexico and they're excellent," she nodded with pride.

"You saw them?" I asked incredulously.

"Oh, yes. I pay attention to your life and I'd like to think I have a little hand in giving you guidance from time to time," she said.

"Are you the thoughts in my head sometimes? Those little voices of sudden realization?" I asked.

"Perhaps," she laughed. "But you don't listen. You've always had an independent nature, which can be good or bad, depending."

"So how would you guide me now?" I asked. "Where do I go next?"

"It's up to you, but I would say take the lessons of your dreams in the cave to heart. Don't forget them as you re-enter the outside world. *It* will be the same, but *you* won't be."

"So what *will* happen next?" I asked with apprehension as well as curiosity.

"Opportunities will be presented to you, as I said. You can do much to make the world better, more than you realize now. Small actions work together to form a better world. It wouldn't be so overwhelming or seem impossible if more people did small things to improve the lives of others, or the state of the planet. Don't miss the opportunities you'll be given, Mishi." She seemed to be knowledgeable about my life, even my future, and this was fascinating to me. "And there are opportunities for love," she continued. "Neil is in your past now. He wouldn't have been a good partner in your new life. It's time to open your eyes and heart to what lies ahead," she smiled, saying the words slowly while pointing to her own heart.

"You were always a wise woman, Grandma."

"You, too, are a wise woman, Mishi. Now you should rest and that means a peaceful, quiet sleep."

She began to sing a lullaby to me that sounded more and more familiar as she sang. It seemed to surface from my infancy, a deeply buried memory. I closed my eyes to listen to her soothing voice and felt myself being rocked. When I opened my eyes, I was in a cradle, and she looked much younger.

"Close your eyes, sweet girl. Grandma wants you to sleep."

Her voice was soft, peaceful, loving and the most comforting sound I'd heard in a long time. I drifted into a deeper sleep as she continued to sing. That's the only dream I remember from that night, but I slept as if I were in the most comfortable bed in the whole world.

39

"Max, time to rise," Reggie said as he tapped lightly on the bedroom door.

On the other side of the door, Max opened one eye in the darkness and replied, "I'm awake. I'll be right down." Mechanically, he pulled himself up, opened the other eye, and tried to get his bearings. *Road work day*, he thought to himself. Reluctantly he turned on the light. He tiptoed to the bathroom and took a quick sponge bath. The house was cool and the night air made his skin go to goose bumps. Showering and shaving could wait. Back in the room, he pulled the elastic brace over his knee and got dressed. He grabbed the camera bag before quietly descending the dimly lit stairs. Reggie stood in the kitchen waiting.

"How about a cup of java to get you started?" he offered.

"Yes. Please," Max responded, still in an auto pilot state.

"Dar made fresh sweet bread, too. Interested?" Max nodded. They sat across from each other at the large table. Reggie was tired but purposeful, knowing it was almost sunrise, the time when they were to join the road crew. Max yawned and stretched after a few sips of the hot, black coffee.

"You've done this sort of work before, eh?" Reggie asked.

"I did construction during my college summers and helped with heavy labor during my travels. How many people are expected?" The coffee was kicking in.

"If everyone shows, it will be around twelve, maybe fourteen. A few of them have more muscle than the others, but they're all tired of the holes in that stretch of road. They should be quite motivated," Reggie smiled.

"I'm anxious to see how this town gets things done."

"Well, you'll be in the thick of it, my friend. Got your camera gear, I see. Good! You can document what we accomplish, and you'll be surprised at how much that is," the Australian asserted.

Reggie filled a thermos with the remaining coffee and they headed out into the cool air. Max knew he'd warm up as he worked his stiff muscles. The first rays of dawn illuminated the stretch of pockmarked roadway they planned to repair. Several vehicles had arrived before they did. The group gathered at the side of the road to discuss their plan of action. Reggie and Max joined them halfway through the initial conversation. Then one of the men, Mexican but speaking fluent English, turned to them and said, "Morning, Reggie. And who is this? Looks like a strong worker."

"This is Max. Max, this is Hugo. Max is a guest at our place. He's also a photographer. Does anyone mind if he documents you while you're sweating?" Reggie asked them.

"What will you do with the photos?" Hugo asked.

"It depends on how they turn out," Max replied. "If they're good, I might sell them. I would identify the location as Oaxaca, Mexico, not Teotenaca. Or they'll just be part of my personal archive. I'll need to have folks sign a photo release. That's an agreement that it's okay to publish their photos." Reggie translated this into Spanish and they all nodded that they'd sign. He introduced each of them to Max. They looked like a small United Nations standing there by the side of the humble road, with only half of them indigenous. Hugo's English had a southern drawl to it, and Max assumed he'd traveled well beyond the state of Oaxaca.

The trucks carrying gravel were to arrive shortly. The plan was for the men to pair up, facing each other on opposite sides of the road. The trucks would drive between them and drop the gravel at intervals. The men would fill the holes with the gravel, then move further down the road to repeat the process. They carried rakes, shovels, and hoes, many of them handmade. One man had a large metal roller for flattening down the loose gravel. The trucks would have the opportunity to sample the newly repaired road as they departed.

As the trucks arrived, Reggie and Max took their places across the road from each other as work partners. Reggie handed Max a shovel he'd brought. The first truck dropped a pile of large pieces of gravel in a place between them while the second dropped finer gravel nearby. Max followed Reggie's example as he scooped up the larger gravel and dropped it in the uneven grooves and holes in the road. Then he put the smaller gravel over that and smoothed it as much as possible. It was a tedious, physical activity, but Max was happy to be there. It occupied his mind and gave him a chance to check out the townspeople at work.

Once the crew filled a section of potholes, they moved further down the line to continue the process. Max took a few photos of the trucks dumping their loads and of the men working. The early light cast a golden aura into the clouds of dust they made. The two partners moved down the line to the next set of holes needing to be filled. They smiled as they passed the other workers. Everyone's clothes seemed frayed or faded so Max was unable to assign them to any particular economic class. He'd assumed the educated foreigners would be better dressed than the indigenous locals. But it didn't show, and it didn't matter. Everyone contributed his share of work and sweat to the project. A few seemed more accustomed to hard labor, but the others gave it their best effort and took the advice given by the more experienced workers.

The road crew worked for a couple hours, but the time went quickly. As the day warmed up Max had the urge to take off his sweatshirt. His brow and the back of his neck were damp. Before long, his clean white undershirt was caked with dirt and sweat. As he focused his lens on the others, he could imagine how he looked. He tasted the dust in his throat, and it burned his eyes. Yet he was invigorated by the physical labor, the pumping of his blood.

Looking back from where they'd started, he saw Diego pulling the roller behind his truck. It was a large, recycled metal drum filled with water, which leaked from fine holes in the rusted, beaten surface, cutting down on the dust. Hugo directed him along the path that needed the pressure of the roller to firm the surface of the road. When they finally ran out of gravel, they stopped. There had been four truckloads that day and Max had no idea how far they'd come. But his feet were tired, his knee was sore, and his muscles were stretched more than they'd been in months. The shovel suddenly felt almost too heavy to lift one more time. But they'd done it. The road looked flat and the old ruts had disappeared in the clouds of dust.

Before they loaded up the trucks with the men who had worked, Max had them pose for a group portrait in front of a truck. Their white smiles stood out from dirty faces and clothes as they leaned on their tools and against each other. Reggie insisted Max get into a second group photograph taken by one of the truck drivers. As a photographer, Max knew the black and white image would intensify those bright, toothy smiles against everything else. He looked around at the rest of the crew and he had to smile just as broadly. Despite his skepticism, he felt part of the community for the first time. It surprised him. And it felt good.

As the others left he saw the first vehicle of the day drive down the newly repaired road toward the town. The mini-van was probably coming from the city. As it passed, he saw the passengers, both men and women. They looked like a little United Nations, too, as if they'd come from different parts of the world instead of being a family or townspeople returning from an overnight trip. He knew why they'd come here and was anxious to tell Angel of this sighting and his experience on the road. But first he had to take a shower. He and Reggie looked at each other and broke out laughing. Max's blue eyes were outrageously bright against his sweaty, dirty skin.

"You've grown darker, Max."

"You remind me of a coal miner, Reggie. Where's your hard hat with the light?" he joked back.

"Reckon I left it at home," he played along.

They brushed off as much dust and dirt as they could before sitting on the seats in the car.

"Well, let's give this road a try," Reggie said and drove a half mile before doing a three-point turn and heading home.

"What do you think, Max?"

"It's great," he laughed. "What a difference!"

"And you deserve as much credit as anyone," Reggie pointed out.

"Hey, I enjoyed myself."

They laughed at their dirty faces once again as they drove down the repaired road, both feeling that something had been mended between them in the process.

40

It was morning again. I knew it without even looking at my watch. In the black environment of the cave, the time of day had seemed irrelevant. But this time my watch confirmed that a new day had dawned, my last day in the Cave of Dreams.

I took my time getting up. It had been the most restful slumber I'd had in a long while. I stretched slowly until I felt that pain in my side again. For a moment I hesitated, then stretched a little more. It hurt less now, but just acknowledging it sparked the memory of that horrible mass grave I'd fallen into. Was the pain in the dream real? Or had I hit myself on a rock and incorporated it into my dream? That was like so many other questions I knew would never be answered. But I could say I was more healed now, both in mind and body, by that long night of rest. As I sat up Father Moran approached.

"Are you waking, Michelle? We have much to do and no time to waste," Father Moran reminded me. "I trust you're feeling better. You've slept peacefully all night for a change."

"Good morning, Father. How do you know that?" I asked.

"You were much quieter. No flailing at all," he laughed. "Are you hungry?"

"Oh, yes," I said, as my stomach growled loudly.

"There's tea and a special surprise for your last day here." I could see his white windbreaker, still looking like a ghost floating in the dim light. In the kitchen, he'd prepared a formal setting on a simple placemat. He lifted small plates from the top of the teacup and top of a bowl of hot cereal that smelled like oatmeal. There were slices of orange on another small plate.

"How wonderful!" I said. "Have you already eaten or will you join me?"

"I had breakfast hours ago, it seems, but I'd like to share your company. Then we must get you ready for your departure. After that we'll work in the dome. What say you to that?"

"Fine. Whatever you say is fine," I replied, then took a bite out of an orange slice. It was divine. The juice trickled down my chin and my tongue struggled to catch it. As I savored every bite of cereal and fruit and every sip of the tea, Father Moran detailed our work for the day. It sounded more like a half day, really.

After the meal he put my backpack near a lantern and asked if everything was in it. I checked and all that was left was Dar's blanket, the flashlight, my baseball cap, the sketchbook and the box of pencils. "Yes," I said. We used our flashlights to find the way to the dome. The size of the place astounded me once again as the cloud of dust continued its slow, circular dance above our heads. It was a pleasure to see it again as the sun colored the dust a soft yellow and lit the inside of the space.

"How does it do that?" I asked my friend, referring to the dust gliding above us.

"I don't quite understand it myself," he admitted. "One can lose oneself when staring into it. The phrase 'the breath of God' comes to my mind sometimes. It seems to be directed by the breezes coming through the cracks up there. At times the wind sings through them, as if the mountain is a great wind instrument."

"I thought I heard singing when I looked in here the first time," I recalled.

"Like the Sirens, the sound coaxes you in, and it's hard to resist. When our group comes together we focus on it and meditate together. It's quite mesmerizing. I suppose I'm not to talk about that process, but that's how it goes," he said.

"Father, would you be spilling the beans if you told me more about the retreat?" I asked.

"Yes, I would be spilling them. I've already spilled quite a few. Sorry."

"That's all right. So how can I help to prepare this room?" I asked.

"This room," he whispered, "this room is the most powerful of all. We'll pray in here every day. So we need to make this a comfortable space. I have mats in the corner. I've cleaned the floor as best I could and put tarps down. Can you help me position the mats?"

"Of course."

We spread them out so they touched and we could get a sense of how much space they would cover. Then he asked me to double them up and place them mostly in the center, directly under the dome.

"We can leave the mats like this," he said. "The group can fit them together as we prepare to lie down here. They'll fit so that we won't get rained on through the cracks."

"How soon?" I asked.

"Tonight. It's only hours away now. Let's pull these together."

I helped him to configure the group of mats so everyone could take one and put it down to align with ones we placed in the center. I could picture them fanning out into a circle.

"Will they have anything else to lie down on?" I asked, knowing how painful the cave floor would be to their backs.

"They'll bring sleeping bags. And we have the air mattresses, just in case," he added.

"Lights?" I inquired.

"Oh, yes," he answered. He had several battery-operated lanterns in a nearby corner. We placed them on a mat in a central location. I knew he would turn them on as the hour drew near.

"What else needs to be done?" I asked.

"I'm not sure what direction they'll be coming from," he said. "I think this is all we can do for now. I just wanted to get it done in case either of us fell asleep again. Is there anywhere you would like to re-visit before you leave?" he asked.

"Yes," I said. "The waterfall room."

We walked back to it. He had an incredible sense of direction in that directionless place. I followed behind and heard the calming trickle of the water. I could picture the fish floating in the pool below.

"Can I have a moment to myself, Father?" I asked.

"Yes, certainly."

"Thank you. I won't be long."

I walked toward the sound until I saw the amazing natural light that illuminated the softly cascading stream from above. I sat down on the stone bench where I'd fallen asleep. But this time I prayed, quietly. I remembered Sunny's prayers at the table and Father Moran's advice about how to pray. I decided to make this a conversation hoping I would receive a reply to my requests and to the questions bouncing around in my head.

"Dear God, please take care of Father Moran. I hope he has enough food, since I ate so much. He's a kind soul. He saved my sanity and blessed me with his insight. And dear God, please guide me toward what

I'm supposed to do next in this world. I still don't understand why I was called here, but I want to do meaningful things from now on. Help me to recognize the opportunities presented to me and give me the courage to respond to them. Direct me to be the best artist I can be. And I pray for love in my life, for a man even better than Neil, one who will be the right partner for the person I'm becoming. And in my heart, I'm glad you chose me. Thank you and amen."

Then I crossed myself and walked to the pool to see what I could of the fish. They darted to the surface and crisscrossed each other's paths in their search for food. I couldn't imagine what they lived on in that dark, isolated place. Then I invited Father Moran to join me. He obliged and we sat together on a bench facing the waterfall. He said the Lord's Prayer and I prayed with him. But I interrupted the silence that followed.

"May I ask you another question, Father, before I go?" I whispered. He nodded. "What is your first name, in case I'm ever in Dublin?"

"It's Michael," he answered, "Michael Malachy Moran is my full name. My name is much like your own."

"It is," I said, dumbfounded. "We're two sides of the same name," I laughed.

"More than you realize," he said softly. "And now can you come with me?"

"Yes," I said, wondering where he was taking me. There was a sense of urgency in his voice. Silently, almost solemnly, we walked down one of the aisles to a place where he had lit votive candles on opposite sides. Above one ledge was the pictograph for water and on the other, the one for fire.

"I believe this is who you are, Michelle. And who I am, too. For me, the water signifies the unconscious, the dream state, the spiritual side of who I am. It's like the waterfall with its calming sound. But there's the other side, too, the fire. For me, it represents the waking state, that place of constant challenges. We sometimes have to walk right through the middle of it and pray we come out the other side intact. But then it's also that sense of being alive and physically active. And fire is what drives me. It's a passion for what I do in the world. I pray it never goes out," he emphasized.

"I hope you find that balance, too. You need both to survive on our troubled planet. Don't cling too tightly to the calming aspects of water, or you will drown in the dream state. But don't be engulfed in the fire, either. It can kill your spirit, if you let it consume your life. I will pray for you and I hope you pray for me, too. You have been an excellent companion and helper. You saved my sanity by being here. I would've been very lonely by myself," he concluded.

Did he hear my prayer? No, I was sure I had whispered it. It seemed we'd been saviors to each other, after all. "Thank you, Father Michael Malachy Moran. You've been an excellent spiritual guide and companion to me as well. I hope we meet again," I said with sincerity.

"We will," he smiled, "even if it's only in our dreams." He touched me on the shoulder and then I felt myself moving toward him until I had put my arms around him. We embraced like the best of friends. Then I followed him back to the dome where he pulled a couple of pillows from a pile and set them near the middle of the mats, below the circling cloud of dust. He set my backpack down next to me.

"When you leave, be sure to take this with you," he said. "You might be startled awake, so don't forget it."

"I won't. And now what?"

"Your release is almost here. You have time for one more dream, a golden dream, I would imagine. Do you have a hymn you know or like to sing?" he asked.

The only one that came to mind was the one I first sang in the cave. "'Amazing Grace'," I answered.

"Let me say a prayer first and then we'll sing it together." We sat down on the cushions facing each other. He whispered the prayer so quickly I could barely catch it all. He was putting in a request for God to watch over and guide me in my post-Cave of Dreams life.

"May you go in peace, Michelle, to love and serve the world." He made a tiny sign of the cross on my forehead in a blessing.

"Thank you, Father. For everything."

"And remember there is only one God, but many ways to reach God, just as the tunnels in the cave all come together in this room. I'm speaking from what my heart tells me and from what I've experienced here. I've never been comfortable believing that God would create so many souls, only to punish them because they don't practice one particular faith. As for you, you will find God, I know, for God has already found you," he said. There was both sorrow and joy in his voice. And then he began to sing slowly and I joined in.

Amazing grace, how sweet the sound,
that found a wretch like me.
I once was lost, but now I'm found,
was blind, but now I see.

He stopped there and I felt that familiar wave of fatigue. "Father," I slurred. "The sleep is coming."

"I know," he said. "Put your head on the pillow now and let it take you to that golden dream. Farewell, my friend."

As my eyes closed, I heard him softly singing his Gaelic prayer and I began to dream of a medieval church with tall white candles burning on the altar in gold candlesticks. Above the altar a golden cloud drifted in a slow, clockwise dance while angels sang in an ancient language I couldn't understand. Did I hear someone calling my name?

41

"So what did you find out, Angel?" Maggie asked about her friend's visit with the local Teotenacan historians that morning. "What are they like?" she inquired before he had a chance to answer her first question.

Angel shook his head and laughed in response. "Let's sit on the veranda and talk about it," he replied. "By the way, what's Max up to?"

"He was trying to stay awake and help Reggie with repairs to a fence, but he couldn't keep his eyes open. If he's not up from his nap soon I'm going to knock on his door. We have to get ready for Michelle soon," she said as they walked through the kitchen. She smiled grimly. "I *so* want to see her back with us," she confided to him.

"As do I," he replied with a nod. "But after talking to them, I know we will," he confided.

"Good! So tell me more," she urged. They sat down facing each other, but both found themselves looking toward El Anhelo, its mass overshadowing the landscape and their conversation.

"Well, for starters, they're local Oaxaqueños who were educated in Mexico City and they've done extensive research in small towns around the state. They've been trying to find the common threads among Mixtecs, Zapotecs and so many others and examine how the Spanish impacted their cultures in smaller communities, like this one. Their names are Guillermo and Rosa Martinez and they've been married for almost twenty-five years. They teach in the city of Oaxaca and have a home there, but they spend their summers here as well as whatever time they can during the school year. Another couple interviews people like Michelle when they're not here."

"Why this community?" Maggie asked. "What drew them here? The cave?"

"Well, as a matter of fact, yes, but not in the usual way. Their interest in this area began a number of years ago when they studied the pottery and other crafts here. They noticed the eyeless fish motif and the bat patterns and surmised there must be a prominent cave around here. But when they asked the locals, they got negative reactions. They were told it was a myth, a superstition, that it didn't exist. The usual deflections. But they both felt there was more to it than that. One night when they were staying at El Refugio, Rosa had a dream in which she was instructed to go to a cave entrance with Guillermo and to bring food and other necessities to last for two days. Guillermo was curious, but he felt her unconscious mind was operating on wishful thinking. But when they discussed it with the owner of the inn, he was quite cooperative, telling them he'd help to assemble what they needed. He was so incredibly helpful, in fact, that Guillermo wondered if there was something to Rosa's dream. And, indeed, they found the entrance where the dream indicated and they were in the cave for two days. Their original entrance seemed to vanish, as it must have for Michelle, but they found an alternate one for their exit."

"So Rosa's faith paid off," Maggie said. "That's reassuring. What are they like?"

"Friendly, but also very professional in their approach. They don't fit the usual profile of people who go into the cave because they aren't local to the town or artists or religious practitioners," he explained.

"So why do they think they were chosen? Was it because of their work?"

"Yes," he nodded. "Through their dreams in the cave, they were told their talents were needed to record people's experiences there. The information could be shared with others who had similar experiences or who knew someone who had. They can supply a comprehensive history that helps people understand their own experiences in the cave and where they fit into a larger context. It's also a process that helps people adjust to their regular lives again. Most of those from outside Teotenaca can't share what happened with people they know when they get home. Those who have shared it are not believed, which is frustrating and isolating for them, unless they connect with others like Darlene and Reggie. I think that's one reason why people come back here, even if it's not to go into the cave. For generations, the only people who went in were local to the area, and they could share their experiences. But now people are coming from all over the world, often summoned here by dreams."

Maggie listened attentively but shook her head. "It reminds me of that Steven Spielberg movie *Close Encounters of the Third Kind* when ordinary people became outrageously compulsive. They were all drawing and painting the image of that huge rock formation, the Devil's Tower. They were on a mission to get to it in time for the arrival of a spaceship. But only a few of them made it. You can accept that kind of thing in a science fiction story, but I can see where people would have trouble accepting the existence of a place like the Cave of Dreams, if they weren't in it themselves. I'm anxious to hear about it from Michelle. It's so mysterious."

"It is," he agreed, "and if you were a respected researcher, would you publish a paper on such a thing? How could you even prove it exists? So Guillermo and Rosa have kept their research here, within the local community. They've done a huge study. And, of course, they want to interview Michelle about her time in there, too."

Maggie looked at the mountain that still held their friend and smiled. "Knowing her, she'll have just as many questions for them." They both laughed in agreement and with relief, knowing in their hearts that the ordeal of waiting was almost over.

"Reggie, where do you get your energy?" Dar asked.

"It must be your cooking," he winked.

"Cheeky," she laughed. "Well, you'd better have some of it before we head over to the trail. Maggie and Angel ate, but I haven't seen Max in a while. Is he still sleeping?"

"I reckon he is," Reggie laughed.

"What did you do to him?" she smiled.

"Put him through his paces, I did. He did well, though. Maybe he didn't get to bed when he should have last night. He's a bit stubborn, that one," he said. "That's the price you pay for staying up late."

Dar set the basket of food for Michelle on the veranda, then called to Sunny who was on the tire swing. "Sunny, do you have the hat and sunglasses for Michelle?"

"Yes, Mum. It will be soon," she said with agitation in her voice.

"Can someone wake up Max?" Darlene called to anyone who would answer.

"I am up," a sleepy voice came from the stairs. "Is it time already?" Max said, rubbing his eyes and stretching his arms as he got to the kitchen.

"It is," Reggie answered. "Are you coming with us?"

"Absolutely. I'm taking my camera." He'd left it near the front door.

"Can we bring Max's sandwich with us?" Reggie suggested.

"I think we'll have to. I'd hate for Michelle to be coming out of there with no one waiting. It's so disorienting when that happens. I'll grab a wet cloth to wash her face and hands. Poor dear. Let's not be late."

Finally, the group began their walk to the trail that encircled El Anhelo. Reggie had his binoculars. They planned to fan out along the mountain and signal each other when there was any sign of the cave opening. "So, how will we know when the cave is opening?" Max asked Reggie.

"Oh, you'll know without a doubt, when that time comes. Trust me." Max only nodded in response as he thought about that issue of trust. But now, was there any other choice?

42

"Michelle," a voice whispered. "Michelle," it echoed. I looked upward into the golden cloud above the altar in my dream. It looked like the one that swirled above where I slept in the dome of the cave. But the dream cloud was made of smoke from the candles and the incense, and floating bits of gold dust. The voice seemed to come from it.

"Yes," I answered, glancing up at it. "Who's calling me?"

"Michelle. Can you see me?" the voice asked. I looked into the cloud but only saw its flickering particles gliding past me.

"I can't see anything but the dust cloud," I whispered. I didn't want to speak loudly, feeling I was in a church where angelic voices sang and ancient prayers were being said nearby.

"It's a matter of perception," the voice replied. "You're seeing what is obvious, but not beyond that. Yet I'm here and I see you." That was creepy. Who was spying on me and why? And why couldn't I see him?

"So how can I see you?" I asked.

"Close your eyes, envision the cloud in your mind. When you open your eyes, things will look different." I closed my eyes and visualized the slow dance of dust in the air. Even imagining it had a hypnotic quality, as if it were putting me into a trance.

"Now open your eyes," the voice said in a whisper.

As I did, the cloud seemed even slower, almost stopped in mid-air. *Will it drift away or fall all over the altar and me?* I wondered. Then I noticed movement beyond it. I saw his body, then his face, and finally his dark eyes. He held my gaze, even from the distance of twenty feet or so. Then he walked toward me, descending through the cloud as if he were on an invisible staircase. I stared back at him as he approached. I couldn't stop staring. He never took his eyes away from mine, either, not even to see where his feet stepped. When he emerged from the golden dust, he seemed to be made of it. He was physically there, yet he wasn't. My perception was more confused since he looked part real and part illusion.

The mysterious man stopped within a few feet of me.

"Your imagination is deep and fertile," he began. "Remember that, always, even in those moments when you cannot reach it, when you feel it has failed you. It is as much a part of you as your lungs or your hands. It is a blessed part of you, like your soul," he said softly, smiling.

"Thank you," I said awkwardly, not knowing who he could possibly be. "And who are you, sir?"

He nodded slowly, his golden-flecked head turning slightly. "One who will advise you when needed," was all he said. "You will hear my words from time to time, usually spoken through the voices of others. It will be your choice to listen and act, or not. But I will be with you."

"I would be grateful for advice," I said, not quite knowing what else to say. "I'll try to listen," I promised.

"Also listen to your heart and your soul. They will not lie or misguide you." With that he seemed to dissipate into flickers of gold that whirled clockwise like a funnel to join the golden cloud above me. I could no longer see him. I felt frustrated since I hadn't found out who he was.

"You will know him when you hear his voice in Teotenaca," a woman said from behind me. I turned to see María, my dream guide, sitting in a pew. I joined her there, comforted by her presence. She wore a white dress flecked with gold. A white veil hung from the back of her head to her shoulders, accenting her dark hair. "You will be leaving the Cave of Dreams soon. But I will be with you whenever you dream," she assured me.

"How shall I dream?" I asked. "Do I merely fall asleep and let it happen? Or can I guide myself to dream a certain kind of dream?"

"I'm sure you've noticed that when you have an issue on your mind, your unconscious deals with it while you sleep, and dream," she reminded me. "Dreams are a means of answering difficult questions that the conscious mind cannot comprehend. If you wish to dream about a particular thing, let it be your last thought as you close your eyes. I'll be there to catch that thought and help you in your quest. We will see each other again."

"You've been very helpful, even when you put me into some frightening dreams. But I've learned so much here," I told her. "I would be truly grateful for more guidance after I leave the Cave of Dreams."

"You're a good student, Michelle. You're more extraordinary than many people I've advised. You withstood a great deal on your journey through the City of Darkness. The lessons of your dreams here will serve you well when you return to the physical world you know. Instead of walking away, you'll be encouraged to interact with those who are in pain. It will take courage, but you are capable of adding your light of hope to those places where little hope exists. Always remember that. And even though you are fearful, do not be afraid. Do not be afraid.... Do not be afraid...."

She sounded like a broken record as her words slowed down and echoed in my ears and then began to fade into a murmur. Then María slowly turned into golden dust and circled around me to join the cloud in its slow dance. But then the golden cloud descended until it covered the altar, and then the altar became part of it. And then it surprised me by whirling in my direction like a slow motion tornado. I closed my eyes thinking I'd be swept away, too, but I just sat there, rooted to the pew, feeling many sensations simultaneously as if the cloud were washing through my psyche. I felt warmth, love, sadness, and hope. I became more energized then and opened my eyes to see what would happen next. Then the cloud swirled back to where the altar had been. The tiny particles came together, turning and tightening into the form of a rotating sun, shooting its rays in all directions. And then the rays tightened and folded into a glowing ball. Finally, the motion stopped and all was still.

But what had seemed sacred and safe suddenly took on an ominous form. I saw that the glowing ball was in the transparent belly of a huge creature shaped like a dragon. The more I followed its form with my eyes, the larger it became. I couldn't see the end of its tail and I was afraid to find its head. I just looked straight ahead at the bright ball in its stomach. The dragon's form moved as if it were sitting down. Its shape grew more compressed and then I saw its immense head turning slightly. Its tail wrapped around its feet, bringing the creature closer to the roundness of the sun within it.

Then I heard María's voice again. "Do not be afraid...." And I heard Reggie and Darlene saying it, too. "Do not be afraid...." And Father Moran's voice joined in the chorus. "Do not be ... afraid." It became a chorus of voices repeating the same phrase. Do not be afraid of this horrible dragon that seemed ready to eat me alive? Would I join the golden ball in his stomach?

"Do not be afraid ... of your *own* power!" the voice of the "golden" man urged as the chorus stopped. It was strong and clear and loud in the cave, echoing in my head. I stared at the dragon and let my fear drop away.

Then I heard María's voice. "Michelle, your own power can overcome your fear. Let it be so and see what happens."

I took a deep breath and called on a deeper place in my heart, or perhaps even my soul. I looked directly into the face of the dragon as it turned toward me. I thought the fire in its belly would spray out of its mouth and transform me into a heap of ash. But as I stared back, trying to see into its eyes, it became something else. It flattened into a Japanese screen consisting of a frame with thin paper stretched over it. The dragon was merely a pattern painted on it, not a living thing at all. But suddenly, unexpectedly, the screen turned like a page in a book, or a door opening, leaving only the ball of golden dust there, glowing like pure fire! It was a sun again and it began to rotate clockwise, faster and faster. It got larger and larger and drew in the air around me, creating a kind of funnel that pulled me toward it. I was suddenly aware of the sound of wind. My hair whipped against my face. The golden circle grew hotter. The sensation was so powerful that it woke me up.

The dream ended abruptly as I opened my eyes, but what I saw and felt in my waking state was the same thing I'd seen in my dream! The bright light of the swirling sun was coming from the end of one of the aisles that led into the dome where I was lying on the ground. I stood up, pulled my backpack on and tried to look into that swirling light. It hurt my eyes, but then it began to illuminate the cave. For the first time I could see without having to rely on my flashlight or any other light source. The rays of the golden ball were warm when they touched me, and then its forceful movement pulled me toward it. I followed the floor of the cave, seeing every rock and groove along the surface. I passed between the pictographs of fire and water and kept moving toward the ball of fire. It happened so quickly! It was huge now and grew hotter as I approached it. I tried not to be afraid, but I wasn't sure what to expect next, since no one had explained this phenomenon to me. I remembered seeing it pictured in the giant mural on the cave wall, and Father Moran telling me I'd see this thing before I left the cave.

And then, as I reached the end of the aisle where the golden disc spun, it stopped rotating and disappeared into the air. Instead of a fiery sun, I saw an opening in the cave wall and found myself standing at that point of transition, that halfway mark between the darkness and the light. Then I saw the green of the wild grass outside. I walked unsteadily toward it, not knowing what I would find as I re-entered the world outside the Cave of Dreams. I was warmed by the real sun at last! I heard the music of bird song and the hum of wind rustling through trees. I had longed for this place, this world where the people I loved were waiting for me to meet them.

43

The group from the Sweet Dreams Bed and Breakfast spread out along the trail that hugged the mountain. Sunny and her mother stayed together, laughing and sharing a story even as they both kept a watchful eye on the rock wall of El Anhelo. Reggie paced back and forth from his point, binoculars at the ready in case he heard any unusual sounds. There were a few trees near him and he kept an eye on the birds resting in the branches. He knew they would be the first to react to sounds of the cave opening. Maggie and Angel weren't sure what to expect and looked over at each other periodically, always returning the look with a shaking of the head, a sign of nothing yet. Reggie and Dar were well aware of what would happen next and knew this was a waiting game, for Michelle's sudden appearance could be minutes or hours away.

Situated between his friends and the Howards was Max, who kept checking his camera equipment. This waiting made him restless and anxious. The sun had a clear path to the back of his neck while he sat on a tree stump. He reached into his pack for sunscreen to coat that vulnerable spot, then pulled his baseball cap further over his face, obscuring part of his view when he looked at the mountain.

How long had they been there, half an hour? There was no sign of anyone along the trail, yet he wondered if they'd arrived too late. Had they missed Michelle? Was she trying to find her way back to the B & B, or was she still in the cave? And, of course, doubts kept creeping into his mind. How long would they wait, if she didn't show up? What if her fate had been entirely different and her body was lying in a gully? But he wanted to see her, hear her voice again, scold her in his brotherly way for hiking alone on the trail and going into the cave. He wanted to believe. And he wanted to capture it all in his camera, document her from the instant of her release, which was why he'd chosen to stay between the two groups, so he could quickly move in either direction.

As he checked his camera one more time, he heard movement nearby. He looked up as a gust of wind blew dust into his face. He brushed it out of his eyes, and then the sound of wind grew stronger. He held his hat down tight and tried to see what was happening. It was coming from the surface of the mountain, not twenty feet away. He looked through the lens of his camera. A huge swirl of yellow light spun counterclockwise there. Was it boring a hole right through the side of the mountain? It grew larger and warmer. He clicked the digital camera several times, not sure of what he'd capture. Then the light and heat subsided and he saw movement. Was it a person? Yes! A person standing in the smoky opening in the side of the mountain, a place that had just been solid rock! He waited for the dust to subside and then he saw her as she gingerly stepped out of the cave, moving slowly, shielding her eyes from the sunlight.

It *was* Michelle! It really was her, after all he'd feared! She looked unsteady and unkempt. He took another couple shots and called her name. She glanced in his direction and then disappeared from his viewfinder into a heap on the ground.

"Michelle," he cried, pulling off the camera and running to her side. Her name went down the line and the others came running one by one. "Are you all right?" he practically yelled at her. She'd landed on all fours and leaned back into an awkward seated position on the ground, trying to open her eyes, but the sun kept blinding her. When she shielded her face from it, there was Max, who looked more than a little concerned.

"Max? Oh my God, it *is* you," she laughed and reached toward him. He removed the backpack and helped her stand. The heat of the sun was too much. She peeled away her sweatshirt and threw it to the ground.

"Are you all right?" he asked again in a softer tone this time. She nodded yes and felt tears coming. They prevented her from speaking. But she reached out to him and he enveloped her in a gentle bear hug. "We were so worried," he said. "You can't imagine what we thought might have happened to you." Gradually, she was able to open her eyes a little more and nodded in reply, the tears still coming. They sunk into the recesses of her smile, which grew broader as she realized this was not a dream. She'd been released into the world again, right into the arms of her friend.

Then the others appeared at her side, one by one. Sunny gave her the sunglasses and hat, which enabled her to see them all. "Thank you,

Sunny," she nodded in gratitude.

And then everyone got a better look at Michelle, and they were shocked. Bloodstains splattered her shirt and pants. Her hair was matted and dirty. The last gusts of wind had tangled it into knots around her face. Her cheeks and chin were smudged with dirt. She was shaking and crying. Maggie stepped forward to have a better look. "Michelle, it's *so* good to see you again. You have no idea how much we missed you!" she said, giving her a warm hug. She whispered in her ear as she held her, "Are you hurting anywhere? Any injuries? Whose blood is all over your clothes?"

Michelle let go and pointed to her head where she'd injured it in a fall. Maggie looked closely and said, "It's healing. Looks like a scratch, but the scab is already healed. Does it hurt?"

She shook her head that it didn't. Then she pointed to her rib cage where the pain had been the greatest after her darkest dream. Maggie lifted her friend's top discreetly, felt the ribs and took a close look.

"It seems slightly bruised, but the bones are in place. I don't feel any cracks or anything out of order. It may just be the bruise. You look a little thinner, too. And the blood?" she asked again.

"It isn't mine, believe it or not, except some from my cut. And I didn't slaughter anyone, either. It's, for lack of a better term, 'dream blood,' which I got splattered with in a horrible dream. I don't know why it's there now," she tried to explain, knowing it didn't make sense, even if it was true.

"We'll talk more about that later. Are you hungry?" She nodded that she was.

"Let's find a place to sit her down so she can eat and drink," Dar interjected. "I've got lots for you to choose from, Michelle," she said, touching the rescued woman's cheek. "You're safe now."

Max had taken that moment to go back to get his camera. He looked through the lens again and took a picture of the group surrounding Michelle. But when he looked at the opening in the mountain from which she'd emerged, it was gone. A dust cloud seemed to hover there, but the "portal" had disappeared as if it had never existed. He took a picture and then ran to where she'd re-entered the world. There was nothing but rock now, the hard, impenetrable wall of El Anhelo stood firm once again. Yet he'd seen it open and release his friend. He shook his head in disbelief and backed away from the mountain.

As Michelle sat down on a nearby tree stump, she was surrounded by good will and the love of her friends. But then she noticed something incredible for the first time. She lifted her sunglasses to concentrate on Maggie's eyes as her friend bent down to reassure her.

"Oh, Maggie, you are *so* beautiful!" she exclaimed. "Your eyes are so many colors wrapped into one." Michelle was fully awake now and aware of everything in a heightened way she'd never experienced before. She shielded her eyes with her hand and took off the sunglasses so she could see her friend in the brilliant light. In Maggie's eyes she detected tones of green mixed with gold and flecks of brown. After the sensory deprivation of the cave, the outside world was greatly enhanced. From that point on, it became much richer for her than it had been before being in the Cave of Dreams. And it all started with Maggie's eyes. She couldn't stop staring at them. They were like fine jewels, like emeralds bathed in gold.

"That's quite a compliment," Maggie said, feeling a bit embarrassed by her friend's attention. She shifted the conversation back. "You've been away a long time now," she responded. "You must be exhausted!"

"No. Not really. I want to see all of you again. Close up," she said, as if in a trance. "Where's Angel?" she asked, putting the sunglasses back on as she looked around for him.

He heard his name. Standing back from the crowd, he now came forward. "I'm here," he said. "I was worried about you, Michelle. How are you after being in there?"

"Oh, Angel!" she cried, standing up. "I've missed you!" She put her arms around him and held on tight. Then she looked into his eyes, too, and smoothed back the hair that fell lazily over his forehead, and she smiled. "My dream was right. You're handsome with your hair off your forehead. You've been hiding behind it all this time," she laughed, pushing it away from his face. He raised the sunglasses enough to look into her eyes. She'd changed in some inexplicable way. He ignored her comment because he didn't understand it.

"I was so concerned about you that I even prayed for the first time in a long time. And now my prayers have been answered," he smiled, embracing her back. As he held her, he could smell the ancient dampness of the cave. Gently, he let go. As she stood in front of him he saw tiny sparks of sunlight on her face and hair as if she'd been sprinkled with gold dust.

Then they set out a feast for her on a blanket. She was glad this wasn't a dream because her stomach growled in anticipation at the sight of so much food. But instead of the juice Dar had brought, she drew out the bottle of water tucked in her backpack.

"Where did you get that water?" Maggie asked in disbelief.

"From the pool in the cave."

Michelle looked at Dar accusingly. "Why didn't you tell me?" she asked.

Dar avoided her gaze and answered, "We couldn't. It's part of our role not to direct people like you toward the cave. They have to find it on their own. Then they have to decide to go in or not. It'd been different if you'd already dreamt about the cave."

"Well, thank you for adding to my food supply. I wondered why the backpack was so heavy. You knew I'd go in, didn't you?"

"Reggie felt strongly that you would," she replied.

"But how did you know when I'd be getting out? And where I'd be?" she looked to him.

"You can thank Sunny for that prediction. Her dreams told her when and where you'd be released," he explained.

"Sunny?" Michelle said, looking for the young girl. She was hiding behind her father's legs.

"Yes?" the girl answered.

"Were you in my dream, the one at the movies?" Michelle asked.

"Yes. But it was my dream, too," the girl insisted. "Angel asked me to dream about you. That was a big bag of popcorn," she smiled.

Remembering that dream again, Michelle turned to her friends. "Max, have you and Maggie reached some sort of understanding?" she inquired, her head cocked to one side.

Max put his arm around Maggie who smiled at him and then Michelle. "Yes," he nodded. "You could put it that way. I love this lady and I'm not afraid to say it," he stated with pride.

"And I love him, God help me," Maggie laughed, kissing Max on the cheek.

"Well, that's good news," Michelle asserted in a soft voice. "Very good news!"

"But how did you know?" Max asked.

"My dreams told me," she answered, letting the mystery of that statement hang in the air. She began eating with obvious delight. The sandwich was consumed in large gulps washed down by the water from her bottle. Then the fruit was devoured along with the juice.

"Thank you, Dar. Sorry if I made a pig of myself just then. But I've been *so* hungry."

"You seem thinner," she answered with understanding.

"I ate in the cave, but not much," she nodded. "But Father Moran is still in there. I hope the pilgrims bring food for him. He shared a lot of what he had with me."

"Pilgrims," Angel said, remembering the assorted individuals he'd seen drive by. "Will they be going in today?"

"Yes, very soon. That's why it was time for me to leave," she answered as she carefully stood up and stretched slightly. "But I missed you all so much that I really didn't want to be in there any longer. So you missed me, too?"

Maggie laughed. "Oh, maybe just a little," she motioned with her finger and thumb held close together. Then she opened her arms wide and wrapped them around Michelle who hugged her back enthusiastically. They held each other for a long time and they both cried silently, joyfully.

"How bad do I look, Maggie? Be truthful," Michelle whispered to her friend who loosened her hug and stood back to take a good look at her.

"Truthful, huh? You look like you could use a bath and a change of clothes. And that hair." She reached out to examine a couple of the worse knots. "Washing will help, but it looks like you've got serious tangles, girl."

"Ow! Should I just cut them off?" Michelle asked nonchalantly, surprising her friend who knew she'd been regularly going to the salon for highlights. Hadn't she had it styled right before the trip?

"I could cut your hair," Dar offered. "I have a lot of experience and it wouldn't be unusual for a person getting out of the cave to do just that. It's a kind of getting rid of the old. Do you remember the snake motif on your vase from Flor? Cutting off your tangled hair is one way of shedding your skin as you outgrow it."

"Yes, please cut it," Michelle nodded and smiled. "That's an easy solution to my hair care problem. And my nails are looking pretty beat up, so it's a good thing I have a nail file with me. But I don't think I can save these clothes. They looked bad in lamplight. They look even more horrible in daylight," she said, shuddering as she looked down at her pants and blouse. "I really am a sight," she said, shaking her head. "But I feel fine, though I could use a night on a regular mattress for a change," she smiled. "My back's a little tired."

"Are you ready to go to Sweet Dreams?" Reggie asked, offering her his hand. He had slung a hammock over his shoulder, brought in case she was incapacitated, but she was far from that.

"I am," Michelle said, taking his hand, "if you mean the B & B. I've had enough sweet and sour dreams to last for a while."

They made their way back down the path toward the house. As Michelle answered her friends' questions, she knew how surreal her story sounded. Yet she spoke the truth. This was only the beginning of a new direction in her life, a journey that had no map. She wondered where it would take her and what other mysteries lay ahead.

44

There wasn't much vacation left at this point, but I was happy to spend it with my friends. I couldn't imagine how difficult the days I'd been missing had been for them, not knowing what my real fate was, trying to believe in what must have seemed like hocus pocus from Dar and Reggie, as well as Flor. And to think that Angel had almost entered the cave to try and find me without supplies or even a flashlight! I was glad Max had stopped him. There wouldn't have been enough food for three of us, after all. Yet I felt his time in the Cave of Dreams might still come, that he, too, could be summoned by a dream one day.

Angel continued to surprise me in other ways. I'd always admired his dedication and his intellect, since he was the most serious of my friends. His mind was always working things out, trying to apply his analysis in many situations. But there seemed to be a releasing of that in Teotenaca. He smiled easily in the Mexican sunlight, a wonderful smile that made him seem more alive and present in the moment. Yet I wanted to tap into his memory and knowledge in an effort to analyze what had happened to me. But first he had a request. He wanted me to visit a couple who researched people from outside the town who'd been in the Cave of Dreams, the very heart of the Mountain of Longing, known as El Anhelo. "I'd like to go with you, if you're up to going," he said. "They have a lot of information on the cave you might want to hear." This intrigued me, so I agreed to go.

But first, I lounged in the tub, soaking off the grime and letting my muscles relax. It was startling to see the cave dust floating on the surface of the water. And then Dar cut away the massive tangled mess on my head that was once highlighted hair that hung to the top of my shoulder blades. I shampooed more dirt away in the laundry tub, followed by a head massage from Dar's amazing fingers. Then she gave me a neater trim, which I liked. It was simple and short. It made me realize I could trim away the excess in my life, too. The haircut was a good way to start.

Then Angel took me to see Rosa and Guillermo, who were anxious to interview me. "You may have questions for us as well," Rosa said. Boy, did I! I knew we'd be there longer than they expected. I agreed to their terms and they began the process. They asked for my name, place and date of birth, citizenship, whether I had a religious affiliation, how long I'd been in town and how much of that time had been spent in the cave. Did I have a dream about the cave or did I just happen upon it? Did I have that pain in my stomach beforehand that Reggie called "the draw of the mountain"? I thought I was a classic case of tourist turned cave dreamer until they learned I hadn't been alone and that my companion was connected to the retreat. Rosa and Guillermo looked at each other. "You helped to prepare the way for the retreat?" Guillermo asked. "We were theorizing that it was possible. In fact, we were hoping it was."

"Yes, I helped. Do you know Father Moran?" I asked.

"He's in our database, I believe. If I'm remembering correctly, he and two other priests were here about ten years ago. But we didn't realize he'd been back," she explained.

"He said this was his second retreat, but this is the first time he got there first to prepare things. Why don't you know that?" I asked.

"The retreat is steeped in secrecy, even from us," she explained. "Those who attend stay at the inn before and after they enter the cave. They're very protective of them there. We have a little information on what happens, but not a lot. Anything you can tell us would be helpful in expanding our knowledge of the cave's history."

That made me a little uncomfortable at first. I wasn't sure why things had been kept secret, but perhaps it was just a privacy issue. I reasoned that if I was there and if Father Moran had told me anything, it was for a purpose. Perhaps I was meant to be there so a smattering of the information could become known. So I told them about the sleeping rooms, the "loo" and the kitchen. They knew a few things already, but when I told them about the dome and how it was set up before I left, that the pilgrims would lie down there together and pray as a circle looking up toward the rotating cloud of dust, that caught their attention. They weren't sure about the retreat's process or agenda, so this was news to them.

But mostly I told them about my dreams. They took particular interest in the "Hell on Earth" dream, and were surprised I'd gone as far into the City of Darkness as I had. While recounting that nightmare, I shivered through the most harrowing moments. Angel wrapped his hand around mine and I held it tightly. He sat beside me, reassuring me and looking just as engaged as Guillermo and Rosa were. He looked horrified when I told them how my side had been injured in the mass grave and that it still ached. "You may always be aware of it," Rosa warned me. "Doctors may find nothing, but it will remain there as a memory of your dream. That physical manifestation is not an unusual phenomenon. There is a reason why it is there, which will become clearer to you." I was not happy to hear that, and I wondered how it would impact my life. Apparently I would know soon enough.

When the interview was over and I'd gone through three cups of hot tea, I turned the tables and began my questions. "Can you tell me how many people enter the cave every year?"

"It seems on the rise," Rosa answered. "We've had at least twenty-five from outside Teotenaca this year so far, not including those on the retreat. Last year, we had only about nineteen by this time. But, of course, the townspeople come and go regularly. We don't keep track of them, but we've recorded many of their experiences and dreams."

"Father Moran said the cave was an ecumenical place, that people of many faiths go there, as well as those who don't believe in God. And Reggie mentioned that many artists have been in it. Is that accurate?" I asked.

Guillermo answered this time. "Yes, it is ecumenical in that way. As for artists, we've had painters, writers, dancers, actors, directors, musicians, so many! And they often come back. The cave and the mountain seem to feed their imaginations. But so do their dreams, no matter where they are."

There were several questions that had crossed my mind again and again, so I finally asked them. "What about people who are atheists or agnostics? Do they find their faith after they've been in there? What do they make of their experiences in the cave?" I asked.

"Occasionally they find faith, especially the agnostics. They feel like they have been given this knowledge for a reason. The people who come here believe in what is just, whether or not they believe in God. The dreams and their messages are custom made for the person who has them. Your dreams unfolded through the perspective of your Christian background. A Buddhist would be in touch with his or her faith, as would a Muslim or a Jew," Guillermo explained. "And in the case of a person who does not believe in God, their faith in moral actions or their respect for others is affirmed. Their faith in what is right is emboldened. Is that clear?"

I could see how things could be shaped in ways that would work for all kinds of people. Dreams come from who we are, after all. And we're all different. "Yes," I said. "I think I understand that now."

Rosa smiled. "You're very inquisitive," she said. "That's healthy. It will help you to understand your own experience on a deeper level. Keep asking questions in your dreams and they'll be answered one by one."

"Can I ask another?" I laughed.

"Certainly," Rosa nodded.

"Are there people who were in the cave who have become famous artists or performers? Have you tracked their accomplishments after being here? I'm just wondering how people who have been here have impacted the world."

"A large couple of questions," Guillermo smiled, "and this is something we often wonder about ourselves."

"It's not always possible to know these things," his wife explained, "but there are a few we know about. Unfortunately, I can't share their names with you, because they want their privacy on this issue. For instance, there is a poet from Brazil who has won several major awards who was here, yet I cannot divulge his name. But there is a poet who lives near you in Chicago that I am able to mention, because she doesn't mind if I do. Her name is Berta Corelli. She has published two or three books and teaches poetry in a university there. Do you know who she is? At times she uses imagery right from the cave, but in metaphorical ways."

"The name is so familiar," I said. And then it hit me. It was Berta Corelli's poem that had turned Max's life around after Anita's death! Her words had given him the courage and will to keep living. "Oh, my God," I exclaimed. "Yes, I do know her work. And I truly admire it."

"If you ever look her up, be subtle when bringing up the Cave of Dreams. Make hints before saying anything specific about the cave. People are very guarded about this experience," she advised me.

"I may very well look her up," I said. "Small world!"

"Very much so," Guillermo nodded.

"In your experience," I said to them, "how does this time in the cave affect people when they go back to their old, normal routines?"

"We only do follow-up research when people come back here, or if they contact us," Guillermo began. "And this part of the journey can vary wildly. It seems that for most people, they can pick up where they were before, but they bring new insight to everything they do. This experience can help them on many levels, professional and personal, dealing with business aspects of their work, for instance. Their dreams are very powerful tools, for advancing themselves, but more likely for advancing others. But there are also those who react by becoming more private, by withdrawing from public contact. Yet their work speaks for them in galleries, on stages and in books."

"And when do they find out about their mission?" I asked.

"Ah, the mission," Rosa smiled. I felt Angel looking at me. He looked deep in thought when I faced him, but he smiled when I caught his expression.

"I'm supposed to have a mission," I said to him, trying to make it sound less than serious, though I knew it could ultimately be extremely serious.

"Keep dreaming and listening for clues," Guillermo said, reaching out to touch my shoulder. "You will learn soon enough. For everyone, the answer is different."

"I will do that," I nodded, "but I hope the answer comes soon. I'm really curious." I laughed a bit self-consciously then and knew I had a lot to think about. There was no need to ask more questions. The complexity of what I'd been told would keep my mind occupied for a long time to come.

45

Angel and I headed toward Sweet Dreams on foot down a dirt road as the sun shed the day in brilliant tones of orange and red. By the time we arrived it was almost dark. I was frustrated not to have my trusty flashlight along. But the lights from inside the Sweet Dreams Bed and Breakfast were visible and inviting, even from a distance. It was comforting to know there was a bed upstairs with a soft pillow waiting for me. *A real bed.* After sleeping on rock and an air mattress in the cave, I couldn't imagine how heavenly that would be.

"I wonder what my dreams will be like now. I hope I'll remember them like I did in El Anhelo."

"I have a feeling you will," Angel said confidently as we knocked and entered the lounge room where Reggie sat reading a Mexican magazine.

"Well, you two have been gone a while," he greeted us. "Did you have an interesting chat with Rosa and Guillermo, Michelle?"

"Very interesting. It's reassuring to know I'm not some kind of freak after all."

"Freak? Far from it," he smiled as he rose. "You're in excellent company. One of the elite around these parts. But not too many outside people will know that. It's part of your cover."

"My 'cover,' eh? For my 'mission,' you mean?"

"Correct, if you want to call it that," Reggie nodded with a sly expression, "whatever it'll turn out to be. If you look back at the dreams you had in the cave there are always clues to your future," he explained. By the way he looked at Reggie, I could tell the idea of a mission still intrigued Angel.

"So Reggie, can I be so bold as to ask what your mission is, or was?" Angel asked him.

"Yes," I interjected. "How did *you* find out?"

"You may be so bold, though I prefer to think of it as a 'calling.'"

Then he pointed to an image on the wall. "It's my paintings. I used to be a frustrated artist, never having enough time between planning lessons and grading papers to make much headway. I taught the French language when it was really the French painters, particularly the Impressionists, I was interested in," he said, glancing at the painting and nodding at the obvious influence of that art movement. "But after my time in the Cave of Dreams, I realized I had to find a way to work on my paintings. I was interested in nature and landscapes, so that was the direction I took. My work is about sharing that awe with others and I hope they appreciate the natural world more after seeing my art. And they often do. My paintings have been auctioned off and reproduced in prints to benefit environmental causes I believe in. There's a part of the Amazon rainforest that my paintings helped to buy as a reserve, and I'm proud of that accomplishment. And how did this come to be? It started with a dream I had one night," he smiled mysteriously.

"Reggie, how did the dream 'call' you?" I asked, anxious to compare my dreams with his.

"I found myself in the middle of a forest. The trees leaned toward me. The birds landed on my hat and sang to me. Even the wild grasses seemed to caress my feet," he laughed. "I felt like I belonged to that place, that I understood it in a way no other human could. I try to share that feeling through my work. I love to paint. It's *my* calling. And, amazingly, people buy it. It's helped to keep us afloat out here. As you may have suspected, we don't have guests all the time," he smiled.

"Well, you have a full house these days," I noted. "But you're sure that was your mission, or calling, or whatever you want to call it?"

"Oh yes," he nodded with confidence.

"What about Darlene?" Angel asked.

He smiled warmly. "Ah, my lovely wife, the spiritual poet. She had published a few poems before we came here, but her focus is more defined now. She has quite the following back in Australia and she's getting one in the UK as well. She still has to crack the U.S., but she's working on it. And she's been trying to make inroads in Mexico, as well, with translation help from native speakers." He stopped for a moment and took a deep breath. It was obvious that he was proud of her accomplishments. "Her work is about hope. She had a dream, too, that pushed her in that direction. In it, someone was pleading with her to help them find their way. She thought they were on the wrong road, but it was their faith that was lost. In the dream she spoke a poem that she'd never heard before, but it turned the person's life in the right direction. When she awoke, she remembered the poem and wrote it down. She was stunned at its power, especially when she realized she must have written it as part of her dream. You could say it turned her life around, too, because she's been inspiring people with her words ever since. At this very moment she's putting the finishing touches to the poems she'll read tomorrow night at the salon."

"Salon?" I said. "What salon?"

"No one told you?" he asked. "We do it monthly in Teotenaca and tomorrow night is our turn to host. Our neighbors share and discuss their projects with each other. And at this go 'round, you'll be the guest of honor," he informed me with a wave of a hand above his head.

"Why me? I'm new here!"

"And newly graduated from the school of El Anhelo, so it *must* be you. Perhaps you could share some of your latest drawings," he suggested.

"Tomorrow is our last full day here," Angel reminded me. "Think about what else you'd like to do, unless you just want to rest."

I had no intention of sleeping away another day of vacation, especially the last one. "I'll see what my dreams tell me tonight and I'll let you know in the morning," I joked. "But I really want to be at the salon to meet these other people."

"You'll feel right at home," Reggie smiled, and I longed for that.

The rest of the day passed quickly and then I felt a wave of fatigue, not like what I'd had in the cave, but from normal weariness after a long day. I said my good nights and slipped into bed, leaving room for Maggie, who was spending almost all her time with Max, it seemed. She kept asking how I was and checking my vital signs, and he would check in with me, too. But every time I said I was fine, they'd vanish again, walking away hand in hand. This time she promised she'd be in soon, but I was too weary to wait up.

I didn't fall right to sleep, though. My mind was busy replaying incidents in the cave. I kept turning every experience over like a puzzle I couldn't solve, trying to see it from all angles, still wondering how and why this had happened to me. Would everything from now on be boring compared to what I'd just been through? Then, from a corner of the room, the gardenia's weakened fragrance wafted over, surprising me that it was there at all. Maggie must have left it for me, a tiny glimmer of hope that I'd return. The flower reminded me of a dream I'd had when I first arrived in Mexico, so long ago it seemed, of coming out of a forest with the withered bouquet in my hand. Now I understood the dream was telling me I'd disappear into a dark place for several days, the passage of time marked by the flowers' withered state. And now I had returned from the deep womb, the heart of El Anhelo. I breathed in the subtle fragrance of the gardenia, happy to be back in a world where flowers could be touched and smelled.

46

It was glorious to be awakened by Rudolfo's crowing the next morning, especially after sleeping in a real bed, which suddenly moved. It was Maggie waking up.

"Where's the snooze button on that rooster?" she slurred. "I bet you didn't miss that in the cave."

"When did you come to bed?" I asked.

"Late. I think I'll sleep just a little longer." I heard her steady breathing a second later.

I lingered in bed for a while thinking about the day to come. But instead of fully waking up, I went back to sleep. Maybe it was the rhythm of Maggie's breathing. Before long I recognized María's smile as a dream began. She was back in one piece, no longer part of the whirling gold ball she'd disappeared into the day before. But the background was hazy and I couldn't make out where she was standing.

"You are wondering what happens next, aren't you?" she smiled, already knowing the answer.

"Oh, yes. And the other question still running through my brain is 'Why me?'"

"Don't preoccupy yourself with those thoughts," she sighed. "People always do. Those answers will come soon enough. Be sure to use the remainder of your time in Teotenaca well. I suggest you go to the church, perhaps to mass this morning, and talk to Father Hernandez. You will get helpful insights and information from him. And tonight you'll meet others who have spent time in El Anhelo, which will also be useful. It will be a sunny, beautiful day. Enjoy your freedom, and your friends, Michelle," she said and the dream ended. I woke up soon after and decided to take her advice.

Dar was already busy in the kitchen. "Good morning, Michelle. Did you rest well?" she asked.

"I did. I slept like the proverbial rock, which is a big improvement over sleeping on a rock," I quipped.

"Oh, yes, that's one thing I haven't missed about the cave," she nodded with a knowing look.

"I'm curious, Dar. Why did you come back here?" I asked.

"The reasons vary. We're more creative here. Living is much cheaper. We love the scenery and our little farm. Sunny is happier than she would be back home, I think. But the reasons don't matter anymore. We've become a part of this community, and I can't imagine not living here. You'll see why tonight at the salon," she hinted.

"I can hardly wait," I smiled. "But in the meantime, I just had a dream directing me to attend mass and then talk to Father Hernandez."

"And I'm sure he wants to meet you, too, Michelle. It's still early so I'll call him in an hour or so to make arrangements for you." She was as good as any concierge.

"Thanks, Dar. Can I help you with anything? I still have to earn that great rate you gave us," I offered.

"When people have been in the cave, we don't charge them for those nights. That would hardly be fair."

"But if I can help you today, or tonight, I'd be happy to do it."

"It's a potluck affair, so I don't have much to worry about where food preparation is concerned. And I guarantee the food will be marvelous. After eating apples and drinking water, it will be quite a treat for you," she smiled. "Perhaps you can help as the hour approaches. Let's say about 3:00 or so. People will come around 4:30. We're an early-to-bed, early-to-rise community, so our parties start early, too."

"I can do that," I said. "Have my friends been helping?" I hoped they had in between worrying about me.

"Maggie has done a lot in between her time with Max. She gets along well with our goats. They like her touch when she milks them. She's talked to them over the fence when they've been out in the pen. And she's helped in the house with entertaining Sunny, who loves to watch her dance. I've caught Sunny striking some flamenco poses now and then," she laughed. "My daughter is not a natural dancer, but she's trying. It's quite precious. As for Max, he worked on the road repair project and did chores around our yard. Angel has stayed away from the animals, but he helped Reggie stretch canvas for a few large paintings. I think he was asking a lot of questions, too. He's got an inquisitive, clever mind, he has. And I dare say you do, too," she smiled. "How about some breakfast then?"

"Ah, breakfast, what a wonderful word. But something simple is fine with me," I explained. My stomach must have shrunk because I didn't feel hungry anymore. She laid out tea, orange juice and a scone. I was halfway through when Angel joined me.

"Good morning, señorita. How are you today?"

"Muy bien. How about you, señor?" I asked.

"Very well, very well," he smiled sleepily. "And what would you like to do now that you're back to being a tourist again?"

"I'm hoping to see Father Hernandez this morning. Dar's going to call him soon."

"Excellent. I was going to recommend that, too. But you must also see the church." He woke up more with that thought.

"What's it like inside?" I asked. I hadn't thought much about it until then.

"It's old, of course, but well taken care of, in a Spanish colonial style that's elaborate in a rustic way. But the carved sculptures of the saints are beautiful. And the crucifix is extraordinary," he raved.

"The crucifix. Father Moran told me he once dreamt he was accompanying Christ to Calvary and Jesus looked like the figure on that crucifix." The memory of that stirred my interest.

"Really," Angel said, sounding reflective. "It's very lifelike. It's startling, really," he shook his head.

"How so?"

"I don't want to spoil the experience for you, Michelle," he teased.

"How about one little clue," I begged.

"Oh, all right. It's *very* lifelike." He said that in a way that gave me goose bumps on the back of my neck.

A little while later, Father Hernandez graciously received Dar's call with an invitation for us to attend mass that morning and meet with him afterward. We changed into our dressiest clothes and Reggie drove us into town. The service was beginning as we entered the church, which was nearly full. We sat discreetly in one of the back pews, but the congregants still turned around as if to say we were rude for being late, or so I thought. Then I realized their expressions were welcoming, their heads nodding in greeting. With relief, I smiled back. I tried to be attentive and follow the service, but I could only read snippets of it, since it was in Spanish. Instead I took in my surroundings: the statuary, the rows of burning votive candles, the hand-carved pews and worn wood floor. Sunlight filtered through the stained glass windows, transforming its beams into warm tones that flooded the church.

Father Hernandez's voice brought my attention back into the service, where it belonged. He wore a green vestment with an embroidered stole around his neck and moved with grace and assurance. Carved and painted saints observed the proceedings from a high wall behind him. There were so many things to see there, which included a large carving of Santa María, the patron saint of the church and the town. But then something else even more startling caught my eye. I was observing Father Hernandez at the altar when I noticed the feet of the Christ figure on the crucifix that hung behind and above him. This was the cross Angel told me about. I took a better look at it and saw the feet gnarled in pain, blood dripping from them onto the wood of the cross. I half expected it to flow onto the floor, it seemed so real. I traced the body upward, along the bruised shinbones, the scratched and bloody thighs, the rough loincloth. I stopped there. I wasn't sure why, but I had the feeling someone was watching what I was doing. I didn't want to seem distracted from the service, so I looked down at Father Hernandez. Even though I couldn't understand what he was saying, his movements were familiar.

"Once a Catholic, always a Catholic," was a phrase that came to mind. I'd been steeped in it from Baptism until I graduated from a Catholic school in the eighth grade. I went to public high school after that, but attended Sunday school as a compromise with my parents. And I joined the youth choir, which was pure joy. But when I left for college my time in church became sporadic. Even so, I always believed in a spiritual realm. I just couldn't decide on its form as I traded the mass for meditation. I tried Protestant and Unitarian Universalist churches, but eventually settled back into a Catholic church. The mass in any language was part of my history.

After a while I decided to look at the crucifix again. I traced the body upward with my eyes, starting with the feet again. It *was* lifelike, wretchedly lifelike, with wounds inflicted on a surface that had the quality of tender flesh. As I got past the loincloth and saw the gash in the chest, I thought I saw a slight movement, like a last gasp for air. But it must have been the light flickering through the windows and onto the statue. I studied the limp arms, the bloody and bruised palms. The overall effect gave me another glimpse into the City of Darkness, into the pain of the tortured and executed. This Jesus represented all those who suffered brutal punishment. And then it hit me that the hard, wooden cross that caused so much pain to so many people during Roman times had been transformed with the dawn of the Christian faith. It had changed into a triumphal symbol of resurrection, of hope and life for those who believed.

As I looked into the face of Jesus depicted on that cross, I began to cry. I couldn't stop since it seemed he was looking right at me as he was about to die. It felt like an appeal, an attempt to connect with someone before he gave up his spirit. Then another thing struck me. The face seemed familiar, even though it was twisted and bloodied. I looked into his eyes and had the urge to ask two questions. I said them silently, slowly, in my head.

"What do you want of me? What do you want me to do?"

As I stared at his eyes, they seemed to move. The light again, I thought. But then I heard a voice whisper inside my head. It reminded me of the one I'd heard in my "golden" dream in the cave.

"Paint and books," it said slowly. "Prayers and actions."

I repeated the words in my thoughts.

"Paint and books?"

"Yes," the voice said softly.

"Prayers and actions?"

"Yes," it affirmed again in a whisper no one else heard.

Had I imagined it? I looked at Angel, who was looking at me anxiously. He must have been looking at me all along. "I'm beginning to understand now," I whispered in his ear.

After mass, we spoke to Father Hernandez, who reassured me that Father Moran was no longer alone. And then I told him of how my questions seemed to be answered during the mass by the Christ figure, which seemed so real to me. He nodded and signed the cross in the air in front of me. "People are enlightened that way sometimes," he said. "If you need guidance, pray for it and it will come to you."

"Thank you, Father. I will pray," I promised him, and myself.

As we left the church, I took one more look at the crucifix. That image will stay with me forever, that powerful artistic rendition of a broken body that changed the world.

47

As we walked back to Sweet Dreams, it felt good to move freely in the light without things like stalactites interrupting my path. It was my last chance to see the town close up. As we meandered along the main street, I was greeted with nods and waves. "They must know about you, Michelle. In a way, you're one of them now. You'll always have a place here," Angel stated with certainty. The attention surprised me, as it had in church, but I responded in kind, feeling like a minor celebrity.

"I'm sorry this trip has to end, Angel. Two days from now I'll be walking into work and I don't know what I'm going to tell them about this trip. I may be more out of place there than I am here," I realized.

He gave my shoulder a reassuring squeeze. "You'll be fine," he said. "Just tell them you hiked and drew and slept a lot. That's all anyone needs to know, and it's true."

"I suppose. I want to take some photos, too, so I have memories of this place, and something to show the folks back home."

"I can take a few shots of you with your camera," he offered.

"You know, Angel, I think one of the first things I should do when I get back is find a faith community. I'm still sad when I think of my old church, which I loved, and how it nearly burned down and ended up being sold to the hospital next door. I get sick when I see that high-rise medical building there now. I have no place to go."

"I remember that. St Margaret's was the oldest church in the neighborhood. Maybe I can help you find another one. Do you want to go to a Catholic church again?" he asked.

"I'm not really sure," I said. "I'm still angry they sold off my old one for a big profit, instead of rebuilding it. It was bilingual and small, but genuine in spirit. I feel lost in that other big, yuppie church a few blocks over. Too much pomp and circumstance for me. I need to find another small church. 'Prayers and actions.' I interpret that as a church that prays, but is active and true to its prayers. Do you know of any churches in Chicago that are concerned with social justice?" I asked him.

"I do," he nodded. "There's Quaker, or Mennonite. But another that you might be more comfortable with is the UCC, the United Church of Christ. It's Protestant with roots that go back to the Congregationalists and the *Mayflower*. There are several UCC churches in Chicago. We can try a few out," he volunteered.

"We?" I said in surprise. "You'd be willing to go, too?"

"Yes," he nodded. "I've been studying religions for a long time and yet I'm not affiliated with one. Ironic, isn't it? Maybe I need to look, too."

"Angel, in your heart, you do believe in a higher power, don't you? It's not just 'theoretical'?" I didn't mean to sound abrupt, but I probably did. He stopped walking just as suddenly, but hesitated before answering.

"For some reason, religions have always fascinated me," he began. "But I'm an academic. I've studied different cultures and customs. It seems every society believes in a superior being or beings, someone or some force that's in charge, even when the world seems out of control," he said, then shook his head. "But none of it reinforced my own faith. I told myself I was being objective, but I realize now that I wasn't sure what I truly believed. All of my research may have only served to confuse me more. Ironic, huh?" He smiled a little, but seemed sad as he glanced away.

"Father Moran told me he believed there was one God, but many ways to reach God, through different faiths and cultures," I said. "That must make sense to you, of all people."

"Yes. If one believes in God."

"Are you saying you don't?" I asked, searching his face. He seemed to be avoiding my question. Then he took my hand and led me into a shady spot next to a building. He took off my sunglasses and looked into my eyes with an intense gaze as if he were searching for something there. I heard people passing by, yet they didn't interrupt his powerful focus on my eyes.

"Before I came here," he said, "I wasn't sure what I believed. But now, after experiencing the mountain opening up for me, that cross in the church of Santa María, and looking into your eyes, which have seen so much when they were closed in sleep, I know that anything is possible, including a higher power. You've changed in a radical way, Michelle. I'd even call it a transformation. For me, you've become one of the bravest people I know. For all my research and travel on the subject of religion and faith, you've come closer to touching the divine than I can imagine. If you believe, how can I doubt you?"

I smiled, relieved and fascinated that our experiences in Teotenaca had touched both of us so deeply. "Then let's be partners in understanding this newfound faith," I said.

He smiled as he replaced my sunglasses. "Partners in keeping it, too," he replied, as we continued our journey arm in arm through the bustling, friendly main street of that humble town.

48

Dar sat with us on the veranda after setting out juice and a snack that included her wonderful goat cheese. I told her about my reaction to the crucifix and how a voice inside my head seemed to answer my questions. "Do you understand what it means?" she asked.

"I work in educational publishing as a graphic designer, but I think it's time to get back to my watercolors," I said. "It could have something to do with my influence at work, too. What do you think, Dar?"

"I think you'll know soon enough," she smiled. "You're getting closer. Don't think too hard about it, Michelle. Such things will be revealed to you when the time is right."

"That's the same advice María gave me," I said, surprised.

Then I heard movement upstairs. Max and Maggie were stirring. "Are they still up there?" I asked.

"They've been very quiet. I think they were up quite late," she smiled.

"It seems they can't get enough of each other," I commented.

"Too true, but they make quite a handsome couple," Dar said. "They seem meant for each other, yet they just found out."

She was right. They looked like opposites at first glance, but they complemented each other in many ways, a real yin and yang duo. Max's blond hair seemed even blonder next to Maggie's dark red curls. Her feminine form and nurturing manner became more pronounced next to his masculine muscles and easy bravado. Yet they fit together like two halves of a complicated jigsaw puzzle. Would they be able to sustain their interest in each other? Or would everything revert to the way it had been, with Max taking off on his own adventures and Maggie pining and angry back home? I hoped they'd turned a corner and were heading down the same road together, a couple at last. But I was also curious about how their children would turn out. Would they favor one or be an interesting blend of the two? In my heart, for many reasons, I really wanted to see their relationship endure.

"Angel, is there anything you've wanted to do while we've been here that you haven't done yet?" I asked. "I know my disappearance was a distraction for everyone."

"I'd like to hike the trail for pleasure, now that I'm no longer in a search party. Are you up to it?" he asked.

"Absolutely. I might bring my sketchbook, too, and my camera."

"Let's not forget to take those pictures. I'll bring my camera, too." But first I had to savor a few more bites of that marvelous goat cheese.

"Dar, do you have a special recipe for this cheese?" I asked as she was going through her to-do list for the salon.

She laughed. "I have a few," she revealed. "I'm glad you like it. I have a growing list of clients who order it here and in Oaxaca city. One of them owns a restaurant where it's featured from time to time. The cheese is our most successful cottage industry."

I gave her an approving glance as I put a large bite in my mouth. "Everything tastes so good to me here," I said, "but the cheese is the best."

"After one leaves the cave, that's not unusual. Everything takes on more significance after you've been deprived in there," she said.

"What about the dreams?" I asked her. "Will they be as realistic and memorable as they were in there?"

"Not always. But from time to time they will be, when it's something you need to know. Dreams are a means of communication, after all, between your conscious and unconscious minds, but also with the highest part of yourself and the highest elements in the universe. I know that sounds a bit lofty, but it happens. I don't know how else to describe it," she said, shrugging her shoulders and looking befuddled and innocent at the same time.

"How often do you hear from those 'highest elements in the universe'?" Angel asked.

She looked at him, then at me, then out the window of the veranda in the direction of El Anhelo. "It varies. It might be every night for a week, a whole series of related dreams. But it might not be for a month after that. Generally, it's about once a week for me. The dreams I get often have to do with my writing. But sometimes they're about guests who will be coming, people in town here or my family and friends back home. If someone is ill or in trouble, I generally know it before they contact me. I often write or call them as they're about to send an email. My family was surprised at first, but now they're used to it," she laughed. "Intuition looms large in my dreams." I wondered if it would in my dreams, too.

Angel and I went upstairs to change for our last hike around the mountain. Maggie and Max were taking turns in the bathroom but were finally ready to face the day.

"Would you like to join us for a hike on the trail?" I asked Maggie.

"That's what we were going to do, too. But we need some food first."

"I miss you and Max," I said, sounding hurt. "I'm happy you found each other. But I miss you."

At that, she gave me a guilty look, followed by a hug. "You're so right! I'm sorry, Michelle. Let's go act like the four really close friends we are," she nodded.

Dar handed Maggie and Max a bag of sandwiches as we walked out the door. Finally, the four of us set out together with sun block, water bottles and cameras in hand. Max made me promise I wouldn't wander off or find any disappearing entrances to the cave. It was a wonderful day, as María had predicted. The sky was a brilliant cloudless blue, a slight breeze kept us cool along the sunnier parts of the trail, the flowers practically glowed with brilliant color, and the birds sang sweet melodies. This was what we had come here for, after all.

Along the trail we took photos of each other: Maggie standing between Max and Angel; then one of me with them; Max and Maggie looking cozy in each other's arms; individual shots of each of us. Max hammed with a manly pose of crossed arms and a huge smile of conquest, as if he'd just come down from the mountain. Angel smiled broadly, looking genuinely happy and totally removed from Academia and his books. Maggie leaned forward, her hands pushing a large, protruding part of the mountain as if she were keeping El Anhelo from falling down. First I just stood in front of the mountain. But then I wrapped my arms around its rocky face and hugged it. I hoped I'd remember that painful longing in the pit of my stomach, that palpable "draw of the mountain," every time I looked at the photo.

As we traveled the trail, we took breaks, sitting down and sipping our water. We were in need of another stop when I spotted the log where I rested before entering the cave. My weathered note was still wedged under it. "This is where I went in," I said in amazement, though they already knew.

"And this is almost where we lost Angel," Maggie replied. "I'm surprised your note didn't blow away."

"I won't go in," I promised again, "and I'm probably not even welcome. But I have to look at this." Max followed close behind me as I approached the vines covering the mountain there. This was where I'd felt the cooler air coming from the cave, where my hand had vanished into black space, where I'd looked in to see a light in the distance and hear music. But now it was a solid wall, impenetrable as a fortress. I was stunned by the knowledge that it had opened to me. "Solid," was all I could say, patting the hard surface before me in disbelief. "It's absolutely solid!"

"Maybe you should sit down, Michelle," Angel suggested. "There's lots of room on this log." I sat facing the mountain and took the sketchbook out of my backpack. I could have taken a picture of this place where I'd entered the Cave of Dreams. But I preferred capturing it through my own eyes and hands. I drew the vines and the rugged surface.

"What did you see when you looked in there?" Maggie asked.

"It was dark, but I saw a light in the distance, and I heard what sounded like singing." I played the scene back in my head, remembering the emotions. "I knew it was a bad idea to go in, but I had to. I can't explain it in any way that would make sense. I was compelled. Something inside me was urging me, almost pushing me, to go in there. When I did, I thought I was being logical. There was a tunnel leading to the light, so I carefully marked the entrance and the tunnel leading back to it. The light came through the cracks in that domed room I told you about. It changed as the sun set. The 'singing' was made by the wind blowing through those cracks, like a gigantic, ancient flute. It was hypnotic. But later I couldn't find the entrance, even though I'd been really careful by marking it."

"I would have been screaming as loud as I could right about then," Maggie said anxiously, hugging herself with her arms.

"I don't know why I didn't," I smiled. "I went back to the dome and fell asleep, exhausted. But then my dreams calmed me down. I felt it would be okay. Eventually I met Father Moran, who's still in there on the retreat."

"What do you think they're doing? What are they praying for?" Max asked.

"He wouldn't tell me. Apparently all twelve pilgrims have their own intentions, but there's also a common one they all pray for. I have no idea what that is," I said.

And then I remembered something I'd wanted to tell Max. "There are some well-known people who've been in there. Guillermo and Rosa are sworn to secrecy about most of them. But they did tell me that Berta Corelli had been in there, before she published any of her books."

It took him a moment to register the name, but then I saw the recognition in his face. "My God," was all he said.

"I may read her work again and look for clues of her being here," I said. "I know she touched *your* life."

I put my sketchbook down and gave Max as big a bear hug as I could, and he hugged back. "The first poem of hers I ever read, I think it was called 'Choosing to Live,' pulled me out of my misery over Anita. I still have the book. I'm stunned! Are you sure?" he asked.

"Guillermo and Rosa mentioned her name to me first. I was stunned, too! That's proof positive these cave dreamers have made a difference in the lives of others," I stated with conviction.

I quickly finished the sketch. But before we moved further down the trail, I went back to where I'd entered El Anhelo and touched the solid surface one last time and said a silent prayer of thanks. I folded the note, and tucked it into my sketchbook. Maggie waited, letting me linger, then put her arm around me as we continued our hike around the mountain.

"I have to get back soon," I said as we sat in the grove amid the gentle music of wind chimes and bells played by the breeze. "I promised Dar I'd help her get ready for the salon. You'll all be there, won't you?" They said they would.

"I want to meet more of the artists here," Maggie said. "It sounds like an international cast of characters."

"All I have are a few sketches to show, but Dar said that's fine," I told them.

"Reggie let me print a few digital shots," Max smiled. "I'm going to share those."

"I'll just be an appreciative audience member," Angel nodded.

Maggie was silent, though she smiled a Cheshire cat smile. "How about you, Miss Maggie?" Max asked, knowing something was up.

"Maybe," she finally said. "We'll see if time permits."

"For what?" he pressed.

"I might recite a poem. About flamenco," was her mysterious answer.

"A poem?" he asked with a quizzical expression.

"Uh huh," was all he could get out of her as she looked off toward the trees.

It has to be flamenco, I thought. "I look forward to your, uh, poem, Maggie," I said, and winked.

"It should be quite an evening," she winked back.

Before we left we took another round of photos of ourselves sitting at the campfire site and standing in front of the trees. "I wonder if anyone will notice we're in the same clothes in all these shots," Max said. "That's a little suspicious in my book."

"We can just tell them we forgot the camera on the other days," I said. "At least we look like real tourists enjoying the scenery. You have taken some of your usual landscape shots, haven't you?"

"Oh, yes. But my lens also fell for a pretty lady named Maggie."

"Boy, did it," she laughed. "He documented me in this grove, practicing flamenco, sitting in the tire swing, petting the goats, talking to Sunny, hiking on the trail, and he took lots of head shots, too. I feel immortalized."

"And you deserve it," Max said with obvious affection.

"I'd love to see those shots. They sound wonderful," I said.

"I saw a few," Angel jumped in. "They're quite good. Max is turning into a portrait photographer."

"It's easy when you have a great subject. I've found my muse," he smiled, in Maggie's direction.

And then I recalled his photographing me. "Didn't you take pictures of me coming out of the cave?"

"I got a few once you were out," he said. "I swear I saw this glowing circle rotating on the mountainside and then you appeared right where it had been. But those shots are a big blur. I can't imagine why they didn't turn out."

Maybe they weren't supposed to, I thought to myself, even as I shrugged my shoulders for his benefit.

49

When we returned to Sweet Dreams, the place had taken on a festive air. Cut flowers from the garden were arranged in ceramic and glass vases on the table and around the house. Dar had placed a long embroidered runner down the middle of the harvest table. "Looks like you've got things in hand already," I told her.

"I could use a little help in the kitchen, if you're willing, Michelle. But before that I have a surprise for you," she said. "I'll be right back."

"This is beautiful," Maggie said. "She's amazing, isn't she?" We unanimously nodded in agreement with the evidence all around us.

Dar walked back into the room with folded clothes in her hands, the same clothes I'd worn in the cave. First she handed me the *milagro* of the eye, wrapped in thin, white paper and still black from oxidation. I tucked it deep into my jeans pocket, grateful that it hadn't disappeared. Then she gave me the clothes and I couldn't believe what she'd been able to do with them. "How on earth did you get the bloodstains out?" I asked in amazement.

"Another one of my special recipes," was her coy answer. "But there was one spot I couldn't get out, over here," she said, taking the shirt back and unfolding it. She held it in place in front of me and I wasn't surprised when the remaining spot of deep reddish brown fell over my left rib cage, where I'd had pain. I winced at the thought of it.

"It isn't an accident," she explained. "I've seen this happen before. You may experience pain in your ribs on occasion, but it will always happen for a reason. You will learn from that pain. And after you do, it will fade away."

"Really?" I said, hoping she was wrong.

"I'm sorry, Michelle. But sometimes we don't have a choice," she consoled me.

It didn't make sense to me, so I just shook my head. I wasn't ready to accept her diagnosis. "I'll be right back," was all I said and headed up the stairs with my friends following behind. In that moment, they felt like a buffer against Dar's prophetic words.

When we got to our room, Maggie asked to see my ribs. They were still slightly tender but the bruising had nearly disappeared. "It seems to be healing quickly," she said. "I hope she's wrong and that this doesn't keep bothering you. That would be a strange souvenir." Maggie's eyes met mine and I sensed her sorrow for me.

"Rosa and Guillermo said the pain might come back, so it's not a total surprise. I accepted what they said. But seeing this shirt really got to me. It feels more real, I guess," I explained the best I could.

I continued, "This vacation has been a strange adventure. Now I have to process the experience and figure out what to do next. If my side keeps hurting, you'll be the first one I consult, Maggie. Besides, how can I explain this to anyone else?" I imagined myself walking into my doctor's office with sore ribs, trying to explain how it happened. "I can see me telling my doctor, 'Well, I had this dream. I was wedged against a dead body in a mass grave and when I woke up I was injured.' Would I get a blank stare or an incredulous, 'But how did it really happen, Michelle? Are you a victim of domestic violence?' And then she probably wouldn't find any sign of an injury. I hope Dar is wrong this time, Maggie, especially since you think it's healing." I hoped the pain wouldn't come back, for any reason. Besides, what kind of reason could there be?

"I can refer you to someone if it becomes a problem," she assured me.

"Of course, I would be happy if it just went away on its own," I said. "But now it's time to change the subject, Maggie. Let's get cleaned up for the party. It's only an hour until show time. I'm nervous and excited to see who's coming."

"I'm a little nervous, too," she laughed, while rubbing my back. It was that flamenco "poem," no doubt.

A little while later, Dar was directing us like a general as we brought out plates and silverware and arranged a platter of sliced vegetables and dip. Reggie and Angel re-arranged the furniture in the lounge room, bringing chairs from the kitchen and setting large pillows on the floor. In the meantime, Max was upstairs still selecting the photos he'd present that night.

Right at 4:30 there was a knock on the door. A friendly female voice announced, "Buenos días, your guests are arriving," as she and two men entered the room. She was a stately woman named Isabella. Her cousins Vito and Francisco, who were from Rome, had been in Teotenaca two years before. Isabella spoke English with a slightly British accent, and translated into Italian for her cousins. The men expressed an interest in seeing Reggie's paintings again as they handed him a bottle of red wine. And then he looked at the bowl in Isabella's hands and smiled. "Yes, it is your favorite pasta," she smiled back.

"You are a fantastic cook," Reggie told her, "and you sing like a nightingale. What a magical combination." She blushed. And then he introduced Angel and me and told them that I'd been released from the cave the day before.

"How are you today?" she asked as she extended her hand.

"Very well," I said, shaking it. "Have you been in the cave, too?" I'm sure I sounded abrupt.

"Most of the people you will meet tonight have been in the cave, Señorita Michelle," Isabella replied. Then she led her cousins to the kitchen.

"What kind of singing does she do?" I asked Reggie.

"She's an operatic singer who has worked in companies around the world. But she's settled in a suburb of Mexico City as her home base. She performs and teaches in the city, but she maintains a home here and visits when she can. She has a wondrous voice, yet she's down to earth. You don't have to be an opera fan to get chills when you hear her sing, believe me. You'll know that soon enough."

"I'm looking forward to it, with a recommendation like that," I said, anticipating her performance.

An hour later the downstairs of the Sweet Dreams Bed and Breakfast had filled with an international mix of those from faraway places as well as those who grew up in Teotenaca. I heard Spanish, indigenous dialects, Italian, English, French and Japanese spoken that night. The dining room table overflowed with the food they'd brought. Maggie and I exchanged looks of approval and delight as we sampled the colorful, aromatic dishes. There were moles, vegetable dishes wrapped in banana leaves, stuffed peppers, tamales, roasted corn and things I couldn't even identify. Isabella was raving about one dish in particular.

"I so love the native cuisine here," she told us before she took a bite, "especially *chapulines*." That was one dish I hadn't tried because of how it looked. "Yes, they're grasshoppers grilled with onions, but they are delicious." Maggie and I just smiled politely but had no intention of joining her.

Even though Dar monitored the opening of wine bottles and the occasional clearing of emptied dishes, she was actively moving from guest to guest, introducing those who were meeting for the first time and giving quick tours of the art on the walls. She radiated hospitality and could have remained the center of attention, but she kept bringing me into the conversation, introducing me and making sure everyone knew I had just "graduated" from the cave. I thought I'd be exhausted from all the attention, but it was exhilarating as I heard the stories of others who'd been there. It was odd to be miles from home in a foreign locale, surrounded by people from around the world who'd all had this common experience. I was part of their community now, because in this small town these people understood something I could never share with those I knew back home.

Flor, Fernán's grandmother, was among the guests. She watched me, smiling as if she knew something I didn't and wanted to tell me. Angel acted as translator when she approached us.

"Flor says you have a glow like new skin, and she's not surprised you went into the cave," he related.

"Tell her I hope I wear it well. But I'm still not sure how all this will affect my life back home. Can she offer any advice?" I asked the question to set up whatever she had on her mind.

"It's the pain in your side she wants to talk to you about. Michelle, this woman knows everything. It's uncanny!" he said, shaking his head.

"What about the pain?" I asked, anxious for her answer. Flor's skin was wrinkled, her hair white, but her eyes were playful and bright. She smiled and Angel translated her words, though he didn't fully understand them.

"She says the pain is a tool. It will guide you along the path you are to take. You will understand this soon enough. It will enlighten you. Do not be afraid, because as you learn its lesson, the pain will fade. If she's right, I hope you learn the lesson quickly, Michelle," he added.

I thanked her, grateful for direction, even if it was mysterious. *Do not be afraid, of the pain, of my own power, of what else?* I wondered.

But before long, after much of the food and wine had been consumed, and both coffee and tea served, it was time to move to the "show and tell" portion of the evening. While Dar was attending to her guests' needs,

Reggie had been talking to them about what they'd present and determined the appropriate order for the sharing. "Can I have your attention, please, everyone? Atención, por favor." He went back and forth between English and Spanish. "Everyone find a seat in the lounge room. We'll come back for dessert. We're too full now," he laughed. People touched their stomachs and nodded in agreement.

Angel and I took a seat on a couple of cushions near the couch, but Reggie approached me shaking his head. "Oh, no you don't, Michelle. We can't have the guest of honor sitting on the floor. You deserve a softer place," he insisted and reached out to take my hand. I looked back at Angel, who smiled and shrugged. Reggie led me to a comfortable chair in a prominent place where everyone could see me. And then someone clapped and the others joined in. I was dumbstruck and sat there with my mouth open, since the applause was for me. Dar kissed me on the cheek. "You're one of us now," she whispered. "And you're about to see what that means."

"We welcome you as one of our own, Michelle," our host echoed. "And you were privileged to meet a priest from the retreat, which is happening right now. This is a special time, indeed. But whenever we get together, it is a special evening. Isabella has offered to start it off for us." There was a buzz around me as people nodded and smiled in anticipation. Isabella's cousin Vito sat down at an electric keyboard as the singer rose and approached the center of the room. There was a round of applause once again. She smiled and bowed slightly in response.

"Gracias, thank you all. It is wonderful to be back with you. I have been composing songs in Italian with Vito, in a classical vein, of course. He has helped me to understand the depths of my voice and how to arrange the music to best suit me. We will perform a new song tonight. In Spanish it is called 'Invocación' and is cleverly disguised as a spiritual revelation as one enters a great cathedral on Easter morning. But it is really about my reaction as I entered the Cave of Dreams. I'm conveying a sense of mystery and awe as well as a connection to the divine." As she tipped her head slightly, Vito began to play a strange and wonderful melody. I tried to imagine her entering the cave as I had. Her voice started softly, like the sound of the distant music I'd heard when I first glanced into the darkness. I don't know that much about classical music, but I understood the emotions she was portraying. Her eyes shone brightly as the power of her voice grew, lifting upward like the cave walls rising to the dome with its cloud of dancing golden dust. She sounded glorious as the melody flowed from one mood to the next, from reverie to quiet reflection. Her magnificent voice deserved a grand piano. The keyboard was no match for it.

There was one last, long lifting of her velvety soprano tones and then she ended with a quiet, reverent hush of a note that seemed to fade into eternity. It was followed by silence from the audience, until someone yelled "Bravo!!!" and others joined in with whoops and thunderous applause. She smiled and took a deep bow, then put the fingers of both hands to her lips, kissed them and spread her arms wide enough to extend the kiss to everyone in the room. She acknowledged Vito as he rose and we clapped for him, too.

"Oh, Isabella, I had no idea you could write, too," Reggie said in an amazed tone. "You and Vito make a terrific team. Very impressive!" He let the mood of the room subside, then continued, "And now we will move to something more visual," he said, turning to the next presenter. "We have some new people here tonight including a photojournalist from Chicago. Max DeBoer is a friend of Michelle's and while he waited and worried about her in the cave, he took some impressive pictures. Max, tell us about them."

Max looked self-conscious as he rose, but was greeted with applause. Reggie translated his words into Spanish. "I don't think of myself as an artist in the sense the rest of you do. I take pictures of scenery when I'm on vacation, but I also document conflicts around the world. Teotenaca is a naturally beautiful area, but I've found the way people treat each other here is also beautiful. Thanks to my hosts, I printed some images I took while repairing the road. I'll let you pass them around." Reggie helped distribute the black and white printouts of dirty, sweating men at work and then standing together afterward smiling at their collective accomplishment. There were nods of approval, some of which came from the road workers themselves.

"And what is left in your hand, Max?" Reggie prompted.

"Another thing I discovered while I was here is that I care deeply about a wonderful woman, Maggie O'Rourke." She blushed as he directed his gaze to her, then threw him a kiss at the mention of her name. "I took lots of pictures of Maggie. Here are a few of them." He gave more printouts to Reggie for distribution around the room. A woman asked questions about technique and a man confirmed he'd seen Max's credit line in a magazine.

Finally, a woman with a New York accent rose to comment, "You're too modest, Max. You *are* an artist. This image of Maggie and the goats is especially well composed. There seems to be a real camaraderie between them. It's quite lovely."

"Thank you. Thank you all," Max nodded, smiling in all directions. "I have a group shot of each of the men who worked on the road repair crew, by the way."

"You must come back again, with Maggie," Isabella persuaded. "I want to see more of these marvelous images," she smiled.

"Well, maybe we will," he said, as if he meant it. As he sat down to appreciative applause, Maggie touched his cheek and kissed him. I could tell he was humbled by the response he'd gotten.

The evening continued with a showing of the work of local artisans, which was a wonderful display of wood carving, pottery and weaving. Besides the bats and snakes and whirling suns, there were motifs of flowers and birds in rich colors. This was followed by Reggie's latest paintings, local folk music, small stone sculptures, illustrated children's books of folk tales, a female rapper from Oaxaca city, even a frenetic Japanese Butoh dance, and more.

At last it was Dar's turn. I'd read a few of her poems but hadn't heard her recite them out loud, so I was looking forward to this. She began, leaving space for Reggie to translate her words into Spanish.

"It is always a joy to have you here and to see the amazing things you've been doing. Most of you know my work, so you may expect something that is simple and, hopefully, inspirational. But I am moving in a different direction lately. I'm anxious to share these words and get your reactions." She began to move around the room as she spoke. "I want my work to move people, to reassure them of divine blessings and guidance, but I also want them to realize they can't just sit waiting for God to do it all for them. We must take an active part in making this world of ours as good a place as it can be. That's a tough order, yet we all must keep at it. My new work is about that pursuit." She took a deep breath before introducing her work. "This first poem is called 'Break of Dawn.'" She began to read, pronouncing the words slowly, with purpose, as she walked among her guests making eye contact and exchanging meaningful looks with each phrase. The murmur of Reggie's translation followed her words.

The cracking open of darkness;
the letting go of emotional weights;
the opening of a door on a locked room;
the shedding of old skin for new;
the regaining of lost dreams;
the sharing of riches with those who have none;
the rebuilding of burned bridges;
the sowing of fruitful seeds;
the nurturing of children who will grow wise;
the lifting up of those who have fallen;
all of these, and more, are the dawning of hope.

After nods of approval and applause, the group grew quiet again. "Now this poem has a bit more bite to it. It's titled 'New Life' and has two parts." She stopped for a moment, turning slowly around to look at everyone.

1
Open up the coffin of your old life.
Let the vermin run out and over the edge.
What remains is dust and ash,
forgotten plans,
intentions dissipated like a trail of smoke
reaching toward the sky.

This is your past,
dead, evaporated.
Turn away and breathe deeply of fresher air.
Fill your lungs with oxygen
until you are lightheaded with hope.

The future is unwritten.
It exists only in your imagination.
It awaits your heart,
your hands,
your sweat,
your vision.

Seek it with strength, not foreboding.
Pray for guidance
and wait humbly for the answer.

2
A smile,
a kind word,
a touch upon a weary back,
a coin placed in an unclean hand:
these are all small acts,
but they widen,
reverberate
like ripples in the great pool
of humanity.

Now move forward into that unwritten future
and know that if you are armed,
not with bullets and bombs,
but with the power of love and compassion,
the strength of mercy and forgiveness,
you can truly change the world.

This second poem was met with even more approval. There was a sense of deep understanding from the audience. They were quiet and reflective. I felt as if she'd spoken every word from her heart to each of ours. She took a deep bow to the applause of her guests.

"Now you know why I married her," Reggie joked, smiling proudly and applauding her as she sat down.

"Now who is left? Who have I missed?" he said. "We still have our guest of honor, Michelle, and our friend Salvador with his wonderful guitar compositions, but is there anyone I missed?"

A small hand shot up near his feet. He pretended not to see as he looked well beyond her and into the four corners of the room. "Dad," Sunny whispered loud enough for all to hear her. "Dad!!!" she said even louder.

Pretending to be surprised, he looked down at his daughter who had sat patiently through each presentation. "Sunny? Do you have something for us?" he said, knowing she did.

"Yes!" she cried and popped up from a cushion on the floor. "I have pots! And Carlita has a drawing." It was clear that Carlita was the quiet one, even trying to hide behind a long braid. There were other children there that night, but only Sunny was brave enough to raise her hand.

As they ran to get their artworks off a shelf, Reggie explained. "Sunny has been spending more and more time at Fernán's house and he has shown her some of his traditional techniques. And I have been working with Carlita to teach her English and more about drawing. They would like to show you what they've done."

Then Sunny added, "Fernán fired them for me. He's a very good teacher."

The guests were genuinely surprised at the beauty and workmanship in the two terracotta pots she presented. Carlita's drawing was a close-up of a flower from the garden. It was a child's drawing, but showed she already had a sense of texture and scale. As the artworks moved around the room, Reggie introduced me.

"When Michelle first arrived, she talked about how she hadn't sketched in a while and that she hoped to do a bit in Teotenaca. But she did quite a lot of it before going into El Anhelo. And now she would like to share these images with you," he said.

Like the others, I took my place in the center of the room. "It's true I hadn't sketched much lately," I explained, "but I was moved to do a number of sketches of the beautiful surroundings here." I passed my sketchbook around for all to have a look at it. "I may go back and use these drawings as a reference for watercolors," I said. "Most of my days are spent being a graphic designer, but I really want to do more watercolors."

"She *should* do more," I heard Reggie say to someone who shook her head in agreement. "We want to see more out of you, Michelle," he smiled.

"Thank you," I said, feeling affirmed as an artist among artists. Sunny and Carlita and my sketchbook continued around the room as I sat down and Reggie unobtrusively rolled up the large carpet that lay on the wooden floor. He talked quietly to Salvador, the guitarist and looked toward Dar who apparently gave him a sign with a nod. I had a feeling something was up. Maggie hadn't read her flamenco "poem" yet. I glanced at her seat, which was empty. Max looked perplexed.

"Now, everyone, we've come to our last artist of the evening. Salvador is a terrific flamenco guitarist. And we have a very special surprise. One of our guests from Chicago, that marvelous Maggie O'Rourke, is a flamenco dancer who will dance this evening to Salvador's music. Maggie, where are you?" And then she appeared to the "Ahs" of people around the room. Her hair was pulled back with a large red comb holding it in place. She wore her simple black practice skirt, but around her waist draping to her right she'd tied a velvety black fringed shawl with a large red rose embroidered on it. She looked sleek and exotic with newly applied makeup that accentuated her features. I looked at Max, who had his camera in hand, and Angel who smiled back shaking his head.

She moved to her starting position as Salvador began to play an aggressive flamenco melody. The energy in the room built with every shift in the music. Soon the crowd got into it with cries of "Olé" and "Toma" and occasional clapping to the syncopated beat of Maggie's feet and hands. She responded by giving everything she had, by keeping up with every musical phrase. She threw her skirt up to reveal black stockings and a long red, flouncy underskirt. Max snapped pictures wildly. The music sounded like traditional flamenco at first, but it had a jazz flavor, too. I responded to the intricate beat by tapping my feet on the floor. The sweat was dripping down Maggie's face as she swirled, skirt in hand, past me. "Alé," I cried. With such a rich ancestry of peoples running through her blood, Maggie had settled on the art of one culture and embraced it with her whole being. She and Salvador got a well-deserved standing ovation. They both bowed, hand in hand. Then Reggie gave his closing comments.

"I thank all of you who shared your work tonight," he concluded. "But there's more. My lovely wife has prepared a table of desserts for your enjoyment. So please, indulge yourselves just a little more."

Max handed Maggie his handkerchief. He didn't seem to mind that her makeup came off on it. She was still catching her breath as we stopped to offer our approval on her masterful performance. "You just keep getting better, Maggie!" Angel laughed. "I'm astonished!"

"You were wonderful!" I agreed. "You must have practiced. But how?"

She smiled her Cheshire cat smile again. "I'm just intuitive," she said and laughed. "But really, when Dar and I were 'running errands' she dropped me off at Salvador's to practice. He was more than happy to engage in our little conspiracy. I would have liked more practice. But his music just swept me into its own little zone. He's one of the best flamenco guitarists I've ever heard. And he was very generous with his time and suggestions. It was an incredible experience to work with him."

Just then, Salvador stopped by to congratulate Maggie on pulling it off. "You have a true flamenco spirit," he said. "You must have gypsy blood. If you ever come back or if you check my website and see I am coming to Chicago you can contact me. Here is my card. It has my email address."

"Thank you for your time, Salvador. Your music is positively moving! I love it! Is it possible to buy a CD somewhere?" she asked.

"Oh yes. You can order them through my website or buy them at the stores listed on it. But I happen to have one here for you," he said, pulling a CD from his coat pocket.

"Thank you," she smiled, "for the CD, and for loaning me this gorgeous scarf and the skirt and comb. I'll be sure the skirt is cleaned and leave it with Dar," she said.

"No, my dear," he said, waving his hand. "Please keep them all. They belonged to my late wife and seeing them on you brings them back to life. Take them with you and show them off to your audiences. It is time for me to let go of such things."

"But are you sure, Salvador? I don't want to take them if they're important to you." Maggie struggled for the words.

"I am quite certain," he said and then turned to Max.

"You, señor, are a very fortunate man," he said while extending his hand. Max took it, but I saw a faint glimmer of jealousy in his eyes.

"Yes, I know," was all he said in reply.

Then the guitarist extended his hand to Maggie, but when she reached out he grasped hers and bent slightly to kiss the back of it. She was surprised and pleased. "It was a delight, Señorita Maggie."

"Thank *you*, Salvador," was all she could say.

As the musician left us, I asked her what had happened to his wife. "It's sad. She apparently died in her sleep a year ago. It was totally unexpected."

"I guess not everything that happens around here is joyous," I said, "just like anywhere else in the world."

Maggie nodded, then gave Max a big kiss. "I hope you got some good shots," she said, brilliantly changing the attention toward his own participation in her performance, subtly reassuring him that he was the man in her life.

"Yes, I did. There was a turn you made about half way through and I got the sweep of your skirt, and those snaky arms of yours. I love it when you do that, Maggie," he said while coming closer to her face, "I got one shot where you're framing your head with them. I can't wait to print these!"

"See you in the dining room," I said and waved as I grabbed Angel's hand and motioned with my head in that direction.

"Do you think they'll last?" he asked when we reached the kitchen.

"Yes, I hope forever," I replied. "I think Maggie knows what she's dealing with in her new guy. But he'll have to figure out a way to stick around instead of constantly disappearing all over the world. There seems to be the right amount of jealousy in him that he may not want to go too far away. I'd say their success lies with him."

Angel agreed. "I think he'll figure it out."

The table was laden once again with luscious food that included custard and pastries. There was a buzz as people congratulated one other. I heard them making dates to get together. This sharing of work and ideas became a networking opportunity of international proportions. Even I was approached.

"Excuse me, Señorita Michelle. I loved your sketches," Isabella said. "You must continue with your work. I would hate to think it stops when you go back. Do you have beautiful places to go near where you live?"

"We have some parks and Lake Michigan in Chicago," I said. "But I would need to get further out, maybe to some state parks or the Indiana dunes."

"Well, then," she said, "let me say this. You have a wonderful eye. I think you could find beauty in the most ordinary of places, even on your own street, and even in the faces of the lowliest of people. Don't stop now, please. You have much work ahead of you." She smiled and touched my shoulder. This wasn't small talk. She meant every word. And then she moved to another person who was signaling to her from across the table, but as she walked away she turned and smiled back at me, as if she knew something I didn't know yet. That was a feeling I kept sensing that night, that these people knew more about my future than I did, and wanted to encourage me.

I talked with Zachary Kimball, the author of the children's books, and told him I worked in educational publishing. I got his contact information and told him I would pass it along to the Reading editors.

Angel was also moving through the crowd and gathering information, probably asking his research questions. I noticed Dar clearing plates and making a new pot of coffee. I went to help her, as I promised I would.

"Did you enjoy the evening, Michelle?" she asked, even though my expression was the answer.

"Extremely! And one of my favorite parts was your reading of those new poems. You're quite expressive."

"Thank you! I keep working at it by practicing in front of Sunny and Reggie. But it's different with other people. I get nervous at first, but once I launch into it, it's as if the words speak themselves. I reckon that sounds daft, but it's true. The poem takes on its own life," she smiled.

"It's like that when I'm doing a watercolor or a sketch," I shared from my own experience, "or even a successful design at work. I try not to think too much and just get out of the way. Is it like that when you write?"

"Indeed it is. You just hang on for the ride."

We both laughed at that as I started washing the plates. It felt as if I'd found a friend I might not ever see again, but I hoped we could stay in touch. "I'm going to miss this place," I said.

"You're always welcome back," she said. "Don't be a stranger, Michelle."

I said good night and went up to bed. I planned to leave a lamp on for Maggie, but first I turned all the lights off in the bedroom. I wanted to be alone with the darkness and the sounds of the night. Off in the distance I sensed the bulk of El Anhelo silhouetted against the blue black sky and its vast array of stars. After all I'd been through, I still asked the mountain, "What do you want from me?"

50

The day began in the usual way, with Rudolfo sounding its arrival. I lay for a while sensing everything around me, cataloging it in my memory: Rudolfo's energetic crowing, the comfortable bed, the early light filtering through the window, the faint smell of the gardenia I'd brought with me from Oaxaca city, the stirring of Reggie and Darlene as they began the day. Then I heard Maggie walk in on tiptoes. "Are you just getting in?" I asked from that warm and cozy bed.

"I've been up for a while. Max wanted to get some shots at dawn. He's fixated on documenting this place and me in it," she laughed. "I'm sorry if I disturbed you, Michelle, but I came back to get that shawl with the rose pattern on it. I'll just grab it and be on my way. Go back to sleep."

"Did you get any sleep?"

"I did. You were deep in dreamland. Did you have more interesting dreams last night?" she asked.

"You know, Maggie, I don't remember any of them, if I did," I laughed. "That's kind of frustrating after having such memorable ones in the cave. Maybe I just needed to rest."

"I'm sure you did. Now get some more. Bye." And then the shadow shaped like Maggie disappeared from the room, gently closing the door.

I didn't get up. But I imagined her running down the stairs and meeting Max out back. I thought I heard their voices and then the sound trailed off. I pictured her standing outside, illuminated by streams of dawn sunlight. He'd found an extraordinary model in her. Part of it had to be Mexico. Then I recalled a book I'd borrowed from Max about the great American photographer Edward Weston and the beautiful, young Italian actress and photographer Tina Modotti, who had come to Mexico with him after the death of her husband. She functioned as Weston's model, muse and lover. When he went back to California, she stayed, until she became embroiled in leftist politics and was deported to Europe. She and Weston had documented churches throughout

Mexico, perhaps even in the state of Oaxaca. Why had she become so radical, championing the causes of the poor? Could she have made a stop in the Cave of Dreams? After Mexico, she'd lived in Spain, where she was a nurse during the Spanish Civil War. At some point, she returned to Mexico City where she lived the rest of her life, leaving a small legacy of her own photography and her sad story.

I stayed in bed for a little longer speculating about who else might have been in the cave and how they'd changed the world. But those thoughts woke me more. So I got up, threw on my clothes and headed downstairs, where Reggie invited me along to milk the goats. The early light was soft, but the air felt stiff. It was warmer in the goat barn, with its musky animal smells. Goats are sweet-tempered creatures, but not sweet-smelling ones. Reggie instructed me again as I sat on the stool and pulled down on the teat of a black and white goat. At first she ate her food, but then she gave me a wary look. Still, he encouraged me until I got the hang of it again and she relaxed.

"Your goats are patient," I said, "especially since they get milked by many hands."

"Oh, they are patient, it's true. But many people won't even try this. And you're doing great, Michelle. I knew you would."

I wanted to look up but I had to concentrate on what I was doing. "And how did you know that?" I asked.

"It's in your nature to try new things. Don't ever stop," he advised. I continued milking in a steady rhythm as the bucket filled. It was meditative.

"So Reggie, what other advice do you have for me as I go back into the big bad world with my newly gained knowledge?" I didn't mean to sound too serious so I said the last three words slowly, articulating each syllable.

He laughed softly. "Do what your heart and your gut tell you to do. Once you start analyzing things with your mind you can talk yourself out of anything. If you want to paint, find a place and a way to do it. If you want to take a class or do volunteer work, carve out a regular time in your schedule. I'm sure it's easy to fill your days with things to do, never having enough time to just relax and let your thoughts drift. But you need to do that, too, so make time for reflection. And if you don't, your dreams will give you time for that," he nodded.

My hands were getting tired and the goat was starting to give me that look again. "I can take over now," he said and finished the job. "This one's done."

As we continued milking the goats, he shared some other thoughts with me. "We both know you've experienced a major shift in your life, but I've seen changes in your friends, too. Angel has become quite animated since you were released from the cave. Were Max and Maggie sweet on each other before?"

"I think they were, but he didn't want to admit it. He hasn't gotten really close to anyone since his girlfriend was killed in an accident years ago. I think he's been afraid of losing someone again."

Reggie nodded and looked up to say, "If you don't have a loved one, you can't lose a loved one. I've seen that logic before. But he seems to have gotten past that. He even warmed up to me, which is saying a lot since he once thought I was a serial killer, disposing of my guests for some mysterious purpose."

My poor hosts! I could picture Max when he found out I was missing. "I'm not surprised he reacted that way. Most people would, but it would be even worse with him because he's a cynic to begin with."

"That's the toughest part of our job," Reggie revealed. "It's not an easy thing to explain. When family members call and you can't tell them what's happened, it's awkward and upsetting for them and us. But it's part of our shepherding. It was our choice to take on that role."

That surprised me. "Didn't you just decide to open a B & B so you could be in Teotenaca again? You make it sound like that's not your real business here."

"Well," he said, stretching the word out, "there was only the inn when we first came, and folks who opened their homes to visitors. But those people felt overwhelmed by the emotional upheaval of preparing their guests for the cave and then dealing with their release. We were living here with our goats and creative pursuits when Father Hernandez approached us. He helped us get a grant from the Lawley Reed Foundation. The community helped us build the bedroom addition over the veranda and we've had guests ever since. We made it official by giving our house a name. It hasn't been easy, but it's rewarding, too."

I wasn't familiar with that foundation, but the name "Lawley" stuck out in my mind. "What's the Lawley Reed Foundation?" I asked.

"Lawley comes from Dennis Lawley, the travel writer who wrote the book that brought us, and you, to Teotenaca. Reed comes from his sister's married name. Mr. Lawley was an adventurer from a wealthy family. His parents and siblings felt his loss deeply and wanted to know more about his travels. They started visiting the places in his books, including this one. People remembered him and revealed that he'd been in the cave. I've heard stories that his brother and sister went in, too, though that may be a rumor. But they came to realize his book was responsible for a lot of people coming here. Apparently a few other communities listed in his books are sacred places, too, yet he never mentioned them as such. Now the foundation supports people like us. It's been a great help to many," he related. "Oh, and they have a new venture they're sponsoring, a publishing arm called Cueva Press. I believe they've gotten permission to reprint his books through Cueva."

"Really! Is there a website?" I asked. Then I could find out more.

"There is, but it says nothing of Teotenaca. Cueva Press has its own site, apart from the foundation's site."

"That's fascinating," I said, amazed at the complexity of connections between a small community like Teotenaca and the rest of the world.

"You know what else is fascinating," he said softly. "There are people who think that Lawley didn't really disappear into a hungry animal's jaws in the jungle. Some think he's still out there, exploring and researching remote places. Or perhaps he's living as a recluse in a cave and receiving visitors seeking wisdom. I'm not sure what to think, but I find it hard to believe he'd voluntarily leave his family behind. But then, who knows?"

As we left the barn we saw Maggie and Max coming from the trail. They looked tired but were smiling and laughing. We waved and caught up. "Did you find a good place to greet the dawn?" Reggie inquired.

"Many," Max said in a weary voice.

"I've been immortalized up and down that trail," Maggie laughed. "I'm going to start charging for my time pretty soon."

Breakfast was waiting. As we sat down Sunny said the grace. "Oh dear God, thank you for all the lovely things we have to eat today. And thank you for bringing our guests to our home. Please take care of them so they get home safely, but bring them back, especially Maggie because I want to see her dance and I want her to teach me, too. Amen."

"Very nice, Sunny," her mother said, reaching across the table to squeeze the girl's hand.

From that point on, the time seemed to evaporate. I took a quick walk to town with Angel while our friends packed. We visited the church one more time where I gazed with wonder at the Christ figure that hung near the altar. I knew he was the man I'd seen in my golden dream. Father Moran had seen this crucifix before he dreamed about seeing the sculpture come alive as Christ heading for Calvary in one of his dreams. But I dreamed about him before I saw him in the church. Such a mystery! I did a quick sketch of the cross to jog my memory later. I was curious about what people of non-Christian faiths did when they wanted to worship in Teotenaca and asked Angel if he knew. He answered by taking me to a chapel at the back of the church, a place Father Hernandez had shown him earlier. We knocked, then walked in, since the door was unlocked. There were pews, chairs, large pillows and prayer rugs. On top of a long, carved wooden table standing against a stone wall, candles were set up in various ways. A statue of the Buddha sat next to a menorah. There were other niches in front of stained glass windows with geometric designs where candles or offerings could be burned. I saw other objects, too, but had no idea how they were used. Yet I knew they were religious objects of some kind.

"What do you think of this?" Angel asked. I was flabbergasted. I'd seen Christian saints and pre-Columbian gods represented in the same room before. But to see objects from so many faiths inside a Catholic church in Mexico was indeed odd. I knew I would never see it anywhere else but Teotenaca.

"You must feel at home here, Angel, since you know so much about different religions. How does this work?" I asked.

"It's quite easy. It can be set up in a variety of ways. I have a feeling what we see here reflects the faiths of those people in the cave right now. This is probably where they came before they went in and where they'll stop before they leave town," he surmised.

We heard the door open behind us. It was Father Hernandez. "I saw you come in," he said. "Perhaps you would like to say a prayer before you leave, Michelle." I'd already said them in church, but I had another idea.

"Father, could you give me a blessing before I leave? Is there a prayer you say for people like me who are about to go back to their normal lives?"

He smiled and took my hands. "Of course," he said, closing his eyes. He prayed in Spanish while holding my hands tightly. Opening his eyes, he signed the cross and placed his hand on my head. In English he said, "May God bless you and guide you in all your endeavors as you go forth into the world. Remember this place, its mysteries and its lessons and take them with you into your world. Amen."

"Amen," Angel and I repeated after him.

"Thank you, Father. And I have another favor to ask. Can you tell Father Moran I'll think of him often? He was a great help to me, a great teacher."

"I will tell him," he nodded.

It was time for our ride back to Oaxaca city. We filled Reggie's vehicle with our bags. It was especially difficult for me to say goodbye to Dar. "Keep in touch," I said. "I would love to read more of your work."

"I'll email it to you, Michelle. And let me know what you're up to, what new adventures you're having back in Chicago." I was about to throw away the spent gardenia bouquet when she took it from my hand. "Don't worry about that. I'll throw it on the compost heap. Your flowers will nourish our vegetables someday," she smiled. We hugged and Sunny gave us a round of hugs, too. And then we were on our way.

As we snaked down and around the mountains, we were all quiet. I looked at my companions and thought I saw a tear in Maggie's eye. Max seemed more reflective than usual and Angel looked lost in thought. I sat next to Reggie and stared out the window at the natural beauty I encountered with every turn. He saw me and said, "Keep it in your memory, Michelle. I fill my canvases with these scenes. Every time I make this journey, something new catches my eye. The world around you will always yield what you need when you need it. You just have to be open and ready to receive it." I smiled and nodded at his words, feeling he was right. And then he asked a familiar question. "Now that you're out of El Anhelo and heading home, what do you long for?"

I remembered that question from my pre-Cave of Dreams days and laughed. "It changes everything, doesn't it?"

"I don't see how it couldn't," he smiled.

I thought back to what I'd experienced and how things had a different perspective for me now. And then the answer seemed obvious. "I long for a world where a walk through the City of Darkness is only a bad dream, not anyone's reality."

"I couldn't have said it better," he responded with an affirmative nod.

Finally we arrived at the airport in the city. As he dropped us off, Reggie gave us box lunches from Dar.

"Thanks, Reggie. You've been a consummate host," Max said as he shook his hand enthusiastically, then gave him a back slapping hug.

"And thank you all for coming. Maybe we'll meet again," he smiled, tipping his straw cowboy hat with the woven headband. We took turns saying good bye. He gently patted my shoulder while his warm smile washed over me. I would miss him, and his family.

It would be a forty-five minute flight to Mexico City, and then a couple more hours until we left for Chicago, making it a long day of travel. I was glad I had a half day off before walking into work the next day.

But the gap between the airport in Oaxaca and O'Hare Airport in Chicago couldn't be measured in miles or hours of travel. It was the bridge between two completely different worlds. I was bringing my new understanding back with me and intended to share it with others in ways I couldn't begin to imagine. I had to be patient and wait for the answers to come, however they would. I wondered what more I would learn in my dreams.

Part Two

If you wish to see the future,
look deeply into the eyes of children,
for one day they will live it.

Berta Corelli
Chicago, Illinois
USA

1

It was nightfall as we circled the bright, bejeweled towers of downtown Chicago. I found it incredible that my city had risen from prairie and swampland long after Monte Albán had been reclaimed by its natural surroundings. But I was happy to be returning to the place I called home. It felt like months had passed.

We were exhausted after traveling on two planes with a long delay in Mexico City between flights. I woke up before the others and saw Max and Maggie sleeping arm in arm across the aisle, their heads almost touching. Poor Angel, who sat next to me, hadn't slept much because of my incessant questions. His was a wonderful, insightful brain to pick after all. Apparently I wore both of us out because we fell asleep in the last leg of the journey. It was odd, but I'd rarely seen him in a state of rest. I studied the curve of his nose, his dark eyelashes, his high cheekbones. In the dim interior of the plane's cabin I detected a glint of silver in his wavy, black hair. Even though I'd known him since college, including taking vacations together, I'd never felt this close to him. But it wasn't easy to categorize our relationship anymore. Circumstance hadn't shifted us in the same direction Maggie and Max had taken. Instead we'd connected on a level where the intellect and the spiritual intersected. He was helping me make sense of my Cave of Dreams transformation while my story was feeding his curiosity, and his faith, I hoped.

And now I had more to tell him. I had a dream on the plane that took me back to the cave in real time. I hovered near the ceiling of the dome. Below me I saw a group of twelve people lying on the mats I'd helped to arrange on the floor. They held hands and their heads formed a circle from which their blanketed bodies fanned out like the spokes of a wheel, an echo of the aisles in the cave. Their voices murmured softly in different languages, offering prayers while votive candles burned at the entrance to each aisle. Scanning their faces, I found women and men, brown and white, and saw Father Moran among them in his white windbreaker. In my dream I prayed with them, for whatever their intentions were. Gradually the echoing voices faded into the sound of deep breathing and quiet snores. Their bodies twitched slightly while their closed eyes moved back and forth. Their prayers transported them into a communal dream state where I couldn't follow. As I woke to the hum of jet engines, I thought to watch the news and check the papers for any surprising happenings in world affairs in the weeks to come.

Then the cabin lights went on and the captain announced our imminent arrival at O'Hare Airport. People stretched and yawned looking bleary-eyed as they checked their watches. It was late. In a short while we stood like zombies around the endlessly rotating baggage conveyor belt, then paired up at the cabstand. Maggie and Max would take one cab, while Angel and I took another. For such a long journey together, with so many twists of fate, it was a quick goodbye.

"Are you really going to work tomorrow?" Maggie asked me.

"Yes, but only for the afternoon. What about you?"

"I have one more free day and then it's back to the clinic in the early morning. That will be tough enough," she replied.

"Will your boss go easy on you, Max?" Angel asked, knowing our photographer friend only had to answer to himself, and his clients.

"Nope," Max said, shaking his head. "He's going to want me to sort my shots right away, especially the ones of Miss Maggie here." While he spoke, he wrapped his arm around her shoulder and stroked her temple. She responded by leaning into his hand and smiling with half opened eyes.

"That may take weeks," she laughed.

"What will you be up to?" I asked Angel.

"I'll be busy, too. I have a lot of notes to go through." I couldn't help it, but I stiffened when he said that, wondering what he would do with those notes once he organized them. He must have noticed because he told me not to worry. "I won't write about you or the cave. I can't reveal that or people would question my credibility. How could I prove any of it? But I have a lot on my mind about the power of prayer." I'd told him about my dream on the plane while we waited for our luggage. I was sure that information would go into the notes, too.

"Let's get together soon. OK?" Maggie suggested. We all nodded, hugged and said good night. Our cabbie dropped me off first, but Angel helped get my luggage past the gated door.

"See you soon, Angel." I hugged him goodbye.

"Good night, señorita. And if you need to talk, just call me."

"You'll be hearing from me soon, I'm sure. Good night, señor." I kissed him on the cheek and he was gone. I waved at the cab as it disappeared into the traffic on Clark Street.

Reggie had fixed the wobbly wheels on my suitcase, making it easier to handle, but also quieter. Still, as I rolled it across the courtyard, the sound echoed against the brick walls. "I'm back," I whispered as I unlocked the door and stepped inside.

2

The next day I woke to the Beatles playing on my clock radio. It was well past the time Rudolfo would have crowed back in Teotenaca. By now the goats would be milked, the chickens fed and breakfast served. I stretched, wanting to be awake, but feeling fatigued. I didn't even notice the ache in my side, anymore. But as I lay there, a dream I'd had that night came back in a flash. It was the third episode of the frightening dream I'd had on the plane heading for Mexico City. Again, I was trapped in a dark place. My arms reached out, but felt nothing. My breath was anxious and labored. I was desperate, until I saw light coming through the small opening in the dark wall. I broke through it with my fingers until the wall crumbled away. Then the light filled the space around me again, blinding me. I lost my balance and fell to the ground as I'd dreamt it all before. Once again the dusty, distorted figure came toward me.

The second time I'd had this dream I was in the cave and it ended with a hand reaching toward me from the shapeless blur of dust and light. After I woke up, Father Moran appeared and became my companion and guide. At the time, I'd assumed the dream meant I wasn't alone and a counselor would guide me. But this time, the dream progressed another notch in the story. I reached up, held onto the outstretched hand and felt myself pulled upward until I stood head to head with the distorted figure. The dust that had hidden the identity of the person slowly swirled upward as my eyes adjusted to the light. But instead of Father Moran, I could tell the figure was a woman. I thought of María, my dream guide, but this woman wore pants instead of a skirt. The white slacks and top reflected a golden glow that came from above her head. Instead of being afraid, I was filled with wonder as the cloud of dust began to lift. Then she gently embraced me, enveloping me inside the lighted dust that surrounded her. I closed my eyes and hugged back. Finally, the chill that shivered inside me fell away, replaced by the warmth of her body. A flood of emotions came to me through her embrace. I was loved and forgiven, filled with light and grace. There was a sense of unlimited energy and hope in that long moment. The warmth grew as if it were a fire burning inside me. It was passion, longing, a flame igniting a torch in a dark room. But the dream ended at that point, so I didn't see her face. Surely the dream would come again and I'd find out her identity. Whoever she was, she'd filled me up as if I'd been an empty well. Now I had a deep reservoir of love and generosity of spirit, as if I could do anything and be anyone I wanted to be. With that realization, my fatigue quickly faded and I rolled out of bed.

It was a workday, or at least a half workday, I reminded myself. I followed my usual routine, but hit a snag at breakfast since there wasn't much food in the house, and certainly no specially seasoned goat cheese. I started a list of things to do with buying groceries at the top.

Being away from home in completely different surroundings always gave me a new perspective when I got back. Often the familiar seemed changed somehow. But this time everything in my home was exactly the same as when I left. There was also a large mound of mail piled on my kitchen table, thanks to my neighbor, and a few calls on my answering machine. But this time nothing seemed different, except me. I was the stranger, transformed into a being living in dreams and seeing everything with a heightened awareness. The familiarity of my surroundings should have been comforting. But it made me realize how different I was and how fitting myself into the old routines, work situations and family visits wouldn't be an easy task. Would I seem the same to the people I knew or would I come across as changed? I'd find out soon enough at work.

But before that, I called my mom to let her know I'd made it back safely. She sounded relieved. "It's so good to hear your voice, Michelle. I got that email you sent from your hotel in Oaxaca. But I thought we might have gotten a postcard from you by now."

Had I sent one? Yes. "I mailed you a postcard from there, but I think the service from Mexico is pretty slow. It'll eventually show up."

"And did you have fun with your friends?" she asked, sounding half anxious and half expectant.

"Yes, and the people where we stayed in the mountains were fantastic. They have a cottage industry making goat cheese and soap. The scenery was incredible, just like we hoped it would be, and we hiked a lot. I met lots of local artists, too. It was great!"

"You must be exhausted. Did you get a chance to just relax, maybe get a little extra sleep?"

"As a matter of fact, I did."

"Well, good. That sounds like the right balance for a perfect vacation."

"Were you worried about me, Mom?" I knew that was a rhetorical question.

She was silent, then said, "Call it a mother's intuition, but I thought you were in danger at one point. But the worry went away. It's good to hear your voice. Will we see you for dinner soon? Let me know when you can come." Call it a daughter's intuition, but I thought she might have picked up on something while I was in the cave.

"I'll try to make it this week, but I have a feeling work will be crazed. I never know what I'm going to find when I get back from a vacation. I may have to put in a little extra time." And I wanted time to myself, too.

"I understand. But don't be a stranger. We want to hear all about your trip. Love you, Michelle."

"I love you, too, Mom. I love you, too."

Don't be a stranger. Hadn't Dar said that, too? *Will I seem a stranger even to my mother?* I wondered.

3

At 2:00 in the afternoon I was standing in front of the electronic door to my office in the suburbs. And from the moment I stepped inside the building I was struck that, just like home, everything seemed familiar, but I felt out of place. My first stop was my manager's office to announce my return. She was on the phone but put up her index finger signaling me not to leave. Her desk was covered with printouts, schedules and illustration samples. The prototype looked changed, but before I could figure out how she was off the phone.

"Michelle! Oh, I'm so glad to see you! It's been wild around here, as you might imagine. How was your trip?" Gwen was an outgoing person who immersed herself full-throttle in her work. She was a tall, African American woman who dressed in hipper clothes than most of the younger people in the company, despite the fact that she was approaching fifty. I couldn't have asked for a better, more inspiring person to work for. She had a reputation for being firm when necessary, but I could always bring my problems and questions to her, unlike a couple of the other managers. I knew I was fortunate.

"It was wonderful. But I feel like I've been gone for months," I laughed.

"Good! That's the best kind of vacation to have. It means you got away both mentally and physically. And you cut your hair! It's cute. It gives you an entirely different look." She grew quiet and seemed to be studying my face for a few seconds. I didn't know how to react, so I just smiled. "That's amazing," she finally said. "You look really good, very well rested, or something. I can't quite put my finger on it. Did you go to a spa?"

"No, but I hiked and slept a lot. The people were friendly. It was beautiful, and peaceful. Maybe it was the mountain air," I laughed. But to myself I thought, *or maybe the cave dust has given me a glow.*

"Well, I have to say it really agreed with you," she smiled, and then changed the subject back to work. "Have you checked your email yet?"

"No. I just walked in."

"Why don't you get settled. We've been thrown a few curveballs by Editorial and Marketing over the prototypes and the covers. Jess has been re-working your designs, but we need your touch. Check your emails and then I'll catch you up on things. It's never easy around here. You think you have a plan everyone agrees with and then someone comes along and changes it! But you know how that goes. I'm *so* glad you're back!" she said, rolling her eyes.

"Thanks, Gwen. I'll go see what's shaking in the emails."

"I really mean it," she said as I got up to leave. "I'm glad you're back, Michelle." For a moment, her smile reminded me of Dar's.

My cubicle was a short distance away. I'd left everything in neat piles with notes on top. But now my office looked like a tornado had ripped through it! My computer had been used and everything on my desk had been moved. There were printouts of my designs stacked to one side with lines drawn all over them. I dreaded what I was in store for.

The emails were another clue. There were well over three hundred of them. A few messages were departmental or company-wide, and a few were personal. But most were about the "curveballs" Nicole had mentioned. There seemed to be a yo-yo effect as one email came from an editor, followed by a designer's reply, followed by an editor's response. Email chains like that made me dizzy, but I was grateful they'd included me in the discussion. I went to the latest of these and read my way through the replies.

It seemed Marketing had added copy and icons to the Teacher Edition prototype. Now they wanted to add even more to pages already overflowing with information. Checking the re-vamped prototypes in my office, I could see what Nicole and Jess had attempted, but it wasn't working visually. The new prototypes were too jumbled for a teacher to navigate. If there was a resolution to this mess, it had to happen soon, since Marketing was about to test the prototype in several important markets, including Texas. From what I could see, the student and teacher covers were being re-designed with images of computers, alluding to digital, interactive products available to the teacher and student.

When I went back to Gwen's office she talked about the printouts on her desk. "Well, frankly, I don't think this design works at all anymore," she said, confirming my own thoughts. "I don't know where to go with it." We talked about various things they'd already tried and then I got an idea. It was a matter of re-balancing the pages. When she heard what I envisioned she laughed. "But that sounds so logical and simple. Why didn't any of us think of that?"

"It helps to be fresh from a vacation," I smiled. They were too close to the problem to see the solution.

"We may have touched on something like that, but nobody latched onto it. If they see it, I think they'll like it. Let me talk to Ruth in Editorial and see what she thinks." She picked up the phone but before she dialed she said, "Again, welcome back, Michelle." I smiled knowingly as I left her office, then checked in with Jess and told him how we might be revising the files. It got his stamp of approval, too.

A little while later Gwen came into his office with a piece of paper. "Ruth likes the basic idea, but she has to see it, of course. This is the re-edited slug line Marketing wants in the banner. Will it fit?" She handed me the page torn from her notepad. It would probably be one more line of type than what I'd planned.

"Another line, huh? I'll see what I can do."

"How long can you stay tonight?" she asked.

"Until the jet lag sets in."

"You're a trooper." She padded me on the back.

And then I was on my own, playing with space and text. Ideas kept popping into my head, so I experimented more. There were at least five page types affected and they had to retain a "family" look. Gwen came by every now and then to check on me and agreed I was on the right track. When she said goodnight she reminded me it was nearly 7:00 and I should be going home so I'd have energy left for the following day. I agreed. But first I printed my proposed changes for the pages and left them on her desk. And, yes, the jet lag was setting in.

4

By the time I got closer to home after leaving work that first day back, I wanted to grab a quick meal. The grocery store would have to wait. I was too pooped to shop. So I stopped at a fast food place to pick up the quintessential junk food meal of a burger, fries and pop. After fasting in the cave, indulging at Sweet Dreams, and tolerating airline food, I knew my stomach would not be pleased.

With my bag of greasy food in hand, I was crossing the parking lot when I was hit by a sharp pain in the ribs on my left side. It came out of nowhere, like a flash of fire. I bent over and tried to catch my breath. The bag of food fell to the ground, but I hung onto my drink. Even though I was in agony, I became aware of a loud exchange going on behind me. As I turned my head to look, the pain subsided a bit. Standing near a dumpster, an older man arguing with a young worker from the restaurant sounded as if he were in pain, too.

"I told you before, don't come back here," the uniformed employee yelled at the man, who looked homeless. "We don't want your kind near our store. You're gonna scare people off. And stay away from the dumpster!"

"But I have to eat," the man pleaded. "Please, can you give me some food if you don't want me to be here? I'll go away then. But I'm so hungry. *Please!* How can you be so mean to me?" cried the old man, bent over almost like I was. His voice was raised, but he sounded weak.

"If you don't get out of here I'll call the police." The young man sounded serious, and a little desperate.

The old man's head fell. "I'll go. I'll go," was all he said as he backed away.

I turned toward him as he approached me and when I did my pain lifted suddenly. I straightened up and, remembering the bag of food on the ground, I picked it up. The old man looked like he would walk around me, but he was walking slowly. The employee, satisfied the homeless man was leaving, had gone inside.

"Excuse me, sir," I said as he passed me, "I heard your conversation. You can have my food, such as it is."

He stopped and shyly looked up at me. "What?" he rasped.

"You can have my food. It's a cheeseburger, fries and a pop. Sounds like you're hungry." I could go back and get another burger, after all.

"You're an angel!" he gasped.

"I wish it could be more nutritious. Why don't you sit down over here on the curb by the sidewalk so you can eat. I'll stay with you so that guy doesn't bother you again," I said, surprising myself. But it seemed the right thing to do.

We sat down on a raised area that bordered the parking lot. Our feet rested on the sidewalk and a streetlight shone down on us. The man reached for the drink first and started sucking wildly through the straw. Then he tore open the bag and began to stuff the fries in his mouth so quickly I was afraid he'd choke on them.

"Sir, I know you're hungry, but if you eat too fast you'll get sick," I warned.

He looked tired and dirty and he smelled like he hadn't bathed in a while. But then I noticed his clothes. Despite the fact they were stained, they were well made. He wore Nike shoes, too, which didn't jive with his homeless appearance. After he was halfway through the burger I asked him his name.

"Jake. My friends call me Jake, but I haven't seen them for a long time. I went to visit them, but I couldn't find them. Now I don't know where I am. Do you know where this is?" he asked, looking around to get his bearings.

"You're on the north side of the city, not too far from Lakeview, but I'm not sure what this area is called."

"It's not Rogers Park, is it?" He sounded sad.

"That's further east and north of here. Is that where you're going?"

"Yes. I took the bus, I think. Or was it the train? I couldn't remember where to get off. I miss my friends and my family. How do I find them?" He started crying as he put the last fry in his mouth and started on the burger.

I hadn't had a chance to read a newspaper yet, but I'd heard a news report on the radio about a man with Alzheimer's wandering away from his home the week before. His family was desperate to find him and the police had put out a missing persons bulletin.

"Sir, what's your last name?" I asked, wondering if he could be the missing man.

"My last name? Cohen. My name is Jacob Cohen."

"Does your family live in Evanston?" I asked. That was where the man on the news was from.

"That's where we moved from Rogers Park," he said. "I think they're still there. But I'm not sure."

I wished I'd paid more attention to the report. I wasn't sure I had all the facts straight. Then I noticed a dispensing box with a *Chicago Tribune* logo on it. It looked like there was a paper in the glass facing outward.

"Jake, can you do me one small favor? Can you stay right here while I go buy a paper over there? I'll be right back, I promise. I'm going to help you find your friends or your family, if I can."

"You are? Oh my God, you're an angel!" he exclaimed, looking at me with renewed energy.

I watched him as I got my change out, then handed him a hard candy from my pocket as he finished the burger.

"Just suck on this, Jake. It's too hard to bite," I said.

Unwrapping the candy occupied his time while I walked the short distance to buy the paper. I was surprised there were any left in the box at such a late hour. It turned out to be the last one. As I walked back, I noticed a small blurb on the front page about the man who was still missing. What I found there was a cleaner, happier photographic version of the man sitting nearby, Jacob Cohen!

"Jake, there's an article about you in the paper. Your family's been looking for you. They've even offered a reward of $10,000. Does that make you feel better?" I smiled.

"Really?" he looked surprised. "But I'm right here."

"Yes, I know. I've got my cell phone and I'm going to call this number in the paper right now. You just stay put," and I motioned for him not to move. Fortunately, I had charged the battery overnight and this time, it worked. When I dialed the number a police officer picked up.

"Hello. I'm calling about Jacob Cohen, the man who's been missing," I said. "I found him. He's sitting right next to me."

"How do you know it's him, ma'am?" the police officer asked, sounding like he didn't believe me.

"He gave me his name when I asked and he looks like the man in the newspaper photograph."

"What's he wearing?" the officer asked.

"A tan knit shirt with a Polo logo, dark brown pants and white Nikes." I tried to be as specific as I could.

"One more thing, ma'am, does he have a scar on his right or left arm?" Now he sounded more hopeful.

"Jake, can I see your arms? Do you have a scar?" He pointed to a pinched, discolored line along one arm.

"Yes, officer." Maybe this would convince him. "It's on his right arm, about two inches long, on the inside of his wrist. Looks like he had surgery there."

"Bingo!" the voice on the other end cried. "That's our man! Where are you? We'll send an ambulance and a car right away."

I gave the nearest cross streets and the name of the fast food restaurant. "We're sitting on the edge of the back parking lot, by the sidewalk."

"What's your name, ma'am?"

"Michelle Hardtke," I said. "I'll stay with him until you're here."

"We shouldn't be more than ten minutes. Don't hang up, Michelle. Stay on the line. But don't let him out of your sight!" His tone had turned to urgent finally.

"He needs to be taken care of really soon. He just ate, but he's dirty and depressed," I explained. "I'm going to set the phone down now." I placed it next to me and turned to Jake, whose attention had wandered to the melting ice in the paper cup.

"Jake, they're coming to take you home!"

"Who's coming?" he asked.

"The police."

"No!" he jumped up looking all around him as if a squad car could come from any direction to haul him off to jail. I calmed him down the best I could, regretting I'd been so direct with him.

"It's all right, Jake," I said, as if talking to a child. "You haven't done anything wrong. Their phone number was in this article in the paper. You were missing is all it says. Don't be afraid, Jake. It'll be all right. They'll take you to your family, not to jail. I'll stay with you until then. I promise. I'll stay with you."

I took his thin, grimy arm in my own and held on. I had to stop him from wandering away or being afraid of the police. "Don't leave, Jake. It'll be all right. I'll stay with you," I repeated. At last, he sat back down on the edge of the parking lot.

"You promise?" he asked softly, then more aggressively. "You promise?"

I nodded emphatically. "Yes, I promise. I won't leave you. I'll come with you."

A couple minutes later I saw the flashing lights a block away and when they got close enough I stood up and waved my hands, as if I were on a desert island trying to stop a passing ship. They saw me and came screeching around the corner to stop next to the sidewalk. There was a parking space open in front of us and I was grateful they could turn the red blinking lights off, since they were agitating Jake.

"Your name, ma'am?" the officer asked.

"Michelle Hardtke. And this is Jacob Cohen."

"Jake," the officer said in a quiet tone, "your daughter has been looking for you since last week. Are you hungry?" the officer asked. Another one was coming around to Jake's left side so he was surrounded on three sides. Jake looked down at the empty food wrappings and then looked up and said, "Yes."

"We can get you a hot meal."

"Okay," he smiled. After my time in the cave, I understood his hunger.

"I promised him I'd come, too," I said.

"We want you to," the first officer said. "We have to fill out a report and there's a reward. We're going to move him by ambulance to the closest ER. They'll be by momentarily. You can come in our car."

"Okay then," I nodded.

Jake was put in the back of the ambulance, despite his protests. I moved my car from the parking lot to the space where the officers were pulling out. They promised to bring me back, so I got in their car and off we went. They asked a few questions to see what I knew and how I was able to find him when nobody else could.

"He looks like just another homeless person," I said. "He blended in and nobody paid attention to him."

"So why did you?" one of them asked. It was that pain in my rib cage that had stopped me or I never would have heard Jake arguing with the employee. And now it was gone. I suddenly realized the horrible ache had disappeared as soon as I offered Jake my food.

"I don't know," I said. "He was arguing with a guy from the restaurant because he wanted some food. It sounded like he was in trouble and

I felt sorry for him. I gave him my food and started talking to him before I knew who he was."

"So you must be hungry," the first officer said.

"Yes, I guess I am."

"We'll get you something," he nodded.

At the ER Jake was getting agitated again and asked for his angel. One of the officers asked if I could stay with him a little longer. "We've contacted his family. They'll be here shortly. I'm sure they'll want to talk to you. You'll be free to leave once we fill out the rest of this report. He seems calmer when you're with him."

"Like I said," I reminded the officer, "when I first saw him he was arguing with a man from the restaurant who said they'd call the police if he didn't leave. I think he must have heard that over and over again. He's still afraid of being left alone, I think. And he doesn't want to go to jail."

"We've got a meal for you on the way, Michelle," one of the officers said.

"Thank you," I said with genuine gratitude. "I could eat anything at this point." I looked at my watch. It was 9:00 p.m.

Jake was moved to an examining room in the ER. A doctor was taking his vital signs when the curtain flew open and his daughter and son-in-law appeared. They were crying. His attention immediately moved from me to them. Fortunately, his illness hadn't advanced to the point where he didn't recognize those he loved.

While I ate a turkey sandwich, Jake's daughter Sarah asked me about rescuing him in the parking lot. "Thank you for being so kind to him," she smiled. Her eyes were red. "I was afraid we wouldn't find him alive. He was a wonderful pediatrician. It's devastating to see him changing into this helpless person. It looks like we may have to put him in a facility where he can be watched. I never dreamed he'd walk away like that."

"I think he was trying to get to his friends in Rogers Park," I told her.

"Yes, and most of them aren't even there anymore. He talks about them all the time. But they've retired to Florida and Arizona or they're in nursing homes, or they're dead. Rogers Park was where he lived when he was a young man. But at least we have him back," she said, "thanks to you. How do you spell your name?"

I saw her opening her purse and pulling out a checkbook. She was about to give me the reward when I got a quiver of pain in my side. I thought about Edgar, the homeless man in my dream who said I wasn't any better than he was, and the other man who lived under the bridge where the cars crashed in the City of Darkness. But there were homeless people standing on the corner where I lived and near the entrance to the store where I bought my groceries. I saw them sleeping in doorways on the coldest nights and on park benches in the summer heat. Suddenly, I knew what I had to do next and the pain began to subside as I addressed Sarah's question.

"It doesn't matter, Sarah. Is that the reward check? I appreciate the thought and the sacrifice it represents, but I don't deserve it and I don't need it," I insisted, surprised at my own words, and yet certain that I meant them.

"But Michelle, you do deserve it, whether you need the money or not. You went above and beyond what anyone else did to bring him back to us. And we advertised that reward. We have to, we want to give it to you. Unless you have an organization in mind you'd like us to donate it to?" she offered.

"Well, I don't know about a particular organization. But I was thinking about all the homeless people out there on the streets. For the days he was missing, your father was one of them." She was surprised by my comment, but then nodded slowly in agreement. "He's safe now, but they're still at risk. You could donate the money to help them. I know there are shelters and food pantries in the city. Will you be all right with that?"

"That's a very generous idea. Yes, I would be happy to do that in your name," she smiled.

"One more small favor, Sarah. Donate the money in your father's name, not mine. I would prefer to remain anonymous, including to the press, if that can be arranged." The last thing I wanted was publicity!

"We'll honor that, Michelle." Then she looked at me and laughed. "You're one of the most extraordinary people I've ever met," she said.

"Well, thank you," I said, feeling totally confused by her response and not knowing what else to say. "But I'm just happy to see Jake back with his family. And safe. Really, that's all."

I finished my meal and said goodbye to them. An officer drove me back to my car and by the time I got home it was *really* late. I pulled the sheet over my head and promptly fell asleep.

5

The next morning I woke up to the news. I'd switched the alarm clock to public radio instead of my usual pop music station in an attempt to catch up with the rest of the world. The big news was about a tropical storm in the Atlantic. The fear had been that it might become an early hurricane and hit Florida hard, then head north along the coast. The weather prognosticators had declared a touchdown by morning, but an odd thing happened during the night. In fact, they all seemed baffled by the storm's behavior, because it had blown apart at sea. Instead of a devastating blow to Florida, a gentle rain was falling on the abandoned beaches and boarded up houses along the coastline. *Hmmm*, I wondered, *is it the Cave of Dreams factor?* No way to know, of course, but I was suspicious.

After the national news ended, the local news began. The first story was about Jacob Cohen being found alive and well in a restaurant parking lot. In a quick sound byte, his daughter Sarah expressed her gratitude to the kind person who'd found him. I braced for the mention of my name, but she kept her promise. "Instead of taking the reward, this person asked us to donate it to help the homeless. We will announce the beneficiary later this week. We're extremely grateful he is safe at last, unlike so many who call the streets their home."

Hmmm, could it be the Cave of Dreams factor? Oh yes, that I knew for sure, and it felt great!

I listened to a local news station on my way to work and Jake's story kept coming up. When I tuned into a talk station I found it there, too. The topic was "Would you take the reward money or give it to charity?" Most people said they would take the money and run. But a few expressed solidarity with my decision. "It gives you something to think about," one of them said. "Why should we expect a reward just because we do the right thing? Shouldn't doing the right thing be the reward?" *Score one for altruism*, I thought.

I wanted to hear more, but by then I'd arrived at work. I wondered if anyone would thank me for doing the right thing on the prototypes, or chastise me for being too radical. I held my breath as I approached my cubicle. When I got there, Gwen was writing me a note. "Oh, there you are, Michelle. I'm bringing these printouts back to you. Ruth and I like them. A lot! I just have a few minor corrections marked here and she has a slight change in the copy. But we're really close. After that, we still have to convince Marketing, of course. But this is the best they'll get from us, unless they have another idea. And if they do, it will have to be brilliant! You did a great job. Let's talk again when you get these done. OK?"

"Fantastic! I'm glad you like them," I smiled. My reaction was not so much celebration, as relief.

While my computer warmed up, I visited the restroom. Someone was getting sick in a stall. She came out the same time I did and it turned out to be Mimi, a designer who worked in the next aisle down. She looked pale and weak. I'd found her in the same state right before I left for Mexico, but she looked worse. I could tell she'd been running her hands through the beautiful straight black hair she'd inherited from her Japanese ancestors, and it looked uncombed and messy.

"Are you all right, Mimi?" I asked. "You're not looking well."

"I feel like crap, too," she whispered.

"Are you pregnant?" I blurted out. She was already the mother of a three-year old named Natalie.

"I am," she said quietly. "But don't tell anyone. I'm not ready to reveal it just yet."

"Is the stress getting to you, too?" That had been an ongoing problem for her.

"Oh, yeah. It's getting harder and harder to come in lately, especially since I've been working with Bill for the last six months. You're so lucky to be working for Gwen."

Bill Close had a reputation for being harsh. He demanded his staff put in extra time, yet he was out of the office more than anyone else. But he still expected excellent work from his team, even if he wasn't there to direct them. I thought he was a terrible manager and I pitied anyone who had the misfortune of working for him. He was stocky with a blustery demeanor that must have made the petite Mimi feel vulnerable.

"I'm stuck here because of insurance and maternity benefits," Mimi continued. "We definitely will need my income, too. But I have to work late to get everything done. Sometimes I feel so nauseous. Oh, oh, like now!" She leaped back into the stall and I could hear her at it again.

"Is there anything I can do?" I asked, not knowing what it might be.

"Just keep my secret, OK?" she coughed.

"I will. But let me know if there's anything else, anything at all."

"Thanks, Michelle. I appreciate it." Poor thing! I felt sorry for her but I had to get back to work on my own crisis.

It only took the rest of the morning to make the changes, have them reviewed, go back in to do minor tweaks, and get an approval from Ruth and Gwen. They were trying to set up a meeting with Marketing. But by lunchtime, I was feeling like it had already been a good day.

In the cafeteria I sat with Nancy, another designer. "So how was your trip, Michelle? Did you find a beach or a pool?" We'd discussed that before my trip. She couldn't imagine going to Mexico without a swimsuit.

"As a matter of fact, there was a pool at one of the places I stayed. I fell asleep next to it, so I guess I was relaxed." *Even though I was dreaming like crazy*, I thought to myself.

"You didn't get too much of a tan, though."

That's because the pool was in a cave. "I used a high SPF because I didn't want to burn." *Lie, lie, lie.*

"Looks like it worked. But you do look good, like you really got away from this place." Considering my late night with Jake and friends, I felt surprisingly rested.

"Thanks. I felt like I was far, far away."

As we sat down at a table, I went on to talk about the city of Oaxaca. While I was describing the winding drive to Teotenaca we were joined by three more people who were already deep in discussion. I was relieved they interrupted my conversation with Nancy. They greeted us and said, "Did you hear the news story about that reward money for the missing man going to charity?" We nodded that we had.

"What do you two think about that?" Rick asked as he sat down. "We're having a difference of opinion."

Nancy and I looked at each other and I gestured that she should talk first. "It sounds like a noble thing to do. But I doubt *I* could do it. I'd probably take the money and go shopping," she laughed.

"Me, too," Camille nodded as she lowered her fork into a pile of mashed potatoes and gravy.

"What about you, Michelle?" Rick prodded. I had hoped to suddenly become invisible and divert the conversation away from myself again.

"Hmmm," I said, trying to sound like I wasn't quite sure where I stood. "I think I could give it away. I know I would want to do that. Didn't she say it was for the homeless? That's a really good cause."

"You mean the daughter?" Nancy asked.

"Uh, or were they quoting the woman who found him?" I asked.

"They never said if it was a woman or a man who found him. Did they?" Camille asked.

The group looked around and they all shook their heads to say "No."

Oops! "Oh," I stumbled. "Then I must be thinking of the daughter."

"You must be," Rick agreed. "She'll announce who'll get the money later. And, personally, I think it was a gutsy thing that person did. First, they had to figure out who this guy was. Then they had to get him to the police. Most people wouldn't even stop or they'd do it just so they could get the money. But it sounded like they just wanted to get him back with his family. You don't see that much concern for a stranger these days."

Thank you, Rick, I thought. His character had just risen in my mind.

"And what about you, Judy?" Nancy asked as the middle-aged mom sat looking out the window at the passing traffic outside. Her smile looked wistful and faraway.

"Oh, well, I've already daydreamed away about $30,000 worth of reward money. I just saw a car out there I'd like to buy. See there's another one in silver."

Rick nodded, "Well, looks like your vote's for taking the reward money and going shopping, too."

From there the discussion took another turn and I breathed easier. We went into reveries of how we would spend vast amounts of money that would unexpectedly find us. There would be long, exotic vacations, second homes, new cars, eating in the finest restaurants downtown, even quitting our day jobs if the pot were big enough. Yet nobody talked about saving the money or paying down credit card debt. Our table was occupied by a bunch of brainwashed consumers. After a while I couldn't stand it anymore so I threw in a zinger to see how they'd react.

"What if we all put 5% of our windfall toward charity? Where would you put yours?" I asked.

"Oh, Michelle, do we have to?" Judy winced.

"No, but what if we did?" I pressed on.

Rick put his hand up and started counting his fingers. "Five percent of $10,000 is $500. That wouldn't go very far," he said.

"Well, maybe not, but it certainly could help someone," I volleyed back.

Nancy threw her hands up. "There are so many people who could use the money," she said. "Where do you start?"

"Where would *you* start?" I asked her.

"Helping the homeless is good," she said. "Or there's all those children who are hungry in Africa."

"Even in Chicago," Judy said. "Maybe I could bring them groceries in my new car."

"Yeah, right," Rick shook his head and rolled his eyes. "But, really, Michelle, it's overwhelming when you stop and think about it. How can $500 make a real difference?"

"Would it help you?" I asked.

"Sure."

"Then think how much it would help a person who's out of work or hungry. It's a ripple toward making another life better," I smiled.

"OK, Miss Generosity," Nancy pointed directly at me. "Who would *you* give it to?"

That was easy. "Maybe a homeless shelter or a food pantry. Or maybe I'd split it up into little gifts and sprinkle them all over the world," I laughed. "Yeah, I like that idea."

"So $25 is going to make a ripple in Botswana?" Camille asked.

"Why not?" I had a feeling that would be a lot of money in Botswana. "If we all did the same thing it might even make a big wave," I nodded, feeling very serious and probably looking it. I must have caught Camille off guard because she grew quiet and went back to her lunch.

Rick nodded right before taking a bite of his buttered roll. "I like that idea, too," he said. "Sprinkling little gifts all over the world. Now if they would just pick my lottery ticket tomorrow night, I could do that." He sounded serious, too.

"Who knows? Maybe they will," I laughed. "And I'll be here to remind you about the 5%."

"Wouldn't that be something," Judy said as she searched the passing traffic for the car she would buy with her imaginary windfall.

6

After lunch, I talked with Jess about the remaining prototypes. There were icons to be approved, final additions to the color palette and images to select that would bring life to our designs. The schedule had slipped and all these things added up to more work than anyone anticipated. We'd be busy right up to focus testing. As we talked, I could hear a conversation between Mimi and Bill Close nearby, since her office shared a common wall with Jess's cubicle. Their voices were low at first, but then I heard Bill's rise suddenly.

"That is *not* what I told you to do. How could you think I would want you to do anything that awful?" I heard him sigh in frustration. "You're just spinning your wheels, Mimi. Go back to that first version and fix it the way I told you. Then we'll talk. I have to leave in an hour. Call me when you're done." Bill sounded disgusted as his voice trailed off down the aisle. I heard Mimi begin to cry. She was trying to be quiet, but I imagined her tears building toward an uncontrollable flood. Somehow she held on. After all, she had work to do.

Jess and I looked at each other. We knew what was going on.

"He's so mean," he whispered. "I don't know how much more she can take."

I nodded, "I know." It wasn't fair. She was one of the hardest workers in the Design department, putting in extra hours whenever she needed to. Besides that, she was a great designer. Yet Bill treated her like she was clueless. It didn't matter how hard she tried to figure out what he wanted. She was obviously under duress. And he wasn't communicating what he wanted very well, from what I heard over the wall. He didn't seem to notice or care about her poor coloring and her faded expression. I felt a slight ache in my side as I imagined her tear-strewn face just a few feet away from where we sat.

Shortly after that, Gwen burst into Jess's office. "I can't believe it, and neither can Ruth! Marketing loved your ideas, Michelle. They bought in

100%. That is so rare!" she smiled. I couldn't believe it, either! I thought the new design might fix the problem. But Marketing never made it this easy on us.

"Really?" I asked.

"Really!" Gwen reinforced her statement. "Now we can get back to work on everything else, thank God."

But first I took a quick break and went back to my office to call Angel. He said he'd been thinking about me a lot and wondered how I was. "Actually," I began, "things are pretty amazing and I'd like to talk to you about it. But I can't do it now. Will you be around tonight?" I had to tell someone about finding Jake and I trusted him over everyone else.

"Sure. But can you at least give me a hint?"

"Okay. I'll give you two words: reward and *dinero*," I whispered.

"Are they one clue or two?" he asked.

"One. Think about it."

"So you can't talk there, can you? Hmmm. Reward money. Now I'm intrigued. Call me later."

"I will. Everything okay with you?" I asked.

"Busy. I'm catching up on some reading. Celia and I have been playing phone tag. I think she missed me."

"She'll have to wait her turn. I have dibs on you tonight," I insisted.

My next hour was spent looking for images we could scan and answering Jess's questions. He'd just left his office when I felt pain in my side as I stood up. Was it physical or another "prod" to act, like the night before? I hoped no one saw me because I was bent over, staring at my shoes. And then I heard Bill Close's voice from the other side of the wall. He was so loud, anyone within twenty feet could hear every word he said.

"Why is this so difficult for you, Mimi? I thought you were a better designer than this. If I have to, I'll take you off this damn project and you can find another manager to annoy! This is ridiculous!" I imagined his face turning red about then.

"But Bill, I did what you asked me to," she answered calmly. "I'm sorry if you don't see it that way. Maybe we just need to communicate better with each other."

"I've tried every way I know how and it just isn't working!" he screamed.

"But, Bill . . ." Mimi tried to engage him in a reasonable tone, but he cut her off.

"I have to leave. I suggest you try one more time, and I don't care if you're here until midnight. I don't care how many fucking tries it takes you. But one of them better be the right one!"

My pain subsided as I felt my anger rise. It gave me strength to do something I'd never done before. I walked quickly toward the aisle where I knew Bill would pass as he left Mimi's office. I saw him round the corner. And then I stepped directly in his path so he couldn't pass. Words flowed out of me like venom. This bully was about to hear what everyone else was thinking, but not saying.

"You may be a manager, but that doesn't give you the right to treat employees the way you've treated Mimi lately!" I was approaching the same volume he had with my pregnant friend. "She deserves your respect! She puts in more hours than anyone else around here! If you're not getting what you want, it's probably because you're terrorizing her! Who can work under that kind of pressure?" I shrugged my shoulders and raised my hands. He stepped back in surprise.

At first he just stared at me. Then, with a nasty look he said, "Who the hell do you think you are?"

I didn't say a word, just stood my ground and stared right back at him.

Gwen's office was three steps behind him. He turned away from me and walked into it when he saw she was there. "Excuse me, but tell your designer here to get out of my way. I have a mind to report her to HR."

What have I done? I thought. But I stayed where I was and waited. Gwen emerged from her office and looked back and forth a couple times between us. Then she said, "I'll ask her to let you pass, Bill. But I agree with Michelle. You're the one who's out of line. And it's no secret. I'm surprised *you* haven't been reported to HR. You're violating the company's code of conduct by yelling at your staff, you know. In HR terms, you're creating a 'hostile work environment.'" Then she looked at me and calmly said, "Let him pass, Michelle." So I did.

But as he did he volleyed an insult at Gwen. "Perhaps you're the one who should be reported, you and this harpy." I'd never been called a "harpy" before!

"Go right ahead," she smiled. "We have lots of witnesses who heard what you said to Mimi. It would be interesting to hear what they would have to say if HR asked them." She was playing it cool.

As Bill swore a few words under his breath and stomped away, Gwen motioned for me to come into her office. She closed the door and sat there shaking her head, until she burst out laughing. I was so tense my hands were fists, but once she started, I found myself laughing, too.

"Oh my God, Michelle. Whatever got into you? That was amazing!" she said, her mouth wide open.

"I surprised myself." And then I stopped laughing. "I don't know what the repercussions will be, but I couldn't stand what he was doing to poor Mimi. She's going through a rough time and it's like he smells blood and wants to hurt her. That man is crazy!" I whispered.

There was a quiet knock on the door. "Come in," Gwen said. Mimi cracked the door and peeked inside. "It's all right. You can come in," Gwen warmly invited. Mimi closed the door behind her and looked at both of us. We smiled back as if nothing had happened.

"I don't want Michelle to get in trouble because of me," she said, biting her lip. She'd been crying again.

"She's not in trouble. Don't worry about that," Nicole soothed her. "It's Bill who should worry. His bad attitude is becoming well known around here. And who knows, maybe he won't want another encounter with your avenging angel here."

"Why did you do that, Michelle?" Mimi's voice was a mixture of awe and anger. I hadn't stopped to think how she would react.

"If I went too far, I'm sorry. But I couldn't stand it. I knew you were in a lot of pain. I guess I snapped," I tried to explain.

"Now what do I do?" she asked. "I still have to finish this Chapter Opener design by tomorrow morning."

Gwen's expression changed then. "You don't look well, Mimi. Is something else wrong?" she asked. Mimi shot a look at me. I shook my head slightly to let her know I hadn't told Gwen about her condition.

"I'm pregnant," she said quietly.

"Oh, Mimi! No wonder this is so difficult for you. Did you know, Michelle?"

"Yes," I nodded.

"You really are an avenging angel, swooping down on Bill like that," Gwen smiled. "Does he know?"

"I haven't told him yet," Mimi revealed. "I thought it would make things worse. I should have, I suppose."

"You really should. And soon. Well, tell you what, we've had a successful day. Maybe our success can rub off on you, too. Is he gone?"

Gwen asked in a conspiratorial tone.

"Yes, thank God. He stomped down the hall on his way out," Mimi reported.

"Let's see if we can figure out what he wants you to do on that design," Gwen offered. We followed Mimi to her office. Scattered about were the printouts that had gotten her in trouble. "This one doesn't look 'awful' at all. But it needs something. What do *you* think it needs?" Gwen asked her.

"It would look better with a thicker banner in a darker color," she replied. "Then it doesn't matter if the page is filled with the image. The title will be more readable. I thought Bill wanted more photo showing."

"That sounds like Bill all right," Gwen nodded. "He's always filling the pages with images. But I think you're right. Why don't you do one like that. And what about you, Michelle?" Gwen asked me. "What do you think Bill wants?"

"To punch me in the nose?" I wondered if he'd have a plan for revenge.

"You're probably right," she laughed, "but what about this design?"

I looked at the various versions and saw potential in Mimi's idea. But then I could see another element that might work. "What about taking the color of the banner and adding it to a rule along the edge of the photo over here. That'll make the image pop even though there's less of it showing," I said.

"Yes. Good idea. What do you think of that, Mimi?" Gwen was gently leading us through this process.

"I like it. I'll try it and see how it looks," she smiled. Then she looked away for a moment and said, "You know, I think he would prefer I move this type, too. He said things look out of balance. Maybe that's what he meant. I'll try that, too." And then she smiled. "I think this will work. Thank you both. I was having trouble thinking this through on my own."

"Therein lies the problem. You really were on your own," Gwen stated. "Let us know if you need to talk things through when Bill isn't around. And take care of your little one," she whispered.

Gwen pulled me into her office one more time. "Michelle, I don't know if there will be repercussions from Bill, but my guess is that he may quiet down now. I think we *both* scared him," she said.

"I hope so," I said. "I'll try to keep my temper in check."

"You have a lot of guts! I'm impressed on one hand, but I certainly hope I don't get out of line or I'm sure you'll let me know!" she laughed. "Now, you'd better get back to work."

As I passed Jess's office I heard him quietly call my name. "That was awesome!" he whispered and he held out his hand to give me a high five.

Now I had even more to tell Angel.

7

I got home at a normal hour that night and called Angel. He was anxious to hear more about the reward money I'd hinted at. But that was only part of the story. "Odd things keep happening to me, Angel. I have to share this one with somebody I can trust and I'm making you my designated listener, if that's okay with you. I can't keep this to myself any longer. Can we get together now? Maybe for a bite to eat?" I asked.

"Sure. But I'm not budging until you tell me a little more," he insisted.

"Well, I've gotten that pain in my side a couple times since I've been home. It's like a signal that a person close by is also in pain, and I can relieve it. When I help them, my pain goes away, too. Weird, huh?"

"But fascinating. Tell me more."

I described how the ache had come as I was crossing a fast food parking lot. "It really hurt, and it came out of nowhere! I was bent over in pain and I couldn't move! That's when I heard a couple of men arguing. Now Angel, I certainly hope you can keep a secret, maybe even from Max and Maggie. Can you promise me that?" I felt like I was about to jump into the deep end of a pool not knowing if I could swim. I was hoping he'd be my lifeguard.

"Yes, if it's that important to you." I listened to every nuance in his voice. "Then what happened?"

I took the plunge. "What happened next made the news this morning. It was even a topic of conversation at our lunch table today. Can you guess?" He was silent for a moment and then gasped.

"You're kidding!" I had definitely taken him by surprise. "You're the one who found that lost man, what was his name?" His voice swung upward in an uncharacteristic way.

"His friends and family call him Jake. Jacob Cohen. He called me his *angel*." I tried to sound matter of fact.

"That's a big secret to keep, Michelle." It got quiet on his end of the line.

"You know what though," I jumped in with a spin on things, "I can guarantee it'll be old news by next week, so just keep it under your hat. People's curiosity will fade away before you know it." Or so I hoped!

The other end of the line was still quiet. Then Angel moved on to the next incident. "So what happened today, Michelle? Will it make the headlines, too?" He sounded like he was bracing himself for another heavy secret I'd ask him to keep.

"No. But it may make our lunch table tomorrow." I told him how Mimi had been verbally abused in her pregnant state and my pain had triggered a confrontation with her manager. "He called me a 'harpy,' but my manager said I was an 'avenging angel.' You're used to being called Angel. But I'm not. It feels freaky to me."

Then I heard him laugh. Maybe he was relieved I wasn't sharing another secret with him. "But it's not a bad thing," he said. "It sounds like you're making waves wherever you go."

"Without even thinking about it," I added.

He suggested we continue our conversation at the Bilberry Café. They had great salads so I agreed. If anyone asked me who my angel was I would simply say, "Angel, of course." He wore a crisp, white cotton shirt from Mexico and sat at a wooden table reading a book, as always, with a latte close at hand. Fortunately, the hum of conversation around the cafe blended into ours, so I could speak freely. "I'm wondering what else to expect from this pain that manifests when least expected. Who else will I have to rescue?" I asked rhetorically.

"I've never heard of anything like it. Maybe your dream mentor, or a spirit guide, is training you by raising your level of awareness in this cattle prod way," he suggested. "It may even be your own psyche doing it. Does everything else seem normal?"

There was more to tell. I skewered a forkful of tender green salad before answering his question. I thought for a moment and said, "I'm also able to solve design problems easier than I did before Teotenaca. I see multiple possibilities and then pick the best solution. I hope *that* doesn't go away!"

He put his book down on the table and gave me his full attention. I noticed the title had the word "prayer" in it. "Sounds like you've acquired a heightened sensitivity. That could help you with sketching and painting as well. Do you feel a need to be doing that again?" He looked into my eyes as if searching for other answers, too.

"To be honest, painting is the last thing on my mind at the moment." Ironically, I noticed the paintings hanging from the mottled yellow walls of the café right about then. They were watercolor paintings, outdoor scenes that evoked beauty and peace. I couldn't stop looking at one of a stream in a wooded setting as I continued. "I'm trying to keep on top of the news," I said, "in case something unexpectedly good happens in the world. Then I'll wonder if it's connected to the prayers from the retreat. But I had no intention of being in the news myself!"

"But you're making 'good' news," he pointed out. Then he looked around us and bent closer, looked me straight in the eye again and whispered, "So what made you decide to donate the money?"

It seemed so logical when I'd made that choice. I had a few second thoughts after hearing people's reactions, but in the end I was glad I'd asked Sarah to donate it in Jake's name. I tried to explain to Angel. "I met a couple of homeless men in my cave dreams, and I see the homeless in my neighborhood all the time. Jake looked like one of them. It seemed fair is all. I don't need the money like they do."

He smiled and touched my hand, "It's a wonderful gesture, señorita. Maybe you'll set a precedent for others to follow." That made me smile. "By the way, I read a piece of 'good news' online today. The U.N. has negotiated with a rebel group in southeast Asia to get humanitarian relief into a remote area cut off for the last year. This is big news. I don't think most people in the U.S. are aware of the situation, but this could save lives."

"Interesting. I wonder if that's connected to the retreat," I speculated.

He shook his head, smiled and shrugged. "There's no way to know. But I'll keep looking for more unexpected 'good news' items. There are probably more of them out there than we realize, if only we'd look for them. In the meantime, I may see your picture on the 10 o'clock news yet," he laughed.

The thought gave me a shiver! "Oh, please. Don't even go there. I'm happy with being the anonymous, charitable person, soon to be forgotten."

"All right, Wonder Woman. Your secret is safe with me." He patted my hand.

After that I reminded him of my search for a new faith community, one where I could merge "prayers and actions." He had a few churches in mind and was willing to go with me. We made a date to attend a Catholic mass in his neighborhood that coming Sunday.

"I can't remember the last time I attended mass there," he said. "Ironic, isn't it, that a heathen like me teaches world religions?"

"But you're a very kind heathen. And your name is Angel, so there's hope for you," I teased.

"Maybe you can counsel me back into the fold."

"Ah, but first I have to find the fold," I laughed.

"Not to worry. I think the fold will find you," he countered.

8

The rest of the week went quickly with no eventful dreams and nothing out of the ordinary happening in my waking hours. I was acknowledged at the lunch table for standing up to Bill Close, who looked down every time we passed in the hall. But then I held my breath when Jake's daughter appeared at a press conference to announce the recipients of the reward money given in her father's name. She split the $10,000 equally between a shelter and a homeless advocacy group. But she sweetened the pie even more by donating another $5,000 to a food pantry. This portion of the money was given in honor of the "Good Samaritan" who found Jake.

"From this point forward, our family will donate at least $5,000 annually to deserving charities in the name of all 'Good Samaritans' who help strangers in need," Sarah Cohen Levine announced to the world. This was more like a big splash than a little ripple! My small investment of time rescuing Jake had blossomed into a blessing for many people. I was overwhelmed by how far my act of kindness had already traveled!

Maggie emailed me that week to see how I was doing. I told her I was fine and had been thinking about her and Max, too. I was glad to hear they were still tight. She wrote, "Max is struggling with how to adjust his life to make more time for me. He may cancel a ten-day trip to the Middle East a few months from now, which is a relief. He still likes taking my picture, for some reason, though I'm always surprised by what I look like from his point of view. He's turned me into a chameleon. There's a gallery that's been interested in showing his photos and they really like the ones from Mexico. He refers to the proposed exhibit as 'The Maggie Show.' Can you believe it?"

I could. And I was anxious to see more of the Maggie photos.

Then Sunday morning arrived and I drove to Angel's neighborhood to attend mass. As we entered the grand, old church with its large stained glass windows and painted statuary, I had a flashback from a dream the night before. The memory had been vague when I woke up, but it came back clearer in that setting. It was an odd image, disconnected from anything meaningful. The strange vignette pictured a small black and white dog prancing down an aisle similar to the one next to where I sat. As it passed by in the dream, it looked right at me. Yes, it was odd to dream about a dog coming down the aisle of a church, but I still glanced around. Of course, there wasn't a canine in sight. Why would there be? A seeing eye dog maybe, but they never looked anything like the little dog in my dream.

The mass that day was well attended. The statues and windows were beautiful. The choir sang an excellent harmony to piano accompaniment. It all felt familiar and sincere, yet I wasn't worthy of receiving Communion, since I'd been away from the church for a couple of years. But the Crucifix didn't move me like the one in Teotenaca. I wasn't convinced of Christ's suffering because he looked too sanitized compared to the realistic and horrific cross in the church of Santa María. But I was also disappointed that the priest's sermon didn't move me. The message was good, but I wasn't called to action the way I was hoping to be. I had to find a community where "action" would be a key word.

Angel and I went out for brunch after church and talked about our experience there. He had a similar reaction to mine. "I think we should look around more. We can always come back. We'll have more of a point of reference that way," he reasoned.

I agreed. We decided to try a Catholic church in my neighborhood the following week. And then I mentioned my vague recollection of the dream with the dog walking down the aisle of a church. "I'm not sure what that would symbolize, Michelle. The good qualities of a dog could be playfulness, loyalty and companionship. I can't imagine how that would fit into a church setting, though. But who knows, maybe we'll see that dog in a church yet. If we do, I'd say we should go back there again," he smiled.

I had one theory. "It might be a church called St. Francis of Assisi. After all, he liked animals. I should look in the phone book to see if there's a church by that name."

"That's a plausible idea," he agreed. "There are lots of churches in this town. One will be the right fit for a couple of well-meaning heathens like us."

"Speak for yourself, partner," I scolded him. I didn't feel like a heathen.

"Sorry. I mean a couple of would-be pilgrims like ourselves."

"Much better. There *is* hope for you."

9

The days began to move along quickly again. When I felt the ache in my side, I acted accordingly when I found the other person who was in pain. It was never as dramatic as the first two incidents had been. But I felt it often when I passed the homeless. I usually stopped and gave them money, but then I wondered if it went for food or alcohol, drugs or cigarettes instead. So I bought gift certificates for fast food restaurants and handed those out instead of cash. When they smiled and said, "God bless you," or "You're an angel," the pain in my side would disappear. But sometimes they wouldn't accept my gift and just mumbled under their breath because they wanted money. I had to walk away from the ones I couldn't help. My pain went away, but I was sorry theirs didn't.

In the meantime, I kept having the dream about the dog and remembered more of it each time. The little guy was mostly white with black splotches and spots. His tail curled and feathered upward, waving like a furry fan. There were children carrying something in their hands as they skipped down the aisle with the dog in what still looked like a church to me. Gradually, I saw pews, too. The people sitting in them varied from teenagers to frail, aged adults. I had a sense that this was the place where prayers and actions came together. I felt strongly that I would know this church when I found it. But I'd given up on the St. Francis of Assisi theory in the meantime.

Angel continued to come with me on Sunday mornings, which was a comfort. We had lively discussions after each church service, but we agreed that none had the right message or philosophy for me. I would have to keep looking.

Then there was a surprising shift. It began when Angel left right after a church service. I thought he was just bored with our search for the right church, or maybe too busy. I didn't say anything. But then I had a feeling it was Celia. He never mentioned her, but I felt she was back in his life. Her presence was usually short-lived before she wandered away again. But Angel was smitten every time. I was wary of what she could do to our friendship. It didn't matter to her if I got together with Angel when I was dating Neil. But now I was single again and I might be seen as a threat. I tried not to think about her, but something was definitely up with Angel. I didn't want to lose his friendship at this critical time, but what could I do to stop it from happening?

10

It was getting close to closing time in the cafeteria at work. I was sitting by myself and about to leave when Rick came by with his tray and asked if he could join me. "Sure. I haven't seen much of you lately," I said. "Is everything all right?"

"Oh, yeah. I'm eating at my desk lately because of deadlines. I'm glad you're still here, Michelle. I've been meaning to email you the last few days. Now we can talk face to face. That's better, anyway." He smiled as if he were relieved and then reminded me of the lunchroom discussion we'd had about sudden windfalls. It was right after I found Jake and made the news for not taking the reward money. As I predicted, the story vanished shortly after that, and I was grateful. So I wondered why Rick was bringing it up now.

"When I mentioned my lottery ticket that day, you said, 'Who knows, you just might win,'" he quoted me. "And you said you'd remind me about donating 5% of the money if I did. So guess what happened."

"You won the lottery?" I said hopefully, and a little loudly. But the cafeteria was empty by then.

"Shhh," he whispered. "Yes, I did. Not that time, but a couple weeks ago."

"That's fantastic!" I congratulated him. "How much?"

"It looks like, after taxes, it'll be around $25,000. I can't quit my day job, but I can pay down my bills and save some of it. I could buy some nicer clothes and take my dates to better restaurants. I've been thinking about joining a fitness club. Or maybe I'll go on an exotic vacation for a change," he laughed happily.

"Sounds like a plan to me," I smiled. I wondered if he was going to ask *me* on a date.

Then he told me he didn't want to share the news with other people at work. "I'm afraid they might get jealous or treat me differently, or even ask me for money. I keep thinking about what you said, Michelle, that

5% of a windfall could make a big difference to people who don't have much. I'd like to share my winnings. What do you think I should do with them?" he asked, as if I was informed on the subject. I was touched that he'd come to me. I took a deep breath and in my head I thought, *María, if you're out there, please help me say the right thing*. And then I got an idea.

"I think you should give away whatever amount feels comfortable to you, Rick, whether it's 5%, less than that, or even more. As for who to give it to, you can give little gifts to several charities or pick one you feel drawn to. Maybe you could split it between local ones and those overseas."

"But, Michelle, how do I find and sort out these charities?" he asked.

He sounded confused and clearly in need of my help, especially now that he'd told me his big news. So I told him to do an online search. "You could type in a key word like 'hunger' or 'refugees.' Specify U.S. or international. Then go to the websites that get your attention and read what they do." He seemed to relax. But he was busy and working long hours, so I narrowed it down. "What sorts of charities would you like to contribute to?"

He impressed me with his empathy when he answered, "I'd like to help feed the hungry and give relief to people in physical or emotional pain. Is that possible?"

"I'm sure it is," I reassured him. Then I offered to research it for him, since I had more flexible time than he did. I could tell the money was weighing on his mind. "I'll email you the links to what I find, and you can take it from there. Can you give me a day?"

"That's fine, and I will be most appreciative if you help me. But please don't tell anyone, Michelle."

I smiled, thinking of the secrets I was already keeping. "Not a problem," I said.

I'd been busy at work off and on, but especially when the prototypes got the final touches before being reproduced for focus testing. Gwen kept her cool head and her warm support for us as we plowed through to the end. Things had grown quieter in the next aisle. Mimi looked better as she approached the second trimester of her pregnancy and Bill was more respectful of her. Maybe he was afraid of being reported to HR. In any case, there was a steady hum of work and a more peaceful state of mind in our little part of the world.

So at the end of the day I talked to Rick I decided to take a break and went online to do research. I found way more charitable organizations than I expected! He'd have to make the final choices, but I sent him links to Heifer International, Oxfam, Bread for the World, the International Rescue Committee, Catholic Charities, Women for Women International, and local links to a food pantry, a shelter for abused women, and an advocacy group for troubled youth. No matter where he decided to invest his windfall, the result would make a difference to those who desperately needed help. I concluded my email to him with "Bless you for doing this, Rick."

The next week I found a small card leaning against a loosely wrapped package on my desk at work. It was a thank you from Rick. He briefly outlined the gifts he'd "sprinkled" around the world. "I hope the tiny seeds of my generosity will blossom into something beautiful for many strangers," he wrote. "Here's a small gift to you for your help." Inside the green and white paper tied with raffia was a white pot containing a healthy ivy plant, its green branches poised to unleash new leaves in all directions.

The next day, and many other days that summer, I went outside after lunch and walked the wooded trail behind our parking lot. It was beautiful, especially on sunny days. The animal and insect sounds seemed louder than the traffic and planes I heard as I left the building. I immersed myself in the natural world again, looking up at tall old trees while I hiked the path. I loved the prairie grasses where clusters of Queen Anne's Lace stood. And the urge to sketch was back again, so I did. Occasionally I packed my lunch and grabbed a blanket or a small folding chair from my car. I moved to a different place each time to vary my subject. Sometimes I concentrated on a single tree or a flower. I learned to draw quickly because of the limited time I had. But there was one place I kept returning to. I often heard the wind there as it moved through the grass and the trees around me. It was soothing to hear the music of birdsong and insects as they created a kind of underlying melody. Even without bells and wind chimes hanging from the trees, it reminded me of the grove behind the Sweet Dreams Bed and Breakfast in faraway Teotenaca.

11

Angel and I were invited to dinner at Max's loft one Saturday night, but traveled there separately, per Angel's request. He didn't tell me why, but I had a theory. I arrived carrying a bottle of wine and my small cache of photos. My Mexican images would pale next to those of Max, the professional photographer, who had captured his scenes in both color and black and white. But I was mostly anxious to see his photos of Maggie, especially the most recent ones. She greeted me at the door with hugs and words of welcome. "Oh, it's good to see you, Michelle. I'm tired of emailing. I can't believe it's been almost two months since we got back in town," she said.

"The time has really flown," I agreed. "How are you?"

"Very, very well," she smiled. "How about you?"

"Doing well," I nodded. But then I changed the subject, "So where's Angel? He's usually ahead of me."

"He just called to let us know he's on the way. He's bringing Celia along."

"Celia! Well that puts a damper on things." It seemed my theory on going in separate cars was correct.

Maggie argued that they'd been together off and on for a while, it was Saturday night, and what was the big deal? I'm sure I rolled my eyes. "Are you jealous, Michelle?" She asked, raising one eyebrow.

"It's not that I'm jealous." How could she think *that*? "But we can't share important details of this trip with people who weren't with us. Of course, I don't know how much Angel's already shared with her, but I would prefer to keep that within our group. I'll have to be careful what I say in front of her," I tried to explain.

"Well, I understand that. But maybe we can just look at the photos and talk about the things we did that didn't involve the cave. Max won't be showing any pictures of you when you came out of it. He's got those tucked away out of sight. I don't even know where they are," she reassured me. *But still*, I thought, *Celia?*

"Where is he?" I asked, looking around for my host.

"Busy in the kitchen. He's always cooking up something. But this time, it's food."

"Authentic Mexican food," he said, emerging with a chef's apron wrapped around his waist. "Here's fresh guacamole for starters. Help yourselves." He set it down on the table next to a bowl of chips. And then he noticed Angel was still missing.

"So where's Professor Fuentes?"

"On his way, with Celia," Maggie replied.

"Celia! I was hoping he wouldn't bring her." He scrunched up his eyes.

"That makes two of you then," Maggie pointed out.

Max and I looked at each other and laughed. "You don't like her, either?" I asked.

He just made another face and shook his head, then reached over and gave me a bear hug like a big brother would. "You're looking good, Michelle. It's great to see you again. It's been way too long."

Then he disappeared back into the kitchen. Maggie opened the bottle of wine I'd brought and poured it into three glasses. "Come back here, Chef DeBoer. We have to make a toast."

He ran into the room again saying, "I have to make it quick. I'm sautéing fixings for the fajitas, and they're close to done. Why don't you make the toast, Maggie?"

She smiled, laughed at him in his splattered white apron, and raised her glass. "To friendships that last forever."

We clinked glasses and sipped the pale wine, so clear it could have been sunlight. "That was beautiful," I said.

"Just like she is," he responded, giving her a quick kiss before he ran off to the kitchen again.

I admired Max's enthusiasm, and his cooking as I savored the guacamole. Then the doorbell rang and Maggie buzzed in the last two guests. "Sorry we're late," Celia said. "We were in the middle of something and lost track of time." I hadn't seen her in a while. She was prettier than I remembered. Her dark curly hair draped itself around her shoulders and back. By contrast, her eyes were a bright blue and her skin pale and flawless. Her smile was wide, revealing perfect teeth. Over her shoulders she'd draped a bright, multi-colored striped Mexican shawl that stood out against her dark top and jeans.

"You're excused, especially since you come bearing gifts," Maggie laughed. Celia handed her a wine bottle that sat inside a hand-woven basket. In the same basket were small round cheeses encased in red wax and a box of gourmet crackers. Angel set a box wrapped in foil on the table and I knew it was one of his incredible desserts. He had mentioned getting the ingredients for a key lime pie the next time we got together, so I was hopeful. For a person who made such rich treats, I wondered how he stayed as slender as he did.

"Thank you both. How generous!" Maggie said, then offered them each a glass of the wine I'd brought. We drank, ate guacamole and started to catch up a bit. "It's been a long time since we've seen you, Celia. Sorry you couldn't come with us to Mexico," Maggie said.

"I had work on the East Coast at that time. Besides, my family's in Manhattan and it gave me an opportunity to visit them, too. But Angel's told me all about your trip. Teotenaca sounds like a charming place," she smiled. I looked at him accusingly, but we didn't make eye contact.

"And beautiful, too. Wait until you see Max's photos. They're wonderful. He's got a great eye for natural beauty," Maggie praised.

"And that includes the lovely Maggie O'Rourke," he praised back as he arrived from the kitchen. He pointed to a large framed black and white photo hanging on the wall. "There she is," he said. "That's the direction I'm going in these days." I wouldn't have been able to identify the model because the image was so abstract. A portion of her bare back was half in light and half in shadow. The patterns seemed to caress the figure as they curled around her muscles and spine. It could have been a painting with a sculptural quality.

"He's also doing a series where he photographs a close-up section of me, like my leg and foot, in a flamenco pose in costume and then the same portion without the costume, then he frames them together. He says my dancer's body inspires him," she smiled and winked at Max.

"Maggie, could you kindly give me a hand in the kitchen?" he asked, indicating the direction with a nod of his head.

"Sure," she said. "Please excuse us."

Celia and I looked at each other. My smile felt awkward. I kept wondering why she was there. But then I glanced over at Angel and I knew. They were back together again and it was Saturday night, after all, just as Maggie said. Celia smiled back and said, "You're looking good, Michelle. I really like your shorter hair. It's very becoming on you." Why was she being nice to me?

"Thanks. Yours is longer than I remember. It looks good on you." I tried to be nice back by stating a fact. I could have said more, that her complexion was soft, that her long nails and makeup made her even more fetching. That she was a perfect embodiment of feminine charm. Was that why her presence was bothering me so much? "That's a beautiful shawl, by the way."

"Angel brought it back from Oaxaca. I love it."

"It brings out the blue in her eyes, don't you think?" he chirped in.

"It does, now that you mention it," I agreed, though her eyes already stood out against the backdrop of her dark hair.

Our stale conversation was thankfully interrupted by Maggie. "Here's our next course," she announced, placing a large ceramic bowl containing a colorful salad next to the guacamole.

"And finally, the main course," Max announced as he set the steaming bowl of chicken fajita fixings next to a traditional tortilla holder. "Dig in! Rice and beans are on the way."

While we ate, I watched our hosts interact. There was an easy familiarity in their movements, an anticipation of what the other was about to do or say, as well as a sense of mutual respect. In some ways, it seemed they'd been together for years. Watching them helped me forget about Celia. *Was* I jealous? Or did I merely wonder why Angel kept taking her back? It had to be an emotional roller coaster ride for my dear friend, after all.

"What are you grinning ear-to-ear about, Michelle?" Max asked me.

"Oh, it just feels really good to be together again."

"So how about giving us a toast," he said.

I didn't know what to say, but out of my mouth came, "To my friends, Maggie and Max, who are the best of friends, especially to each other, to Celia, who is with us tonight, and to Angel, who is my partner in faith."

We clinked glasses, sipped wine, and then I saw Max looking at Angel. "Your 'partner in faith'? What does that mean, exactly?"

"We're going to church together, trying to find a faith community for Michelle," Angel explained. "She's looking for a place where she can worship, but also where she can put her prayers into action."

"And Angel is looking for a community where he feels in touch with his own faith," I said. "By the way, this is going to sound weird, but I've been having a dream about a dog and a group of kids walking down the central aisle of a church. I know it sounds absurd, but the image is getting clearer, so I think we're getting closer."

"As a matter of fact, I have a good feeling about where we're going tomorrow," Angel said. "We tried a few Catholic churches, since that's the religion we both grew up with. We have no complaints with Catholicism, but we haven't found the right fit yet. So we're going to a United Church of Christ service tomorrow. It's a group concerned with social justice, and I find that intriguing. Instead of just applying their faith to their own lives, they turn it outward, toward the world and its problems, to deal with important societal issues." There were times when Angel sounded like the professor he was.

When he explained where it was, Max said, "Is that the church with the anti-nuke sign on one side of the building and the peace banner hanging from the front?"

"That's the one," Angel confirmed.

"If it hadn't been for those signs I don't think I would have even noticed it. It just blends right into the block of buildings around it," Max nodded.

"I know what you mean," I agreed. "It'll be our first time inside. Angel says I should feel comfortable and accepted there, even if I'm not Protestant."

He smiled and said, "They're a very open and inclusive group, from what I've heard. I don't know if they accept canine members, but if your dream comes true, that will definitely be a sign." I saw him wink at Max and they started laughing.

"Hey, stranger things have happened in my life," I countered. And they knew that for a fact.

"A dog in a church," Celia said, laughing a little too loudly. "I'd like to see that for myself."

After dinner we saw more Maggie photos. Some were stark and minimalist while others were lush with color and movement. Max was exploring the multiple layers of her persona: healer, dancer, lover, muse. It was an open-ended collaborative adventure between them, the best kind of relationship. When I left the loft, the world seemed magical again.

Before I went to sleep that night, I prayed, "Dear God, please bring me to the place I belong, where I can find my faith and the path to take.

Help me understand how I can alleviate the pain of others. I put myself in your hands, God, Jesus, María, whoever is listening and can help me. Amen."

I fell asleep quickly that night. It was the same wave of fatigue I had in the cave, always followed by vivid dreams. As it happened, I had one of those dreams that night. I was in the City of Light looking out over the blue sea from an opening cut out of a high gate. María walked across the courtyard where I stood.

"How has your journey been lately, Michelle? Do you have questions?" she asked.

"Oh, María. You know I always have questions. Life has been surprising and eventful. But much of the time it's pretty much the same as before. From your point of view, how am I doing?"

She smiled warmly. "You're doing very well. You're understanding where you can make changes for the better in the ordinary things around you. As I've said before, you were right to stay anonymous when you found Jake and asked his daughter to donate the reward money to the homeless. But there are other things you've done that may seem small, yet are just as important in turning things toward the good. The pain in your side will continue to alert you to the pain of others. But someday you'll know they're there through your intuition and the pain will no longer be necessary to guide you." I was relieved to hear that!

"You are getting closer to the place that can help you broaden your scope and become more active. You will find it with Angel. He is an important part of your life and you are an important part of his, even if it seems another is closer to him than you are. You were always meant to be partners in faith, and you will be."

That left me with a thing or two to ponder. But I had another pressing question. "María, can you tell me if or when my art will become important?"

"Just keep sketching and when you feel the urge to paint again, do it. Yes, your artwork will become very important, not only to you, but to those who you can help," she said. I probably looked confused because she continued by saying, "Don't worry. You will know who and what to paint when the time comes. Use your watercolors because you're comfortable with them and they will be the perfect medium for your subjects." Then she walked back across the courtyard and opened a door. "Just follow the path of your instincts and intuition. Listen to them and take the opportunities presenting themselves to you." She entered the doorway of the house and was gone.

And then I heard the gate open onto the bluff. I walked through it and stood at the edge of a patio above the sea. I felt the pull of the wind in that high place and looked down to the blue water that could have been the clearest sky. It seemed that it all had become one. I couldn't tell where the sky and sea met. My next sensation was one of floating, but was I on the water or in the air? I couldn't tell, but I let whatever element it was take me where it would. Rather than struggle, I surrendered to it, to the flow of where my life would take me next.

12

The next morning I waited in front of the Lakeview United Church of Christ, looking down the street in both directions for Angel. When a bell rang inside the church I realized it was 10:30, time for the service to start. I thought back to our conversation the night before. Yes, it was absolutely this Sunday and this place we were meeting. But where was my friend? I was about to go in when I heard him call my name. He must have come on the El. Maybe he was running because the train had been delayed.

As he approached I felt a sudden ache in my side. But why? What was wrong? His face looked red and streaked on one side. When he stopped, smiling and out of breath, I was shocked to see his left cheek swollen and bruised and he'd bled slightly from several scratches. "Did that happen to you on the way here?" I asked with concern. He winced when I touched his cheek, then shrugged his shoulders as if he had no idea. "You look awful!"

"That bad, huh? I was hoping it didn't look as bad as it feels," he said, covering the wound with his hand. Still catching his breath he said, "Michelle, I'm sorry, but I can't go to church with you anymore after today."

And then it hit me. "Is it Celia? Did she do this to you?" I was outraged on both counts.

He nodded sheepishly and said, "She's jealous. She thought I was being evasive about our trip to Teotenaca. I hadn't said anything about Max and Maggie getting together, but now she knows. Last night she asked about what you and I were doing when they went off together. A couple times I stopped talking abruptly because I was afraid I'd give away too much. I told her you were always sketching and that you slept a lot, but she got suspicious about what we might be doing without them around. I tried to reassure her that nothing happened between us, but it doesn't matter now."

"But we're just friends, really, really good friends," I protested, wishing I could be saying those words to her in his defense.

He stopped for a moment, as if he wasn't sure what to say next. "I know this sounds crazy, but she thinks we had an affair in Mexico and she's worried it's still going on. It's absurd to think we're going to bed when we're really going to church! Last night she stayed over and this morning she didn't want me to leave. But I promised you I'd be here. We talked about it at Max's last night. I had no intention of breaking that promise, no matter how hard she protested. I even invited her along. It was about then that she slapped me. I think she scared herself when she did it. Then she slammed the door and stormed off."

This had happened to him because he covered for me, which made me feel partially responsible. She'd forced him into a murky place and he didn't budge. He kept my secrets. But would she have believed the truth? "How could she do this to you? Why do you stay with her, Angel?"

Another shrug. He scratched his head as he looked away with a distant smile on his face. "I find her exciting. It's not about abuse. This is a weird manifestation of her temper I haven't experienced before, and hope not to again," he explained as he pointed at his cheek. I imagined it throbbing in pain. "She's a creative, intelligent woman with a passionate side unlike anything I've experienced in other women. Unfortunately, I'm learning that passion can be a double-edged sword."

"No kidding! I don't know which edge she used, but it looks like she hit you pretty hard with that sword of passion!" *Pathetic male*, I thought to myself.

He smiled slightly and nodded at my joke. "It was her bare hand that did this. She slapped me and her nails scratched my cheek. I may cut them off while she's sleeping one of these nights. But I haven't any illusions. Celia comes and goes out of my life because of her work, she says, but I think it has to do with how things suit her at any given moment," he said, looking down at the ground. "Right now I've become more desirable because she thinks I'm involved with you. Having a perceived rival for my time and attention has made me more attractive to her, I think. But this morning I'm with you and we're going to church. But I won't be able to see you for a while after this." He hesitated while judging my emotional state. "It's nothing between you and me, Michelle. It's just an effort to keep the peace with Celia, the madwoman I'm involved with." We took turns rolling our eyes at each other.

I couldn't imagine my life without Angel in it at that point. And especially after what María had said in my dream the night before, that we would be partners in faith. Now I had to keep the faith that we would stay friends, somehow. Maybe I just had to wait out this untamed woman of his.

"I don't want to lose your friendship, Michelle. Maybe this will be the right church and you'll be on your way. I don't want to put restrictions on seeing you, but for now I have to. Eventually Celia will probably get bored with me again and leave, like she always does. Maybe I'll be strong enough not to take her back next time. It may sound corny, but I'm still under her spell." He shook his head as if to clear any thoughts of her and then he said, "But for the next hour and a half, I'm all yours. We'd better go in."

He took a deep breath and offered me his arm. I looked into his eyes and saw both sadness and determination. There was no room for argument. I put my arm around his and we walked up the steps and through the double door. As we entered a long narrow room with a large table near the front windows, a cheerful middle-aged woman greeted us and handed each of us a green program. Angel crossed his arms and positioned the program in front of his cheek. "Is this your first time here?" she whispered, since the service had begun. I heard a female voice coming through a microphone. We nodded that it was. "There's a coffee hour following the service and we'd love it if you could join us. Just take the stairs over there to the basement." She pointed in the direction we'd just come from.

"Thank you," we whispered back. Entering the sanctuary down the side aisle, we found a spot a few rows from the altar. At that point people were standing and singing so we weren't noticed. Angel had warned me not to genuflect, but it felt odd when I didn't. The church was small inside and not even half full of worshippers. It had a tall ceiling with long, cylindrical glass lamps hanging from it. The slender stained glass windows were much plainer than any I'd ever seen. A pale cream with art nouveau flowers, they were probably from the Arts and Crafts period, early twentieth century, and must have been original to the building. The front pews at the left and right were turned to face toward the altar, which was only slightly elevated from the main floor. There was an organ on the left and a grand piano up high on the right. But compared to the Catholic churches we'd seen recently, including Santa María, this was a much simpler space. There were no statues, just wood paneling behind the altar, and a squared-off cross, minus the body of Christ, painted on the back wall above a granite baptismal font. A short distance in front of that, suspended high above the altar, hung another version of the cross. It seemed to be made of two concentric metal circles united by strips of colorful cloth woven together to form the same shape as the painted cross on the back wall. Was it American Indian or Guatemalan? I wasn't sure, but I'd never seen anything like it before in a church.

We found a hymnal, turned to the song in the program and joined in the singing. There were no kneelers so we could only stand or sit. Would there be a Communion? It wasn't listed in the program. Angel assured me the service would not seem strange, but I already felt like a foreigner.

When the music stopped we sat down along with everyone else. A woman, the liturgist according to the program, spoke from her own personal experiences and how they related to the scriptures of the day. The message was one of receiving the word of God and then trying to deal with the aftermath. Do you listen? Do you doubt? How do you know what to do next? In her case, it was deciding whether she should take a vacation to Europe or go to Central America to work. She'd been planning the European trip for a long time. But then a friend asked if she could help establish a medical clinic in Central America. The liturgist had a nursing background and could do the job, but could she give up her long-awaited trip to Europe?

"This was a difficult decision. I saw my vacation time as a reward for all my hard work. I never imagined a vacation where I'd do even harder work than my job. But when I looked into the faces in the photos my friend showed me, it was an easy choice. I went to Guatemala. I know in my heart that was God's calling. I have no regrets. And yes, it was hard work. But it was uplifting and joyous as well. As some of you know, I've made the trip back a couple times since. Each time I've decided Europe can wait, but Guatemala cannot."

Then we read the "Prayer of Confession" together, which was written by the liturgist. Her words could have been mine, especially those that said, "I realize I am only human and do not possess your wisdom. I know that you will lead me to the place where I can do your work." Was I standing in the place where I could do my Cave of Dreams-inspired work? My discomfort was replaced by excitement at the prospect.

Then she read a passage from Paul and said, "Like Paul, we may be blind to the path we are meant to take. But we can trust in God to lead us in the right direction, even if it doesn't seem like the right one at the time."

Then we passed the peace, familiar enough, though I was used to only shaking the hands of those standing closest to me. But in this church, people only started from there. Then they walked down the aisles greeting everyone they possibly could with hugs and kisses on the cheek. I liked that a lot, especially after Angel's warning that I wouldn't see him for a while.

"Peace," I said, not moving from our pew and only offering my outstretched hand.

"Peace of God be yours this day," they said and shook my hand.

I took the opportunity to give Angel a hug. "Peace be with you," I whispered in his ear.

"And with you," he said and kissed me on the cheek. We held each other a few seconds more.

Then the minister rang the bell. With a smile in his voice, he said, "OK. OK. Enough hugs. Take your seats and let's sing!"

The next song was "Amazing Grace," my favorite hymn and the one I'd sung in the cave. As we sang, several children came up the central aisle and dropped money into a basket on the altar. According to the program, they were to give their offerings before going to church school. But this simple act was also part of my recurring dream coming true right in front of me, children walking down the aisle with something in their hands.

Would there be a dog, too?

Then I heard Angel gasp. I turned to see him glancing toward the entrance to the church, then at me in disbelief. When I looked in the same place, I was shocked, too! In the next wave of children, there it was, a small black and white dog prancing along with them all the way to the altar! The dog's tongue hung out slightly and as it passed, it seemed to be smiling right at us! My mouth dropped open and I covered it self-consciously. A hand touched my shoulder. I turned to the young woman in the aisle behind us who urged me to come closer to her. She whispered in my ear, "Don't be shocked. Pearl is a regular here. The kids love her."

I had to laugh, though I put my hand over my mouth so I wouldn't broadcast it. This absolutely had to be the place, the faith community I was meant to enter! There was the liturgist's meaningful message, that powerful, familiar hymn, and then, of course, there was Pearl and all those children with their church offerings. By the time I turned back to Angel, I was in tears.

"This is it," I whispered. "It *must* be."

He reached over and squeezed my hand. "*That* qualifies as a sign in my book," he whispered back.

I didn't think it could get better, but I didn't know what was coming next. Reverend James Horsley, who wore a woven stole around his neck like something out of Teotenaca, stood up as the song concluded. He was in his forties, tall and slender except for a slight bulge around the mid-section.

As he spoke, Reverend Horsley engaged his audience with friendly humor, but the sermon took on a serious tone as he got back to the same gospel the liturgist had referred to. He vividly recreated Saul's experience on the road as he was struck blind by a flash of light that knocked him from his horse. As he regained his vision, he changed his name and his attitude. He became Paul, no longer a killer of Christians, but an advocate of their beliefs. I'd heard the story before, but Rev. Horsley's words gave me a sense of Paul, the flesh and blood man. Then he said, "If you're waiting for the big flash of light to knock you out of your chair before you take a more active role in the world, it may never come. But it doesn't have to, if you're paying attention. There are flashes of light in our lives every day, on TV, on the radio, at the grocery store or the bus stop, at the office and even at home. God is always dropping opportunities in our laps. We need to notice them, even seek them out, and act accordingly.

"I know that many of you certainly have. But we must remember that even the smallest acts can make a difference in our unjust and violent world. Let us become the bearers of light, seeking out the dark corners of fear, despair and ignorance, and let us bring hope, even to those who would be our enemies. Amen," he concluded. Then he sat down and the congregation grew silent, reflecting on his words. My heart was pounding so loudly I wondered if anyone else could hear it.

After a short time, the minister stood in front of the altar calling for "the prayers of the people." There were many requests: restored health for a sick father, a job for a friend out of work, guidance for finishing a Ph.D. dissertation, mercy for two men on death row awaiting execution in the coming week. After each request we prayed for God to hear our prayers. While the others verbalized their hopes, I prayed silently that

Angel would come to his senses and break with Celia once and for all, for his own good. *And mine*, I added, feeling only slightly selfish.

Then Rev. Horsley asked God to grant all our spoken and unspoken prayers. As we said "The Lord's Prayer" together, it was slightly different than I'd learned it. We said "debts" and "debtors" instead of "trespass" and "trespasses," in remembrance of the poor countries with extraordinary debt, it explained in the program.

As the collection plates were passed around, a young tenor sang a song I didn't recognize. But I kept hearing the words at the end of each verse, "Let me be a messenger of hope." My spirit was lifted by his soulful voice. I felt lighter, as if I could levitate to the ceiling and peek out the tops of the stained glass windows.

After that, the liturgist, Sheila Nelson according to the green program, asked if there were guests or newcomers present. Angel and I looked around to see what to do next. Of course, everyone was looking at us. I raised my hand and Sheila motioned for us to stand. "Could you introduce yourselves, please?"

"I'm Michelle Hardtke and this is my friend, Angel Fuentes. We're here because I've been looking for a new faith community in the area," I revealed.

"Welcome," Sheila said while everyone clapped. Once again, we were invited to coffee hour, and to sign a guest book. We nodded and smiled as we took our seats.

This was followed by announcements concerning everything from volunteering for the next fundraiser to marching for immigrant rights. These announcements went on for a while until Rev. Horsley turned to the pianist in a quiet moment and said, "Hit it!" The last hymn began and we all sang, "This little light of mine, I'm going to let it shine!" He and Sheila headed down the central aisle during the last verse. After we concluded the song, no one moved. Then the minister's booming voice came from behind us.

And now, go forth into the world in peace,
be of good courage,
hold fast to that which is good,
render to no one evil for evil,
strengthen the faint-hearted,
support the weak,

help the afflicted,
honor all people,
love and serve the Lord
rejoicing in the power of the Holy Spirit.
Amen.

More moving words to take with me! The woman behind us asked a few questions and said it was wonderful that we'd come and stayed for the entire service. "It's a good thing we didn't have Communion or a Baptism today to lengthen the service. We might have lost you," she smiled. I'd already decided they weren't about to lose me. But I regretted Angel wouldn't be around to take the journey with me.

Angel stopped to compliment Rev. Horsley on the service as we left the sanctuary. The minister asked about his wounded cheek and the reply was an outright lie. "It was an accident. I fell on the way here when I ran to catch the train. Thanks for your concern," he said, smiling dimly with his injured cheek.

"If you need to clean it, there's a men's room downstairs," he suggested. "I hope it was worth your running and slipping to get here," he smiled. "Do you have time for coffee hour today? If you do, I'd recommend it. Annie makes wonderful finger sandwiches and pastries. You should check it out," he urged.

Angel and I looked at each other. Food as a bribe usually worked for both of us. I nodded in approval. "Thank you, Rev. Horsley," he said, "we'll take you up on that offer. I was wondering, and I know this is a long shot, but would you be related to Richard Horsley who wrote *Jesus and the Spiral of Violence*?"

"That's a fascinating book. I'm familiar with his work, but I can't lay claim to knowing the man. Maybe we can discuss the issues in his books sometime," the minister smiled, appreciative of my friend's intellect.

"I hope so, too," Angel responded, sounding like he meant to be back. I smiled at the thought.

Then we dutifully headed down the stairs. Besides, I was hungry and curious about more than those finger sandwiches. On the way down Angel asked how bad his cheek looked. The redness had faded and the swelling had stopped. I assured him it had stabilized. "It's not any worse than when I first saw it," I told him.

The downstairs was brightly lit with overhead fluorescents as well as natural light filtering through horizontal windows on both sides of the hall. The main table was set with two platters of tiny sandwiches piled several layers high, a huge bowl of fruit salad, and assorted pastries on other platters. It all looked homemade and delicious. Taking a plate, I filled it as people kept smiling and saying hello to each other, but also to Angel and me. It was the most welcoming church I'd visited since Santa María in Teotenaca. "I didn't realize radicals were this friendly," I said. "I always pictured them as shouting and carrying signs, like they do in the news."

"Oh, I'm sure they do that, too," he said. "But at their core they're just ordinary people. As you can see, they include mothers and grandmothers." And their children and grandchildren, who were chasing each other around the tables. Pearl the dog stood quietly next to her owner, a tall man with close cropped salt and pepper hair and a thick mustache. Pearl's head turned back and forth following the movement of children as if she were watching a tennis match, but keeping her distance. I motioned toward her and Angel followed me to meet both man and dog.

"Hi. You have a very cute dog," I said.

"Thanks. She's friendly, too, if you want to pet her," he smiled.

As I leaned down, she turned her attention to me. I petted her head and she seemed to smile while she wagged her tail from a seated position. "I don't think I've ever seen a dog in a church before," I said to her owner.

"Oh, you'll see all kinds of things in this church," he laughed. "This is your first time here, right?" I nodded. "I'm Mel Berriman. What were your names again?"

"I'm Angel Fuentes and this is Michelle Hardtke." We shook hands with him.

"Nice to meet you both. You were looking for a faith community, wasn't it?" Mel asked.

"Yes," I replied. "Angel's been suggesting churches in the area. I'm looking for one where people are actively involved with social justice issues. I was raised Catholic, so this is a change for me."

He nodded. "I was raised Catholic, too. And so were a number of people here. This congregation is a real crossroads of Christian denominations, and others, too. We're an open and affirming church, which means we don't turn anyone away."

"Including dogs?" I smiled.

He glanced down. "Pearl's a special case. She's very well behaved." He didn't sound defensive, just matter of fact.

And then a young woman with long red hair leaned into the conversation to get Mel's attention. "Pardon me, but can I talk to you, Mel? It's important."

"Sure. Excuse me, folks." He stepped away with Pearl right behind him. When he came back a couple minutes later he seemed upset.

"Is there a problem?" an African American woman asked.

"Looks like we're going to have to find a new assistant cook for tomorrow night. I just found out Dina's grandmother is very ill so she's leaving for Indiana this afternoon. She's not sure when she'll be back. Do you know anyone who could do it? I'm already one person short."

"I can't do it," the woman replied. "Is Sam still here? He might be willing."

There was an urgency in Mel's body language as he tried to locate Sam in the crowd. Apparently he had already left the church.

"Excuse me," I said. "What kind of cooking are you doing?"

"We cook dinner for a local homeless shelter two Mondays a month. But we need at least four people to do it. Right now we only have two including me. I'll need help tomorrow night."

I didn't have anything planned, but before I was willing to volunteer I wanted to know what I was getting into. "Do you need a professional cook?"

"Not at all. It's basic cooking, but at a large volume. I can work with anyone who follows directions well." He was answering my questions while he continued to search the crowd for worthy assistants. And then he trained his gaze on me. "Do you know anyone who might be willing to help?" he asked.

"Maybe." Angel and I exchanged looks. He rolled his eyes, knowing what I had in mind.

"I can't make it tomorrow night," he said.

"But I can," I said before I realized I had just made a commitment.

"Really?" Mel looked at me with a dubious expression. "But this is your first time here. Once you start volunteering you'll be asked to do it again," he warned.

"Tell me more about it and then I'll know for sure," I said, backing off a little. As Mel laid out the time, the process of preparing the food, and the location of the shelter, I knew I could handle it. And I wanted to help. But it would be a late night for a Monday. "I'll do it," I said.

"I'm overwhelmed," he laughed. "It's almost as if someone sent you."

"Maybe someone did," I smiled.

As Angel and I left the church with full stomachs I heard my friend chuckle. "What's so funny?" I asked.

"I'm just amazed at your jumping right into the assistant cook position. I know you like to eat, but I didn't think you liked to cook," he said, shaking his head.

"I should be fine. He needed a *basic* cook and that's exactly what I am," I tried to reason.

"A basic cook, maybe, but one with a very big heart," he smiled and put his arm around me. My heart was the place where a new pain had deeply embedded itself. I leaned closer to him as we walked past boutiques and coffee shops to the El, then gave him a long, goodbye hug.

"I'm going to miss you, my friend," I said. "Take care of yourself. At least stay in touch by email, when Celia's not watching over your shoulder."

He hugged me even longer and said, "I'll miss you, too, señorita. I'll think of you often. I'm glad I was able to take you to this point in your journey. Now you'll have a faith community to cheer you on."

13

The day after my first visit to Lakeview UCC I was back, this time cooking in the church kitchen with Mel. I chopped vegetables, stirred a large pot of stew and scrambled to do whatever he asked of me. He'd never found a fourth helper so it was just Mel, Lea and me. I got an adrenaline rush that reminded me of my job. After a quick two hours, we packed loaves of bakery bread and chocolate chip cookies, containers of cooked vegetables, gravy and a huge mound of mashed potatoes into large boxes for carrying. Mel poured the stew into two deep containers, then put the lids on tight. Lea cleaned lettuce for salad and whipped up a vinaigrette dressing with Italian herbs. Unlike the other groups that cooked for the shelter, the philosophy of the Lakeview UCC was to do things mostly from scratch instead of using canned and frozen food. It was more work, but the effort paid off. Everything was fresh and smelled delicious. We'd sampled and tasted what we'd made, but my stomach still growled as I took in the aromas. Hurriedly we loaded up Lea's trunk and drove the mile and a half to the shelter. There was a long line of men, women, and even children waiting outside. Other volunteers unloaded the food and set it up cafeteria style, along with other donated food. When the doors opened at 9:00 p.m., the hungry people poured in for the meal.

The other part of Lakeview UCC's philosophy was for the cooks to sit at the tables and share fellowship with the recipients of their efforts, the homeless. We stood in line with them, then filled our trays and sat down at a table.

"Thank you for helping me do this," Mel said with a look of great relief on his face.

"Not a problem." I meant it. It was satisfying to watch the faces of the people as they got their food.

"For a first timer, you hung in there, gal!" Lea said with her southern twang. She was a little older than I was and more down to earth than most people I knew.

Even while I ate I felt that familiar ache in my left side, but only as a dull pain. When I looked around at those who were hungrier than I, it was easy to know what it meant this time. I was surprised I hadn't doubled over from the misery in that room. But then I realized that by bringing food to those who lived on the edges of society, we were showing we cared about them. As they ate, the pain in my side faded away.

When several men sat at our table, we asked their names and told them we had prepared the food that night. "Bless you," said one between devouring large spoonfuls of mashed potatoes.

"I don't know what I'd do without this meal. Thank you so much," said another who attacked the stew.

Their gratitude made our huge cooking efforts seem small. But the real reward for me was our interaction with those at our table. I'd never had a close-up look at the homeless like this before, except in my dreams in the cave. Instead of begging for money, they were talking to each other, sharing their stories, and even a laugh. A few spoke softly instead of cursing or talking to themselves, as I'd seen them do on the street. The man who sat nearest Mel was surprisingly young, probably in his early twenties. He was missing a tooth, needed a shave, and his skin had a weathered red tone to it. But his mannerisms, his dark hair and his knowledge of the latest music had given away his age. As if he knew I was thinking about him, he looked intently at me, then cast his eyes downward. When he fixed his gaze on me for a few seconds, I smiled back.

"Excuse me, ma'am. I don't mean to stare," he said. "It's just that you remind me of my sister. I haven't seen her in two years."

"That's a long time. Where is she?" I asked him.

"Back in Kentucky. I came north looking for work and I haven't been home since," he said with a drawl.

"Does she know where you are?" I asked.

"Yes. But we don't talk much. I can't afford to call her and she can't reach me," he said, shaking his head and shrugging his shoulders as if the situation was hopeless.

"Could you call her collect?" I asked, trying to find a solution.

"She's poor, ma'am. She'd have to refuse the call."

"I'm sorry," I said. "Can you write to her?" There was always good old snail mail, I reasoned, if he couldn't email her.

"I write when I can get my hands on an envelope and paper, a pen and a stamp. She writes me sometimes and sends the letters here, to the shelter. I wish we weren't so far away from each other. But then, well, I don't want her to see me like this." He winced when he said that.

I asked if he could go back to Kentucky. "I got halfway home once, but then I ended up here. I was in Minnesota for a while. It's beautiful up there. But I've had a run of bad luck, you see. I was hoping to get back to work, but I've been kind of sick lately. I'm feeling a little better today."

"I hope things turn around for you," I smiled. And then I remembered that I had what he needed in my purse. As I reached into it, he probably thought it was for money. He seemed surprised and grateful with what I gave him – a small, plain note card and envelope, a pen and three stamps.

"Here you go. No more excuses not to write," I told him like a big sister would.

"Why, thank you, ma'am," he smiled for the first time. "That's very kind of you. *Very* kind. My sister's name is Clarice. What's yours?"

"It's Michelle."

"It's a pleasure, Michelle. My name's Danny."

"Good to meet you, Danny." We nodded to each other.

After the meal we gathered up the empty containers and boxes and put them in Lea's trunk for the ride back to the church. Mel thanked me again as we drove off. "I may have been able to find someone else at the last second, but none of them could have worked as hard as you did, Michelle. Or Lea, for that matter." She nodded with a smile.

"It *was* work, but I enjoyed it. I'd be willing to do it again any time you need me, as long as I'm available," I offered.

"You shouldn't have said that. Now I have to ask you again, you know," he laughed.

"And where's little Pearl tonight?"

"Home with David, my partner. He's back from the West Bank after a month on a CPT assignment. That stands for Christian Peacemaker Teams. It's good to have him home. He and Pearl are getting re-acquainted."

"I see. So tell me, what other kinds of things do people do in your church?" I was downright curious.

"If there's a cause, you'll find one of our members there," he laughed. "We've got a group going to City Hall in a few weeks to lobby for more affordable housing. There's another group working on closing down detention sites for immigrants about to be deported. It's part of our immigrants' rights initiative. Besides cooking for the homeless, we do monthly collections for local food pantries. But we get global, too. There's a CPT training session about to begin. Two of our members with CPT will go to Afghanistan soon. I have a feeling that's where David will be heading one of these days." He raised his eyebrows and sighed after that thought.

"That will be a tough one, Mel. I know he's highly motivated to take those risks," Lea said, patting his hand. "And hey, let's not forget the School of the Americas," she added. "Every year we join the protests against it at Fort Benning. That's a military school that teaches torture and interrogation techniques to Central and South American soldiers. People come from all over the place for that. We publicly read off the names of their victims."

"But we do normal church things, too," Mel insisted. "We have a committee working on events like the Christmas bazaar. It will have a fair trade theme and we'll have a silent auction, too. And there's a youth group working on their own projects. We've been brainstorming fundraising ideas so we can get ourselves back in the black, too. Is there anything you would be particularly interested in plugging into?" he asked.

"I have a background in visual art and publishing, if that helps anywhere. I'm a graphic designer," I offered.

"Hmmm, we can always use help with publicity. Sometimes we need posters or ideas for T-shirts. I'm sure we can find a place for your skills, if you're interested," he nodded. "And I can always use an assistant cook, especially one with your work ethic," he smiled.

"I'm your gal then. I have a feeling you'll be seeing me on a regular basis," as would the other members of the Lakeview United Church of Christ, since I felt in my heart that this was the faith community I'd been seeking. "Prayers and actions" could have been written right under their name on the sign outside the stained glass windows.

14

As it turned out, I continued to help Mel cook the shelter meals every other Monday, which is how I got to know several of the shelter's residents. Danny did write to his sister, who had recently married. She scraped up the money for a bus ticket that took him home to Kentucky. Then there was Frankie, a wrinkled older man who was great on the harmonica and occasionally played after the meal. From time to time, he was joined by Oscar, who had a gift for singing the blues. Pete was a nervous, wiry type who could talk your ears off with his stories of an adventurous life on the road that had gotten him in trouble now and then. And then there was the quiet Johno, a Vietnam vet with twitchy eyes. I got him to laugh with my bad jokes.

They had interesting faces and sad lives. For me, homeless men and women were no longer just gaunt shadows with outstretched hands haunting city street corners. They had personalities and stories. One night I began to dream about them. When I woke up I made sketches of them. Before long I was able to paint their images from memory, which was quite an accomplishment for me, since I'd never worked without a reference in front of me. But now I'd found a fascinating subject for my art. The more I painted the homeless, the more I dreamt of them and the ideas for paintings kept coming. I wasn't sure what to do with these watercolor portraits of street people, but it didn't matter. My artistic block was gone and I was in a compulsively creative state of mind. It felt great!

Another benefit of being consumed by making paintings was that I didn't think about things that upset me, like how much I missed Angel and wanted to tell him about where my life was heading. We kept in touch with occasional emails, but it wasn't the same as having a live conversation with my dear friend. I wanted to see him, hear his voice, exchange ideas and news of what was happening in our lives. He never mentioned Celia, but I sensed her presence in his guarded words. I wondered how his cheek had healed and if it bore the scarred impression of her fingernails.

And there were times when I thought of my ex-boyfriend Neil, but more out of curiosity than regret or anger. After being in the Cave of Dreams my misery over losing him now seemed frivolous. I was happy to leave him in my past. Yet there were times when I missed having the companionship of a boyfriend. Father Moran had warned me about maintaining balance in my life. At times, I knew I was working so hard that I wasn't leaving time for anything else. I would have to make room for someone new to enter my life, somehow.

In the meantime, I was making it to the Lakeview UCC services most Sundays. I found the monthly Communion to be especially moving. The congregation gathered around the altar, passing the peace and sharing bread and wine. It was always a beautiful, sometimes poetic liturgy. A collective murmur of approval always followed the consumption of the home baked bread. Most of these Sunday services inspired me, whether it was the music, the sermon, or the sense of community. I was connected to the place I belonged, a place where I could continue the education I began in the Cave of Dreams.

One service I'll always remember was when Mel's partner David and a woman named Diana were leaving for Afghanistan on a Christian Peacemaker Team mission, as Mel had foreseen. They would connect with a group of young Afghan peacemakers there. During that month, they'd "bear witness," then share their experiences through their writing and photos on a blog. Reverend Horsley spoke of their sacrifice of time, security and the comforts of home, as well as the sacrifice of their friends and families in letting them go. We were told to think of "hope" as an active word, one requiring participation by people like David and Diana. He said to give them our support emotionally, spiritually and financially. We prayed for their safety and gave them a grand send-off during a service commissioning them to do this work. At the end they knelt in front of the altar where their red CPT hats were placed. We gathered around them and down the center aisle. Rev. Horsley laid his hands on them as he spoke the commission. We each touched the person in front of us until our hands touched Rev. Horsley, Diana and David. We were all connected in those moments of physical touch and our common intentions that their mission be successful and they'd come home safe.

At coffee hour, I could tell Mel was both proud and frightened for his partner, David, who seemed upbeat, even though he knew the serious risks he faced. Someone mentioned Tom Cox, a CPT'er who'd been killed by his captors in Iraq.

As plans were being made for the Christmas bazaar, my name came up in a meeting and I was asked to help. There were three queries. Did I have art to sell at a booth? *Not enough yet.* Would I be willing to put something in the silent auction? *Yes.* Would I be willing to help with an artistic project the youth were working on for the event? *Probably.* Finally, I decided to frame one of my homeless portraits, which I'd never shown before, and put it in the silent auction, and to use my artistic skills for directing the youth project.

The painting I donated was of Pete, the man with all the stories. I had put him in his typical storytelling pose in the foreground while the background was a depiction of a tale I'd heard him relate. He stood out in more detail while the story part was diffused and mysterious. It was the kind of image that kept you guessing. Who was this man and who were these people behind him? I liked the ambiguity of the piece.

During a few Sunday services I was down in a large classroom, helping the youngest to the oldest of the children create gift cards with pictures of goats, sheep, cows and hens on the front, decorated with tempera paint, then enhanced with crayon, colored pencils and glitter. On the inside, the older children glued the message "A gift has been given in your name to Heifer International, to aid the hungry children of the world." Even though the church needed money, all the proceeds of this project would go to the not-for-profit group. I learned that Heifer supplied farm animals to enable people to feed themselves and make a living. Each card cost $10, the normal price of a share in an animal. It was only paper and paint, but it made a difference in the lives of people I'd never meet.

On the day of the bazaar, I was grateful for the attention my portrait of Pete was getting. In the end, someone paid $115 for it, all of which I donated to the church. As I gathered up the gifts I bought, the bags of fair trade coffee, the handmade soap and beaded jewelry from non-profits, the peace calendars and, of course, several of the Heifer cards, a woman I'd occasionally seen, but never met, came up to me.

"Michelle Hardtke?" she asked. I said I was. "I'm Alicia Marino. I'm the one who bought your painting. And I'm very impressed with your work. But I'm curious about the person in this picture. Who is he?"

"It's good to meet you, Alicia." She was a longstanding member of the church who had been involved in the sanctuary movement back in the '80s as well as the anti-nuke campaigns. Her latest efforts on behalf of a non-government organization, or NGO, had taken her all the way to South Africa. She'd been missing a lot of Sundays at the church since I'd been coming there. "His name is Pete. He's homeless. I met him while I was helping Mel cook for the shelter. He's quite a storyteller and so I painted him with one of his stories."

She pulled the painting out of the paper it was wrapped in to view it again. "You have quite a talent, Michelle. Do you have a series of these you're doing?"

The magic question! "Oh, yes. I can't seem to stop doing them lately. These men are haunting my dreams. I *have* to paint them," I said.

"Well, don't stop," she laughed. "I'm on a fundraiser committee for the shelter you've been cooking for. In fact, our event will benefit a shelter for abused women and children, too. We've been trying to come up with new ideas. I'd like to see your other work, but if it's as good as this I'd like to make a proposal. I think we could feature it at a benefit party, maybe even reproduce a piece for sale, if that would be all right with you. You could take a share of the profits, of course. That's your choice."

"I'd love to show you my work, Alicia, if you think it will help the shelter. I haven't shown these before today," I confessed.

"Well, believe me, it won't be the last time, if it's up to me," she smiled.

We made a date for her to see the other pieces I'd done. I bumped into Mel and Pearl as I was leaving.

"So who bought your painting, Michelle? Was it Alicia?" Mel asked. When I confirmed that it was, his mouth dropped open. "That's fantastic! Do you know about her art collection?"

"No. She *collects* art?" I was stunned.

"Yes, mostly works on paper. It's an incredible collection. She loans pieces out to museums for special exhibitions. There's a chance your painting could be hanging next to a Whistler or a Warhol in her living room."

"You're kidding!" I couldn't imagine being in such grand artistic company.

"It's true. This is wonderful news! Congratulations!" He gently slapped me on the back.

"She said she wants to feature my work at a fundraiser for the shelter."

"Do whatever she says. In the end, she'll be helping you, too," he advised me.

"Thanks for the tip, Mel." I couldn't believe my good fortune!

15

The next week Alicia was looking through my work and bubbling with compliments and ideas. "Besides using these to promote the fundraiser for the shelter, I think the Paul Reilly Gallery might be interested in your work, Michelle. It's an outsider art gallery in River North, but they also feature art by those who connect to marginalized people like the homeless. Would that interest you?" she nodded with a big smile, as if she knew what my answer would be. "I can arrange a meeting with Paul, if you'd like."

"Absolutely!" I smiled and nodded back. "But do you really think these paintings are worthy of a gallery in River North?" That would be a giant leap for a former Sunday painter like me.

"I wouldn't say it if I didn't mean it," she stated with conviction.

Later, when Paul Reilly saw the paintings he had a similar reaction to them. "Are you showing with anyone right now?" he asked.

"No," I answered and kept it at that.

"Good. I would like to be your exclusive gallery for this series on the homeless." I couldn't believe my ears! He explained his commission would be 40% and that he'd take care of the framing, which sounded fair to me. He'd show a few pieces at all times and eventually give me my own show, though he was booked well into the future. "Do you want to think about it?" he asked.

"I've already promised a couple pieces to Alicia for a fundraiser. Would that be a problem?" I asked.

"Oh no, that's fine. If you decide to show with us we could arrange a sign at the fundraiser saying we represent you. She shouldn't mind that," he assured me. That would give more credibility to my work, of course. We talked over the details, including how much the work would be worth, which was much higher than I expected, especially for an unknown like me. I told Paul I'd get back to him in a couple days.

Then I took the proposal to Max and Maggie, my own committee of advisors, to see what they thought I should do. I'd already shown them a few of the paintings.

"Go for it!" Maggie said without hesitation.

"This is a golden opportunity," Max agreed. He was the most knowledgeable person I knew in the business of art. "Besides being beautiful, haunting works of art, they give a face to the homeless. You have to do this," he said. They convinced me. I called Paul the following day and my new career as a professional fine artist was born.

As for the shelter fundraiser, Alicia convinced the committee to use my painting of Danny for their poster. It depicted his ravaged face in the foreground with the unmistakable storefronts of exclusive North Michigan Avenue shops behind him. The contrast was startling and it drew a lot of attention. As the event approached, I saw the poster displayed in the store windows in Lakeview and I heard they appeared in a few places downtown, too.

I was given two tickets to the fundraiser, to take place at a ritzy banquet room on the north side. It was about that time that I had a dream where María reminded me of keeping my "balance" the way Father Moran had advised. I had found the fire, that creative energy that burned in my soul, as well as my new passion for helping others. "You need to find the water, too, that place of calm where you can renew your own spirit. It's time you got back with your partner in faith. You know his name has a water reference in it, don't you?" she asked.

I thought about that, and then it hit me. "Fuentes means fountains. Lots of water!"

"Exactly!" she answered. "You need someone to escort you to the event. Ask him. You may be surprised," she smiled, as if she knew something I didn't.

Of course he was the person I wanted for my escort, but I was doubtful he could come. Still, I emailed Angel and he did surprise me by saying he'd be happy to join me. He hadn't heard from Celia recently. She hadn't even returned his calls or emails. "Looks like she's bored with me again. I'd love to see you, Michelle. I've missed you. A lot," he wrote.

"I've missed you, too," I wrote back. We had a lot of catching up to do.

On the night of the fundraiser, I stood out in the cold waiting for Angel to pick me up. It was winter, so we were both bundled up. When he took off his coat at the coat check, I couldn't believe his handsome, well-fitted black tuxedo. In all the years I'd known him, I'd never seen him in a tux. I was glad to be wearing my dark blue party dress with its shimmery taffeta skirt. Around my shoulders I draped a woven shawl from Oaxaca with a similar shade running through it, hoping the blue would bring out the color in my eyes. *Take that, Celia!* I thought, suddenly remembering Angel's comment about the blue in the Oaxacan shawl he'd given her.

My dear friend looked fantastic. His cheek had healed, his hair was shorter and styled with a cut that revealed his cheekbones and wide forehead more. He reminded me of a dream I'd had in the cave. He looked like the horn player version of himself at the "Club of Dreams." This was a suave version of the Angel Fuentes I'd known for years. How could Celia get bored with *him*? His presence gave me comfort and stability as I was greeted like a well-known artist, when I wasn't one at all. Besides the poster, Alicia had reproduced another of my paintings as a smaller print for sale. Through her persuasiveness, she'd gotten the printing donated. It was announced that all the auction profits from the original paintings would go to the shelter, which helped sales of the posters even more. It gained me more attention, which was exciting, but strange. I wasn't used to being recognized for my art work after all. But I was enjoying my moment.

The banquet room was beautiful, with chandeliers, opulent curtains and a parquet dance floor. There were long buffet tables on either side with every sort of appetizer one could imagine, as well as a chef slicing roast beef onto small bread rolls and a sweet table brimming with chocolate treats. How ironic, I thought, to feed people so they would donate money for helping to feed the homeless. The place was filling up quickly with the well-dressed and, hopefully, the wealthy. The table settings were draped with turquoise and white linen, with centerpieces of pink and white flowers. The light from votive candles reflected patterns in the cut glass vases. The auction featured local celebrity auctioneers who helped to get the most from each item. I couldn't believe my original painting of Danny fetched $500! And the other painting brought in $400. I was in shock! I held tight to Angel's arm to get my bearings.

"You've got a stranglehold on me, Michelle! What if I have to go to the men's room?" he laughed.

"Then I guess I'm going with you. Otherwise, I may just float off into space," I said, half serious.

"Don't worry. I'll hang on so you don't levitate through the roof. Just don't let your head get so big your hat doesn't fit anymore," he advised.

"If you ever see that happening to me, just give me a good shake, OK? Besides, this isn't my work alone, you know," I acknowledged.

"You really believe that, don't you?" he asked with a quizzical look.

"Of course," I shrugged. I was convinced my creative and spiritual sides were intertwined.

About halfway through the auction an announcement was made by the fundraiser's co-chair, an elegant silver-haired woman in a sequined red gown. "Excuse me everyone. I just wanted to remind you that we also have a silent auction going on in that back corner behind the sweet table. We are taking a break from the main auction now, so please check that out. You'll also find a talented writer who will be seated back there selling and signing her books of poetry, with all profits going to the shelter. And here she is to read her work for us. I am pleased to introduce a wonderful Chicago poet, Berta Corelli."

A petite woman in her forties strode to the microphone amid much applause. Her wiry dark hair was loosely pulled back, exposing long earrings that sparkled against the backdrop of her simple black dress and lavender scarf. I knew her words, but couldn't remember her face from the photo in the book of poems Max had worn out long ago. Angel groaned as I tightened my grip on his arm.

"Sorry," I said. "But it's Berta Corelli! Do you believe this? How did I not know she would be here?"

"Maybe you can meet her later," he suggested. I was already planning our conversation in my head.

"I'm certainly going to try," I said, glad we were seated near the stage.

"I'm pleased to be here tonight," Berta began. "My friend Alicia Marino invited me to come, and anyone who knows Alicia knows I couldn't refuse her. But I am truly grateful for this opportunity. So to get you in the mood to buy my books, I've been asked to read," she smiled. "I'm going to start with a poem I haven't read in a while, but it's been on my mind lately so something is telling me to read it. It's entitled 'Choosing to Live' and is from my first book *Too Near the Fire*, which is for sale tonight."

"That's the poem that helped Max," I whispered to Angel.

"I know," he whispered back. "Did you know your mouth is wide open?" I took his hint and closed it, but I think it continued to open involuntarily as I listened to words that had a new clarity for me.

Ghosts glide in the second floor ballroom,
circling softly amid the shadows,
specks of dust illuminated
by shafts of stolen sunlight.
They move quietly, bound
by their common fate.
Are you with them,
drifting in that dance after death?

We were loving partners once,
yet are forever separated by our choices.
I still breathe each day in
with longing for the next.
As the sole survivor of our conspiracy,
I regret you'll never know this peace,
this hope.

When my conscious mind drifted into darkness,
toward an open grave,
my dreams saved me
by carrying my soul into wakefulness.
I grasped the hands of hope and grace
as I stood at the edge of the abyss.
Gazing into that dark chasm, I chose life,
creating a place for myself
where none had been before.

I learned that throwing one's life away
is easier than the hard labor of survival.
There is nothing to gain
by giving up the world.
While compelled to re-discover it,
I felt the need to help others.
This work began when I saved myself.

Each of us carries a seed of hope in our hearts.

With a small amount of water and light,
the beauty within us can blossom
and shine upon this weary earth.
Each of us contains the power to bring humanity
one step closer to heaven.

If you are there, my dearest friend,
dancing with the golden dust
forever turning in the second floor ballroom,
do not wait for me.
I cannot join you because
I am of the living and
there is still too much for me to do.

"The dusty ballroom of ghosts must have been inspired by the dome in the cave," I whispered to Angel amid enthusiastic applause. "I could picture it while she was reading." He nodded as if he heard me, but I wasn't sure he did.

Berta continued, unfolding a sheet of paper. "I'm working on a new book, so this next poem is one you can't buy yet. But I really would like to share it because I think it's pertinent to what we're doing here tonight. I'm using the metaphor of a cave to illustrate hope. Now I know that sounds contradictory. A cave can be a dark and treacherous place. But it can also be a shelter from storms and the outside world. My point is that even in the darkest of places one can find hope if one believes it *is* there. It's the element of belief that can make all the difference, and faith, of course. This poem is called 'Pool.'"

Angel and I looked at each other not quite knowing what to expect. I was getting goose bumps as Berta directed her eyes to the paper in her hand.

Water ripples down the rocks,
wears them to a polished smoothness
like marble in a church.
The constant murmur of the flow is
like whispered prayers
that never cease.
Below the source, the pool shines

like onyx or black pearls.
Eyeless fish float past like dreams.

Yet in this darkness, there is hope.
In this sunless place,
all possibility lies dormant.
In this cave, spirit calls us
to look beyond the shadows.
Here, days are not measured
by the sun and moon,
nor the changing seasons.
Time is still, keeping watch
while we stumble from day to day
in the sunlight.

It was another familiar place, the room with the pool, the stone benches, the blind fish. I pictured the Cave of Dreams and wondered if anyone was there as she read about it. Now I *had* to talk to her.

"Thank you all for being here tonight," she concluded, smiling and bowing slightly amid much applause. She was a classy lady, confident and poised. Her words had moved me years before, but her reading of them now had me in tears. Angel handed me his handkerchief.

"Looks like the cave had its effect on her, too," he said. "You two have a lot in common, but I don't know if you'll be able to speak privately tonight. There's already a line waiting for her back there."

"If I can't speak to her tonight, maybe Alicia will help me arrange a meeting," I reasoned.

He smiled, "That's true. You have a friend in common, too."

"Will you come with me?" I asked him.

"For moral support?"

"And physical support. I'm feeling a little weak in the knees right now," I admitted.

"Of course," he smiled. He walked me to the restroom where I freshened up. Then we stood in the line waiting to buy a book and have it signed. Alicia saw me standing there and came over.

"Now Michelle, when you get to the front of this line, be sure to introduce yourself to Berta. I told her about you and your wonderful paintings and she said she wanted to meet you tonight. I probably should have introduced you two before she read, but I've been working this room all evening trying to get people to cough up more money. It feels like a full-time job! And, by the way, your prints and posters are selling quite well. I'm most appreciative of your generosity," she said, touching me on the hand.

"And you're most welcome, Alicia. I'm very happy to be a part of this." I was going to introduce her to Angel, but before I could, a woman whispered in her ear and she was off to another part of the room. Walking away, she pointed toward Berta and then to me and moved her fingers and thumb to signify talking. I nodded that I'd introduce myself.

"How are you doing?" Angel asked with concern. I must have looked disoriented by all the activity swirling around me.

"Wonderful, really. I feel as if I'm in another dream. Tonight just seems totally fantastical," I shook my head with a silly smile on my face.

"It's always a mystery to me how people and circumstances can be connected to each other," he said. "It's that 'small world' sensation. It must be feeling particularly small for you right now."

I nodded and said, "Oh yeah."

"By the way, you look wonderful tonight," he smiled.

"Excuse me?" I responded with surprise.

"I said you look wonderful tonight," he laughed, speaking closer to my ear and putting his arm around me.

"You're looking quite handsome yourself," I noted, turning more of my attention to him. I had to smile at the man who was my dearest of friends, grateful that I'd gotten him back in my life. "I should get out more," I said and he nodded in agreement. I suddenly realized that I hadn't dated anyone for a long time. *Priorities*, I thought. Where would I even fit a boyfriend into my wildly busy schedule?

When we finally got to the table I purchased Berta's first book, then waited for my chance to have her sign it. She was taking time with each person, making sure she answered questions and spelled their names correctly in the dedications she wrote before she signed the books. I turned to Angel and whispered, "Can you stand behind me in such a way that no one can see or hear me talking to her?" He agreed to try.

As I approached her, she took the book from my hand and I bent close to her face. "Alicia Marino told me to introduce myself to you. I'm Michelle Hardtke. I did the poster for the event."

"Oh, Michelle," she said in recognition. "It's a pleasure to meet you.

I admire the two paintings I've seen tonight. They're quite expressive in terms of what life is like for these men. But they also give them a sense of dignity and personality. I like that. Tell you what, I'll sign my book for you if you sign your poster for me." She pulled out the poster she'd bought and we took turns with her pen. I was hoping Angel had seen that, but he had begun a conversation with the people behind him.

As I handed the poster back to Berta I leaned down closer. "Berta, I was in Teotenaca last summer, in the cave. I was told that you had been there, too, and that you were approachable about discussing it. I know the dome with the floating dust and the room with the pool. Your poems reminded me of them." Her reaction to my words was extremely subtle. I was the only one who could see it in her eyes, a look of exposure, fear and longing.

"Tell me something else about the cave or the town," she whispered.

"There are stairs behind the waterfall and the pool that lead up to another large space. There's a mural painted on the wall there that is very old. The dome is like the center of a wheel. The spokes are passages in the cave. The town is small but spread out. People from all over the world come there, mostly artists. The church is old and has a huge, very realistic and brutalized Jesus on the crucifix behind the altar."

"What is the cave called, and why?" she asked.

"The Cave of Dreams. You can't help but fall asleep and have the most vivid and memorable dreams there. Mine often began at a place called The City of Light where a guide advised me before or after the dreams. Her name was María," I explained, trying to be concise and quick.

"Why were you in the town?" she asked, looking into my eyes hopefully.

"I was on vacation with friends, including the man I'm with tonight. Through circumstances, I got there first, went hiking, found the cave and went in. I was in it for four days before it released me," I explained.

She grew quiet and then said, "I didn't know about the mural. How did you find it?"

"Another person was in the cave when I was. It was his third time there and he showed it to me."

Finally, she smiled and surprised me with her next statement. "You are just the person I've been hoping to find. No wonder I felt moved to read 'Choosing to Live,' as well as 'Pool.' Will you stay a little longer,

Michelle? Don't leave without talking to me about a project I've been working on lately. It has to do with my new book and your painting ability. And your dreams." She held out her hand and I told her I would stay as I shook it. We looked into each other's eyes and smiled knowingly.

Then I turned to Angel, who was still deep in conversation, and said, "It's their turn now." He said goodbye to his new friends and we walked away. I waited as long as I could stand it before I blurted out, "I told her, Angel. She wants to see me after she's done signing books. She says she has a proposal for me. She even had me sign one of *my* posters for *her*?" He just smiled and put his arm around me again.

As we crossed the room I almost bumped into a woman who looked familiar, but I couldn't place her. We both did a double take. And then she smiled with recognition.

"Michelle? If it weren't for you I wouldn't be here tonight. I'm Sarah Cohen Levine. Remember me?" she smiled with a warm expression.

Then I did. She was the daughter of Jacob Cohen, the lost man I'd found. It seemed so long ago now. "How's your father?"

"He's doing much better, thank you. He's in an excellent facility for Alzheimer's patients and he has lots of new friends. I meant what I said, though. I got the invitation to come here because I donated money to the shelter as you wished. I'm doing a good job of giving more to them tonight in the silent auction," she laughed.

"Sarah, this is my friend, Angel," I said. "He's the only one I told about finding your dad. I'm enjoying the anonymity. Thank you for that," I smiled.

"And we'll leave it like that," she said, nodding to Angel. "But thank you again. I know you saved his life. And now, I'm sorry, but my husband is waiting for me over there so I have to go. Take care, both of you."

I waved as she disappeared into the crowd, and then I said to Angel, "It's a *really* small world tonight."

Later, when I talked with Berta near the end of the evening, we had a lot to discuss. She was convinced I was the genuine article as far as what I'd told her about the cave. Since I seemed to be able to paint from my dreams, I was a worthy candidate for her latest project. "I'm putting together a proposal for Cueva Press. Have you heard of them?" she asked.

"A branch of the Lawley Reed Foundation?" I asked, remembering hearing that from Reggie.

"Exactly. And you know the cave is steeped in mystery and secrecy. So that makes what I want to do controversial. I don't want to expose that specific place in any way to the public. I just want to use the idea of a cave as a metaphor. But *that* cave is the one I remember, so my imagery is specific to it. It's been years, but I still see it in my dreams, more and more lately. Do you dream of it, too?" she asked me.

"It's only been months since I was in it, so the memory is still fresh. But I do dream about it at times. I'm sure I could program myself to dream of it more, if I tried," I offered.

"I prayed I'd find a visual artist who'd been in the cave and who could paint it from memory if necessary. By making the images specific, it will inform the writing better. And it will send a message to anyone who has been there that they're not alone in this crazy world," she explained.

"You want *me* to illustrate your cave poems?" I asked in disbelief.

"Yes, if you're willing. I would like to see more of your work, of course, but I think you're capable of this from what I've seen tonight. I'd like to put your participation in the proposal to Cueva, so I would need to know fairly soon." There was an urgency in her voice.

"Could you put me in tentatively?" I asked. "I've only recently begun to paint again and I've been immersed in doing portraits of the homeless. Sometimes I feel like they're haunting my dreams. You should see more of my work so you feel comfortable with your choice."

She looked at me thoughtfully and smiled. "I have a proposal right now, Michelle, if you're game. If I were to give you this poem about the pool, would you be willing to paint an image of it? I don't want it to be photo-realistic. It just has to convey the essence and the mood of that place. If it's slightly abstract or mysterious, that's even better. What do you say?" she asked with enthusiasm.

I looked at Angel who smiled and nodded. He knew I couldn't say no to Berta.

"I'll do it," I said. "But I'm not sure how soon I can have it for you."

"Let me know where you are in the next couple weeks," she said. "Let's exchange phone numbers and email addresses."

We did and then she had to leave. "It's been a long day," she sighed, and it had been a long one for me, too, though the evening was almost over. A DJ played a few slow numbers as time ran out on the event.

Angel squeezed my hand and said, "I know you're probably tired, but how about a dance or two, señorita, to bring you back to earth?" I nodded and followed him to the dance floor. As he put his arm around my waist I glanced over his shoulder and did a double take. Was that my ex-boyfriend Neil across the dance floor? I couldn't be sure and stared, then exhaled. "What's the matter?" Angel asked.

"Nothing now. I thought I saw Neil over there. It startled me. I've barely thought about him in the longest time. I must still have a vulnerable spot in my psyche," I realized.

"Haven't you dated anyone else lately?" my dancing partner asked, pulling me closer.

"Are you kidding? I work all day, then come home and paint, then dream about what I'm going to paint next. On the weekends I paint, do errands and visit family. That's a too full life! No time for dating these days."

"Well, that's a shame," he frowned as he moved me in a circle across the floor. "Any prospects?"

"Maybe, but I haven't thought about it lately."

"You may as well be choosy. What are you looking for in the next man you date, Michelle? What are the qualities you prefer the most?" he quizzed me.

I looked across the room at the man who reminded me of Neil. What was it that was so great about him, anyway? "My ex was sophisticated, which I liked. He knew how to make money, which was helpful, of course. I think ambition is a good quality, if the person keeps his priorities straight. But to be truthful, he was getting too materialistic, too showy. That was starting to rub off on me, too."

"So what do you want next time?" he asked again.

"Angel, I haven't thought about this in a long time!" I protested. Why this line of questioning, I wondered.

"That's all right. It's better not to think too hard," he smiled. "What pops into your mind without thinking about it?"

"Hmmm, well, I'd like to find an intelligent person, one who's supportive of what I'm up to these days. I'd like a man with a good sense of humor, who's kind and generous and willing to understand what's important to me. I'd want him to have the same values I have, to be a person I can talk my heart out to and feel it won't come back to haunt me. A person I can trust. Yes, that's really important to me, too." It was easy to come up with the qualities I'd be looking for in my next man, once I got going.

"Those are all good qualities, good choices. Anything else?" Angel asked.

I looked at him not knowing why he was questioning me. Was he making fun of me, knowing I'd been too busy to even think about these things? I decided to try another tact. "Yes. I hope I can find a man just like you. You're my friend, but you have those qualities and a whole lot more."

He smiled broadly. Maybe that was what he was fishing for. But then he threw me a curve. "You don't have to look any further then, señorita. Why go looking for someone like me when you're already dancing with me? Isn't the genuine article good enough?" he winked.

What? I didn't know how to respond, where to look, what to say. I think I stepped on his foot right about then. All he did was laugh. "What's so funny?" I asked, incredulous at his behavior.

"I don't think I've ever seen you speechless before, Michelle," he smiled. "But you haven't answered my question. Shall I repeat it?"

"I'm just trying to wrap my brain around it. Are you serious? We're friends!" Now *this* was disorienting!

"But isn't that a great place to begin?"

He had a good point, of course. But what about *my* point? "It's hard for me to think of you as anyone other than my best friend," I explained.

But that only helped his argument, "Ah, I'm your best friend, am I? That's even better."

"Angel, you're confusing me. Are you trying to seduce me?" He was starting to scare me a little.

But he just smiled and slowly shook his head from side to side. "I'll be whatever you want me to be," was all he said, and then he gently pulled me closer toward him so we couldn't make eye contact. My first urge was to pull away, but it felt comforting to be in his arms. Without thinking, I relaxed into his grasp. Our bodies moved in the slow rhythm of the dance as he guided me along. I'd never known anyone else like him, dedicated to his work and teaching, curious about many things like I was, but on a more intellectual level. Yet he was earthy, human, dependable and caring. And he knew about Teotenaca. Could I share that with anyone else? I already loved him on one level. But could my love for him grow even deeper?

"Angel," I whispered into his ear.

"Yes."

"Aren't you afraid, if we go further?" I asked.

"A little," he whispered back, "but I've been thinking about you a lot lately." He loosened his grip so we could face each other. His eyes were more serious now.

"I've been thinking about you, too," I admitted. "I do care a great deal about you. I missed you so much! But what about Celia? What if she comes back? Or what if we do something we regret later? How will it affect our friendship?" I asked.

Again, he smiled. "I had to let my relationship with Celia play out. As far as I'm concerned, it's done. Inconstancy is not a trait I admire and I'm sick of it. End of story. As for my friendship with you, that's been constant for years. I don't want it to end, no matter what."

I was light again, feeling like I could float away if he didn't hold me. I made a bold suggestion. "What if I said, come back to my place tonight and we'll see what happens. Maybe we'll just talk about this. Maybe we'll play Monopoly. I don't know!"

He seemed pleased at that. "Yes, I would gladly go back with you. But again, it's whatever you're comfortable with, Michelle. The last thing I care to do is push you into a situation you don't want."

I knew he meant that. I trusted his word. And as he spoke, I felt warm inside, like a flame in my heart had re-ignited after a long winter. He took my hand and we walked back to the table to gather our things. He helped me with my coat, then held the door as I breathed in the chilly night air.

16

Angel and I stayed up talking hours after the fundraiser. We munched on popcorn and drank mismatched beers. He draped his jacket and tie over a chair, and abandoned his shoes next to the couch. I thought he'd have to rush his rented tux back in the morning, but he said he owned it, had bought it for special occasions like the fundraiser. I hadn't had a special occasion in a long time. My blue dress went back to its usual position in the closet and I was happy to trade it for jeans and a sweatshirt.

We talked about everything imaginable, but avoided mentioning the possibility of becoming lovers, even though it filled the room like a heavy mist. We played with it by discussing places in the world we'd like to see, reasons to stay in Chicago, things we wanted to do but hadn't yet. Finally, it got to the point where I couldn't stand it anymore. It was getting later and later. I knew Angel was waiting for me to make a move, so I did.

"And where do you see yourself in a few years, Angel? What do you want your life to look like?" I slid a little closer to him, since he was sitting on the opposite end of the couch.

"Hmmm, it would be nice to have a partner in my life, a woman I could share it with, good times and bad. I'm happy to keep the teaching job I have, as I said, but to be doing more research, maybe in Mexico. I'd like to be working on a book by then. So far I've only published essays. But my partner would be the most important part of the picture, if I want my life to be truly fulfilling. And I do," he concluded, leaning toward me for emphasis.

"Tonight you asked me what I wanted in my next boyfriend, and you pointed out I could have it all with you," I said. Maybe I was tired, but that sounded blunt to my ears, which I hadn't meant it to at all. My friend's earlier boldness seemed to dissipate when his response was merely to clear his throat. Was he getting cold feet as the night pushed on toward dawn? He'd started this whole thing. Where did he want it to go? "What are *you* looking for in a partner, Angel?" I asked. "Someone like me? If so, why so?" Yep, that was blunt, but I didn't care anymore.

He slid over near me then and looked into my eyes. His tone turned serious, "I have a confession to make." Had he changed his mind? Made a mistake? Was it time for him to leave?

"All right then. Put it on the table," I said, taking a deep breath and holding it.

"Celia was right," he began. "You and I didn't do anything sexual in Mexico. But I discovered how much I cared for you, Michelle. You could even call it a longing or a yearning. It comes from a deeper place than sexual need." He paused, looking toward the dark window while my heart began to race. I touched his hand and he turned back with a sudden intensity. "Maybe it was always there," he continued. "But when you went missing, it was horrible! I was worried I'd never see you again. And then these odd things kept happening: I almost walked through solid rock; Flor seemed to know all of us intimately; Sunny reminded me of my own childhood; the crucifix in the church looked like a real person; and there was this whole odd story of the cave in El Anhelo. I went from feeling all was lost to anything was possible." He smiled and caressed my cheek. "When you emerged from the mountain, it was like witnessing a miracle. You underwent a transformation in there, Michelle, a re-birth. Even your appearance changed. You may have been covered with dirt and grime, but you were radiant. There was a new depth in your eyes, and I was transfixed by that. I'm still reeling from the mystery of it all." He shook his head and came closer. "For me, you make the Divine… palpable."

As he gazed into my eyes, I was the one who was transfixed. He kissed me, first on the cheek, then on the mouth. I felt myself surrendering to him as I floated on a wave of my own yearning. We'd both felt the draw of that sacred mountain. It linked us together even while it separated us with its solid rock walls. But this time the magnetic pull came from our longing for each other. Maybe my need for Angel had always been there, too. I just hadn't recognized it for what it was.

All at once, the couch seemed too confining for such a powerful force. I took his hand and led him into the bedroom, where we explored our mutual longing until sleep overcame us.

17

When the alarm went off at 9:00 a.m. Sunday morning, I hit the off button. I felt bad about not going to church that day, but when I laid my head back down on the pillow and turned toward the sleepy man next to me I knew where I was meant to be. "Are you getting up?" he asked with eyes still closed.

"Not yet. Are you?" The only reply was a slight snore, which I took to mean, "No."

I didn't last long, either. We probably slept another couple hours before my eyes opened again. I focused on the sunlight coming over the top of the curtain and the patterns the trees in the courtyard made on the ceiling. I'd just slept with my best friend! Now what? *Where do we go from here?* I wondered. As I watched the light and shadows shifting above me, I imagined how our lives would intersect, how schedules and priorities might change to accommodate our new dynamic. It was an interesting development that had dropped from out of nowhere. Then I imagined a camera suspended above us, like it had been in the film *When Harry Met Sally*. Would I be smiling like Meg Ryan had been? Would Angel be looking shocked and terrified like Billy Crystal had?

"Angel," I whispered, "are you awake?" I kept gazing at the ceiling, at the invisible camera.

"Barely," he mumbled.

"I have a question for you."

"Being you, that's no surprise. What's up?" he asked with a yawn.

"Do you remember that scene in *When Harry Met Sally* when it's the morning after they slept together for the first time?" I asked.

"Do I remember. . . yes, yes, I do. Why?" he asked, stretching.

"They had different reactions and you could read them on their faces. I'm just wondering how we'd look if someone was filming *us* right now. What would they see on your face after you'd slept with your best friend?"

He laughed. "They'd see a guy who can't believe his good fortune, who's smiling like a lunatic, even though he's weary after a long and tumultuous night. How about you? What would they see?" he asked back while looking up at the ceiling.

"I'm smiling like a lunatic *and* I'm still in shock! But that's because I can't believe my good fortune, either," I laughed, trying not to sound as giddy as I felt. We turned to face each other then. He looked rumpled and I'm sure I did, too.

"Good morning," he smiled.

"I hope it still *is* morning," I laughed.

"I thought we'd never go to bed, with or without each other," he said, running his hand through his hair.

"You could have gone any time you wanted," I teased.

"No, it was a waiting game, and I'm glad I waited," he smiled. I was glad, too.

"So what do you do on Sundays these days?" I asked.

"I get up, make coffee, have a little breakfast, read, have lunch, read, grade papers, make dinner, grade papers, read. You get the picture." *Busy guy*, I thought, *and a recluse*. Fortunately, he had a few books in his car. When I asked about clothes, he surprised me by saying he had a gym bag in the trunk, too, but hadn't gotten to the club in a week. The clothes would be clean, but wrinkled.

"I didn't know you were going to the gym, Angel. I thought maybe those muscles came from lifting heavy books," I joked. "But I'm glad you're prepared for any eventuality, including this one. That is, if you'd like to hang out with me today, at least for a while."

He leaned on his arm and stroked my hair with his other hand. "I was hoping you'd want me to stick around. My papers are all graded, by the way. Do you have plans?" He looked hopeful that I wouldn't.

"I have to call my folks later, but they're getting together with friends, so I'm free. Otherwise, there's laundry, housekeeping, and a painting waiting for me to finish it. But if I don't get to any of it today, oh well."

"I really do have good fortune then," he said as he kissed my mouth. If I'd known he kissed that well I would have suggested getting together a lot sooner! Breakfast could wait.

The rest of our day went like that. He read while I painted, interrupted by another kissing session. That was followed by a discussion of our favorite foods and the preparation of a late lunch. He helped with the cleanup. But while I rinsed the plates at the sink he wound his arms around my waist and snuggled my back, followed by another kissing session. It was amazing we got anything done as we got to know each other in a whole different way. By dinnertime it was getting late. We ordered a pizza and discussed how we'd insert ourselves into each other's lives. We could clear part of the weekend and share an occasional week night. We could take turns at each other's places, but Angel was more mobile. He could read or grade papers while I painted, but I couldn't bring my studio with me. Over time I knew his books would take over corners of my apartment, and that was just fine with me.

18

In the week following the fundraiser, the usual images I saw in my dreams were of the homeless, although Angel made a few appearances, too. I might do a quick sketch of them when I woke up, then paint from it in the evening after work. But one night, right before I fell asleep, I read Berta's cave poem again. The next thing I remember is being back in the cave, alone, but not completely in the dark. Candles were burning in their usual place near the stone benches where I sat down and faced the waterfall. I could hear its steady trickle running down the face of the mountain and into that hidden place. It was a soothing sound that echoed in the grotto-like space. Its familiar rhythm pulled me back to the time I'd spent there. In that moment of the dream I almost felt as if my waking life was the dream and my place was really in the cave. I remember the image, the sound, and that thought quite clearly. And I knew I could paint that scene from memory, as I made a mental snapshot from where I sat. I got up and slowly walked to the water, where I saw tiny objects swimming back and forth. The pale bodies of blind fish absorbed the dim light and turned into small beacons gliding through the dark water.

"You've come back!" I heard a familiar, surprised voice from the other side of the candles and spun around to find my former companion.

"Father Moran?"

"Yes," he laughed. "How have you been, Michelle?"

"Very busy," I said as I walked back to the bench. "I've joined a new church. It's Christian, but not Catholic. Sorry. But its main focus is social justice. I love it there. It's been a guiding light to me."

"Then you've found a suitable place for yourself. No need for apologies," he insisted.

"It does suit me," I agreed. "I've been painting portraits of the homeless, too. They're mostly people I've met at a local shelter where I volunteer. I never thought my paintings would benefit others, but they did at a fundraiser for the shelter. One thing leads to another, it seems. I even have a gallery showing my art work. It's all happened so fast my head is still spinning! Oh, and the latest development is that Angel and I are closer, shall we say, we're more than friends now," I sighed.

"I could tell you had a close bond with him. That's good. I think he would be a grand partner for you."

"And how have you been, Father?" I asked, suddenly realizing I missed his humor and his wisdom.

He stood up, stretched, and sat back down. "Oh, I've been quite busy in my parish. But I dream myself back here now and then. I think the retreat was probably my last physical visit to this place. It's time for younger people to have their turns and pray for the things they care deeply about."

"Was the retreat successful, in terms of having your prayers answered?" I asked the man who sat before me, though he seemed to float in the subtle light. He no longer wore his white windbreaker, which had given him form in the dark surroundings.

He hesitated before answering. "In many ways it was a success. But it may take years for our prayers to make a difference. They must be followed by more prayer and deliberate actions, a concerted effort by many. But I believe the process has begun," he nodded with conviction.

"That sounds positive. I often wonder how powerful prayer can be. How much of change is effort and how much of it is prayer? Do you believe prayer can save this violent world of ours, Father?" I hoped his answer would be yes, but I had my doubts.

He looked away and shook his head. "I can't answer that question. But I believe if not for prayer the world would surely have been blown to bits by now. Humanity has that capability, you know. And it could still happen." That was a chilling thought. "When one enters this cave, one is given an opportunity, and a responsibility. We're reminded of the good that can be accomplished, of what we are capable of doing to elevate the planet in a spiritual way. And there are others who share our vision. Surely you've found occasions to help those in need, but one must be open to the effort." He shook his head and sighed. "Sadly, if people don't care about those in their own communities they'll have no interest in helping those on the other side of the world. Still, it happens occasionally and people from around the world join together over a common cause. In your case, being in a social justice church, you could do something every day, if only there were time to do it all," he laughed with a sad tone in his voice.

He was right, of course. "All I had to do was say 'yes' once and that's how I got involved with feeding the homeless. I find the work very satisfying. One of our latest projects at church is giving sanctuary to human rights workers who are at risk in their own countries."

He nodded and said, "They're homeless, too. There are more refugees now than most people realize. That's a particularly tragic form of homelessness, people who had homes and lives and countries, all brutally taken from them. They must leave all that has meaning behind with no certain future."

I thought of them, the streams of refugees pouring into camps not knowing what to expect next, as well as those coming into our own community searching for a future among strangers. The photograph of a young woman carrying her baby that I'd seen in the City of Darkness flashed through my memory then. I wondered if I could paint these refugees, too. "We're such a tragic world, Father. How do we break the patterns of poverty and war?"

"You're not very sleepy, Michelle. You're thinking of difficult questions tonight," he laughed. "Most people are too busy living their own lives to even think about that. But for those who have the extra income or time, why not share it? Money can be a powerful tool if applied to a place of need. And volunteers can soothe the pain of others as you have. Keep following your opportunities, my friend. They're there for a reason. But what has brought you here tonight?" he finally asked.

"Another opportunity, Father. I'm trying to remember what the cave looks like so I can paint scenes from it to illustrate a book of poetry for Berta Corelli," I explained.

"I don't know her work, I'm afraid. I take it she's been here then, if she wants you to do research here. Does she want you to paint *this* cave?" He sounded apprehensive.

"She'll never name it specifically. She wants the images to match her word descriptions. She's trying to sell the idea to Cueva Press and that's why she wants a painting as a sample. But I'll use a wash technique to abstract the details of the cave," I promised him. "Besides, that's the only way Cueva would let her do it. Her book's message will be that even the darkest, most remote place can hold the promise of hope and grace. Those who know the cave may recognize it in the book, and that's meant to be encouraging for them."

Then he seemed distracted. "I hear my alarm going off. I must be going. It's time for me to awaken and prepare to say mass. Now you can study this space before you leave this dream. It's wonderful to see you. I hope we find ourselves in the same dream again, Michelle."

"I hope so, too, Father Moran." Before I said his name, he disappeared back into the waking world. I turned to the pool and took a close look again, trying to memorize its contours and light patterns against the shadow. After that, the waterfall's rhythmic sound put me into a deeper sleep with no more dreams.

19

I woke up a little earlier than usual that morning and went to my drawing board to sketch and make notes about the pool in the cave. I had an image in my mind of how I could blur it, but still make it specific enough for the person reading the words to imagine it. And that blurring, I suddenly realized, would make the painting more dreamlike in a conventional way. I knew it would work for Berta's book.

I called her a couple days after I'd completed three paintings of the pool and its surrounding area. We met the next night in a café that was halfway between our homes. As I pulled the watercolor paintings out and laid them on the small table I could tell she was pleased.

"Yes," she said. "All of these are wonderful. This is exactly what I had in mind! I knew you could do this, Michelle, but these are even more masterful than I hoped they'd be." She smiled as she traced the path of water into the pool with her finger.

"I'm glad you like them, Berta. They were fun to do, something different for me. My other paintings are much more specific. It felt good to loosen up a bit. And I think the images do resonate with your words. They're dark, yet there are these bright fish swimming through the darkness like the pieces of hope in your poem."

She smiled. "I want the message to be subtle and simple, but very powerful. I want it to inspire people to think and to dream of what could be. I think Cueva will have to say yes to us. And it will be an unusual and beautiful book. You'll be paid for your efforts, of course."

"That would be frosting on the cake! Any idea how many paintings you'll need?" I asked.

She weighed the question in her mind, moving her head back and forth. "If Cueva goes for the proposal, it would be about a dozen. Maybe a few more. I'm still writing, but I already have over forty poems on the cave to choose from. You won't be illustrating every one. It's more about creating a mood. We'll use interesting type and design for the poems themselves and the images will be interleafed with them. I'd like a beautiful cover, too, which may need another of your works. This is an unusual concept for a book of poems, but I think people will be drawn to the beauty of it. And the images will help readers to imagine a mysterious place," she smiled with a wink.

I was psyched. "I'm very interested in this project, Berta. I hope you're right about Cueva."

"I'll let you know as soon as I hear. Thanks to your efforts, I can include color copies of these images in my proposal."

"By the way, I mentioned it to my gallery and they were supportive," I said.

We talked a bit more about the project and shared a little of our experiences in the cave. And then I remembered a question I had had for a long time. "Berta, the poem 'Choosing to Live' reminds me of the dome in the cave. But there's a story there, too, of one person who didn't choose life, and another who did, who I think is you. Who was the person who died, if you don't mind me asking? If I'm getting too personal, just say so."

Her expression grew pensive, as if she were trying to go back to the time she'd written the poem years ago, before Max lost Anita in the auto accident. And then she drew back a bit, raised her chin and held it steady. "It goes back to a time when I was young. The other person was my boyfriend then. We both suffered from depression. It was as if his sickness fed mine and vice versa. We wallowed in it, bathed in our own negativity. It was quite sad, when I think back on it. We often talked about a double suicide, how romantic it would be, like Romeo and Juliet. We played with the idea, but there were occasions when it seemed more real. It would be a terribly dramatic end for both of us. We saw ourselves rising above the misery of this world to find relief in the next one together.

"But, thankfully, I'd made plans to go to Oaxaca with my cousins before the suicide pact came to pass. On my way there I thought the trip might be the last thing I did before making my big exit with Matthew. But one of my cousins had a dream about Teotenaca, so we went there when we found it really existed. Through unexpected circumstances, my cousins and I found the cave, went in, and I was changed completely. That experience brought me out of my depressive tendencies. Everyone who knew me couldn't believe I was the same person when I came back home. Thank God! The last thing I wanted to do was take my life!" She shook her head at the absurdity of the thought, then continued her story.

"I *had* to change. I was needed and that's why I teach. I want to instill a deeper insight of the world into my students so they can put that into their writing. More than a few are published authors, I'm happy to report. The drive to write and teach saved me. Unfortunately, I couldn't save Matthew," she sighed. Regret lingered in her eyes. "I tried to get him into therapy. But he decided to take his plunge into the afterlife without me. There are times when a situation is truly hopeless, but you still have to try to turn it around. I was deeply saddened by his death. I hope he found what he was seeking, but suicide is a seriously negative act. My poem is about salvation, which I found for myself, but not for him."

And then I had something to share with her. "I have a friend who was depressed after the accidental death of his girlfriend. He blamed himself. And then I found your poem in a library book and gave it to him to read. I was afraid he was thinking of killing himself, too. But your poem worked. It reminded him that he had a lot he still wanted to do in life. There were other things he had to work through, of course, and that took years. But he's doing much better now, thanks to the love of a good woman."

She smiled. "The love of a good woman. Now *that* is a powerful force in the universe."

Berta stayed in touch with me as we waited to hear from Cueva Press. Their response was positive, but only on condition that she and I never reveal the location of the cave in the poems. Surely there would be questions about it, but she was already anticipating the answers as she wrote more cave poems. "I may become a fiction writer as a result of keeping this secret," she joked.

But the poems were beautiful and easy to illustrate in this looser, dreamy style that was emerging from my watercolors. I painted more than the book needed because I enjoyed doing them. I dreamt myself into the cave more often after that, but I never saw Father Moran again. Occasionally I heard movement or noticed lights in the distance along the aisles that projected from the dome. One time I lit candles on the ledges under the fire and water pictographs, then said a prayer. And once I whirled like a slow motion dervish below the dome, echoing the movement of the golden dust that spun above me.

It was around this time that I had another instance of the recurring dream I'd first experienced on the plane going to Mexico City. How far would the story go this time? My arms flailed in the darkness, as before, and again I saw the light coming from beyond the wall. The rocky surface gave way as my fingers tore into it. Then the bright light filled the space around me, blinding me as before. I fell and once again an outstretched hand lifted me up. It was the woman in the dazzling white clothes again. But who was she? Her white slacks and top reflected the glow of the swirling dust cloud that had slowly revealed her form, but not her face. Once again she gently embraced me and I hugged her, closing my eyes. The chill that shivered inside me faded away with the warmth of her body. I felt a flood of emotions in that embrace. I was loved and forgiven, filled with light and grace. There was a sense of unlimited energy and hope in that long moment. The warmth grew as if it were a fire burning inside me. It was passion, longing, a flame igniting a torch in a dark room.

Even though the intensity of my feelings subsided, the emotions lingered. But the mysterious woman was gone, as if the dust had carried her away with it. When I opened my eyes my arms were crisscrossed over my chest but I wasn't embracing anybody. As I oriented myself in the golden light that surrounded me, I realized I was facing toward the pile of rubble left by the crumbling wall, looking back into the dark room where I had been trapped. As I glanced down, I realized I was wearing the same clothes the woman wore, the white top and pants. And then it hit me, the most amazing revelation. I had become *her*, that loving woman! There was no trace of the old me now, the one who was trapped in that dark place. It was as if that fearful, anxious person I was had been absorbed into this new person I had become. Or perhaps the old me had been shed like a skin that no longer fit. But now I was someone else, a new Michelle, new and improved, pulled out of the darkness. I turned around and headed into the golden light in front of me. No longer blinding, it felt warm and comforting on my skin as it lit the unknown path that lay ahead. In the distance I heard a faint sound like a waterfall, or was it the laughter of children?

20

One busy work day I got to the cafeteria late in the lunch hour. Most tables were empty, but then I spotted Rick sitting alone and went over to keep him company. "Mind if I join you?" I asked.

"Please do." He looked really good, like he'd lost a few pounds and was wearing new clothes. But there was another thing, too. When I passed him in the hall, he was smiling more lately.

"Aren't you busy on Reading these days?" I asked, wondering how his stress level had lessened.

He nodded, "Insanely busy."

"But you look like you're not letting it get to you," I said. "You look calmer or something."

He laughed. "Maybe it's because I'm in love. When it's right, that makes everything easier." So that was it.

"Congratulations," I said. "You do seem happier, so I'm not surprised. Who is she, if I may ask?"

He reached into his wallet and took out a picture of a smiling woman with long brown hair. "Her name's Ramona. We met at the club. You remember when I told you about winning the lottery? One thing I did was buy a membership to a health club. Ramona and I met during an aerobics class there. Turned out we had a lot of common interests. I'm hoping she'll marry me someday," he said, holding her picture in his hand. "She's really special," he said as he stroked the edge of the photo.

"How wonderful for you, Rick. I'm happy to hear that," I said.

During the course of our conversation he got back to the subject of winning the lottery and sharing the money with charitable organizations. He was glad he'd done it, but then he discovered, as I had, what happens when you make a few donations. Before long you're on mailing lists for worthy causes of all sorts and the requests seem endless. I told him that I'd picked a few that I gave to regularly. And when I saw a request I couldn't say no to, I gave them something, too. "Every little bit helps," I said. "And look on the bright side, we'll never run out of address labels," I laughed. He rolled his eyes. The labels were regularly tucked in with the letters of request he'd received, too.

"Do you remember that ivy plant you gave me?" It was a thank you for my helping him figure out how to donate 5% of his lottery winnings. "It must really like the lighting in this building because it's extremely hardy," I told him. "I gave a few cuttings away and those did well, too. If you walk around our area you'll see little pots of ivy in many of the offices. People have been sharing it with each other. I overheard a sales rep the other day say, 'What's with all this ivy?' I had to laugh."

Rick laughed at the thought of all those plants being born from the one he gave me. But then his expression changed. He looked a little shocked. "You know Sarah Milkwood just gave me a little pot of ivy last week. She thought my office could use some green, she said. I wonder if..."

"Sarah? I gave her a cutting from that plant a while back."

"Isn't that weird?" he asked.

I smiled and said, "Your gift came back to you, Rick." He nodded and we both laughed at the irony of that. "And maybe in more than one way," I said, motioning at the photo of Ramona that sat next to his tray. He picked it up, shook his head and sighed.

"If that's true, it came back to me in spades."

21

I'd stayed in touch with Dar over the months since I'd left Teotenaca. She shared her poems, tales of Sunny's precocious adventures, photos of Reggie's recent paintings, and stories about a few of her guests and their experiences. It was wonderful to share what I was up to, also, including my newfound love for Angel, and my dreams. She was particularly interested in my paintings of the cave and when Berta's book would be coming out.

I continued to work on the muted cave images, though they played with my sense of reality at times. But then I was painfully reminded of the real world when I went to the shelter or listened to speakers at church or turned on the news. BBC News seemed to hold nothing back so I grew to prefer it over my local stations.

At this point, I'd become an official member of the Lakeview United Church of Christ. I attended classes with readings and discussions, but it was far less rigorous than the catechism classes from my young days of Catholicism. We read *A Private and Public Faith* by William Stringfellow and were urged to continue on our own by reading *The Cost of Discipleship* by Dietrich Bonhoeffer. There were five of us in the class with Rev. Horsley and we were presented and celebrated during a Sunday service. I felt honored as my name and abbreviated life story were read to the congregation. Angel was there, cheering me on, but he wasn't ready to join up himself.

Being a member of an activist congregation opened up my eyes to the issues behind the causes that people championed there. My consciousness was raised on many levels, some of which made the world even more frightening to me. Humankind had devised countless horrific ways of treating one another in an effort to keep power or feel powerful over the vulnerable. And we didn't spare the planet, either, in the quest for land, oil, or whatever resources we could exploit. Industrialization trumped the environment most times, it seemed. Cruelty was more commonplace across the world than I had realized. The enormity of this fact was paralyzing on one hand, but then I remembered the lessons I'd learned in the Cave of Dreams. Undermine the darkness with light whenever you can, even if the light seems small and insignificant. Like the ivy Rick had given me, I shared that light whenever I could. That's what we all did at Lakeview UCC. And there were times we could see it grow brighter, as our efforts changed policies and attitudes and touched the lives of others.

After completing the paintings for Berta, I went back to painting images of the homeless. In the area around my drawing board I'd laid out a few of the things I'd bought or found in Mexico as a reminder of my time there. I had a small stone from the trail along El Anhelo, a photo of all of us in front of the Sweet Dreams sign, as well as one of Dar, Reggie and Sunny, a painted ceramic cross I'd bought at the airport in Mexico City, and a small box containing the tiny *milagro*, shaped like an eye, that I'd found in the cave.

One day while I sat at the drawing board not sure what to do next on a painting, I glanced over at my little assembly of souvenirs. I had just placed a gardenia candle there the day before. I lit it and said a prayer for guidance, then sniffed the air as its fragrance was released. Gardenia always reminded me of Mexico. I lifted the lid of the box with the *milagro* inside it. Dar had retrieved it from my pocket right before she washed the clothes I'd worn in the Cave of Dreams. She'd wrapped it in thin, white paper and in all the time since then, I hadn't unwrapped it. But now I wanted to see it again. As I opened the folded paper, I was surprised to find some of the black oxidation had flaked off its surface to reveal silver underneath. Unlike the *milagros* I'd seen before, this wasn't a blend of silver with cheaper metals, but real silver, shiny and bright. That was impossible, I thought. The black surface would have to be polished with a cloth in order to be removed. But as I rubbed the *milagro* with my fingers, more of the black residue sloughed off in my hand, shedding like old skin. *Whoever bought the* milagro *was praying for vision*, I thought, looking at its abstract eye shape. All at once I realized that *I'd* received that gift. I found a silver chain and pulled it through the open circle at one end of the *milagro* and placed it around my neck. From then on I rarely took it off. It became a reminder of my gift of vision, a gift to be shared.

Then there was that intangible souvenir of the Cave of Dreams, the ache in my rib cage that meant someone nearby was in pain and I could help them. Like the black oxidation on the *milagro*, the intensity of that pain had eventually worn off. What remained was an occasional dull ache. But instead of an injury that had taken a long time to heal, I understood it as a tool to boost my awareness of other people's suffering. I must have learned the lesson because I'd become more empathetic, even intuitive, about such things. Because the tool was no longer needed, the pain had lifted, much to my relief.

My job was filled with its usual craziness, its tight deadlines and occasional long hours. But I was less stressed by it all when I thought about the real life and death struggles going on in the world. One co-worker called me "an island of calm in an ocean of chaos" and others came to me for advice on work matters, as well as personal ones. Gwen gave me a glowing review that resulted in a better raise than I'd expected. But then I took on more responsibility, too. I began supervising younger designers, but approached this new challenge as if I were their mentor. It was extremely satisfying to watch them grow in confidence and skill. It surprised me that even my job had taken on a dimension I hadn't foreseen.

And there was Angel, my dear friend and lover, my partner in faith. We had great discussions at Sunday brunch after church, often frequenting the neighborhood restaurants. He would share stories from his classes or an essay he'd read that fascinated him. I'd always meant to learn more from him, and now I was. I could tell he was happy to be able to discuss these things with an interested listener, too.

One day our discussion got me thinking about how to weave it all together, the common threads of the world's great and minor religions. When I asked him if that was possible he told me about a book called *A Global Ethic*, which was a declaration published by the Parliament of the World's Religions. "I can loan you my book," he said. "It gives the background and lists the principles. It was adopted when members of many religions met in Chicago in 1993. It's a minimal ethic that they could all agree on."

I took him up on his offer and read the short book. There were echoes of the principles I knew from my own upbringing. But there were new insights, too. *How could anyone argue with this?* I wondered. Yet I just didn't know how the world could change so that people truly lived this way. It was an ideal, a way of shaping one's choices in life. But still, I took a few of the tenets and posted them from time to time on the walls inside and outside my cubicle. And I made them part of my signature in personal emails. At least I could share these wise words.

We make a commitment to respect life and dignity, individuality and diversity, so that every person is treated humanely, without exception.

We must have patience and acceptance. We must be able to forgive, learning from the past but never allowing ourselves to be enslaved by memories of hate. Opening our hearts to one another, we must sink our narrow differences for the cause of the world community, practicing a culture of solidarity and relatedness.

We must strive to be kind and generous.

We must move beyond the dominance of greed for power, prestige, money, and consumption to make a just and peaceful world. Earth cannot be changed for the better unless the consciousness of individuals is changed first.

When the human rights workers began coming, seeking sanctuary in apartments and homes made available by members of our congregation, these words took on a deeper meaning for me. Here were ordinary people who had put their lives at risk against intimidating forces. They were squeezed between rebels and paramilitaries, threatened by both drug lords and corrupt politicians. Their voices were silenced through arrest, torture, rape and even murder. They became martyrs because they sought fair payment for the coffee growers, peace for the quiet villages constantly raided by rebel and paramilitary forces alike, and the right to speak openly. I learned from them, too. There was gratitude in their eyes as we passed the peace in our Sunday service, but there was so much more that could not be spoken. Every time I came near them I would feel the dull ache in my side. I looked into their eyes and tried to pass on my own thoughts. *You are safe here with us. We love you. We will try to understand your pain. We will do what we can to make this your home, too.*

Many had lost friends and colleagues. By coming to the States they had saved their own lives, but they had lost their country, as well as everyone and everything familiar and meaningful. What had been gained? Perhaps nothing. But they'd resisted those who would crush them. They'd done what they could and there was honor and dignity in that.

One of the women was getting psychological assistance at the Chicago

Center for Victims of Torture. I asked a parishioner, a Latina woman named Silvia, if she knew what the woman had been through. "She hasn't told me directly, but I know what has happened to people during interrogation. Gang rape is not uncommon. Electric shock may be applied to the most sensitive parts of the body. I have seen scars, maybe from burns, on Antonia's arms. Yet she's fortunate she wasn't disappeared. But she has no country now and that is a terrible loss."

Refugees. Displaced persons. Exiles. They were homeless people trying to find a safe place in the world, a means of survival after waking from their real life nightmares in the City of Darkness. Now they began to invade my dreams. I saw the pain in their eyes, but in my dreams I began to see and understand what had caused that pain. I saw their stories unfolding before me along with the scars of their physical and emotional wounds. The faces of the homeless were replaced by these others from time to time. I began painting portraits of refugees, mostly women and children, from around the world. The colorful clothes of an African woman were contrasted with the bare bones of shelters behind her. A Middle Eastern woman with a black head scarf and dress held her young son in a protective embrace so that only his face, mostly his frightened eyes, could be seen. There were people of all races who came to me in my dreams, all of them living away from their homes in refugee camps. Sometimes I cried as I painted them and my tears bled into the paint or onto the paper. *These paintings have a terrible beauty*, I thought. And Max agreed when I brought them to his loft.

"Have you shown these to your gallery?" he asked.

"Not yet. I'm not sure what to do with them or if the gallery will take them. They're disturbing, yet it's cathartic for me to do them. I'm seeing these people in my dreams now. I have to paint them," I explained.

"They're incredible images," Max said, shaking his head. "Have you thought about going bigger or working in oil or acrylic instead of watercolor?"

"I've become really comfortable with watercolor and I don't have a lot of room to work bigger in my apartment. But I've thought about it," I admitted, though it had been a long time since I'd painted on canvas.

He looked into the air past me. "If you wanted to set up a small studio, I probably could find enough space here. You wouldn't have to pay me anything. I'm buying part of the loft next door. There are two of us buying it and we're going to split it between us. So I'll have more space in a few months."

I couldn't believe his offer! "That's incredibly generous of you, Max," I gasped.

"As an artist you're growing by leaps and bounds. I hate to see you confined to a space that can't accommodate that. So now you really have something to think about," he laughed.

"Boy, do I! But it's a wonderful thing." I could hear myself choking up a bit. I closed my eyes and buried my face in his shirt as I hugged my tall friend. He hugged back, then made another observation.

"We've both come a long way since Mexico," he said, squeezing my shoulder. "My life keeps unfolding in ways I never expected, especially since Maggie and I got together. She's the biggest blessing I've ever known."

He shared his work with me, too. He'd been busy photographing her in his studio, but the photos he'd taken in Mexico were pure magic. Among them was one he'd forgotten in the pile of matted pieces. It was me, released just seconds before from the Cave of Dreams.

"I look terrible!" I said in shock. "You're not putting this in the show, I hope."

"I promise not to show this one. Here, you should have this," he said, handing it to me. "But why wouldn't you look dirty and bewildered after all you went through in there? For us it was an incredible moment of relief to see you at all. To us you looked absolutely beautiful." Now Max became the teary-eyed one. "It was hard to buy that weird story about the cave Reggie and Dar told us when we arrived. But it turned out to be true and it helped restore my faith in possibility. The world may get wackier every day, but I'm less of a cynic than I used to be," he smiled.

I looked at his photos of Maggie spread out on the worktable in his studio. "These are images taken by a man in love. How can anyone be a cynic when they're as happy as you are?" I commented.

He just nodded in agreement and smiled. "Touché." Then he handed me an invitation to a gallery opening.

"Be there or be rectangular," he said. "Take one for Angel, too."

"'The Maggie Show'?" I asked as I read the title.

"'As well as other recent photographs,'" he added.

"You didn't tell me you were having a gallery show so soon! Angel and I will be at the opening. Count on it."

"I am," he chuckled.

22

I spent part of the next weekend at Angel's place. I brought my sketchbook and got to work while he graded papers. The view from his front window inspired me to try my hand at urban landscapes. I could see a portion of the neighborhood from the fourth floor and below to the busy street. It was different than drawing nature. Instead of soft, curving lines I drew straight, squared off ones. It was good practice for me.

As we were pulling a meal together that afternoon I noticed a new postcard on his refrigerator door. The dark background surrounded columns of round, stained glass windows. I pointed to it and said, "Where is that?"

"It's somewhere I have to go one day, Saint-Chappelle in Paris, the church of King Louis IX, also known as Saint Louis. It's historical, but it's mostly known for those windows. They are beautiful, aren't they?" he asked.

"Yes. I haven't been there, either, but I'd love to go to Paris one day," I sighed. "There are lots of museums, and churches, of course, and wine and chocolate. So who went to Paris?"

He smiled slyly and said, "Go ahead and read it. You'll be surprised when you see what it says," he added.

I moved the round black magnet and took down the card. The date was a couple weeks earlier and it was signed "Celia." If I had hackles, they would have gone up. I looked at Angel, but he smiled and shook his head.

I read it out loud, but stopped periodically so I could take in the enormity of her words.

Dearest Angel,
I'm sorry I haven't written or called, but things have taken an unexpected turn. I've made a major life commitment. You may not hear from me again. On my last trip to New York I ran into a dear old friend, Charles Montgomery. He has a successful law practice. I shared my writing, including my latest play.

He said he first fell in love with the play, and then with the playwright. We had a whirlwind romance and decided to marry. We're in Paris on our honeymoon as I write this. I won't be back to Chicago, except to close my apartment. Please don't think badly of me. You know I'm impetuous. You'll always be dear to me, but I'm Mrs. Montgomery now. Adieu, sweet Angel. I wish you the best in life.
   Celia

When I looked up he was still smiling, but his eyes were sad. "How did this make you feel?" I asked.

"It was a shock at first. But then I thought something was going on in New York for a while. It may not have been this Charles guy, but I think Celia had quite the social life there. In the end, I'm not surprised. But I am disappointed. She could have called or emailed me. Sending a postcard from Paris while she's on her honeymoon is just mean. I wonder if anyone else got one of these," he said, sounding a little angry.

"If what you say is true, you're probably not the only one, my friend. I'm sorry she hurt you." I meant that, but at the same time I felt like the Celia shoe had finally dropped and a shadow had been lifted from my life. I'd dreaded the possibility that she might show up at Angel's door, ready to claim him again. I was grateful not to have to think about that anymore. I put the postcard back on the fridge, turned and wrapped my arms around him. He kissed the top of my head and embraced me, then said, "At least she wished me 'the best in life' and she let me know what happened to her. That's civil. But she was one frustrating woman, I have to say. I could never measure up to her economic standards like Charles Montgomery can. That's really what that's about, if you read between the lines."

So that was where the real hurt was hitting him, that he didn't measure up to her class standards, that he just wasn't good enough in her mind. She was so wrong! I tried to divert that thought. "Hey now, you don't have to be rich to go to Paris, señor. I hear you can get great rates these days, if you look online. Maybe we'll make it there yet. I would love that."

"Me, too," he said. I could tell he was looking at the postcard.

"Angel, I can't speak for Celia, but in my opinion you're a brilliant, fascinating and very sexy man. She may have taste on one level, but she missed the boat when she let you go." But, of course, I was glad she had.

"Actually, she couldn't have done me a better favor," he said, and then he kissed me on the forehead and proclaimed, "I already have the best in life, and that would be you."

23

Finding street parking in the city was always challenging, but during art openings it was doubly tough. I circled the Lenbach Gallery a couple times. No luck. So I gave up and parked three blocks away. But we were feeling a touch of spring at last, so I didn't mind the walk. I liked the suburb where I worked, but I missed the energy of downtown Chicago. I soaked it up along the streets of River North. When I passed people with wine glasses in hand I knew I was getting close.

There were two large rooms in the Lenbach Gallery. The wall leading to the one on the left bore an unfamiliar name in oversized type, "Thomas O'Neill," with the smaller title, "Recent Paintings." The canvas below his name was abstract with a complicated web of paint blobs and lines that reminded me of a map. Then I read the wall to the right. "Max DeBoer: The Maggie Show" it said in large red letters with "and other recent photographs from Mexico" as its subtitle. I felt right at home with the image that hung there of Maggie conversing with the goats at Sweet Dreams, including ones I'd milked. The large photo gave me the first wave of déjà vu. But the rest of Max's work gave me that same goose-bumpy feeling. Here was Maggie in her black practice skirt, her back against the red hen house while brown chickens cavorted close to her bare feet. And in the grove of musical chimes and bells Max had photographed her in black and white from above as she lay on a wooden bench near the ashes of a campfire, her hand masking her eyes from the sun. In another, the first red rays of dawn illuminated her face and a shoulder draped with a black shawl embroidered with a red rose. Salvador had given her that shawl the night of the salon. And next to that photo was another close-up of the flamenco-dancing Maggie, arms writhing on either side of her stern face with its upturned eyebrows and down-turned eyes. Max had found his muse, and her name, indeed, was Maggie. His photographs were character studies, laying out different aspects of her personality while capturing her energetic beauty.

But there were other memorable images as well: the mountain trail; the men with grimy faces working on the road; Teotenacan landscapes; a portrait of Sunny Howard proudly holding out her first clay pot; the Zócalo in the city of Oaxaca and the remains of the ancient city of Monté Albán.

Max held court in a corner of the gallery, surrounded by a throng of well-wishers. I tried waving but I knew he couldn't see me. I walked around a wall to view the remainder of the show and nearly bumped into Maggie herself. It was an odd, startling sensation after seeing her face and body displayed all over the walls of the gallery.

"Michelle!"

"Maggie!"

We caught our breaths and then hugged each other, laughing. "It's good to see you," she said. "I was beginning to wonder if we would."

"Sorry I'm so late. I got stuck at work and the traffic was bad getting down here. And don't get me started on the parking," I laughed.

"Well, now that you're here, how about a glass of wine?" she smiled with a gentle hand on my back. We walked to a table where I was given a plastic cup filled with a nondescript white wine that hit the spot. My tense muscles relaxed.

"This is a wonderful show, Maggie. I'm impressed!" I said.

"Did you see the red dots?" she asked with an excited voice. "Max has already sold three of my pictures! And they're selling the show's promotional poster with the goats. I've seen several people walk out of here with it. The gallery seems quite pleased," she smiled as she scanned the crowd.

A woman from behind me cried, "You must be Maggie!" Before I knew it, I was standing on the outskirts of a conversation. My friend shrugged her shoulders helplessly at me so I smiled and walked back into the show to try to talk to Max. I waited in what seemed a line to get my chance when I felt a friendly tap on my shoulder. It was Angel, who greeted me with a kiss.

"I haven't had a chance to talk to him, either," he said, looking toward the crowd that surrounded Max. "I'm glad it's going well for him. Maggie is already stunning, but he's a master at bringing out her dramatic side."

"It's an amazing show," I agreed. "It brings back Mexico for me. There are lots of memories here."

"How is that for you?" he asked.

"It's good. It makes it real again," I realized as I said it. "Sometimes I wonder if all of it was just another fantastic dream. But here's the proof that it wasn't. Looking at these images makes it seem like nothing has changed from that moment until now."

"And yet everything has," he smiled.

"And it continues to," I added. "Every week brings a new adventure. There's talk of bringing me up to a higher level at work. I think Gwen will be the next director, so they may be grooming me to replace her as a manager. Do you believe it?"

He smiled and shrugged, "Why not? Anything seems possible with you."

"Anything, huh? Just call me Wonder Woman then."

"It's bigger than that," he smiled.

"It's way bigger than I am. It scares me sometimes!" I whispered.

"You know that old saying about God doesn't give us more than we can bear?" he asked.

"I've heard it, but I'm not sure I believe it." He put his arms around my waist and brought me closer. Our conversation had suddenly become intimate and quiet despite the activity around us.

"You can bear more than you think, Michelle. I see you do it over and over." His expression got more serious. "On the way here I discovered something that'll stir up those Mexican memories even more. It's right out of the dreams you had in El Anhelo."

"What are you talking about, Angel? Where?" I demanded.

"I'd rather show you than try to explain," is all he would divulge. *Why the mystery?* I wondered.

"Then show me," I urged, raising my voice. We looked back at Max, who had been joined by Maggie. The gallery visitors were still hovering.

"They're not going anywhere," he said, stating the obvious. "It's just around the corner. We won't be long." He held my hand and said, "If you see what it is and you don't want to go further, we won't."

Now he was scaring me. "Show me and I'll decide. *Please*," I insisted.

Max's show was on the second floor of a large building with three levels of galleries. We walked down and entered the stream of people that led up and down the stairs. All the galleries had openings that night. I felt a wet splash against my hand and wasn't sure if it was my wine or someone else's. We walked out the main entrance and stood on the street. The warmer weather had brought a lot of people out that night.

"Max isn't the only photographer having an opening tonight," Angel informed me. "You must have come from another direction or you would have seen that. It's not far, over this way." We walked around to the next street and a few storefronts down. Then Angel stopped and said, "Here."

Right in front of me, on street level, was a window displaying a large black and white photograph of a woman holding a baby. It reminded me of my own recent work of refugee mothers with their children, and was reminiscent of a Madonna and child pose. The woman looked like a Central American *indígena*, poor and in desperate straits. I saw the concern and love she had for her child, who was wrapped in the same shawl that surrounded her head. The image was darkly beautiful. Above it, against a white backdrop, were the huge maroon letters that formed the name of the photographer, Rodrigo Guzmán. I had carefully carried what remained of my wine all the way there. But now the plastic glass dropped from my hand, splattering wine across my leg and the sidewalk.

"Oh my God!" I gasped in disbelief and Angel asked if I was all right. I wasn't sure how to answer. I just stared at the photograph. I heard him pick up my cup and throw it in a nearby receptacle. But he seemed far away, until I heard his voice next to me.

"We don't have to go any further, Michelle, but I thought you should know about this," he said.

"Guzmán! He's right out of my City of Darkness dream! I knew his work was real, but I didn't know he was coming to Chicago." I must have been too busy to pay attention to such things.

"Want to go in?" Angel gently asked.

"I think I have to," I replied. I knew I had to.

"But this time you're not alone, señorita," he reminded me. "You've got back-up!"

I smiled at that thought and turned to him. "I love you, Angel."

"I love you, too," he whispered, kissing my cheek.

We entered the door to the Andrea Gallery and stopped at the receptionist's desk. On a counter there were copies of a price list for Guzmán's work and a biography in a binder with photos of him in the field shooting images of people around the world. I examined each of these elements trying to get my bearings, trying to understand more about this man. The two people behind the counter were talking about him.

"His work is so moving, even disturbing, yet it's so beautifully photographed. How did you get him to come here?" a young man in a gray shirt and black tie asked.

"Actually, he approached me," the woman answered. "Can you believe it? He said he wanted to find a place to show in Chicago. That was fortuitous for me. His work is hard to forget."

Then she turned her attention to us. "Good evening. Welcome to Andrea Gallery. Have you been here before?" she asked. We shook our heads that we hadn't. "We are primarily a photography gallery. We bring in work from the Americas that you won't see anywhere else in the Midwest. You seem very interested in Guzmán, miss. Do you know his work?" she asked me.

"Yes. I saw it in Mexico," I explained. "But I don't know anything about him."

"He's a fascinating character," she said. "He was born in Mexico, but lived in Los Angeles for a time. He's been everywhere, it seems, all over the world. He lives near Mexico City now, but he's here tonight so you can meet him. You'll recognize him from this photo," she said, pointing to a page of his biography.

I already had. He was the same man who had been in my dream, the same man I encountered inside a photograph of young Afro-Colombian refugees on the road. *If only you knew*, I thought to myself as the woman continued.

"He brought copies of his latest book." She reached over to a place further down the counter and picked up a slim volume with a photo reproduced on the cover. The title was *In Search of Tomorrow*. "Here's a copy you can look through. We've sold quite a few tonight." Angel and I turned each page together. I recognized the images. They were the same framed photographs that hung in the Crossroads Gallery on the edge of the City of Darkness.

"I agree with what you said," I told the woman. "These aren't easy to forget. I remember them quite vividly. I'd like to buy this book," I said as I opened my purse and curled away the bills from inside my wallet.

"Most certainly, miss," she said, taking the money and giving me change back. "I'm sure he'd be happy to sign it for you. If you need a bag for it, stop by as you're leaving," she smiled. "I'm Andrea, by the way, if you have any questions. We have a mailing list, also."

"I'll think about that," I said, motioning to the list. "Thank you, Andrea." I knew my tone of voice was flat, but I couldn't help it.

"Thank you," Angel echoed, but with more enthusiasm, and then we walked a short distance away. I opened the book to see who the publisher was.

"It's Cueva Press," I told Angel. That made all the difference in the world.

"Do you still want to go in?" he asked in that serious tone again.

"Oh, I must." I was anxious to see the work again. But when I looked at the first image, it shot through me like lightning. I turned to Angel in disbelief after scanning the rest of the photos. "It's as if I'm back in the dream. This gallery is set up exactly like the Crossroads Gallery was, with the same images in the same places. It's all coming back." It was surreal, as if reality and my dreams were intersecting. But this exhibit couldn't go as far as the dream had. "There's one photo I *have* to find," I said as I plunged into the show. I walked through, peeking over shoulders and in between people. But in an unattended corner, just as it had been in my dream, I found it, the photo taken in Colombia of the desperate young woman holding a baby and fleeing in terror, the young man at her side. Seeing Max's photos from Mexico had brought back memories of the physical world I'd experienced on our trip to Teotenaca. But these images put me back into a realm my friends couldn't understand. Seeing them disoriented me. But the photo of the young woman especially held me in its power. I tried to explain to Angel.

"Do you remember the photo I said I was pulled into? This is it! This is the one. Look at her face. She's so young to be put through such an ordeal, and with a child," I said, gesturing toward the tiny form. But I was so overwhelmed I began to cry. No. I began to weep! I saw the horrors of the world up close again and I couldn't look away. Poor Angel tried to console me, but I also felt him trying to push me gently in another direction.

"I'm sorry, Michelle. I shouldn't have brought you here," he apologized.

"No! It's all right. But I can't leave yet!" I stood my ground. He loosened his grip on my shoulders, then reached around my back to support me. We stood staring at the photo, which blurred through my tears.

"Excuse me, madam, but are you all right?" a man with a slight accent asked. I blinked several times so I could focus and saw it was Rodrigo Guzmán himself, sounding much kinder than he had in my dream. "My work can be difficult to view, I know. But what has upset you so?"

I tried to speak. I sounded awkward to myself. "It's just that. Oh. I've seen this photo before and this young woman's face, her circumstances, were really disturbing to me then. And they still are. It's as if I'm connecting with her emotions, what she was feeling when you snapped the picture," I tried to explain.

He seemed puzzled. "And where did you see this before? I've never shown these photos in Chicago until now."

"In Mexico." What else could I say?

"Ah. And where in Mexico, might I ask?" He and Angel looked at me, both wondering how I would reply. I could sense my friend's anxiety for me.

"This may sound strange, but I'll be honest. I saw this photo in a dream I had while I was staying in a town called Teotenaca. Do you know of it?" I asked, taking over the role of inquisitor. I was getting my bearings again.

His expression changed and I could tell he knew of it. He looked more intently at my face as if he were trying to place it. "Yes," he said quietly. "I was there a long time ago. And I had dreams there, too. I still have them. And now, I am wondering if I know you from a dream I had last year. But if you were that person, you looked very different then. Do you know what I mean?" he asked, shifting the questioning again.

"Yes. My hair was longer then. It would have been tangled. I would have looked dirty."

"And what else?" he asked gently.

"I would have looked gruesome, bloodied," I said, remembering what had happened in the dream right before I found the gallery.

He nodded, "Yes. I remember you now. And where did we meet in the dream?"

I turned back to the photo. "Inside of this photograph. Everything was life-sized, three-dimensional, black and white except for you and me."

"That is how I remember it, too," he said softly. "I was talking to you and then you disappeared. What happened to you?"

"You said something like, 'What if this girl were you?' and then I found myself outside the photograph looking at my face on her body. After that I woke up. It was horrible! I was sweating and shaking. I felt so cold in the cave after that dream."

When I mentioned the cave Guzmán pulled back a little. Then he came closer and almost whispered in my ear. "For those who dream in the heart of El Anhelo, the world is a different place upon waking. Have you found your voice, your vision?" he asked. "It hasn't been long for you."

"It's becoming clearer to me all the time. Yes," I nodded.

Angel hadn't said anything, as if he were eavesdropping on a private conversation. But he added to my reply. "She's touched many lives since then," he told Guzmán, who smiled.

"Good. Perhaps we will meet again in a dream. And your name is?"

"Michelle Hardtke. I'm stunned that we're having this conversation," I almost laughed.

"It surprises me, too," he said with a smile. "But I'm glad to meet you, Michelle. You look much better than you did in the dream," he whispered. We both laughed with relief. "Here, let me sign your book." He took a pen from his pocket and opened to the title page. I helped him to steady the book while I spelled my name. Then he wrote a few lines in Spanish and handed it back to me.

"It is a special message to you. Thank you for coming. It is always an honor to meet someone who knows the Cave of Dreams," he smiled, looking me in the eye for another few seconds.

"My honor as well," I smiled. "Thank you for your incredible work."

Then he looked away and saw people standing near us who obviously wanted to talk with him, too. I wondered how much of our conversation they'd heard, or understood.

"I must go," he said. "Vaya con Díos, mi amiga. Take good care of her, señor," he told Angel. "She will bear much on her slender shoulders," he whispered to my companion.

When he turned away from us, he was surrounded by a crowd, as Maggie and Max had been. We walked away unnoticed. I opened the book as we stepped outside the gallery and stood on the street.

"What did he write?" Angel asked.

"I'm not sure if I'm getting it right. It's in Spanish. What does it say?" I turned the book so he could see it next to a nearby streetlight.

"To Michelle Hardtke,

"From one dreamer to another. Always remember, we do the work of a loving God.

"Your friend,

"Rodrigo Guzmán."

24

After leaving the Guzmán show, we returned to the Lenbach Gallery where the crowds around Max and Maggie had dwindled. I had hoped we could get together with our friends after the opening, but they were obligated to go out with the gallery owner and his friends. "We would invite you, too," Max said, "but this is all about schmoozing. It's business and I don't think it will be much fun."

"I've got an idea," Maggie said. "Let's meet for dinner tomorrow night to celebrate. We'll make Max pay, since he sold so many pieces tonight."

"I'm not a rich man. Yet," he replied. "When I am I'll take us all out on the town."

Then he noticed the book in my hand. "What did you buy, Michelle?"

The cover said it all. "Oh my God!" Max and Maggie said, almost in unison. When I had described the dream to them in Mexico, Max confirmed that Guzmán existed and was a Mexican photographer. Then he added, "I was so busy pulling my show together I didn't even notice he had an opening, too. I'd heard he was coming to town and meant to tell you, but I didn't know when. Sorry."

"She met him," Angel said. "It was a heavy dose of weird reality."

"I'd rather talk about it tomorrow," I said dully. We decided to meet at a tapas place in Logan Square. Maggie would make the reservation and call us to confirm the time.

Back in the car, I was exhausted and hungry, so I let Angel drive. He'd come from school via public transportation. Angel suggested a Thai restaurant I hadn't tried before. He pulled out of the tight parking space and drove to the expressway. We sat in silence with only the radio playing. It was a classic rock station I'd turned on to keep me awake through the slow, heavy traffic on the way to the gallery. They were playing "Imagine" by John Lennon. I'd heard it many times before, but the chorus took on an entirely new meaning. Yes, I was a dreamer, but like the song said, I wasn't the only one.

"From one dreamer to another," I whispered. "I forget that I'm *not* the only one. There are lots of us, all over the world: the Howards, Father Moran, Berta Corelli, Rodrigo Guzmán and the people of Teotenaca. That's comforting to remember." All of us cave dreamers were adding our light to the world, and waking it up.

"I'm glad you made that connection with Guzmán tonight, even if it was tough for you," he assured me. "You know I didn't go in the cave like you did, but my dreams are more vivid and memorable since we were in Teotenaca. I've been dreaming about the grove behind Sweet Dreams lately, that place with the campfire and chimes in the trees. It's become a dream 'sanctuary' for me. I always wake feeling rested after I dream myself there. It used to be rare for me to remember my dreams, but now it isn't."

"Fascinating!" I said. I had run into Father Moran in a dream and began to wonder if I could consciously do the same with Angel. "Maybe I'll visit you in the grove one of these nights," I laughed.

"You're on. Want to try tonight? That would be *really* fascinating if it worked," he mused.

"Do you think you can program your dream to go there?" I challenged him.

"No guarantees, but I'll give it a try," he promised.

At the Thai restaurant we were escorted to a table next to a fish tank that served as a room divider. After we ordered I noticed that the frilly gold and black fish gliding through the tank behind Angel had huge, protruding eyes. *Google eyes*, I thought. *So that's what that means.* Just looking at them swish their extravagant tails made me laugh out loud.

"Is it what I'm wearing?" Angel asked, looking from side to side at his jacket.

"No, silly. It's those fish behind you." He turned to see what I meant and started laughing, too. It was a relief to laugh. I suddenly felt so relaxed I could have put my head on the table and gone to sleep right there. But I couldn't stop staring at those amazing fish. They were such a contrast from the blind cave fish I'd painted. Unlike them, these city fish could see quite well, especially since their tank was lit from above.

"Ah, Michelle, it's good to hear you laugh again," Angel said while exhaling slowly. "Seeing your reaction to that photograph gave me a glimpse into what your time in El Anhelo must have been like. Those dreams were intense to have left such a strong memory." He stroked my hand with his thumb.

"I don't know what came over me in that gallery tonight," I said. "Seeing everything laid out the way it had been in my dream was strange. It made everything in the City of Darkness seem more real. It all came out of the conscious world, after all. That woman walking along the road in Colombia was real, her situation, her suffering, the baby in her arms, it was all real." I almost started crying again, but took a deep breath to get control of my emotions.

"Most of us are numb to the suffering we see on the news every day," he said while I exhaled. "But I think for you there's more insight and concern. You understand it on an empathic level, so it must be difficult to watch at times."

"BBC News isn't sanitized like U.S. news is. The suffering is more obvious. Sometimes I cry, but most of the time I get angry. And then I write emails or donate money because of what I've seen. Or I paint. It's a great motivator for that," I nodded.

Angel smiled and enveloped my hand in his. "I have to tell you that I always thought you were special, Michelle, well before we went to Mexico and you went down the rabbit hole into El Anhelo's cave. I want you to know that. Even if we had never gone to Teotenaca, even if you came back exactly the same person you were before, with the same goals in life you had before all this happened, you would still be a special person to me. But because of Teotenaca, you've become *very* special to me, an exceptional person."

His honesty touched my heart. "I could say the same of you, Angel. You really are my best friend. You know my secrets and understand my fears better than anyone else. And I know they're safe with you. *I* feel safe with you."

"I want us always to be the best of friends," he said, "no matter where our lives take us, rabbit holes and missteps included."

My friends and I were always big on toasting. When our jasmine tea arrived, I raised my blue and white cup and said, "To us, two of the best friends the world will ever know," and I gingerly clinked my hot cup against his.

"Salud," he smiled and slowly sipped his tea, then raised his cup.

"I'd like to make a toast, too," he said. "To my best friend, who also happens to be the best lover I could wish for. I hope we're lovers and friends for a long time to come," he winked.

"Cheers," I said as we clinked cups again and sipped.

More and more I saw a mischievous side to his personality, with a hint of the Latin lover thrown in for good measure. I had always appreciated his intellect, his kind and gentle ways. But this other layer was seductive and fun. I had truly fallen in love with him as I'd gotten to know him intimately.

"You're thinking about something important," he smiled. "I can tell."

"Maybe," I said, afraid that I had a smirk on my face. "What are *you* thinking about?" I asked.

He looked around the room in a clockwise motion, then simply said, "You," as his eyes linked with mine again. "We spend a lot of time together on the weekends," he began. "Frankly, it feels like that's the way things should be, whether we're at your place or mine. Do you agree?"

I smiled and said, "I do. You're incredibly supportive, and a much better cook than I am. We give each other space when we need it. I think we have a trusting, healthy relationship. Do *you* agree?"

He smiled, laughed a little, and picked up my left hand. Then he bent his head down and kissed it. "Absolutely," he asserted. "So what should our next step be? Have you ever thought about moving in with the man you love?"

That was a question that Neil had raised not long before we broke up. I wasn't ready with an answer then, but this time I was. "Yes, I've thought about it before. If I were twenty-five I'd be more inclined to do it. But I'm in my thirties now. At this age, I would want more of a commitment. And I'm hoping to still have children one of these days."

He looked down at my hand and kissed my ring finger. "I understand," was all he said as he put my hand back on the table. Then he picked up his teacup and didn't say anything more. Our conversation had hit a big bump in the road.

"Angel, my dear Angel, I'm fine with where we are right now," I said, stroking his arm. "There's no rush to do anything. Are you all right with that?"

He smiled gently and whispered, "I am. For now."

The waitress stopped by to ask how we were doing. I didn't want to say anything more about our relationship, but I vowed to dream myself into his "sanctuary" dream that night.

When we met on Friday nights we usually stayed overnight together.

But he had to meet with a colleague early the next morning. And I was taking care of my parents' cat while they were away, so I had to go home to feed him and keep him company. I drove Angel to a nearby train. He gave me a long hug in the car. Burying my face in his hair, I thought I smelled rainwater. He pulled away and kissed me on the mouth, and then the eyes. I didn't want him to leave, but he had to.

"Good night, my special friend," he said. "Perhaps I'll see you in my dreams tonight."

"Until then, good night, Angel." I waved as he disappeared past the door of the train station.

25

I was exhausted, exhilarated, happy and probably a little confused when I got home. Angel and I had known each other for over ten years, as friends. We'd been lovers for less than a year, and everything had changed between us. I knew in my heart that this was the man I wanted to share my life with, but on whose terms? He and Celia hadn't lived together or been engaged. I'd assumed it was her doing, her inconsistency, perhaps even her infidelity that hurt their future together. But now I was wondering if I'd dropped a bomb on our relationship. Maybe commitment wasn't in Angel's vocabulary, either. Yet from all he'd said, all the feelings he'd shared, I couldn't believe that. A little patience on both our parts would be necessary to let our future unfold in its own way, I thought.

As I walked through the door, I was greeted by Mr. Kitty, my parents' black and white cat. It seemed he was always hungry. First he rubbed against my leg, then looked toward the kitchen, then back at me. "I get it," I said. "I may be human, but I'm not stupid." So I spooned his favorite flavor of cat food onto his dish.

While he ate I walked into the small bedroom that had become my studio. I'd kept the door closed so Mr. Kitty wouldn't be nosing around everything or walking across my new painting with dirty paws. I sat down and turned on the light over my drawing board. The piece I was working on was a portrait of a homeless American mother and child. Perhaps it was time to focus on the youngest of the homeless, including refugees and evacuees, those who were the most vulnerable, after all. Their stories needed to be told, too. And what would *their* futures look like? The world was a scary place for most of us, but for them it had to be terrifying.

I thought about working on the painting despite the late hour, but my friend Mr. Kitty didn't want to be alone anymore. He scratched the door and meowed loudly. So I watched the news instead. My furry companion found my lap to be an excellent place to sleep. Once he got settled he looked up at me with dreamy green eyes. He always made me laugh. He was big and white with infrequent black splotches on his sides. The markings on top of his head resembled a bad toupee sitting slightly askew. He also appeared to wear a fake mustache with one end higher than the other, but on his chin was a perfect black goatee. I assured him that he was loved by rubbing his toupee. He purred and closed his eyes as BBC News began.

"Our top story tonight concerns recent terrorist attacks in the Middle East," the blonde woman in the black suit began. *More unnecessary death and destruction*, I thought. *Why can't there be news about peace breaking out in the world?* But it didn't get better after that. The rest of the news was the usual mayhem of social and political unrest, scandals, and a plague of natural disasters.

But right before the sports report they went to a story that gave me hope. It was probably just getting on the radar in England, but it appeared to be making an impact in other parts of the world already. I liked the way BBC News spent time on each story, bringing in experts to comment. This story was about three men traveling together around the world and speaking in mosques, churches, and synagogues. They were holy men from three religions: Islam, Christianity and Judaism. And they were from three different countries. They hadn't given their movement a name, but Christians were dubbing them "The Three Wise Men." They promoted religious and cultural tolerance and the peace that could grow from mutual acceptance. Each man spoke briefly on camera in quick snippets as another voice translated. The Pakistani Sufi said the same God made us all and would not want us to fight in his name. The Russian reformed rabbi said if we wanted God's favor we should work as brothers and sisters, not enemies, that it would be better to use our resources to help those in need, not waste them on weapons. The Christian priest from the Armenian Apostolic Church said the world had seen dark times before, that there was hope even in our time for a better world. But we must find commonalities, not resent each other because of our differences. Tolerance was our only hope, they all agreed.

They were sponsored by donations from all three religions, bringing their message to dangerous places. I marveled at such faith in action. Among their plans was a visit to the United Nations in New York and a stop in Washington, D.C. to meet with religious leaders. "Plans are being made for visits in several American cities as well, but they have not yet been disclosed," the newscaster said. *A road tour for peace*, I thought. *May God keep them safe!* There was footage of them speaking to congregations and at candlelight vigils in parks and stadiums. They'd spoken in the Middle East and Europe and were about to enter the U.S.

Then the newscaster began asking questions of a man whose image was streamed in by satellite. He was British, in his fifties, with gray hair, glasses and a friendly face. He represented the World Parliament of Religions.

"So, Geoffrey, what can you tell us about these 'Three Wise Men,' as they're called? How did this movement begin?" the newscaster inquired.

"Well, Fiona, it's a bit fuzzy, but it is rumored that all three of them met at an interfaith retreat in a remote location, possibly in Mexico or South America, possibly in the last year or two. But they're not confirming or denying this rumor. So no one is quite sure about its validity."

I gasped. Mr. Kitty screeched his protest as I stood up suddenly. I don't know how, but I knew in my heart where they'd met, at a retreat in the Cave of Dreams!

"Their philosophy is that the leaders of the world have failed to find peace through war and violence," Geoffrey continued. "Therefore, it's necessary for ordinary people to do what they can through dialogue and prayer. Since much of the world's conflict centers around religious differences, they feel tolerance and knowledge of other cultures are a powerful way to approach this problem."

Fiona asked more questions. "Do you think they're getting that message across to people, through these vigils and visits to congregations? How are people reacting?"

"They are getting many reactions. Those who believe there's only one true faith, and it happens to be their own, are skeptical, even outspoken against them. But there is clearly a groundswell of enthusiasm and interest among many people, particularly young people." He smiled and said, "It reminds me of how youth reacted in the past to Pope John Paul II and Pope Francis more recently. The three are having to book larger venues to accommodate their audiences."

And then Fiona asked a question that was on my mind, too. "What happens after they've gone from a city? Does that enthusiasm carry on afterward?"

"Yes," Geoffrey nodded. "I've heard of congregations from various faiths, including Buddhists, Hindus and others, I might add, who are conducting joint services in which they incorporate elements from each of their faiths. Often, they are praying for peace. I've attended a couple of these services and they're quite moving."

"Thank you, Geoffrey. We'll continue to watch The Three Wise Men, as they're popularly known, to see where their message takes them," Fiona ended.

I was dumbstruck! I just stood there. "The process has begun," Father Moran had said when I saw him again in my dream. Was this what he meant?

I turned off the TV and walked to the bookshelf where I kept my photo albums. I brought the one from Mexico back to the couch and opened it. I'd documented what I could: the city of Oaxaca, the ruins of Monte Albán, the grounds of the Sweet Dreams B&B, Sunny with the goats, a photo of Dar singing to her chickens as she fed them, the garden, Reggie's studio, the trail around El Anhelo, the church, the market, and my friends.

There was a photo of Angel smiling with a wide grin as he stood in front of El Anhelo. He looked full of joy, his hair long and tousled. I remembered that moment and why he was smiling. I wanted to think it was because I was back from the cave and safe. But it was also a kind of freedom that shone through his expression. He could be so serious, yet there was this other side that was open to life. He was an intellectual. But he was also an adventurer who wanted to explore the world and delve into its mysteries, especially the spiritual ones. I'd seen the months since the trip as my own personal journey, but now I realized it was Angel's journey, too. My partner in faith and love was keeping me safe at times, but pushing me, too, as he had at Guzmán's show.

I turned the page to see more photos from Mexico. There were my friends sitting in the grove and laughing as they stood beneath the large wind chime hanging in a tree. I pulled the photo out of the album and stared at it, trying to recall everything about that place. I closed my eyes and pictured it as I remembered the gentle breeze that blew through the tall trees, the sound of birds and bells, the dappled warmth of sunlight on my face. I put myself in the memory, too, and closed my eyes as I sat down on the couch.

All at once I felt a wave of fatigue come over me. It was the same sensation I had in the cave right before I dropped into my dreams. I stretched out on the couch and it didn't matter that the lights were still on. I fell asleep clutching the picture from the grove in my hands. And I began to dream. My mind raced from images of Maggie and the goats to Max surrounded by people in the gallery. He seemed to stand behind a high fence I couldn't get through, because I couldn't find the gate. I waved to him and to Maggie, who had also gone behind the fence.

And then I remembered Angel as I played back the scene at the Andrea Gallery. Here he was standing at my side as I talked to Guzmán, translating what the man wrote in my book, sitting in front of the aquarium with google-eyed fish floating behind him, hugging me goodbye in the car. I was swallowed whole by the thick, dark shadows of his hair. And then I smelled rain and felt the heavy air of a humid forest surrounding me. It was dark and filled with vines and tall trees. I had no idea where I was. I saw a light some distance ahead and slowly made my way toward it. As it got brighter I heard music, though it had no particular melody or rhythm, but sounded familiar.

As I reached an opening in the forest, I realized the light was the sun with its warm rays beating down on a clearing in the woods. I heard birds and chimes and bells and I knew I was in the grove behind Sweet Dreams. I could see the rough benches that surrounded the campfire, which was dully burning. I stepped out from the thick vines into the clearing and was alone. Walking to the benches, I sat down, closed my eyes and turned my head in the direction of the sun. The back of my eyelids turned a golden crimson. The sun bathed me in its warmth and I was at peace.

Then I heard another sound mixed in with the breeze, bird songs and chimes. Someone was breathing deeply nearby. I opened my eyes and looked around. A man sat opposite me who was doing exactly the same thing I was, sitting with his eyes closed, soaking up the sun.

Angel!

Had I summoned him into my dream or had I invaded his? He hadn't been there when I sat down. But it didn't matter, since he was sitting there now. I watched him for a time and then he mirrored what I had done by opening his eyes and looking directly at me. "Buenos días, señorita," he smiled. "You found me!"

"Or did you find me?" I smiled back.

"I think we found each other," he laughed. Then he got up, walked around the campfire and straddled the bench where I sat. I threw my leg over the bench so I could face him.

"So now that we've found each other in this dream, what are we going to do about it?" I asked. I knew it would be interesting, whatever it was.

"There are a few things that were on my mind as I fell asleep tonight," he said. "I'd like to share a little of that before anything else. Now don't be upset with me if I bring up an old girlfriend, but do you remember my attraction for Celia's passion?"

"Yes, the passion that left its mark on your cheek," I recalled.

"Ah yes, that painful memory," he winced. "Michelle, one reason I love you is because you're a loving person who is both beautifully passionate and passionately beautiful," he gushed.

"You're becoming a poet, Angel."

"A man in love is subject to becoming poetic," he smiled.

As we sat there, I studied him. He truly was "dreamy." I became more aware of the essence of who he was. His beautiful soul was shining through, revealing his own passions, including his love for me. Even though my activism hadn't rubbed off on him, I knew in that moment that he cared about the same things I did.

"Is a woman in love subject to becoming romantic in a place such as this?" he asked. He leaned a little closer. Picking up my left hand, he stroked his cheek with it, kissed the back of it, then turned my hand over and kissed my wrist. These were slow, wet kisses that climbed gradually toward my elbow. And with each one he pulled me closer. He stopped to say, "I'm waiting for your answer."

"What was the question again?" I asked, not wanting him to stop. "Oh. Yes, of course she is."

He let go of my hand. I wrapped my arms around him as we kissed. "Why did you come here?" he asked.

"Because I wanted to see if I could do it. It was an experiment. Remember?" I asked.

"But there's something more," he whispered in my ear.

"And what would that be?" I asked, not sure what he was getting at.

He stroked my hair. "Perhaps you're testing the boundaries of our love, wondering if it can exist even in this unconscious state of being."

"An interesting theory, but I hadn't really thought about it before you said it. I think that's a romantic notion, too. I've found that the unconscious state usually reveals more than the conscious one does, so you may be on to something, Professor Fuentes."

"Quite possibly," he said. "Do I pass the test?"

I laughed. "You're more irresistible than ever, señor. You get an A+."

"And so do you, señorita. So do you."

We sat in that embrace a long time. I felt completely at peace. The heat of his body against mine replaced the warmth of the sun. The sounds of the grove enveloped us in their gentle rhythm as well. When a breeze blew by, stoking the campfire to a higher flame, the heat of the place intensified. It was like a blessing, a moment of grace bestowed upon our relationship. After a time, he loosened his arms and cleared his throat.

"I have a confession to make," he said.

"Have we had this conversation before?" I asked, remembering the feelings he'd revealed to me the night our friendship evolved into a more intimate state. But he shook his head to say no.

"I wanted you to come here, to be with me. It may have seemed like part of a casual conversation, but I was more calculated than that. I put it out there and you went for it," he smiled.

I recalled our conversation earlier that evening. I thought trying to get into Angel's dream had been *my* idea, but now he was saying it was his. "Why couldn't you have just asked me? Were you testing me?" I asked, a little peeved.

"I was testing your curiosity, and anxious to see if this would work. If it did, I had another thing in mind."

"Like what?" I asked, feeling impatient.

"I have something very important to talk to you about. I find it difficult to say in the waking world. I thought being here might give me more courage," he revealed. He held my hands in his and I felt him shaking. Again, he cleared his throat, then he gently scooted further back on the bench.

"I've never done this before," he said. "You're better at this dream control than I am. I have to focus on what I'm about to say." He took my hand, kissed it and looked into my eyes. It was almost a stern look, he seemed so serious. He looked as if he was about to open his mouth to speak, but then he leaned forward and began to lick my face! I was totally repulsed!

"What are you doing?" I cried. And then I heard another familiar sound.

"Meow."

I was suddenly back on my couch with the lights on bright and Mr. Kitty laying on my chest licking me with his sandpapery tongue. There were no more trees, no more warm sun, burning campfire, or gentle breeze, and no more Angel. The dream had completely faded away! It was after 1:00 a.m. so I went to bed. I fell asleep in a state of disappointment. What had Angel wanted to say to me that required extra courage? I had my theories. But then I wondered if I'd made the whole dream up. Whatever the truth was, it would have to wait until we saw each other again. I fell asleep with Mr. Kitty's warm body at my side.

26

When I woke the next morning, my memory of the dream in the grove was faint. But then I remembered our embrace, the calm, peaceful feeling as we held each other on the rough plank seat. I wanted to keep that part of the dream inside me until I grew old. The experiment had been worth trying, whether it was really Angel or my dreamed-up version of him, because the most important part of the dream stayed in my conscious mind, ready to replay when I needed to be there again.

But I couldn't dwell on it because I had a lot to do that day. There were errands to run, laundry to wash and dry cleaning to pick up. I even bought a new shade of lipstick in an effort to look a little sexier that night. It was part of my plan to jog Angel's memory of the dream, if he'd been in it. As I was walking in the door that afternoon Maggie phoned.

"You're my last call," she said. "Max and Angel are okay with 7:00 at Bernardo's tonight. Sound good?"

"Sounds great," I said. "I love their food."

"Wonderful. I'll go ahead and make a reservation, just in case. And Angel said he could pick you up around 6:30. Does that work for you?"

"That's fine."

"Good. Then I don't have to call anyone back, unless I can't get a reservation. I have a lot to tell you, Michelle, but I'm going to save it for tonight."

"Really? Can you give me a hint?"

"No," she laughed. "I'm not giving any of it away. You just have to wait until then. We have a few things to celebrate is all I'll say. And, by the way, I'm sorry we couldn't talk much last night."

"But that meant Max had a successful opening, so don't worry about it. We'll make up for lost time at Bernardo's," I reassured her.

"Thanks for your understanding, Michelle. See you then."

Before I did anything else I checked online to see if my parents had dropped me an email. They were staying with my aunt and uncle who had just retired near Las Vegas. I couldn't picture my parents at a roulette table. But no email yet, so I sent one to them to say that Mr. Kitty was doing just fine and said hello.

Then I checked my messages. The amount of junk mail leaking through was getting worse, it seemed. There were also the usual messages from not-for-profits asking for more charitable contributions, as well as political messages urging me to call my congressman or sign the petition on their website. That didn't leave too much else to read, except a message from the Lakeview UCC. Being on the church's list serve was one way for all of us to keep in touch. The email's title read, "Please pray for the family of Jorge Pintero." That was a name that sounded vaguely familiar, but I couldn't place it. I wondered if he was part of our sanctuary program for activists. I hurriedly clicked the message open. It was written in both Spanish and English.

Carolina, who is in our sanctuary program, just heard that her dear friend Jorge Pintero has been found dead. He was an activist in the movement to re-gain land taken from Afro-Colombians by the paramilitary. Jorge had been invited to participate in a conference in Chicago, but was denied a visa by the U.S. He disappeared on his way back to his village and was apparently kidnapped by known members of the paramilitary. His body was found in a river two days later.

He was an outspoken leader in the people's right to hold onto their land. Many people in the region have lost their lives this way and whole communities have been displaced by paramilitary groups who allegedly work with large international companies that want the land for planting African palm oil trees. He will be missed by his wife Ana and their six children, as well as his community.

Horrible as this is, his family has some comfort because his body was retrieved. In many cases, the disappeared are never found and there is no sense of closure. There is nothing more that can be done for him, but Carolina asks that we pray for his family. We will be taking up a collection this Sunday to send financial support to them.

We are also considering a fundraiser that would add to the coffers of the sanctuary program for at risk activists. We're looking for creative ideas. Please direct your thoughts on this to Jeri Byrd who has volunteered to head this event.

Yours in peace,
Rev. James Horsley

Six children. Six fatherless children. I wanted to cry, and scream, and yell at my elected representative for not paying attention to what was happening in countries where our tax dollars were going. I went back to a message with a link to my congressman's email. There was a form letter to sign about a completely different issue. I filled in the necessary blanks with my name, address, and other vitals, but instead of adding my personal comments about the issue at hand, I cut and pasted as much of the Jorge Pintero message as it would allow. I began my message by saying. "Please look into this issue as well. Why do things like this happen?" I hit send and was thanked for my participation. I went offline and put the computer on sleep. My drawing board was a few feet away. I saw my painting of the homeless woman holding her child. Where was her husband, or was he just the child's father? Had he left them or died? Ana Pintero had a home and six children, but no husband. Why was it that women and children were often the ones to carry the burden of survival? On a stack of books next to the computer I'd placed Guzmán's book of photographs. Paging through them I found the image of the woman with the shawl wrapped around her baby and the young Afro-Colombian woman walking down the road holding her baby. As I glanced through the book I found another of a thin African refugee woman with her malnourished child. I saw these same faces on BBC News and in my weekly news magazine. They were on cnn.com and other online news sites. Why were we numb to their suffering? Was there just so much of it we stopped caring?

Then I did the only thing I could besides pray for the Pintero family or donate to their fund. I painted. I poured my frustration and anger into my own rendition of a mother and child living at risk on the streets of a U.S. city. It was done an hour later. I felt it was more important for people to see the image, to be struck by their own emotional reaction to it, like I was by Guzmán's work, than it was for them to buy it. I knew my gallery might disagree with that, but that was why I did it. That was my mission, my calling, to shed light in dark corners and help the world see and understand these things. But the image was too fresh for me to judge it properly. I closed the door and went back to the rest of my life.

27

Later that day, after straightening up my place and petting Mr. Kitty profusely, it was time to get ready for the evening. I wondered if Angel would remember our mutual dream at all, and if he did, would it bear any resemblance to mine? I would give him a chance to bring it up first, but if he didn't, I'd ask. If he had no memory of it, then there'd be no way to know if it had happened at all, except in my own imagination.

I took a shower, washed my hair and prepared myself for what I hoped would be a spectacular date. I lived in slacks on the weekend, but this time I put on a dark gray skirt that hit above my knees and a V-necked orange sweater that fit snugly and showed off a few curves I usually didn't advertise. It was all done in good taste, I told myself, but I hoped the effect would be flirtatious. I added panty hose and black heels with skinny straps, which I'd been saving for a special occasion.

My hair had recently been cut and was really short this time, except on top. I squeezed as much curl into it as I could with the help of extra hold gel. Then I carefully applied eye shadow and liner and put another layer of mascara on for good measure. My new shade of lipstick worked well with the orange sweater, as I hoped it would. Then I dug out a pair of hoop earrings I hadn't worn in a while, put them on and stood in front of the mirror on the back of the bathroom door for a full-length look.

Ooh, la la! Mr. Kitty gave an approving purr as he ran his cheek against my leg. "Hey, watch the stockings, please!" I warned him. He just looked up and did it again, still purring.

I was even thinking about doing my nails, but by then it was just after 6:00 p.m. As I scooped cat food onto a dish for my feline guest, the doorbell rang.

"Hi, Angel," I greeted through the intercom. "Do you want to come up or shall I come down? You're early."

"I found parking. Can I come up? We have time."

I answered by buzzing him through the courtyard gate and then into the door of my building. "Hi there! How was your day?" I asked as we exchanged kisses. It was good to see him in the flesh this time.

"Hi there, yourself. It went well. Dan and I are off and running on our article, so I spent a good part of the day doing research for that. And time flies when I'm doing research. How about you? How was your day?" he inquired.

"Busy. I finished my latest painting, thanks to an email that got me angry." I told him about the death of Jorge Pintero. He hung his head and sighed.

"I'm sorry to hear that," he said. "Guzmán has plenty of material to work with, doesn't he? And how did your painting turn out?"

"Would you like a private showing?"

"Of course," he shrugged.

I opened the door to my studio, formerly known as the guest room. Mr. Kitty had gone into hiding the moment the doorbell rang, but I closed the door behind me again, just in case he snuck in. I turned on the light above the drawing board and Angel sat down to get a better look. He didn't say anything for a few seconds. I was about to ask what he thought of it when he turned toward me. "I'm amazed! Your talent is huge, Michelle! Who would have thought paintings of the homeless could be this hypnotic? Who is she?"

"Her name is Ida. Her son's name is Nathan. I've never met them in person. I dreamt about them and they told me their story. I can tell you that little fact, but how do I explain that to anyone else?" I said, shaking my head.

"Just say you saw them on the street and filled in the rest with your ample imagination," he suggested while looking it over closely. "This piece is quite moving. A homeless mother and child. People don't realize they're out there, too. Or maybe they don't want to know that's possible."

"I may not have met them, but I know they're more than my imagination at work!" I emphasized.

"How do you know for sure?" he asked. How to answer that question?

"I just know. In my gut, I know they're for real. Are you playing devil's advocate with me or are you doubting the reality of my dreams, Angel?"

"I'm just curious about the process. You seem a bit on edge tonight," he observed. "That email about Pintero's death?"

I took a deep breath and exhaled. "I suppose," I said. Then I changed the subject. "I could use a drink of water before we leave. Would you like anything?"

"Water sounds good, and then we should be going."

He followed me out of the room and I gestured toward the couch. I drank some water as I stood at the sink, then brought him a glass and set it on the coffee table. He was smiling at a piece of paper in his hand. It was the photograph of him with Max and Maggie standing in the grove behind Sweet Dreams. I must have dropped it the night before when I fell asleep there.

"Where did you find that?" I asked.

"I almost stepped on it. It was on the floor peeking out from under the couch. Looking at this is giving me a sense of déjà vu. Did I dream about this place last night? You know, I think I did." Well, that was a hopeful sign.

"Do you remember anything else about the dream?" I asked him.

He looked straight ahead, then shifted his eyes to the left, the right, and then back to the photo in his hand. "So Michelle, you must have dreamed about it, too, like you said you would. I forgot all about that, I've been so busy today."

"I did. That photo's there because I used it to focus on my memory of the place, the sounds of the bells and chimes, the birds, the breeze. Do you remember the dream?" I smiled innocently.

"Uh-huh," he said, nodding slightly. It was coming back to him.

Then he looked up at me and said, "Wow!"

"Wow what?"

"I'm just looking at you. You look fantastic!" He stood up and embraced me. We stood like that for an entire minute, not saying a word.

"I remember this," he finally whispered. "I remember holding you like this in the grove. We were sitting on a plank around the old campfire site. I didn't want it to end."

"Neither did I."

"It worked then," he said as he loosened his arms.

"What else do you remember?" I asked.

"It's too blurry, I'm afraid." He frowned in frustration.

I looked at my watch. "Whoa, time to go," I said. "Drink up and let's get out of here."

That seemed to be the end of the discussion about our mutual dream.

At least he remembered the most important part of it. I wondered if it might come back to him in little bits that night. Even if it didn't, I still wanted to know what was on his mind, what he was about to ask me before Mr. Kitty interrupted our conversation. Angel's earnestness in the dream was very real to me. But I decided not to mention it. Maybe he'd get the courage to say whatever it was before the night was done.

We got in the car and headed out into the crowded Saturday night traffic. The day had been unseasonably warm again, so I only put on a short jacket with no hat, because I didn't want to ruin my hair. But the air outside had gotten cooler. Angel turned on the car radio, as well as the heater, and we let the music fill the space where our conversation had been. I couldn't believe it, but "Imagine" was playing again. "By the way, I found time to do a little John Lennon research today, too. Did you know he was in Oaxaca in the sixties?"

"I had no idea," I said, very surprised at that fact.

"He was in the town of Huautla. It had to do with magic mushrooms. But still."

"You don't suppose he happened on Teotenaca, do you?" I asked. That would be something!

"I suppose it's possible. We'll never know for sure. If nothing else, at least he was in the same Mexican state."

That gave me something to contemplate. Lennon's anthem to world peace played on, becoming the background music to my picturing the rock star turned pacifist entering El Anhelo and disappearing into its cave. I thought about the rest of his lyrics. He outlined the things that divided us, our national and religious identities. I interpreted the song as saying we should focus on our relationship with each other in the here and now, instead of worrying about what divided us, or concerning ourselves with heaven and hell in the afterlife.

Then Angel got my attention by saying, "By the way, you smell great, Michelle. What's that fragrance? It's familiar, for some reason."

"It's gardenia," I answered. "Body lotion."

He gave me a sidelong glance at a red light. "What did you do to your hair?"

"I washed it and used extra hold gel for more curl," I said, wrapping a tiny wisp of hair around my finger.

"You look especially wonderful tonight," he said to me and then turned back to the traffic. "You know I seem to remember you were very attractive in that dream last night, too. You practically glowed. Were you putting a spell on me?" he laughed.

"I don't do spells, Angel. Don't blame that on me. It was your own imagination at work, or you were seeing beyond the physical, the way I do sometimes," I tried to explain, though I knew he'd need more information.

"Beyond the physical? What do you mean by that?"

We seemed to be hitting all the red lights. It was slowing us down, but it gave us a chance to look at one another when we spoke.

"You know, you were glowing last night, too," I told him.

"I was? I don't remember that."

"Well, you wouldn't. That's *my* memory of you. It's like seeing into a person's soul. Another way of putting it would be to say that you gave off very positive vibes. I've met a few people in my dreams who had really negative ones, like their souls were sick. Ugh. Bad memory," I recalled with a shiver.

At the next light he turned to me and just stared, mouth still open. I thought something was wrong with him. "Are you all right?" I asked with real concern.

"This is fascinating. You don't do spells, but your insight or intuition is developing. I wonder if that ability will move from your unconscious mind into your conscious one," he theorized.

"But in a way, it already has," I laughed. "I remember my dreams when I'm awake."

"I know. But what I'm trying to say is that maybe someday you'll pick up those vibes from people in your conscious state," he said as the light turned green. He looked ahead and reminded me about our favorite Teotenacan psychic. "Flor was incredibly intuitive. Maybe that's how it developed for her."

"Sunny's already got it, too. I hadn't looked at it like that, since it seems so natural when I'm dreaming."

"You're one amazing woman, my love. I wonder what else you're capable of doing," he said, eyebrows raised.

We found a parking space not far from the restaurant, which was surprising for the area. As we walked the half block Angel stopped and looked at me again for about five seconds, then shook his head.

"I wish I could remember more," he said.

"That's all right," I assured him. "Your memory is better than I thought it would be."

We walked in to find our friends already seated at a round table. We greeted each other like long lost comrades. "I was beginning to wonder if I said the wrong time," Maggie confessed. "We almost lost the reservation. Did you have trouble finding a place to park?"

"Sorry." I said. "We got lost in conversation and then we must have hit every red light between Lakeview and here."

Max gave me a knowing look, as if "conversation" was a code word for a whole lot of kissing and maybe more. I looked at him and said, "Conversation means conversation, Max."

He looked me up and down and said, "You're looking good, Michelle. And you're a lucky man," he nodded to Angel, giving him a pat on the shoulder.

Maggie handed us the menus. "I'm hungry," she said. "Let's order."

We picked out an exotic combination of dishes and ordered a bottle of Spanish red wine. "Olé!" Max shouted when the waiter popped the cork.

"You're in a celebratory mood," Angel said to him. "You must have done well at the opening."

Max tasted the wine. "That will be fine," he nodded and the waiter poured it.

When the first plates arrived, they included goat cheese and toast with a red sauce. Angel took a bite and then stopped chewing in the middle of it.

Maggie noticed and asked if he was all right. He nodded that he was and then he looked at me and said, "It's coming back to me," he smiled, recalling more of the dream. He looked over at my hands and then up to my face and smiled again. I raised my glass of red wine and he reached over with his. We nodded once in unison as we clinked our glasses together.

"Hey, no fair making private toasts," Max said. "Let's make a public one."

"Go for it," Maggie encouraged me.

"To my dearest friends," I said, "whether they're asleep or awake." We laughed and clinked glasses. Angel gave me another of those nods as our glasses touched.

"And now we have a special announcement to make," Max began. "May I have your hand, Miss Maggie?" She brought her left hand up from under the table. I saw a flash in the dim light. A diamond ring! I had to have a closer look. It was beautiful, a large square stone with baguette diamonds along the sides.

"It's lovely!" I said. "Congratulations, you two. When did this happen?"

"Late last night," she said. "Max kept the best for last. And it was quite a night already with all the sales he had."

"I'm glad the opening went well for you. But this is fantastic." Angel said, "Congratulations!"

We got up and took turns hugging the two of them.

"And to make this weekend even more perfect, we've decided who our maid of honor and best man should be, if they're willing," Max said with an enthusiastic grin.

He paused and then Maggie added, "We were thinking of both of you. You are our best friends, after all." Angel and I looked at each other and smiled.

"I'd be honored," I said.

"And so would I," he replied.

"Fantastic!" Maggie responded, all smiles. "We're thinking about December so we can have a winter wedding. We don't want to wait until next spring."

"A winter wedding could be really beautiful," I agreed.

And then there was even more good news from Max. "Do you remember that I was trying to find a gallery that would show Reggie's paintings? Well, I did. The Lenbach Gallery wants to represent him in Chicago. They really liked the digital images he e-mailed them. And he and family are hoping to come to the opening, whenever it is. I told him they could stay at my loft."

"Do you have any idea when?" I asked.

"Probably next spring," he replied.

"I'm looking forward to seeing them again," Maggie nodded.

"They were wondering if Dar could do a few poetry readings, too," Max added.

"Maybe I could introduce her to Berta Corelli," I suggested. "They'd have a few things in common, after all."

"That would be awesome," he agreed. "And while you're at it, maybe you could introduce me to her, too."

"Sure. Why not?" I laughed.

The tapas were delicious and the meal went by too quickly. We stretched it out by ordering more dishes one at a time, as well as another bottle of wine. Now and then I caught Angel smiling at me. When our eyes met he would nod and I would smile back. Something was on his mind and I wondered if it was that important thing he wanted to say at the end of our dream. Finally, he made an announcement.

"Ah, excuse me, my friends, but there is something on my mind and I can't hold back any longer. I have to interrupt our meal." He cleared his throat and turned to me. "Michelle, I've been meaning to ask you something. I tried last night in our dream, but you disappeared. What happened to you?"

"I thought you were licking my face. That's why. I found it offensive, of course," I laughed.

"What? I didn't do that!" he protested.

"Of course you didn't. It was Mr. Kitty, and he woke me up, the rascal," I explained. "That's where I went, back to consciousness."

"Wait just a minute," Max jumped in. "Are you saying you two were in the same dream last night? No way!"

"Way, Max. We were in the grove behind the Sweet Dreams B & B," Angel insisted.

"And what were you about to ask this lovely lady?" Maggie asked with a mischievous smile.

Angel cleared his throat and looked back at me. "I've been inspired by our friends here to go for it, Michelle." He took my hand and focused on my eyes. Then he stopped and pulled out a small box from his coat pocket and set it on the table. "Will you, could you, oh, how do I say this? I love you very much."

"Angel, do it right," Max interrupted. "Down on your knee, man!"

"Of course," Angel said, clearing his throat, as he pushed the chair back and went down on one knee. He reached out for my hand again. A shiver went down my back in anticipation of what we was about to say. "Michelle," he started again, then whispered, "will you marry me?"

"The ring, Angel!" Max coached. Angel opened the box and presented me with an elegantly simple diamond ring. It flashed in the candlelight.

I swallowed and whispered back, "Oh my God!" Then I couldn't help myself from nearly shouting, "Yes! Of course." He slipped the ring on my finger, a perfect fit! Then he stood and kissed me. I heard applause around us. This was a far cry from the privacy of our dream the night before.

Maggie applauded, too, and said, "Now it's our turn to congratulate you two!"

"Congratulations!" Max echoed, slapping Angel on the back and kissing me on the cheek. "What a night, huh?"

"Indeed!" Angel said. I sat there silent and stunned, but smiling broadly, like I'd just won the lottery. My hunch had been right on.

"How are you?" Maggie asked, coming over to give me a hug.

I was shaking a bit. All I could say was, "Can you believe this?" And then I burst into laughter, and so did Angel. It was relief and joy and love and the beginning of another adventure, for all of us. I raised my left hand and pointed at the ring with my right index finger. "God sure works in mysterious ways!" I said, shaking my head in disbelief.

"Doesn't she, though?" Maggie laughed, gesturing to the engagement ring on her hand.

"Indeed she does!" Angel repeated, nodding with wide eyes.

"Hmmm, I wonder what other mysteries are in store for us," Max pondered out loud.

It was time for another toast. "To the journey that lies ahead," I said, raising my half-filled wine glass, "wherever it takes us."

I wondered if it might lead us all back to Teotenaca with its mountain and hidden cave. And surely we would have children, beautiful children.

"To the journey," they joined in, as we raised our glasses to the sky.

Acknowledgments

There are plenty of people to thank who helped me during the writing of this book. I particularly appreciated the detailed advice given by Jacqueline Lee and Joseph Shepley who read my first draft. Their comments and ideas resulted in essential changes to the structure of the book.

Barbara Anne Bost, who also read my first draft, and Jacqueline Lee were instrumental in bringing Rubin Pfeffer on board. He was working for our mutual employer at the time. Despite his busy schedule, Rubin found time to read my huge manuscript and offer his helpful comments, as well as forward an updated draft to a New York literary agency. Even though they chose not to represent the book, their review was encouraging and extremely helpful. So a very big thank you goes out to Rubin.

My brother Michael Dilsaver read most of the first draft and remarked that "it reads just like a novel," which was encouraging to hear from him.

A big thank you to my husband Clinton Stockwell, who read both the first and final drafts and added his helpful comments and ideas to both. With his knowledge of the Bible and world religions, he's *my* "Angel Fuentes." His many academic degrees make him the expert in many areas in our household and way beyond.

A special thank you goes to Jill Zylke. She was one of my first readers, but has been so much more. When I was creating my characters, I'm sure she inspired me, since she's a talented watercolorist as well as an accomplished flamenco dancer. But she also agreed to help me with the design and production of this book. It's a blessing to work closely on a project like this with someone who can bring so much to it.

Thanks to Bill Farrell for giving me ideas on how the road repair project would be handled. It made it more plausible, given the conditions and the location.

Thanks to Phyllis Salata for reading my last draft and for making a good argument to change the title I was using. I like this title much better, too. And thanks for accepting my packages all these years!

Thank you to Brian Salata for advising me on self-publishing this book. He's been through the process with his close friend Jessica (J.A. Redmerski) and helped her to achieve success on her books with his editing and advice. So his expertise is much appreciated.

Samantha Hoffman and I exchanged parts of our rough drafts a long time ago. I hope I gave her some good advice on her manuscript. Her novel was published in 2012. Her comments to me were very helpful and I took them to heart.

I would also like to thank my fellow congregants at Wellington Avenue United Church of Christ, as well as its pastor. Thank you for sharing your experiences and knowledge regarding feeding the homeless, the School of the Americas, Christian Peacemaker Teams, the plight of Afro-Colombians, and the inspiration of your many works that contribute to social justice, both locally and globally. Special thanks to Pam Richart, Roland Dehne, John Volkening, and Reverend Dan Dale. The people at Wellington are an amazing group that I feel very honored to know. Much of what inspired this book came from my experiences in that church. The benediction (from the *Book of Common Prayer*) that includes the words "Honor all people," is one of the most powerful statements I know. It has a way of grounding me and setting me on the right path when I leave church after Sunday service.

And thank you to anyone else I'm not mentioning that I should be. Writing this book has been a long journey of its own that has taken twelve years. So if I missed anyone else who contributed to its completion, please know that I am grateful for your help along the way.

Author's Notes

This is not the first novel I've tried to write, but it is the first one I've completed. I started several when I was much younger, but always ran into a roadblock, like needing to do research and not having the time, or not being able to write consistently over time to keep track of the story. Now I can say I've learned two things about writing: it takes a whole lot of discipline to see a manuscript through to the end, and the biggest part of writing is really editing.

This book started as a bold experiment back in May 2001. Those were pre-9/11 times. I've watched the world change in so many ways since I started that first draft that I hope I've captured this story in a place that others can relate to in coming years. The first thing I wrote was Michelle's release from the cave. After that, I had to figure out all the rest of the puzzle of who she was, where she was, what she was doing there, and what would happen next. This is a work of fiction, but I pulled from many of my own life experiences in putting the pieces together to form this whole.

I had visited Mammoth Cave shortly before I wrote that scene. It had massive rooms and beautiful drippy formations. But the thing I remembered most was how absolutely black it was when they turned off the lights. What could be more terrifying than to lose your light source in a cave? So I gave the Cave of Dreams a filtering of light in several of its spaces so it wasn't a completely dark place. And that works well as a metaphor for undermining the darkness of the world with light, of course.

When I was 31, the same age as Michelle, I went to Australia for five weeks by myself. I was supposed to be traveling with a group, but the members dropped out one by one until I found out four days before departure that I'd be going it alone. Fortunately, I had connections in Sydney, Adelaide and Melbourne and was housed and fed. I found Australians to be some of the friendliest people I've ever met. So why not have them run a bed and breakfast in a small village in Oaxaca, Mexico?

I have a graduate degree from the School of the Art Institute of Chicago in Modern Art History, Theory and Criticism. In the early days of researching my Master's thesis, my adviser gave me the address of Filemón Santiago, a Mexican painter who was living in Chicago at the time. It turned out that we would both be in the city of Oaxaca during the

Day of the Dead holiday in early November. He gave me a phone number where I could reach him in Mexico. When I called he was getting ready to visit his hometown in the mountains. I went along for the winding ride and found myself in a small indigenous village. His mother made tortillas on a stone for us. It was rustic, but very welcoming. That was the seed for what would become the town of Teotenaca, which I turned into a larger, more cosmopolitan and modern place. I also remember watching artists outside the façade of the cathedral in the Zócalo of Oaxaca city, including Filemón, as they created Day of the Dead images on the sidewalk with colored sand (I think), with each of their art works bordered by the orange flowers of the dead. Mexico is a country of contrasts. It's culture is a blending of the ancient and the modern, of the pre-Columbian and the Christian. Even many of the people are a mix of native peoples and their Spanish conquerors. I haven't contacted Filemón in many years, but he is living in Oaxaca now. Much of his work depicts his hometown. His paintings can be found in many collections, including the permanent collection of the National Museum of Mexican Art in Chicago.

Of course, other settings came from my own life. I've worked for a textbook publisher for many years in production management. I know the stress of that world quite well and could understand it from Michelle's point of view.

I've been a member of Wellington Avenue United Church of Christ for almost as many years. That's where I was married. From time to time I've written and delivered liturgies there and am currently a member of the choir. There is much more that can be said about that century old church and its congregation. It has served as a day care center, a sanctuary for Central American refugees, a homeless shelter, and a place that was occupied by members of the Occupy movement protesting the NATO summit who needed a place to stay. As I finished my final edit of the manuscript for this book, I attended a memorial service for Michael McConnell. He was ordained in the church and commissioned to be a peacemaker. He followed that calling by organizing peace vigils, marches and rallies as the Regional Director for the American Friends Service Committee. His best known exhibit was "Eyes Wide Open," which represented fallen American soldiers in the Iraq War by their combat boots lined up in formation, each one tagged with the name of a real person who had died in the war. The many more Iraqi civilians who were killed were symbolized by pairs of shoes. The exhibit was seen around the nation, adding its visual impact to the dialogue for peace. Michael was a poet who wrote beautiful, metaphoric Communion services. Seeing the church packed all the way up to the balcony at his memorial service made me realize that there are many who work for social justice and make it a central part of their lives. There will always be a need for people to work for the good of all. And there will be many challenges ahead with war and terrorist attacks around the world, climate change, overpopulation and scarcity of resources on the horizon.

The fictional death of Jorge Pintero, the Afro-Colombian activist who went missing and was later found dead in a river, is based on the actual murder of Orlando Valencia in 2006. The facts of his death are the same. He worked for land rights for his people and for that he was killed.

When I was trying to picture my main character, Michelle Hardtke, I couldn't form a physical image of her in my mind. That is, until I met Stephanie Sinclair. I had heard her interviewed on NPR and saw her in a documentary on the War in Iraq. She is a photojournalist who covered the invasion. After that phase of the war was over, she planned to document the rebuilding of Iraq. But things didn't quite work out that way, as we all know. Al-Qaeda in Iraq stirred up sectarian violence between the Sunni and Shiite communities and a civil war ensued. Stephanie documented that, too. I saw her photographs at the opening of her show at the Peace Museum in Chicago. She's petite, but courageous, just as I knew Michelle would be. So I kept her in mind as I defined my heroine. You can visit her website to see her photography at www.stephaniesinclair.com.

The social issues mentioned in this book are real. Some of them happened during the time I was writing this book and may no longer be current, but I chose to leave them in, anyway. There is a School of the Americas that you can read more about at www.soaw.org. Afro-Colombians have been pushed off their land by paramilitaries so that African palm oil trees could be planted there. The oil is used for cooking, but can also be converted to biofuel.

Much of the City of Darkness dream came from actual events. The Guatemalan woman holding Michelle's arm as she and other indigenous women and children were gunned down represented over 200,000 Mayans who were slaughtered. More of that horrific story is coming to light. The torture chamber episode was influenced by the Leon Golub paintings I saw at the Chicago Cultural Center, but there is also the story of Jon Burge, a Chicago police officer who used torture methods he'd learned in Vietnam to gain false confessions from suspects who were convicted of crimes they did not commit. And the images that came from the prison of Abu Ghraib in Iraq reminded us all of the horrors of torture and our country's involvement in it.

Sebastião Salgado, a Brazilian photographer, was the model for the character and work of Rodrigo Guzmán. Salgado uses natural light when shooting his black and white photos, but Guzmán used a flash in order to stop that moment in time as the Afro-Colombians fled their village. I was influenced by Salgado's work of displaced people shown at the Chicago Cultural Center and met the man at a book signing there. You can see that work in his book, *Migrations*. I also viewed his current work, entitled *Genesis*, at the Royal Ontario Museum in Toronto recently. His images of the wild places and indigenous people who populate our planet are a moving reminder of what is still out there, and at stake. He is also one of the best examples of what I envisioned a Cave of Dreams artist could be.

Of course, I have to mention two other characters I incorporated into this story from real life. Sadly, both have passed on. But Pearl the dog really did exist as part of the Wellington community. Originally I changed her name to Opal, but when I read a segment of my manuscript at a church event, her owner John Volkening assured me that Pearl wouldn't mind if I used her real name. So I gladly did. She was precious in real life, after all, and in moving my story to its next phase. Mr. Kitty belonged to our friend Reverend Jacqueline Ziegler. I loved his markings. So when I needed some comic relief and a cat that would interrupt an important dream, he seemed like the perfect feline to do the job.

A Global Ethic, The Declaration of the Parliament of the World's Religions (The Continuum Publishing Co., NY, 1993) is a real book that came out of a conference of the world's religions in September 1993 in Chicago, Illinois. I would encourage you to find a copy if you'd like to learn more about the commonalities of religions. And there are other books out there on that subject, of course. Matthew Fox explored this in his book *One River, Many Wells* (Jeremy P. Tarcher/Penguin, NY, 2000). I found the perfect quote for my dedication page from the Kabbalah in that book when I couldn't sleep one night. He has a long list of other titles that are worth delving into as well.

When it came to the seasons, whether the growing or liturgical ones, I used artistic license to tell my story. I bought a gardenia bouquet in late fall in Oaxaca, which may have been grown in a greenhouse faraway. But I decided Michelle should get one, too, but in the spring. That beautiful white flower truly has a magical fragrance.

Pop culture is full of super villains and heroes. But there is plenty of real evil in the world as it is, so I didn't need to make any of that up. My "super heroes" are ordinary people who have imagination, talent and empathy and who have been called to use those qualities to bring more light into a dark world. If you see even a tiny opportunity to do the same, I hope you will. Small acts of kindness and respect toward others (and don't forget Mother Earth) can make a huge difference.

This great experiment of a book has a lot of other connections to the world I know and the experiences I've had in it, but they are too numerous to mention. Suffice it to say, the experiment is completed. It's time to move on to completing another manuscript I've started. But I enjoyed this journey, and I hope my readers gain something they can carry with them on theirs.

ABOUT THE AUTHOR

In her creative life, Karen Stockwell has been a visual artist, a journalist, a poet, a singer-songwriter, a jewelry designer, a fiber artist, and now, finally, a novelist. She's made a living by working for advertising agencies and an educational publisher. She holds a B.A. in Art Education and a M.A. in Art History and has taken many classes and workshops in the arts. Her craft work and articles have been published in *Belle Armoire* and *Altered Couture* magazines. As a product of a Catholic mother and a Protestant father, she has been a member of both churches, but now attends Wellington Avenue United Church of Christ in Chicago. With her husband Clinton Stockwell, she divides her time between Chicago and Galena, Illinois. You can find out more at *www.karenstockwell.com*.

Made in the USA
Columbia, SC